The Cracked Mirror

The Cracked Mirror

CHRIS BROOKMYRE

abacus
books

ABACUS

First published in Great Britain in 2024 by Abacus

1 3 5 7 9 10 8 6 4 2

A CIP catalogue record for this book is available from the British Library.

Hardback ISBN 978-0-349-14579-2
Trade Paperback ISBN 978-0-349-14580-8

Typeset in Adobe Caslon Pro by
Palimpsest Book Production Ltd, Falkirk, Stirlingshire
Printed and bound in Great Britain by Clays Ltd, Elcograf S.p.A.

Epigraph on page vii © 1993 Kali Nichta Music,
lyrics reproduced by kind permission of Greg Dulli

Papers used by Abacus are from well-managed forests and other responsible sources.

MIX
Paper | Supporting
responsible forestry
FSC
www.fsc.org   FSC® C104740

Abacus
An imprint of
Little, Brown Book Group
Carmelite House
50 Victoria Embankment
London EC4Y 0DZ

An Hachette UK Company

www.hachette.co.uk
www.littlebrown.co.uk

For Mark Billingham

Tonight I go to hell
For what I've done to you
This ain't about regret
It's when I tell the truth

Greg Dulli, 'Debonair',
from *Gentlemen*, The Afghan Whigs

PART ONE

The Corpse in the Confessional

I

There was a body in the chapel of St Bride's.

This was, of course, not unusual. That the body should be in the confessional booth rather than a coffin most definitely was. And that the body should be that of a gentleman who had been strangled, more unusual still.

The red sandstone church sat proudly at the head of the Main Street in the village of Glen Cluthar, just past Tayview Brew, which had twice been shortlisted for Perthshire's Prettiest Tearoom despite not actually affording a view of the Tay. Poor Father Driver had made the discovery when he was undertaking preparations for Sunday mass, a service that had to be cancelled for the first time in parish record.

Much of that Sunday morning was instead spent in agitated speculation as to what could have necessitated a police cordon, and the conspicuous absence of Father Driver at the church steps had led many to fear the worst. Then Judith Houston had spread the big news.

3

'It's Mr Gault,' she reported, just the wrong side of giddy. 'He's been murdered.'

Perhaps it was relief at who the victim was *not* that had coloured Mrs Houston's response, but equally it could have been because Mr Gault was not well liked in the village. And that his demise should have been a commissioned act was undoubtedly a factor in the speed with which she spread the tidings.

However, it had to be said: a murder in Glen Cluthar or its wider environs was altogether less unusual than ought to be the case for a settlement of its size, location and prosperous demography. Despite its sleepy pace of life, its cosy insularity and its old-fashioned ways, this little corner of Perthshire was a place where a great many people met their untimely ends. More happily, Glen Cluthar was also a place where murders seldom went unsolved, and this was generally attributed not to the region's under-resourced and frequently befuddled police force, but rather to the presence of one redoubtable long-term resident.

A couple of days after the unholy discovery at St Bride's, the resident concerned was receiving a visit from her nephew, William.

Ms Penelope Coyne lived in Silverbank Cottage at the north-western edge of the village, overlooking an oxbow lake that had once been a tributary of the Tay. She often considered that Glen Cluthar itself was something of an oxbow lake, formed in faster-moving times but now cut off from the flow, and reassuringly placid as a result. Apart from all the murders, obviously.

Penny, as she preferred to be called, was in her early eighties, but did not like to specify further, or to dwell upon how elastic-ally one might stretch the definition of 'early'. It sometimes seemed like she had been in her eighties for a very long time, though physically she did not feel she had aged much in recent years. Mentally was another matter, but she opted not to dwell on that.

She was a slight woman, always had been, despite her appetite for sweet things, something jealous observers attributed to a fortunate constitution, but which Penny put down to seldom being at rest. She liked to be busy, in mind and body.

She was standing in her living room, dressed in her favoured combination of Harris tweed trousers and a cream twin-set (though she disliked this term, a twee-sounding description for an elegant pairing of warm and comfy garments). In her hands was a document. William had presented her with a glossy brochure advertising an admittedly pleasant-looking retirement home, a facility he had mentioned before.

'I am not ready to leave this place quite yet,' Penny told him.

'No, no, absolutely. I'm not doing this to pressure you. I just want you to know that this is an option, and that if the time comes when you feel . . . in need of such a move, I will be here to help you make the change.'

It would be easier if he were some impoverished rake and she could attribute his motives to avarice. A desire to buy her little cottage out from under her and turn it into some hideous apartment block perhaps, blocking Mrs Houston's view down to the water. But her nephew was a successful and wealthy man, even if she never did quite understand what it was his company did. Something in computers, was all she grasped. William was dutifully attentive, visiting her frequently and sometimes fruitlessly, for she often didn't have time to see him, or would return home to find he had called when she was out.

There was no question but that William had her best interests at heart. But she did not always like to dwell upon what her own best interests might entail.

. . . in need of such a move . . .

They both knew what that meant. She could not stay in this place for ever, and nor should she wish to. But whenever Penny contemplated the quiet ease of moving on, she was beset by this lingering sense of unfinished business, of a troubling mystery yet to be solved. It beset her like a wound to the soul, then it would be gone. All that remained was a ghost of a memory: the echo of a sound half heard, a shadow of something merely glimpsed.

'I will have a closer look at the brochure some other time,' she told William. 'But for now, I simply have too much to do.'

'So I see,' William acknowledged, indicating the suitcases out in the hall, yet to be unpacked. 'You're barely in the door again.'

'If you ever think you're too busy with work, William, just you wait until you retire. Then you'll know what busy truly feels like.'

As she spoke, there was a creak and a clatter from the front door, the sound of a letter being popped through the slot by the postman. She saw him walk back up the path, giving her a wave as he retreated.

'Let me get that,' William said, fusspot that he was.

He returned from the hall bearing a crisp white envelope with silver embossing. 'You're not kidding, are you,' he said, handing it over. 'That looks like an invitation to me.'

Penny reached for her letter knife and sliced it open. She could not abide messy tearing. It spoke of carelessness and impatience, both of which carried more risk than people appreciated.

She stared at it.

Mr Martin Deacon and Mrs Catherine Deacon
invite you to
the wedding of their daughter, Ms Lilian Deacon,
to Mr Sebastian Gossard,
at Crathie Hall, Perthshire, on Saturday, 17 May

William had a look, his curiosity piqued by how long Penny was taking to read it. Perhaps she was having another of the episodes that had occasioned his presentation of the brochure.

'Who is it from?' he asked. 'I mean, is it someone on the groom's side you know, or . . .?'

'I have no idea,' Penny confessed.

William gave her *that* look.

'No, I don't mean I've forgotten,' she chided. 'I've just spent two months travelling halfway around the world on my own, and I managed without incident. Or at least, without incident to me. I'm saying that these names are not familiar and consequently I have no notion why I've been invited. It must be an administrative error.'

'The envelope is definitely addressed to you,' William pointed out.

'Curious,' Penny observed, putting the card on her bureau, and checking the time on her wristwatch as she did so. It was almost nine forty-five.

'How *was* your cruise, by the way?'

'Gratifyingly eventful,' she replied, though she did not have time to elaborate on what would have been highly complex details. She had somewhere to be. 'I'm afraid I can't tarry,' she said.

'Where on earth are you off to now?'

'St Bride's. For mass.'

William looked nonplussed. 'It's Tuesday.'

'Yes, but the church has just reopened.'

'Oh, after the . . . Oh dear, you're not involved in all that business, are you?'

She fixed him with a look. 'As you just pointed out, I'm barely in the door. So no, I'm not involved.'

But she fully intended to be.

The Corpse in
the Confessional

II

Penny had only met the late Mr Brendan Gault a couple of times before departing for her cruise. He had recently moved to the village from Dundee, and had bought up the premises vacated when Blue Skies Travel finally succumbed to the inevitable after gamely hanging on for an improbable number of years. As she remembered it, Mr Gault was planning to open a patisserie and coffee shop.

He had been a slight man, a little over five feet tall, and 'seven stone soaking wet', as the postman described him. Penny thought that it rather militated against the success of a patisserie if the proprietor looked like he seldom sampled the merchandise. He had also struck Penny as an inappropriate person to be around so much coffee, as he seemed a right restless individual. Which was not to say that he lacked all charm: there had been a boyishness about him, a vulnerability that she knew some ladies found attractive.

It was difficult to imagine him incurring anyone's wrath,

certainly not sufficiently to strangle the poor man, but Penny had long since learned that even the most mild-mannered and predictable people contained multitudes if you bothered to peel back the surface.

Penny strode along the Main Street, enjoying the spring sunshine and the welcome sense of the familiar, the sights, sounds and smells that comprised a typical Glen Cluthar morning. There was something irresistibly reassuring about finding herself back here after a trip, a comforting warmth that made it difficult to imagine ever being tempted by William's brochure.

She stopped to look in the patisserie, which was of course closed and unlit. Through the windows she saw that it did not look recently closed either. The tables and chairs had been stacked against the walls, and there was a saw-horse sitting in the centre of the room, opposite the counter.

Penny's dalliance came at a cost, as Mr Toal emerged from his newsagent's just as she resumed her progress.

'On your way to St Bride's?' he asked.

'Yes. Are you going there too?' she asked. Penny knew it to be a rhetorical question and that she would be stuck with him for a hundred yards.

It was said that hope springs eternal in the human breast, but seldom by anyone who had met Mr Toal. He was a dedicatedly miserable fellow, one who seemed to be under the impression that every new development reported in the papers he sold was both a precursor to and herald of the imminent collapse of society. The fact that society had continued to muddle along, subsequent to all of the previous heralds and precursors, never sapped him of the certainty with which he embraced each new omen.

'A terrible business,' he said, locking the door of his shop; ostensibly against theft but possibly also against asylum-seekers, transgender athletes and zombies. 'What's the world coming to if there's murders happening in church now?'

'Well, at least St Bride's is open again,' Penny said, reckoning this was as much of a silver lining as Mr Toal would allow.

'Aye. There won't be a funeral for him, though.'

'Mr Gault? Why not?'

Mr Toal bowed his head and shook it, as though a great burden was hung about his neck. A stranger might think this indicated troublingly portentous news, but he could affect such an air when informing you that there were temporary traffic lights on the Perth Road.

'He was one of those militant atheist types,' Mr Toal said, much in the way Penny imagined 1950s Americans might discuss alleged communists.

'How do you know that?'

'You must be the only one who doesn't. He was far from discreet, and it made him no friends in the village, I can tell you.'

'That sounds a lot like you're saying he was ostracised for his beliefs. I didn't think we were censorious that way here in Glen Cluthar. Not any more, at least.'

'It wasn't his beliefs, more his conduct in expressing them. He told Father Driver he wasn't welcome in his establishment, apparently. Started ranting about the Catholic Church and child abuse. All this in front of customers.'

'Dear, dear,' Penny said. 'That truly is indiscreet.' And unintentionally revealing, she thought. It was one thing to be angry at an institution, but it was an act of bigotry to act as though all priests were guilty by association.

'Aye,' said Mr Toal. 'And whenever certain types start banging on about child abuse, I can't help thinking they're trying to deflect from some hideousness of their own.'

The Corpse in
the Confessional

III

Penny paused briefly in the vestibule, that neutral space between the public and the holy, part of the building and yet not the church proper. People tended to pass through it quickly and quietly on the way in, but to linger there on the way out, its walls echoing with friendly chatter.

She had a complex relationship with faith. Increasingly she was drawn to St Bride's as a local institution more than to the Church itself as a global one, believing that the church, like the village, was its people. She paid scant attention to the content of the services, but she enjoyed the occasion, the sense of coming together, and the predictable order of it.

William once asked how her love for reason, evidence and deduction sat with her belief in God, to which she simply answered that somebody had to be in charge.

'From where I'm standing,' William had said, 'it doesn't much *look* like there's somebody in charge.'

'Then just imagine the chaos if there wasn't,' Penny had replied.

She had missed this place on her travels, but there was another reason Penny was coming to this morning's service. She believed there was a likelihood that the murderer would be among the congregation: returning to the scene of his or her crime out of perverse pride, an anxious need to find out what was known, or perhaps simply because they might be conspicuous by their absence.

One individual conspicuous by their presence was Mr Gault's widow, whose cheeks must surely have been burning under the glare of so many surreptitious glances. Penny had only met Brendan Gault a couple of times, but Helen Gault, née Dewar, had grown up here in the village. She was conspicuous also by being a good twenty years younger than her late husband, which caused Penny to remember that she had not been his first wife.

The church was as busy as Penny could remember it, more so than Christmas and Easter combined. It seemed the whole village was here, including those of other faiths and none. It was a gesture of solidarity towards those whose sacred place had been violated, and in light of what Mr Toal had told her, perhaps in solidarity with Father Driver also.

Penny saw a lot of herself in Father Driver, someone else who kept on going despite his advancing years, partly because he was needed, and partly because what else would he do with himself? He was a tall and well-built man, someone who still looked to be in good shape, but that was the thing about age: you looked to be in good shape until suddenly one day you didn't. Because it happened by increment, people's lingering perception of a person interfered with what was right before their eyes. And that included your perception of yourself.

When Penny looked in the mirror, she saw the same woman looking back as she always had, but she knew that couldn't be

13

true. Too much time had passed, and despite what she told William, she worried about the condition she was in, in particular her memory. She could remember fine details about places she'd been and conversations she'd had sixty or seventy years ago. And yet when she tried to remember specifics about her past, it was often like rooting through an attic full of jumble. She could not for the life of her find the thing she was looking for, but might happen upon a memory she had been seeking a week ago, or something she had not thought about in decades.

She had pretended otherwise to William, but the wedding invitation troubled her. She accepted there had been no mistake, and that she was the intended recipient, but she hadn't recognised any of the names. It would have been easier had she no notion whatsoever of who might have sent it, but there was this nagging sense that she ought to know. That she *used* to know.

When Father Driver ascended to the pulpit for his sermon, he was warm and assured in his tone, but Penny could tell he was having to dig deep. And in the vestibule afterwards, greeting the parishioners, though he came across as if everything was normal, Penny suspected he was putting on a brave face. She wanted to understand how he was really doing, which was why she sought out the person best placed to know.

'Dorothy, how are you keeping?'

'Och, you know,' Mrs Crichton replied, as though her own welfare was insignificant weighed against the things that mattered. And chief among those things was Father Driver.

Mrs Crichton was the priest's housekeeper. She had held this post for so many years that by Penny's estimate she had shared a house with Father Driver longer than she had with her late husband. Nonetheless, she spoke of her long-ago bereavement as though it had happened within the past fortnight, and affected

14

a wounded demeanour that gave the impression she was the world's first widow. Those who remembered Mr Crichton might note that for a man she so professed to miss, she had never shown him a fraction of the devotion she had subsequently shown to Father Driver, and far less than she showed to the Church itself.

'I haven't seen you in a while,' Mrs Crichton continued. 'I gather you've been away somewhere exotic.' She made this last sound like an accusation.

'And what a shock to come back to. How is he holding up?' Penny asked, nodding towards Father Driver, who was now shaking hands with Mr Toal, God help him.

'He's a man of the world. Given his line of work, it's not the first body he's seen, so it would take a lot more to knock him off his stride.'

Mrs Crichton had a few tiny red specks in her hair. Penny recognised them as flecks of candle wax. She would have dutifully scraped the votive shrine clean this morning, the church having been out of bounds since Sunday. Penny wondered when the police had lifted the cordon, and how many seconds later Mrs Crichton had been inside, reasserting her control and dealing with what it must have pained her to neglect.

Penny respected that. She had a fixation with the order of things too.

'It's just, I heard there was some prior unpleasantness concerning Mr Gault,' Penny said.

Mrs Crichton's expression turned sour. 'Disgraceful, the things people feel they have the right to say. He paid the price for it, though.'

Penny's expression conveyed her shock at Mrs Crichton's tone.

'Oh, heavens, no. I didn't mean, you know . . . I'm talking

about before that. It doesn't do to insult a man of Father Driver's standing when you're trying to get a new business off the ground. Anyway, that was weeks ago. Water under the bridge.'

'So do you have any notion what this nasty business was all about?'

Mrs Crichton glanced in the direction of the confessional. It would be a parishioner in sore need of absolution who wanted to be first to use it again now. She looked back at Penny.

'This is no time for gossip,' she said, her tone unmistakably admonishing. 'A man has died.'

And with that, she huffed away in a spoor of self-righteousness, but not one that impressed Penny. Mrs Crichton was an incorrigible gossip. 'You know me, I'm the soul of discretion,' she would say, before sharing some juicy nugget that she always claimed to have heard from someone else. She took pride in keeping the church immaculate, but had a tendency to be polishing the pews closest to the booth whenever Father Driver was hearing confessions.

If she knew nothing she'd have said so. That she had all but chided Penny's sense of decorum indicated otherwise. Dorothy Crichton had information, and Penny knew she wouldn't be able to keep it to herself for long.

Everybody Dies Alone

Chapter One

The light comes searing through a small crack where the blinds are bent. It's like a laser-sighted scope firing a high-velocity round dead centre into Johnny's aching head. Most days the LA sunshine is Johnny's best friend, there to cheer him up and remind him he lives in the best place on earth. But some days even your best buddy can go fuck himself, because it's too early in the goddamn morning and anybody being cheerful is doing the devil's work.

The blinds are unfamiliar. So is the wallpaper and the framed photograph of Santa Monica Pier. He hears the sound of breathing and feels movement beside him on the bed.

Holly golly.

Johnny doesn't recognise the room. He hopes to hell he recognises whoever owns it. He turns his head, the mere movement enough to send a spike shooting through his eyeball. It looks like she's coming to, which means the clock is ticking on remembering her name.

She rolls over and sits up. Takes a couple seconds, like maybe the room is still spinning or she's trying to wrap her brain around this situation too. She pulls a t-shirt over her head, squirming a little to get her mushroom of thick curly hair through the tight neck. The t-shirt is crisp white against her dark brown skin.

It's starting to come back. He's thinking her name's Shawna. And with that he susses the pain in his head ain't a hangover; or at least not *all* hangover. Everything's a bit of a blur but he's pretty sure he rolled an unmarked vehicle.

Or is it Sandra? Either way, she's the nurse who stitched up the cut on his forehead, last job before she finished her shift.

'You can discharge yourself so long as there's somebody who can watch out for signs of concussion,' she had said. 'You need to take it easy. Get some rest. No alcohol.'

'I can manage maybe a quarter part of that,' Johnny recalls saying. 'With your help.'

'Which quarter?'

'The one where someone stays with me to monitor whether I got concussion.'

He remembers a bar. More than one.

She seems pretty sanguine about waking up with him in her bed. On a school day too. Johnny ain't sure that's a good thing. Any broad who's prepared to take a guy home a few hours after meeting him – a few hours after stitching a head wound – gotta have her issues. Or maybe he's just so damned irresistible.

Yeah right.

She turns around and looks at him quizzically, like she's trying to make sense of *a lot* of different things.

'Did we . . .?'

Johnny can't decide if her incredulous tone is in self-reproach or pleasant surprise. Ten years ago it would have been the second. These days it's more likely the first.

In all honesty he doesn't remember. He takes a gamble on giving the answer that will most reassure her.

'You already took care of me once, sugar,' he says, pointing to his head. 'Would have been greedy to expect anything more. We were both pretty tired, pretty drunk. Went straight to sleep.'

'Then why did I wake up in only my panties?'

'Ain't that just how you normally sleep?'

'Sometimes,' she decides. 'Whatever. Anyway, you want coffee?'

'I'd refer you to my previous answer re you taking care of me enough, but yeah, I could really use coffee.'

She gets up and walks delicately out of the room into the adjoining kitchen-diner, leaving Johnny still struggling to piece last night together. Two things strike him as particularly problematic. One is that he is due back on shift this morning, and the other is that he has no idea where he is. Both of these become that little bit more pronounced as he hears his phone buzz and sees that it's Captain Nimitz. He swipes to ignore the call, nostalgic for the days when cell phones were for Wall Street assholes and Hollywood suits.

'Hey, what's your address?' he calls out to her.

'Man, you already here. What you need my address for? You gonna send me a postcard?'

'I need to get to work and I don't know where I am. I don't even have a car.'

'Oh yeah, you sure don't,' she replies, with a giggle that suggests she remembers more details than he does. 'Maybe you could ask the guy outside.'

'What guy outside?'

Johnny opens the blinds. Winces as the morning sunshine hits him with everything it's got.

There is a guy outside, standing next to a grey Dodge Charger.

Johnny recognises the plate, even recognises the scratches on the fender. Doesn't recognise the dude. He's on the job, though.

Dude looks up at the window, gives Johnny a curt wave and a friendly smile. Sonofabitch looks about fourteen years old. He's probably twice that but what would Johnny know. The range within which he can accurately judge keeps shifting upwards.

The kid has a keen expression, too keen maybe, like he's being ironic.

Johnny grabs his watch from the nightstand and checks the time. Turns out he ain't on the clock officially for ten more minutes. Let the asshole wait.

'Can I get that coffee to go?' he says.

'Oh, yeah, for sure. Just as sure as you're gonna call me. You even remember my name?'

Johnny takes a moment.

'Shawna,' he ventures.

She gives him an appraising nod, inscrutable though. She neither confirms nor denies.

He likes that.

Everybody Dies Alone

Chapter Two

'Lieutenant Hawke,' the kid says, opening the door for him.

'What are you, my chauffeur?'

'I'm Ibanez.'

Figures. He's Black but there is some Latino in the mix that makes him look real pretty.

'I'm your new partner,' he adds.

Johnny doesn't have an immediate response to this. Reckons he'll give himself a little time to process it, let the kid wait a while for feedback.

'I heard you might be short of a ride,' Ibanez says, starting the Charger and pulling away. A street sign tells him he's on Montana, which puts them in Echo Park. Yeah, he wasn't gonna be walking to work from here.

The kid knows he's digging Johnny out of a hole. Doesn't look like he's gonna milk it, but Johnny ain't ready to get down on his knees in gratitude either. He hasn't decided if this Ibanez is gonna be a problem yet; or rather, going by long-established precedent, he hasn't decided what kind of problem Ibanez is gonna be.

21

One thing intrigues him though.

'How'd you know where to find me? *I* didn't even know where I was.'

Ibanez gives him a weird little knowing smile, taps the side of his head.

'Just follow the trail of destruction.'

'No, seriously. Somebody got a low-jack on me, back at the department?'

'I guess that's a matter between you and Captain Nimitz,' he replies.

So it's like that.

'Ibanez, you say? Like the guitars? That's Spanish, right. Figures.'

'How so?'

'I feel like I'm working my way through every kind of ethnicity and minority in my partners. Like somebody's ticking off a list.'

'You mean like limeys and hebes, maybe? Who else? Fat dagos?'

It's a good thing Shawna *didn't* give him the coffee to go, because he'd have sprayed the windshield with it at this point.

'What the fuck? Why would you say that shit?' he asks, interrupting before Ibanez can get to the worst part. Hard R incoming.

'I was referencing.'

'Yeah, I know. *Dirty Harry.*'

'Just running a shorthand check on your values.'

'And what kind of values do you think I would have?'

'Well, you're white and this is the LAPD.'

'Point,' Johnny concedes.

'You a *Dirty Harry* fan, Lieutenant Hawke?'

Johnny doesn't know where the kid is going with this. Some kind of declaration of intent, perhaps.

'Always been more partial to James Bond, myself. How about you?'

'I like Doctor Who.'

More quixotic weirdness. At least they've taken an exit off the n-word expressway and left that shit in the rearview.

'Doctor Who ain't any kind of cop.'

'No, but he's a lot like James Bond.'

'How you figure?'

'Different iterations. The same character and yet not the same character. Sean Connery to Daniel Craig, William Hartnell through Ncuti Gatwa, whoever inhabits the role defines the personality, but they're still playing the same person. You accept each one as a continuation and yet also a distinct entity. It's a weird paradox.'

Johnny has no idea where the kid is going with this either.

'People nowadays gotta intellectualise everything. Used to be simpler. Connery and Moore. Fuck the girls, fuck up the bad guys. No paradoxes, no "iterations". What's your deal anyway? How come I ain't seen you before?'

'Just got transferred from out of town.'

'How far out of town? Barstow?'

'Mesa, Arizona.'

'Who'd you piss off to get your ass hooked up with me?'

'I don't know, but I'm not going in blind.'

Kid was telling Johnny he'd pulled his file. The way he said it, it sounded like a warning. Or maybe a threat.

'So what do you know about what went down last night?' Johnny asks him.

'I know you were chasing a suspect named Istvan Kulic. Guessing from the handle he ain't from South Central or East LA. I understand he's extremely accomplished in the

23

unauthorised unloading of freight. Particularly partial to high-end electronics.'

'His name is Kulic but we call him the Jackrabbit, because every time we get close—' Johnny blows on his fingers '—pff. He's gone. But I finally got a lead. Took me a long time to cultivate this particular informant, but it was worth it. The info was solid, including where Kulic was stashing his latest score. We hit it last night, and man, that place looked like the inside of RadioShack.'

'What do you mean: completely empty because it closed down a decade ago? How old is your frame of reference, man?'

'Hey, fuck you, junior. Okay, like the goddamn Genius Bar or some shit. Anyway, we got the goods but . . .' Johnny sighs and dabs tenderly at the stitches on his forehead. 'You know how houseflies seem like they're telepathic? They're sitting there, you're about to strike, but the fly always moves just before you do. Long story short, I came pretty close last night. Till I had a little accident.'

'Word is you didn't wait for back-up. You pulled some kind of hot-dogging manoeuvre and flipped about forty thousand dollars' worth of department wheels.'

'If I'd waited for back-up, all we'd have seen was his taillights.'

'And yet,' Ibanez says. Like Johnny needs to be told.

Johnny feels his cell vibrate. Nimitz again. Technically he's on the clock now, but he swipes 'Ignore' again. Patchy reception, what you gonna do.

'What I'm trying to work out is, did you come to hand-deliver me to Nimitz so you could score points with your new captain, or did you pick me up when I had no wheels to score points with me?'

'I'm here to serve,' Ibanez says.

'Good answer,' Johnny tells him. 'I never rated anyone who

put their cards on the table right away. Speaking of which, take a left down Alvarado.'

'For what?'

'Because I didn't play all of my cards last night.'

Ibanez nods and makes the turn. He grins approvingly.

'You didn't only get where Kulic was keeping his gear, did you?'

'Mr Kulic had a bad break-up,' Johnny replies. 'And nobody will sell you out faster than a woman scorned. I got a line on Brer Rabbit's address in the briar patch, the secret crashpad where he lies low when things get too hot. After last night's fun and games, he'll be there now, dug in like a tick.'

Ibanez accelerates as the lights change and they pass beneath the Hollywood Freeway.

'Okay. Where we headed?'

'It's a condo in Mid-Wilshire. He chose it well. Multiple exits from an underground garage.'

'Can't we just go there and kick the door down?'

'Problem is, I don't know exactly which door. The ex who gave me this was only there once, late and drunk. She didn't get the apartment number. She couldn't even rightly remember which floor, just the building. So we're gonna need to get as many units down there as we can spare, but quiet and inconspicuous.'

Johnny reaches for the radio handset.

Ibanez grips his hand before he can press the talk button.

'Wait.'

'What?'

'Kulic got a thing for electronics, right? And he's always one step ahead. Takes off like a fly, just before you move. This guy's monitoring your frequencies.'

Johnny laughs. 'What do you think this is, the eighties? I

don't know what they're using in AZ, but here in LA we're on a smart-radio system, digitally encrypted, so without verified credentials you're hearing nothing but static. You ain't telling me a guy like Kulic hacked the whole LAPD radio network.'

'Verified credentials,' says Ibanez, nodding. 'Okay, who's the dumbest cop in your precinct?'

Johnny's gonna have to think about that. It's a wide field.

'Because that's how smart your smart-radio system is. Kulic doesn't need to hack the whole network. He just needs one guy's password.'

Shit. Ibanez is right.

'What am I supposed to do? Call them all individually? Send a group-shot email? What if he's on that too?'

They were on South Alvarado now, heading for MacArthur Park.

'You want me to head back to base?'

'So Nimitz can ground me while somebody else uses my intel to put the bracelets on a guy I been chasing for months? Fuck that.'

'Well, we can't go in there and start trying doors,' the kid says. 'I figure a guy who can hack into our radio network can hack into the CCTV in his building too.'

Johnny allows himself a smile.

'That's why we're gonna make him come to us.'

Everybody Dies Alone

Chapter Three

The condo is on Wilshire Boulevard, close to the LA County Museum of Art. The Charger slips quietly down the north-western ramp into an underground garage that serves three buildings.

Johnny directs Ibanez to park out of sight of the elevator. The garage is expansive but largely empty. First thing in the morning is the right time for doing this. Most of the residents are out at work, leaving maybe a dozen cars in the place.

Johnny scans the vehicles and sees something he likes.

'I'm betting the blue Corvette Stingray,' he says. 'Kulic likes a V8 engine, something that lets him get away at high speed. Last night he was in a Subaru, also a V8.'

'My money's on that white Tesla,' says Ibanez.

Johnny sees a chance to make some easy money. 'Care to make it interesting? A C-note?'

'Fifty. I haven't had my first pay cheque yet.'

'Fifty it is.'

Johnny picks up the handset. 'All available units. This is Lieutenant Hawke. I have a twenty on Istvan Kulic, wanted for multiple hijackings. Suspect is in an apartment building, junction of Wilshire and South Fairfax. No lights, no sirens, and do not approach within sight of the building until directed. My ETA is four minutes. Repeat: no lights, no sirens.'

Then they wait.

It takes Kulic less than ninety seconds to vacate his apartment and reach the garage. Johnny hears the chime and sees the light flash on the elevator, heralding his arrival.

'Jeez, he really is a jackrabbit,' says Ibanez.

They wait until the elevator doors have closed before making a move. Kulic is already haring across the concourse, heading for the Tesla. Ibanez gets there first, Johnny flanking him from the other side a couple seconds later.

Kulic sees they got two guns on him. He knows he ain't gonna make it.

Johnny orders him down on his knees with his hands behind his head. The click of the cuffs feels particularly satisfying on this one. Almost as satisfying as when his phone buzzes again, showing Nimitz's name a third time. This call he *will* take.

'Hawke. You wanna explain why you've been ghosting me all morning?'

'My pleasure,' Johnny replies.

He tells him the news, lays it out matter-of-fact. Nimitz responds by acting like it's nothing, all in a day's work.

'Don't I get an attaboy?'

Nimitz ignores this. Figures. Maybe if he hadn't rolled that car.

'Ibanez with you?' the captain asks.

'Yep. What I do to get him foisted on me?'

'Ask Gina Hoffner.'

'That was a low blow, Captain.'

'You asked. How's he working out so far?'

28

'I'll tell you when I've known him more than five minutes. We're recruiting from Arizona now?'

'Arizona? I thought he was from San Diego. Anyways, there's a unit on its way to your location to pick up Kulic.'

'What you talking about? I want to book this one myself. You know what I went through for this piece of shit?'

'Job's done, Johnny. I got something else I need you on urgently. Now that you've reminded yourself you can bring in a suspect without making too much noise, your reward is I'm gonna trust you with something delicate.'

'What is it?'

'Suicide. Some guy ate his gun at a movie studio in West Hollywood.'

'Suicide, or apparent suicide?'

'Sounds about as clear cut as it comes. Guy even locked himself in a closet to do it. Got two uniforms on-site now.'

'Why can't *they* write it up? What do you need me for?'

'Because it's delicate. You fuckin' deaf? It's at Kingdom Pictures, as in Dominique King.'

'That *is* delicate,' Johnny admits. He knows Dominique King has friends in high places, including on the Board of Police Commissioners.

'No shit. It's been impressed upon me that this needs to get processed properly but without it turning into any kind of circus. You know how it goes with the politics of these things. I need to send an officer of sufficient rank, but one who's gonna notice if this thing isn't what it looks like.'

'To be clear, you want me to do this by the book. Investigate it thoroughly, but discreetly enough that I don't piss off anybody important?'

'Your basic poisoned chalice, Johnny. Attaboy.'

29

There is a squad car coming down the ramp as Johnny hangs up the call. Two officers get out and bundle Kulic into the back, chaining him to the cuff-anchor.

'What's the deal?' the kid asks.

'You're a lucky guy, Ibanez. In the job five minutes and you're already going to Hollywood.'

Johnny opens the door of the Charger and gestures Ibanez to drive.

'Aren't you forgetting something?'

'Like what?'

'I believe you owe me fifty bucks.'

Johnny sighs. He'd been hoping the kid had forgotten, or written it off as just talk. He pulls out a fifty.

'Don't you have Venmo?' Ibanez asks.

'The fuck is Venmo?'

Ibanez tuts, then leans across the roof of the car and takes the note.

'How did you figure it?' Johnny asks, indicating Kulic's vehicle.

'I reckoned stealth over speed. A Tesla's about the least conspicuous thing he could own in this neighbourhood. Plus the profile: he's really into tech and he's an asshole – of course he's gonna be a Musk fan.'

Johnny nods. 'Played.'

'This is how it goes with you and partners though, isn't it?' Ibanez says, smiling. 'Nimitz told me you start off wary and then they gradually earn your respect.'

'Don't get ahead of yourself, kid. Just because you're smart don't mean I got any reason to trust you. And when he was telling you about my partners, there's something Nimitz left out.'

'What would that be?'

'That they keep winding up dead.'

The Corpse in
the Confessional

IV

Penny was in the Tayview Brew enjoying a cup of what these days was described as 'English breakfast tea', or as it used to be known, tea, while nibbling on a miniature Devon finger, in the company of Dougal Keogh. Dougal owned the little art-deco cinema on Leven Square, as well as managing the Glen Cluthar amateur dramatic society. They were discussing his imminent production of *The Government Inspector*, in which Dougal would be playing the lead.

'I am always fascinated by what goes through your mind on-stage when you are in character,' she said. 'Are you detached from yourself entirely, feigning emotions, or do you tap into your own feelings to make it authentic?'

'It's a strange symbiosis,' he replied, holding one half of a fruit scone in either hand. 'You're inhabiting the persona of someone else, with their concerns, their memories, their needs and regrets, and yet you're still entirely yourself. The result is an amalgam of what is already written and the properties you yourself bring

31

to it, so Khlestakov is always Khlestakov, but he would be a completely different character if he was being played by anyone else.'

'Fascinating,' Penny said. She watched him butter one half of the scone and let him take a bite before moving on to her primary purpose.

'I saw you at the service,' she said. 'You're not normally a church-going man.'

'Showing my neighbours I'm there for them at a trying time. And hoping they remember to be there for *me* at a trying time. Such as opening night.'

'You'll be doing well if you get half that turnout. It seemed like most of the village was there.'

'Yes. Though not all of them would have been weeping at the loss of Brendan Gault. This pair, for starters,' Dougal said. His eyes subtly indicated the Tayview's proprietors, who were working behind the counter.

'How so?'

'They haven't changed their menu for twenty years. Wish I could say the same about their price list. Then this fellow comes along and sets up a patisserie.'

'You're not saying . . .?'

'Oh, don't be daft, no. Gault was competition, but he was no threat. Especially after the unpleasantness with Father Driver. That was bound to torpedo all local goodwill and trigger an unspoken boycott. But ironically, he might have upset fewer people had his patisserie been a success.'

Penny put down her cup. 'I don't follow.'

Dougal glanced back and forth conspiratorially.

'When the patisserie failed, he was raging at what he saw as a conspiracy, the locals circling the wagons against an incomer.

So he planned his revenge. He was planning to open—' Dougal dropped his voice '—a franchise.'

'One of those American coffee places?'

'Worse. Much worse. We're talking bakery here. You know, a . . .' He mouthed the name much as though he might a swear word, a smirk on his lips in acknowledgement of the disproportionate outrage.

'Goodness. That can't have gone down well.'

'The idea of an outsider coming in and ruining this picture-perfect, award-winning thoroughfare, four-time finalist for Scotland's Prettiest Street, with *one of those*. They had an emergency meeting of the town council. The provost was fit to be tied. "We don't want people coming here and thinking they've strayed into Fife," he said.'

Penny giggled at Dougal's impression of the provost, who was a retired banker and an inveterate snob.

'And what did they decide?'

'They decided they were snookered. When they checked the bylaws, it turned out they had no power to stop him. It would have been a desecration. But fate intervened.'

'Yes,' said Penny. 'Fate does that a lot in Glen Cluthar.'

Everybody Dies Alone

Chapter Four

Johnny sees a queue of traffic up ahead as they proceed north on La Cienega. The lights are out and there's a resultant fender-bender blocking the intersection.

He tells Ibanez to hang a right.

'After this block?'

'No. Right now.'

Ibanez looks at where Johnny is pointing.

'That's not even on Google Maps. It's not a street. It's barely an alley.'

'It'll get us around this. Trust me, I could draw this neighbourhood from memory. I used to work these streets, back before . . .'

'Before what?' Ibanez asks. 'You still work here. Robbery-Homicide out of North Wilcox. Have done twenty years, according to your file.'

Everything feels fuzzy for a moment. Johnny touches the wound on his forehead. He must have got banged up more than he thought. He recalls what Shawna said about concussion.

He had a memory of something that was there and now it's

gone. A real jolt, something fucked up, something *he* fucked up. And then there was nothing, like when you have a nightmare and can't remember it after you wake, just the relief that whatever it was isn't real.

Ibanez drives them along the alley, the bushes close enough either side to brush the flanks of the Charger as it passes. The sat-nav is happy again once they're back on Rosewood heading east.

Kingdom Pictures occupies half a block close to Fountain and Fairfax. It's a sizeable lot, set back from the street and bordered by stretches of concrete wall interspersed with blue-painted fencing. There are signs warning of anti-climb paint, in case you miss the barbed wire on the fencing and the embedded glass on top of the walls.

There's a black-and-white parked in front of the gates, stopping any traffic going in or out. Johnny recognises both the uniforms standing next to the car: Dunn and Ramirez. He tagged Ramirez as smart but in a conceited way, like she knows this stage of the job is beneath her, and grudges having to mark her time before moving on to greater things. Dunn, by contrast, was one of the first names that popped into Johnny's head when Ibanez asked who was the dumbest cop in the precinct.

Johnny hopes to Christ they haven't touched anything. He's more worried about Ramirez than Dunn, because the problem with people who think they're above the basics is they're the ones who get the basics wrong.

'You been inside?' Johnny asks, rolling down the window.

'No,' says Ramirez. 'Our orders were to secure the gate.'

'Good. Anybody try to get inside?'

'Yeah. Someone who was due to shoot here today. Guess she didn't get the email.'

Dunn moves the squad car so that Ibanez can approach the gate, which rolls aside with a rumble in response.

There's an office building taking up maybe a quarter of the compound, a larger two-storey structure accounting for half, with the rest for parking. The bigger building has a double-height loading bay with concertina doors, marks on the tarmac before it warning TRUCKS ONLY.

On one wall Johnny can see the faded ghost of an old sign stating Kingdom Production Facilities. He remembers being here once before, back in the day, interviewing a wit. Dominique King started her business down the street, renting out cameras and sound equipment, then expanded into this lot as a studio space for hire. Eventually she had the idea of the company making its own flicks. Started off with straight-to-video fare back in the nineties. That got their toe on the ladder to becoming, not exactly a mini-major like New Line or Miramax, but at least one of the bigger indies.

There's a man walking towards them as Johnny and Ibanez get out of the car. White, mid-thirties, tall, handsome. He's extending a hand as he approaches. The welcoming committee.

'Peter Godfrey,' he says. 'Chief financial officer, Kingdom Pictures.'

'Lieutenant Johnny Hawke. This is Detective Ibanez.'

The guy's wearing Johnny's mortgage. His haircut alone probably cost more than the best suit Johnny owns. It's not doing much for him today, though. Godfrey's looking gaunt, worried. Johnny makes a note to find out what he's worried about. Being shocked about finding a dead body in your building is a different thing to being worried about why.

'The body is in the . . .' Godfrey glances towards the bigger building. 'This is our soundstage. Do you want me to take you there right away?'

36

Dude clearly wants the answer to be no.

'If you wouldn't mind.'

Godfrey nods, like he's bracing himself. He leads them across the lot, pulling out a set of keys as he nears the door.

'It's through here,' he says, redundantly. Nervous.

Godfrey unlocks the door and they enter a dark corridor. He flips on the lights and Johnny rears up at the unexpected sight of blood streaking the walls. Not just streaking: it's smeared, spattered and dappled.

'Christ. I thought it was one guy. How many people died in here?'

'That's all corn syrup,' Godfrey says. 'They shot a zombie movie a couple months back. This part of the corridor leads from the make-up department to the soundstage.'

A few yards down on the left is a heavy door with an unlit red bulb above it. Godfrey holds it open, revealing it not to be a door but a portal.

As soon as he walks inside, Johnny is transported. He's in a different world, or at least a different time. He just stepped into 1950s LA. He's standing inside the Formosa Café, or at least three sides of it, even though he knows the real thing is still standing up on Santa Monica Boulevard. It's been recreated in fine detail, the red upholstery looked down on by the rows of black-and-white ten-by-eights. Johnny remembers the first time he went in there, maybe twenty-five years ago. It looked like the 1950s then too. It's more than just the look, though. It even smells right: a mix of old leather, spilled alcohol and decades of cigarette smoke.

Johnny touches one of the cushions, puts his fingers to his nose. There's nothing, just a hint of something chemical, like cleaning product. He realises how much the imagination automatically fills in the blanks if you give it something to work with.

'Wouldn't it have been cheaper just to rent the Formosa?' he asks.

'They might have objected to us firing two thousand rounds of blank ammunition and spraying a hundred blood squibs around the place. That's what was due to shoot today. When the Formosa closed down in 2016, we bought all the fixtures and fittings they were throwing out.'

Johnny remembers reading about that. The new owners gutted it, then, when their business failed, the next owners spent a shitload to make it look exactly like it used to. It made Johnny think of that time he went to Italy and saw that the ruins in Pompeii had a maintenance crew. How do you maintain a ruin? 'Okay, guys, leave everything the fuck alone. And don't let me catch you repairing any shit.'

Godfrey leads them out of the Formosa into a grand ballroom with a bandstand at one end, set for a jazz orchestra. Chandeliers hang from the ceiling, though with less head clearance than Johnny would have expected. He guesses camera perspective makes the ceiling appear higher. Magic of the movies.

He notices that the ballroom tables are covered with empty bottles and glasses, the dregs of drinks in many of them. He sees pizza boxes and uneaten bao buns, neither of which look very 1950s.

'Was there an actual, like, real-life party in here?'

Godfrey pauses, looking at the floor, looking at the evidence, then reluctantly back at Johnny.

'We were having, I guess, a double celebration. Sort of a wrap party, even though today was supposed to be the last day of filming. Shooting up the diner was the last scene on the sheet.'

Godfrey seems self-conscious discussing this soirée. Something he's not comfortable about.

'What else were you celebrating?'

He takes a beat.

'We had acquired a script, a real hot property, in the face of a lot of competition. Co-written by two up-and-comers: Crawford Nicholson and Jed Mahoney. The majors were after it too, so it was quite a coup.'

'How'd you swing it?'

'We were able to offer a degree of control that the big studios would never agree to. Even director approval. That still wasn't getting us over the line though, so we offered the writers a three-picture first-look deal, and that sealed it. We had shaken hands ahead of formalising terms, so we invited them to watch yesterday's shoot and hang around for a party.'

There's a tone of regret in Godfrey's voice, like this story has a second act. Johnny reckons this might be what the guy's worried about, and why Dominique King has been calling in favours.

'You worried this morning's discovery is gonna put a spanner in the works?' he asks.

'Oh, it's already done more than that.'

'How so?'

'I'm taking you to Jed Mahoney.'

They follow Godfrey onto the bandstand and through a gap in the screens behind, back into a world of bare brick and gypsum partitions. A steel staircase leads up to a second level.

'When was the discovery made?' Johnny asks.

'Building superintendent was doing his rounds at seven a.m. He noticed blood under the doors of the lighting storage bay. When he tried to open them, he found they were locked.'

'He was the super, he had the keys, right?' Johnny says.

'That's the thing. There *is* no lock on those doors. But they had been padlocked from the inside. The super had to use a crowbar to open them.'

At the top of the stairs, they proceed along a low-ceilinged corridor lined with open doors, the space divided into storage units for props and costumes, as well as workshops for painting and carpentry.

Walking behind Godfrey, Johnny smells it before he sees it: the tang of spilt blood. As their host steps to one side, he gets how the super couldn't have missed it, congealing but not quite dried on the black-and-white tiled vinyl flooring.

The double doors are partially open, enough to see a section of the body lying just inside. He is dressed in grey cargo shorts and a blue t-shirt. Both doors are gouged and splintered from the super's crowbar, which is lying just to the side.

Johnny and Ibanez pull on gloves and plastic overshoes.

'Where's the super right now?' Ibanez asks.

'He's in one of the production offices. There's a paramedic with him. He's pretty shaken up.'

'Don't let him leave. We'll need to speak with him.'

'He understands that.'

Johnny nudges the doors open and steps cautiously through the gap, making space for Ibanez to follow. Godfrey doesn't need to be told to wait in the corridor.

It's gloomy inside. Johnny noticed the workshops along the corridor all have skylights, while the storage spaces only have corrugated aluminum above.

He finds the light switch, flips it on. There are rows of lights, gels, stands and brackets wall to wall, floor to ceiling, but that's not what he was brought here to look at. He turns around.

The inside of the door is real Jackson Pollock shit. A mess of blood and brains.

'Tell me what you see,' Johnny says.

Ibanez stares at him like it's a trap. 'What am I looking for?'

'It's not a trick question. Tell me what you see. And what you don't.'

Ibanez takes in the scene.

'White male, twenties. The body is lying on its back, cause of death appears to be a single gunshot wound. The face is unharmed. I can't see the back of the head without moving it, but it's clear the round went in through the open mouth. There's a nine-mill in the dead man's right hand, still held in place because his index finger is tangled in the trigger guard.'

'What about the door? And I don't mean the blood.'

'There is a length of chain looped through both door handles and a padlock hooked through two of the links. Right door handle ripped away and dangling from the chain. The padlock and the chain must have held while the crowbar dislodged the screws holding the right handle's base-plate.'

'Okay. Now what don't you see?'

Ibanez takes a moment.

'No signs of a struggle. No ligature marks or bruises to the body. No windows or skylights in the room. No visible means of ingress or egress apart from the door, which was padlocked from the inside.'

Johnny nods.

'Mr Godfrey?' he calls.

Godfrey steps reluctantly into the gap between the doors.

'The deceased's name is Jed Mahoney, you say?'

'That's right.'

41

'When did you last see him?'

'At the party. He was there, then he wasn't. I don't mean he stormed out, I just mean, you know what it's like, a whole lot of people milling around. I assumed he had gone off with Blake, but I saw her later and she asked me if I'd seen him.'

'Who's Blake?'

'Blake Astor. She's our head of development. She was instrumental in bringing in the script. She's also his fiancée. They're real close. That's why I just don't understand what's happened. I really can't paint a more vivid picture of someone with everything to live for.'

'And yet,' says Ibanez.

'Did they have a falling-out?' Johnny asks.

'Not that it looked like.'

'Nobody heard a gunshot? Even thinking it came from outside, or a car backfiring?'

'The music was pretty loud last night.'

'How late did it go on?'

'I left around two or three.'

'Which was it?' Ibanez asks. 'Two or three?'

'I remember looking at my watch around two and deciding it was getting on. But you know how it is, trying to get out the door when everybody's drunk, and you know, talkative.'

'Who has access to up here?' Johnny asks.

'Anyone who's got access to the building. We're security conscious about getting in the lot, but after that it's never really an issue.'

Godfrey's phone buzzes.

'I have to take this,' he says apologetically.

'Don't worry about it. But don't go too far.'

Johnny looks around again, then at Ibanez.

'They teach you anything about the sound of hooves back in Mesa, Ibanez?'

'Same thing they teach you in LA. When you hear it, look for horses, not zebras.'

'So what do you figure?'

'Only one way in or out of this room and it was padlocked from the inside. Single gunshot, no other damage or signs of disturbance. Short of a note, he couldn't have made it more blatantly a suicide.'

Johnny frowns, looking at the chain and padlock again.

'Yeah. That's the part that bothers me.'

'How so?'

'I feel like somebody's taken a lot of trouble to make sure we see a horse.'

The Corpse in
the Confessional

V

Penny understood the protectiveness the locals felt towards Glen Cluthar's beautiful Main Street. She loved its character and its bustle, even enjoyed slaloming the tourists as they fell upon its gift shops and cafés with the spatial awareness of blind hippos. But her favourite thing about the Main Street was that if you turned left off it, onto Marshall Street, you would reach the library, where Penny worked as a volunteer.

She might even say that while Silverbank Cottage was her home, the library was where she lived. Reading allowed her to lead infinite lives, to access someone else's thoughts and memories: memories that did not fade, curated by minds that did not fail.

On this particular morning, Penny was perusing the society section of *Scottish Field*, in search of answers to the mystery that was disconcerting her far more than the murder of Brendan Gault.

Lord and Lady Stonebridge say they are very much looking forward to their forthcoming visit to Perthshire for the wedding of Sebastian Gossard, Lord Stonebridge's son, to Miss Lilian Deacon. Jonathan Stonebridge, who was ennobled two years ago, heads the Stonebridge Publishing empire. Sebastian Gossard is Lord Stonebridge's son by his first wife, and carries her surname.

Penny had now at least seen a name she recognised, but she remained unclear as to why she had been invited. Many years ago she had worked for Stonebridge Publishing, and had known Jonathan Stonebridge as a rather ineffectual editor. He was, however, the son of Arthur Stonebridge, the firm's founder, which explained his subsequent rise.

She remembered and yet she didn't: names that made sense, buildings she could picture, but with only the most fragmentary memory of her time there, a scrapbook with most of the pages torn out. Among the missing sections was the one covering whatever she had done to so endear herself to this peer of the realm that she should be invited to his son's wedding.

A part of Penny understood that the place in William's brochure was an inevitable destination, but she still wanted to put it off as long as possible. In that respect, her mind was a lot like this library. By rights it ought to have closed down years ago, but she wasn't letting it go without a fight.

The library faced a constant struggle to raise funds, not merely for acquiring new titles, but literally to keep the lights on. It was a struggle that had Penny weary, and she sometimes wondered whether she ought to choose her losing battles more selectively. The owner of Blue Skies Travel used to say: 'When the internet arrived, they told us our time was up, and yet here we still are.' But he wasn't there any more, and in time, inevitably, nor would the library be.

For now, though, it remained a going concern, and one which, right then, she could see Inspector Sattar striding purposefully towards.

Penny rose automatically to put the kettle on.

'I was wondering when you would appear,' she said, as Saeeda walked through the swing doors.

Inspector Sattar had been in the post almost five years now, and had made a highly favourable impression on Penny. She had proven considerably less obtuse than a succession of male prede-cessors who resented the meddling contributions of an elderly librarian, even when those contributions prevented a miscarriage of justice or a monster walking free.

Saeeda had what was these days known as emotional intelli-gence, or in the old tongue, a keen instinct for reading people. It was not infallible, otherwise she would not have become involved with that last boyfriend, but still served her well enough to decide that being a single mother was preferable to saddling herself with a no-user as a father to her child.

She looked tired, and Penny suspected she knew why.

'And how is little Humsar today?'

Saeeda inferred from Penny's tone precisely why she was asking.

'Little Humsar was very close to spending a night in the cells. He's teething again, and I barely got a wink last night. I have seldom been so happy to hand him over at the nursery.'

Saeeda threw her jacket over a chair as Penny presented her with a mug of tea and a Bourbon biscuit.

'As you intimated, we both know why I'm here,' Saeeda said.

Penny put her hands in the air. 'I'll cop to it. Or should I say, I confess.'

Saeeda rolled her eyes.

'It's hard to miss the symbolism,' said Penny. 'A body left in a confessional.'

'Someone clearly felt Mr Gault had something to repent.'

'Yes, but I think it poses a larger question. Which is what an outspoken atheist was doing in that church at all.'

'I didn't know that about Gault,' said Saeeda. 'What can you tell me?'

'Not a great deal. As you know, I've been away for the best part of two months. I'm only catching up myself.'

Penny told her what little she had found out.

'Even in Glen Cluthar, I can't see someone offing him just because he was threatening to bring down the tone of the Main Street,' Saeeda said.

'No,' agreed Penny. She had heard of people murdered for the most petty and seemingly incomprehensible reasons, but in her experience, motives tended to ultimately come down to variations of greed, jealousy and revenge. 'What can you tell me, by way of quid pro quo?' she asked.

'We've been pursuing lines of inquiry pertaining to Mr Gault's previous business dealings in Dundee. He had a number of creditors following a historic bankruptcy. When he set up a new business, accompanied by a degree of press fanfare, it's possible some long-simmering resentments might have been stirred up.'

'That's surely not all you have,' Penny said, her tone warning Saeeda not to take her for a numpty.

Saeeda gave a knowing smile. She leaned forward, even though they were alone in the library. 'In the strictest confidence I can tell you that there is a detail we've been keeping back from the public. There was a card in his suit pocket. A mass card, in fact, with a message inside. It said: "This is your last chance. Do the decent thing or I will destroy you." It was written in all caps, but we're still hoping to identify the handwriting.'

'So there was a direct threat. What of your forensic-science eggheads? Have they come up with anything useful?'

'The pathologist says a ligature was used. Something soft and strong: cloth as opposed to leather or rope. He wasn't strangled by someone's bare hands. We've also heard rumours that he was something of a ladies' man, so one possibility is a jealous husband. That would fit with the card, but . . .' Saeeda sighed.

'What?' Penny asked.

'I don't know if it's the ligature detail, but sometimes you get a feeling around a case, and for whatever reason, I'm getting a sense that this was a woman.'

Everybody Dies Alone

Chapter Five

Ibanez tries the doorbell one more time. Like that's gonna make all the difference.

They're at the address Peter Godfrey gave them for Crawford Nicholson, the dead guy's writing partner. The apartment is on the second floor of a six-unit complex in Marina del Rey. It's a retro art-deco building, fifties design but nineties construction, a return staircase winding between the landings, and glass bricks in the centre.

Godfrey told them he hadn't spoken to Nicholson since the party. They can't be certain he even knows about Jed Mahoney being dead until they speak to him, but the guy isn't answering his cell. It keeps going straight to voicemail.

'Could be on DND?' Ibanez had suggested. 'After a late night.'

'This is Hollywood,' Johnny told him. 'Not answering your phone is a big deal. My gut says he knows.'

Johnny has the impression Godfrey was the up-and-comer who got landed with the shit detail on a bad day because they knew he would go along to get along. He told them Dominique King had flown out to New York that morning for some big meeting. There were rumours of a hostile takeover and she needed to shore up support. Johnny might have asked what kind of tragedy it would take for her to cancel the trip, but figured he wouldn't like the answer.

There are footsteps on the stairs, the scratching of paws too. A woman ascends to the landing, dressed head to ankles in Lycra. Johnny figures she's around Ibanez's age, late twenties or early thirties. She's got one of those dogs that look like they're mass-produced in a factory and sold in a boutique: soft, short hair, hypo-allergenic, even temperament. The next stage is they breed one that don't need to take a shit.

She looks them up and down with disapproval, like she's afraid they're here to tell her about Jesus. She has her keys out, heading for the door opposite.

'We're looking for Crawford Nicholson, your neighbour,' Johnny says, flashing his badge. He can tell a lot from how someone reacts to that. Your white-bread law-abiding taxpayer gets tense. They want to cooperate, they don't want to be on the wrong side of the law.

She gets tense.

'Is he in some kind of trouble?'

'No, ma'am. We just want to make sure he's okay.'

'Why wouldn't he be?'

'We're not at liberty to discuss that. Do you speak to him much, or just to say hi?'

She strokes the dog, glances at Nicholson's door. 'We've had drinks a few times. Him and his writing buddy, me and my roommate.'

'Jed Mahoney?'

'That's the one, yeah.'

'Did they talk about Kingdom Pictures?'

She smiles. 'Oh, yeah. *They* were buying the drinks that night. They got offered a three-picture deal.' Her expression changes. 'Is everything okay with that?'

'Why wouldn't it be?' Johnny asks.

'I don't know. Just asking.'

'If you had to guess . . .' Ibanez prompts. His tone is warm, unthreatening.

'Last we spoke, Crawford mentioned Jed was having second thoughts that Kingdom was the right move. He didn't say why, just said Jed could be like that, always sweating the details.'

'When did you last speak?'

'A couple days ago. Here on the landing. I was coming in, he was going out.'

Johnny produces a card. 'If you see him, can you ask him to give me a call? It's very important.'

'Sure thing.'

She takes the card and slips inside her apartment.

'What now?' Ibanez asks.

'I want to talk to more of these Kingdom Pictures people. The ones who were at the party. I want to know who might have spoken to Jed last. Starting with his fiancée.'

'Seriously?' Ibanez says. 'You're not happy just to put this down as a suicide?'

'Not quite yet. Nimitz said he wanted it investigated properly, so that's what I'm gonna do.'

Blake Astor's phone has also been going to voicemail. Johnny's left a couple messages. He's not optimistic she'll get back to him, and not just because as Kingdom's head of development, she's gotta be Olympic standard at dodging unwanted calls.

Johnny phones Peter Godfrey as they walk back out to the car.

'Are you still on-site?' he asks.

'Yes. They've been to uplift the . . . to take Jed away. The coroner.'

'Who else is there from your company?'

'Nobody. I was told to close things down until the body had been . . . you know. I'm only here to hold the fort.'

'Do you know where I'd find Blake Astor?'

'I haven't spoken with her today. She isn't picking up. She was due on set for a location shoot in Santa Monica.'

'And where would I find—' Johnny reads from his notes, listing the senior Kingdom Pictures execs '—Tom Lennox and Damien Lennox? Are they related?'

'Brothers. Tom Lennox is due on the same shoot. Damien, who knows.'

Johnny ends the call and tells Ibanez they're headed for Santa Monica.

The kid looks sceptical. 'Her fiancé just killed himself. Surely she doesn't go to work after that?'

'This is Hollywood. You'd be surprised. But call in and get me a home address for her anyway.'

The location is only ten minutes' drive away. The shoot is taking place on the terrace outside a restaurant off Ocean Park, a green screen masking off one side. Johnny doesn't know if it's a special effects kinda picture or if they just want a prettier street in the background. There are two actors at a table, deep in conversation, two cameramen shooting them in shot/reverse shot while a director in a baseball cap crouches feet away. Behind him are about a dozen other people, watching in silence.

There are three trucks parked around the corner, Kingdom Production logos on their sides, and a couple security guys making sure curious passers-by don't get too close.

One of them puts a hand up as Johnny and Ibanez approach.

Johnny flashes his badge discreetly, but not so discreetly that a nearby production assistant doesn't notice. She swoops in, clutching an iPad, a headset and microphone wrapped around blue-dyed hair.

'We need to speak to Blake Astor,' Johnny says quietly.

'Blake isn't here. She—' The assistant clocks the significance of who she's talking to. 'I'm guessing you know why.'

'What about Tom Lennox?'

'I'll talk to Tom but we're rolling.'

Johnny nods and watches the shoot. He's too far away to hear what's being said. Looks like a break-up scene, though. Johnny knows pretty good what they look like.

As soon as the director says cut, the assistant speaks into her mouthpiece.

Johnny scans the crew, sees a guy in deck shorts and a polo shirt look up. He strides towards them briskly, a solemn expression on his face. He looks stressed.

'Tom Lennox, Kingdom Pictures,' he says. 'I take it this is about Jed?'

'Yes, sir. We were hoping to speak to Blake Astor.'

Lennox sighs, like dealing with Johnny is just another turd on this shit mountain of a day.

'Blake is taking a personal day. For reasons I assume you understand.'

'I do understand, but we'd still like to speak to her. Do you know where she is?'

'You tried her cell?'

'She's not answering.'

'Well, there you go. She doesn't want to be disturbed.'

'She might answer if it's someone she knows.'

Lennox considers, makes a quick decision.

'I can try.'

He puts his phone to his ear. Johnny is not convinced he actually dialled.

'Voicemail,' he says after a few seconds. 'She's screening calls. I can leave a message.'

'No, we'll drop by the house. She lives in the Canyons, right? Be good to know if she'll actually be there, and to give her some notice, but . . .'

Johnny lets it hang. So does Lennox. Stand-off.

'We're having trouble locating Crawford Nicholson,' Johnny says. 'He's not answering either, and he's not at home. Do you know where he might have gone?'

'No. I don't know him that well. We've spoken a few times, but Blake had more to do with him. You should ask Peter. They worked together before Peter came to Kingdom.'

Johnny's getting a strong sense of deflection, the guy happily offering up Godfrey, and a connection to the victim that Lennox accurately guessed Godfrey hasn't mentioned.

'Were you at the party last night?' Johnny asks.

'Sure.'

'And did you speak with Jed Mahoney?'

'A little, yeah.'

'How did he seem?'

Lennox's expression is blank. 'It was a party.'

'What does that mean?'

'It means everybody wears a happy face at something like that. So if I tell you he looked fine, it doesn't mean shit.'

'You saying there's a reason it wouldn't be fine?'

'I'm just saying, I hung out with them a few times, but I didn't know Jed or Crawford particularly well. Blake is the one who brought in their script.'

'Were Jed and Blake an item before that?' asks Ibanez.

'What do you mean?'

'I mean, did they become close because she was talking to him about the script or—?'

'Oh, I see what you're saying. No, Blake was already seeing him. I mean, Blake knows everybody. She's a ninth-dan black-belt networker. But yeah, she and Jed were already seeing each other. To be honest, Blake's the only way Kingdom were gonna get a sniff of such a hot script in the first place.'

'We spoke to someone who suggested Jed might have had reservations about the deal,' Johnny says. 'You know anything about that?'

'Not that Blake ever mentioned. But it doesn't surprise me. I always assumed they had other offers that they hadn't quite closed the door on.'

'We had the impression it was specifically Jed who was getting cold feet.'

'I can't speak to that,' he says.

'I'm just trying to garner impressions. A young man took his own life, with seemingly everything in front of him. We're trying to understand why that might be.'

'Look, I'm doing three people's jobs today. And one of those people is Blake, who does three people's jobs every day. I don't have time for speculation.'

Lennox glances across to the terrace. They're waiting. He gestures to someone that he'll be two minutes. Cute that he reckons he's in control of that, Johnny thinks.

'I figure if you've had to come in on a day like this, there can't be much slack in this picture's schedule,' Johnny says.

'You got that right.'

'With that in mind, do you know how little it would take for me to shut down this location today? I make one phone call and I can get like three permits revoked inside ten minutes. Would that make you more talkative?'

Lennox looks to the terrace again. This time he signals that they should go ahead without him.

He turns back to Johnny and sighs, resentful but resigned.

'Okay. For what it's worth, if you'd told me one of those guys was going to kill himself, I'd have picked Jed every time. Not that I'm saying I ever thought he was suicidal, just . . . They were yin and yang. Crawford only ever saw positives, Jed negatives. But that was how they worked as scriptwriters. One dreams up ideas and the other anticipates pitfalls. You need both halves of that.'

'It's kind of a stretch to equate a negative mindset with shooting yourself during a party,' suggests Ibanez.

'I'm not saying I'm not shocked. I'm just saying I'm less shocked that it should be Jed than anybody else. Jed had this dark side to him. Blake isn't going to admit that, but it was there.'

'Did anything else strike you as odd last night?' Johnny asks. 'Anyone behaving strangely? Anyone leave early?'

'*I* left early,' Lennox replies. 'I had to be on set down here at seven. You should talk to Peter Godfrey. I'm sure he'd have been there pretty late.'

He's nudging them towards Godfrey again, Johnny notes.

'We already did.'

'Or Damien. Damien's always the last to leave a party.'

'He's not answering his phone either.'

'Yeah, my little brother will be taking a personal day too.'

There's a side to this, an edge of resentment.

'*You* don't need a personal day?' Johnny asks. 'You seem like you could use one.'

'Somebody's got to keep driving the bus. Even at a time like this.'

'Can you tell us where Damien lives?'

'I could. But it won't be any use to you, because that's not where he'll be.'

Johnny wonders if he should raise the permit threat again, then understands it won't be necessary. Whatever loyalty Lennox is feeling towards Blake Astor does not extend to his little brother. And you don't say for sure somebody won't be home unless you got a pretty good idea where they'll be. Sure enough, a moment later, Lennox coughs it up.

'One last thing,' Johnny says. 'This script you guys were buying from Nicholson and Mahoney. What's it about?'

'It's about someone who steals a screenplay and kills the writer.'

The Corpse in the Confessional

VI

Father Driver's devoted housekeeper still lived in the wee two-storey terraced house on Faskally Street that she had moved into with her late husband several decades earlier. Penny was of the opinion that Mrs Crichton would be better off letting out her property and actually moving into the parochial house, given that she spent most of her time there: cooking, cleaning, ironing and generally ministering to the more enduring love of her life. For that reason, Penny waited until late in the evening to call upon her, when she would finally be at home. She wanted to speak to her away from the church because she suspected that proximity to the confessional booth might be the thing staying her tongue.

'Ms Coyne, what brings you here at this hour?' Mrs Crichton asked, swiftly ushering Penny inside as though fearful that the sight of her might cause tongues to wag. Those who most traded in gossip were also those most worried about being the subject of it.

Mrs Crichton was a strapping woman, at least a foot taller than Penny, and might have been an imposing presence were it not for a permanent air of servitude that would have made Uriah Heep seem arrogant by comparison. Her apron was lying across the back of a chair, strings dangling almost to the floor. She wore it like a vestment, the symbolic attire of her sacred order. Penny admired her selfless devotion in pursuit of no earthly reward. When Mrs Crichton died, she would surely go to heaven, though Penny doubted God would measure up to Father Driver.

'I need your assistance, Dorothy. Or rather, the police do, and I thought you might prefer to speak to me than to Inspector Sattar directly.'

'But I don't know anything,' she insisted.

'I think you do.'

Mrs Crichton glanced again towards the church that she lived in permanent sight and service of.

'Honestly, I'm in the dark as much as everyone else. I was here at home on Saturday night, but it's not like I saw anyone come and go from the church. I've already told the police this.'

'But it's not Saturday night I'm talking about. I think you might have heard something before that, something of relevance.'

'I talk to the same people as you and anyone else,' she replied defensively.

Penny understood. This was why she wanted to speak to her here, and not in the church itself. It was not that Mrs Crichton needed to protect what she knew, it was that she needed to protect how she knew it. That was what Penny had to find a way around.

'We both understand that the sanctity of the confessional is absolute,' Penny said.

Mrs Crichton looked anxious, as though this was an accusation.

'Absolute,' she affirmed.

'And that you would never violate that. You would never *intentionally* eavesdrop upon someone's confession. But is it possible that, without meaning to, you accidentally overheard something regarding Mr Gault?'

Mrs Crichton glanced out the window again. When she turned back, there was a certain relief in her expression, less of that quiversome look about her.

'I didn't mean to overhear,' she said.

'Of course not.'

'It was Mrs Gault. The poor woman sounded like she was at the end of her rope. She wasn't so much confessing as needing someone to listen to her, and Father Driver is such a compassionate man. She said she thought her husband was having an affair. Poor thing, she grew up here, as you might know, and she'd come back hoping to settle down. But her standing in the village was damaged by the incident with Father Driver and the failure of her husband's business. If people also found out her husband was unfaithful, she knew she'd get sympathy, but living in pity is no way to exist. She thought she'd be better off without him.'

Mrs Crichton dropped her voice, concern darkening her face.

'She didn't confess any sins of her own, which I didn't think anything of at the time, but after what happened . . . I couldn't help wondering if she was at confession not because of something she'd done, but because of what she feared she *might* do.'

'Goodness,' said Penny. She thought of the symbolism of the death, and of Saeeda's intuition that the killer was a woman: an intuition that chimed utterly with her own instincts. A wronged wife was but one side of such a deadly triangle, however.

'I don't suppose she mentioned who she thought her husband was having an affair with?' Penny asked.

A wistful, faraway look came upon Mrs Crichton.

'She didn't say, but she'll know,' she said. 'Wives always do. They might tell themselves they've no idea, but deep down they know fine.'

Everybody Dies Alone

Chapter Six

'What kind of permits can you get revoked inside ten minutes?' asks Ibanez, pulling into the parking lot of a health club in Pacific Palisades, the address Lennox had given them. Johnny reckoned they should talk to his brother while they were at the coast, then head for the Canyons and hope Blake Astor was home.

'None. But he didn't know that. He was stressed and under pressure. Out of his depth despite his fancy title. Otherwise he might have called my bluff. Even if I could make that call, Nimitz told me to tread delicately around this one.'

'So firing threats around is treading delicately?'

'Long as they're fake threats.'

The parking lot looks like a showroom, high-end vehicles glinting in the afternoon sunshine. Johnny worries their Dodge Charger might get towed just for bringing down the vibe.

They walk into a glass-walled, air-conditioned reception vestibule that smells of citrus and money. There's a guy behind the desk who looks like he stepped off a teenage girl's bedroom wall, his smile flickering only briefly at the sight of the two cheap suits that just walked in.

When Johnny flashes the badge, the guy looks relieved, like there were a dozen worse explanations for who they might be.

'We need to speak to one of your guests. Damien Lennox?'

The Adonis nods and glances at his monitor.

'I think they're having a late lunch on the terrace. Would you like someone to escort you to—'

'No, we're good.'

'If you're sure. It's down the hall, all the way to the other side of the building.'

'Thanks. Oh, and did you say "they"?' Johnny asks.

'That's right,' the Adonis answers brightly.

'Just checking.'

Johnny heads down the marble-floored corridor. He can hear squash balls and the squeak of sneakers on a court somewhere behind the walls.

'You making a thing about someone's pronouns?' Ibanez asks.

'Did you miss the part about me working West Hollywood?' he replies. 'Nimitz said to tread light. So I don't want to piss "them" off by mistake before I've had the chance to piss them off intentionally.'

They stride out through a set of glass double doors into a courtyard where the sun is sparkling off an infinity pool that appears to bleed into the Pacific. It is bordered by immaculate lawns interspersed with topiary. Johnny wouldn't mind some personal days here himself.

A maître d' is waiting behind a podium, scrolling his phone because the terrace is notably quiet. Johnny quickly susses that he won't need to ask where to find Damien Lennox. He also realises that 'they' actually meant two people.

Peter Godfrey is sitting at a table, supportively clutching the hand of his dining companion, a guy maybe ten years younger. There is an unmistakable intimacy about it, solicitous and tender.

He lets the hand go rapidly when he sees Johnny and Ibanez approach.

'You must be Damien,' Johnny says, as Godfrey's companion looks round to see what has sparked this reaction.

Godfrey stands up awkwardly. 'Lieutenant Hawke, I, er—'

'You did err. When you lied and told me you didn't know where Damien would be.'

Damien stands up too, like he doesn't want to leave Godfrey facing a two-on-one.

'These are the police officers who are dealing with—'

'I understand.' Damien holds out a hand. He's in a robe, lettered with the club's initials. He looks tired, like he didn't get much sleep last night. 'Please forgive Peter's omission. It's a delicate situation. Workplace relationships are a minefield these days, and as we're both on the board of the company, it's even more complicated. Not everybody knows, so I'd appreciate your discretion.'

'My discretion tends to have a corresponding relationship with other people's candour,' Johnny says.

A thin smile tells him Damien gets the point.

'You mind if we take a seat?'

'Sure. Can we order you something?'

'No thank you.'

Johnny and Ibanez sit down.

'I appreciate it's a difficult time, but we need to ask you about—'

Before Johnny can finish, Damien's phone buzzes on the table. He glances at it then lifts it, standing up.

64

'I'm so sorry, I absolutely have to take this.'

He steps away from the table, but stays close enough that Johnny can still hear him speak above the trickle of water from the infinity pool.

'Understood. No, absolutely. I haven't said anything.'

He ends the call and turns around.

'I'm sorry. We can't speak to you. Neither of us.'

'What?'

'That was my . . . my boss. Dominique. Her lawyers have instructed us to say nothing further about this matter.'

'Her lawyers? Personal lawyers or lawyers for Kingdom Pictures?'

'I've been instructed not to answer any more questions.'

Before Johnny can respond, his cell buzzes. Unrecognised number.

'I think you should take that,' says Damien.

Johnny answers. It's a female voice.

'Hello, Lieutenant Hawke? You're speaking to Dominique King. I have instructed all of my employees not to speak to you without our lawyers being present.'

'Ma'am, there is really no need for—'

'I spoke to the coroner and to the deputy chief first thing today. I was given assurances that we would not be put through any unnecessary rigours merely because we have been adjacent to tragedy. Your superiors acknowledged that we've experienced something highly traumatic and we need to be allowed to deal with that. Instead, what I've got is you harassing my staff on-set, threatening to shut down a production, and disturbing grieving individuals while they're taking time to heal.'

'Ma'am, I can assure—'

'I've been assured: assured this would be dealt with professionally and sensitively. I was prepared to extend our full cooperation, but I will not let my company or my colleagues become a vehicle for whatever personal bullshit you're dealing with. Do you understand me?'

Johnny waits a moment to see if he'll be allowed to answer this time. It's long enough for her to hang up.

He pockets his phone and gestures to Ibanez that they're leaving. He can't stop himself from glaring at Damien and Godfrey by way of saying this ain't over.

'Best get one of those forensics bunny-suits,' he tells Ibanez as they reach the car.

'We got another body?'

'No, we're going back to the station. Where I'm about to get twenty gallons of shit dumped on me.'

Everybody Dies Alone

Chapter Seven

There's some kind of demonstration going on as the Charger approaches the precinct house. Nothing major, maybe a dozen or so people standing with placards. Somebody's always protesting about something these days. At least this one looks peaceful, more of a vigil kinda deal. Johnny hates it when they got the drums and whistles and shit. Hates it all the more when they got a point too.

One of the protestors turns just as Ibanez slows the Charger ahead of the corner. She is holding up a sign, plain black text on a white card. It says: 'Justice for Jayden Freil'. Johnny reels, feeling it like a migraine. He closes his eyes as though it's too bright, the sign painful to look at, but that's absurd.

Johnny forces himself to look again. It says: 'No Justice No Peace'.

He thinks it said something else a moment ago, but what's weird is that he now can't remember what. There was a name. A sentiment, one that cut him to the quick. Now all that's left is a kind of emotional residue.

Fortunately they don't have to walk through the protesters to get into the precinct. Ibanez drives around the building and they park underground.

'Which ride do you figure for mine?' Johnny asks as they pass a line of cars. 'Just want to see if Kulic's Tesla was a lucky guess.'

Ibanez scans the models.

'Black late-nineties Mustang Cobra,' he replies. 'Gimme something harder next time.'

'Son of a bitch.'

They go up the stairs and emerge opposite the door to the locker room.

'Fuck,' Johnny mutters.

'What?'

He has spotted Arlo Waters walking towards them down the hall. Never a welcome sight, or a pretty one. He's threatening to bust out of that cheap suit. Been hitting the roids again. Johnny keeps his eyes down, but his unguarded reaction causes Ibanez to look up.

'You must be Ibanez,' Waters says, all fake friendly. 'Yeah, I heard Johnny got a new partner. Seems appropriate he should be giving you a guided tour. We call this the Johnny Hawke Gallery.'

Ibanez takes in the photographs lining one side of the hallway leading to the bullpen. The nearest shows Gina Hoffner. She's smiling out at them in her dress uniform. Johnny figures it won't have taken Ibanez long to suss the significance of that second date under her name. Christ, it was less than two months ago. Already seems like another era, and yet still feels raw.

'Never works out too well for Johnny's partners,' says Waters. 'Though it would be unfair to say they *all* end up dead. One of 'em only ended up in a wheelchair.'

'I can think of one who didn't get injured at all,' Johnny replies coldly. 'Remind me what happened to that guy?'

Waters ignores this, gestures along the corridor. 'Take a good look, Ibanez. Plenty of space on this wall for your picture too.' He gives Ibanez an ugly smile then clatters through the locker-room door with an angry shove.

'Who was that?' Ibanez asks.

'Arlo Waters. Asshole.'

'Oh, I liked him. What's his beef?'

'One of my former partners was his brother.'

'Does he blame you for getting him killed? Or is he the one in a wheelchair? Shit, I'm sorry, Johnny. That's none of my business.'

'His brother's walking and breathing just fine. Arlo's pissed because he's doing all his walking and breathing in California State Prison since I sent him down for murder.'

'Shit. Who did he kill?'

'A witness about to testify against him on a corruption charge. What I've never told Arlo is that the wit was gonna testify against him too. Anyway, he's fulla shit. I've had a lot of partners, and they don't *all* get shot. Only the ones who decide they like me enough to stick around.'

When they reach the bullpen, through the glass of the captain's office Johnny can see that Nimitz is on the phone. He figures he can stealth his way through and buy a little time before the inevitable. But though the guy is riding a desk, Nimitz proves his peripheral vision is still as good as it was on the street. The captain doesn't even look up as he jabs a finger first towards Johnny and then towards his open office door.

Ibanez sees it too.

'It's okay if you want to sit this one out,' Johnny tells him quietly. 'This is all on me.'

Nimitz's hearing is as sharp as his eyesight.

'No, Ibanez, you get your ass in here too. I want to hear if you got any mitigation to offer.'

'Don't say shit,' Johnny tells Ibanez as he follows him across the floor.

Nimitz waits until Ibanez has closed the door.

'You want to know who I just got off the phone to, Johnny?' he asks.

'Should I start the bidding at the deputy chief?'

'Higher. Kingdom Pictures might only be an upstart independent, but Dominique King punches above her weight politically.'

'It's my understanding that the law applies the same to everybody, sir,' Johnny replies.

'She ain't *breaking* any laws,' Nimitz yells. 'Her daughter's fiancé just shot himself. I told you to tread lightly.'

'Blake Astor is her daughter?' Holly golly. It gets worse. How had he missed this?

'Yes. Astor is her married name.'

'So how could she be engaged to Jed Mahoney?'

'She's divorced. Married young and hung on to her ex's name for professional reasons, none of which matters. What matters is that her fiancé's dead, she's in pieces and her mom is pissed, which means I'm getting shit from on high, shit I specifically asked you to avoid.'

'You asked me to deal with this professionally, sir.'

'So what the hell are you doing? The coroner is happy this is a suicide. Nobody wins from you spinning this out, Johnny. Guy locked himself in a fucking closet to blow his own brains out. How much more obvious do you want it?'

'What's not obvious to me is why he would bring along a

70

padlock and chain if his intention was to kill himself. He already went off someplace private, where nobody knew he was.'

'Maybe he didn't want to be interrupted. And maybe he didn't want some asshole drawing the wrong conclusion, so he thought he'd best make it as obvious as it can fucking get that it's a fucking suicide. But that's just my two cents. What do you think, Ibanez?'

This is a typical Nimitz move, putting the new guy on the spot. See which way his loyalties fall.

Ibanez takes a moment, but from his regretful expression, Johnny can tell it won't go his way.

'My problem is, if this isn't a suicide, how does a perp chain and padlock those doors together then end up on the other side? There was only one way in or out.'

The kid makes a good point, one Johnny has been wrestling with. The captain can tell he doesn't have an answer.

Johnny glances up at the strip lights and the shitty polystyrene ceiling tiles, discoloured since the days you were still allowed to smoke in here. How many times has he stared at that same ceiling while getting chewed out by Nimitz and by half a dozen superiors before him?

That's when it hits him.

'The chandeliers,' he says.

'What chandeliers?' Nimitz asks.

'The ones in the movie set downstairs. It was done up like a hotel ballroom.'

'So?'

'They were way too heavy to be hanging from that fake ceiling. I'm betting there's some kind of gantry above that. Mahoney was found in the lighting storeroom. There's gotta be a hatch or something for getting lights into position above the sound-stage. I'd like to take another look.'

Nimitz is shaking his head. 'Not gonna happen, Johnny. Now that the body's downtown, Dominique King has made it clear her doors are closed. You're not getting back in there without a warrant.'

'So can't you make a call to a judge? Or does she have pull with all of them too?'

Nimitz is laughing. Never a good sign.

'Call a judge? For *this*, Johnny? You're out of your mind. This case is over. Write it up as a suicide. I want the paperwork on my desk by tomorrow morning.'

Johnny takes a seat in the bullpen, reflecting on how hard it is to stay in credit in this job. Taking down Kulic hasn't earned him much slack, but when was it ever different?

There's a shadow across his desk. Ibanez standing there, still hanging around like he's got no place to go.

'I'm sorry,' he says.

'For what?'

'I didn't back you up in there.'

'You called it like you saw it. That's more valuable to me than you keeping your mouth shut when you think I'm fulla shit.'

Ibanez glances towards Nimitz's office.

'"I want the paperwork on my desk by tomorrow morning." Did he really just say that?'

'Yeah. What's wrong with that?'

Ibanez laughs at a joke Johnny doesn't get. 'Forget it,' he says. 'Can I buy you a beer?'

Johnny checks his watch. He's off the clock but he's not ready to quit today just yet.

'It troubles me that we still ain't been able to find Crawford Nicholson. For all we know, the poor bastard might not even know his buddy's dead.'

72

'His cell's still on voicemail. We went by his apartment. What else can we do?'

'I'd like to get a check on where he last used his credit card.'

'Which we can't do because he's not a suspect, Johnny. And we've no evidence to consider him one.'

'And what if he's not a suspect, but a second victim?'

'I think that's a hell of a stretch. I get why he's not answering his cell: he's not just lost a friend, he's also just lost his writing partner. It might be worth driving by his place again, though. See if there's a light on now.'

'Okay, you do that.'

'What are you gonna do?'

'What the captain told me to. Close the case by tomorrow morning.'

'That's not what he said.'

'There are fine distinctions in this job,' Johnny replies. 'Me and Nimitz are both instruments of the law. But there's a difference between the law and the rules. People say that without rules, there would be anarchy. But from what I've seen, there already is anarchy, hidden behind an illusion of order. Unless I can apply the law to everyone equally, then any rule stopping me doing that is part of the illusion.'

The Corpse in
the Confessional

VII

It was the following afternoon when Inspector Sattar returned
to the library with an update of sorts, if not exactly a development. She looked altogether brighter today, wee Humsar
evidently having granted both of them a more restful night.

Penny appreciated how hard it must be for Saeeda, juggling
her childcare arrangements with her shifts, which was why she
occasionally helped out. They were both easy with it now, but
there had remained a lingering awkwardness after the first time,
when Penny agreed to stay overnight at Saeeda's flat in Perth
while her parents were abroad on holiday.

Much as Penny had admired Saeeda as a single mother from
afar, up close she had been appalled at the laxity of her child-
safety arrangements. Everywhere Penny looked there seemed to
be potential hazards or outright death-traps. When Saeeda
returned the next day, she found that Penny had installed safety
latches on all the cupboard doors, covers on all the plug points
and a safety gate at the head of the stairs.

It had not been well received.

'What do you think I am?' Saeeda had demanded. 'Some negligent heidthebaw? I don't want my child growing up walking on eggshells, worrying that death lies around every corner. And I don't want to live my life trying to head off danger from every source I can think of.'

What was difficult for Penny was that she knew death *could* lie around every corner, and that the greatest dangers came from the sources one *couldn't* think of. They had got past it, though, and when Penny babysat again, she noticed that some of the safety measures remained in place. It had nonetheless taken an effort of will for her not to reinstate the other ones.

'I talked to Mrs Gault again,' Saeeda said, leaning against one of the library's huge front windows. 'Given what you told me, I had to be careful not to burn my source, or more specifically yours, but I managed to get her to admit she suspected her husband of having an affair. She got rather nippy when I asked who she thought it might be. She said: "Take your pick. Perthshire is a big place." Seems he was serially unfaithful.'

'The curse of the second wife,' said Penny. 'When a mistress marries, she creates a vacancy.'

'From what I gather, Brendan wasn't many people's image of Casanova, but she said women were drawn to his vulnerability. They wanted to mother him. Which is ironic – or maybe not.'

'Why?'

'Because his real mother didn't. He grew up in care. Not far from here, as it turns out. A place called St Serf's, over in Kincraig. It closed down decades ago. It's probably flats now, or a hotel.'

At the mention of the nearby town, Penny felt suspicion lurch at the core of her. It was not the usual exhilaration she experienced when glimpsing a potential connection, but rather a queasiness at an unpleasant possibility.

'Surely not,' she said.

'What's wrong?'

Penny did not answer. Instead, she crossed the room and walked through the stacks to the section where she kept the archives. She thumbed the spines until she came to the parish records covering the village of Kincraig, pulling a volume carefully from the shelf.

Penny flipped through the pages and felt a growing relief. With every year further back that she looked, she found the same individual listed as the parish priest for St Serf's church, which shared its name with the children's home. A Father Sheehan. Not the name she feared.

Twenty years back. Twenty-five. Twenty-six. Twenty-seven. Still Father Sheehan.

Then she read that twenty-eight years ago, there had been no priest in post for four months. It was recorded that Father Caird of St Kentigern's in Blaircowal was travelling to conduct services each Sunday. This indicated that the previous priest must have left St Serf's suddenly.

Penny saw her fear realised in elegant calligraphy. The parish priest who had left abruptly, and whose time at St Serf's overlapped Brendan Gault's years at the children's home, was Father Colm Driver.

Penny walked numbly to the library counter and placed the open volume down in front of Saeeda.

'You won't need to identify the handwriting on that mass card,' she said. 'It wasn't a message *to* Brendan Gault. It was a message *from* him.'

76

Saeeda looked at the parish record, the name and the dates Penny had presented. Her eyes widened.

'When Gault threw Father Driver out of his patisserie,' Penny went on, 'people called him a bigot for accusing all priests of child abuse. But he wasn't. He was accusing one priest.'

Everybody Dies Alone

Chapter Eight

Johnny heads back to Fountain and Fairfax again once darkness has fallen. He takes his own car as he's off duty and he's got enough paperwork to be dealing with, to say nothing of not wanting a visit to this location logged on the system.

He drives up to Kingdom Pictures' gates, which this time remain closed. He can see only one light on in the office building. That's what he's counting on.

He parks on Fountain, walks back to the gates, and raps with his telescopic nightstick. He waits.

A minute or so later, a security guard comes ambling out of the office suite in no particular hurry. She's chewing on a Hershey bar. Looks like it might be her staple diet.

'Sir, you can't be here. The offices are closed.'

She's a rentacop with a private security firm. Her nametag says Lori Bolger.

Johnny flashes his badge. He knows that's not enough for what he wants here, because if he asks to come in, Lori's gonna refer it up the chain. He's got a game plan, though. People like

Dominique King think if they've flexed their muscles and handed out an order, that's enough. She might have said no police were to be admitted without a warrant, but it's not like they'll have Johnny's picture pinned up.

'We got a report of someone on the roof. Just want to check it out.'

'I didn't call in no report.'

'No, I think one of your neighbours saw something suspicious.' Johnny nods towards the apartment buildings that overlook the compound. Lori glances across too. 'I just need five minutes to check it out. It's probably a cat or something. Is there roof access from inside the building? Not sure I'm up to a climb in this suit.'

'Sir, I'm afraid I can't just let you into the offices. They got strict policies regarding computers and data and such.'

'No, no,' he says. 'Not the office suite. That other building there. The report said it was the big one. If you can open the door for me, I'll be five minutes and then I can go home.'

Lori thinks about it. She looks Johnny up and down, taking in the suit he just drew attention to.

'You ain't no beat cop. Ain't this kinda below your pay-grade?'

Shit.

'Truth be told, I just finished my shift, but I heard it over the radio just as I was passing and thought I'd save somebody a job. Kinda hoping to pay it forward, if you get me.'

Her expression softens. 'I hear that,' she says.

She walks him to the entrance. Keys in a code. Looks like 5732.

As Lori steps through the door ahead of him, Johnny realises she intends to tag along.

'You got somebody else minding the store?' he asks.

'Oh, shit,' she says.

'Just in case this is some classic distraction. Call in a bullshit report to get you out of the way . . .'

'Good thinking, Officer . . .?'

'Waters,' he replies. 'Arlo Waters.'

Johnny switches on the lights and makes his way through the soundstage, through the Formosa again, and into the ballroom. He takes another look at those chandeliers and that ceiling.

He crosses the bandstand like he did earlier, but when he passes behind the screen at the end, this time he turns left, into a narrow channel.

Johnny flicks on his flashlight. He follows a narrow passage that broadens out into a space dominated by one side of a huge metal structure. Diagonal ladders ascend a complex framework that is supporting not only the chandeliers, but the ballroom's entire fake ceiling. Above it there is a platform running more than half the length of the building; definitely far enough along for part of it to sit beneath the lighting storeroom.

The walls of the ballroom are bolted to the framework too. From this side it all looks so flimsy: canvas screens and balsa-wood. Work here long enough and it's easy to forget that everything in this town is an illusion.

Johnny starts climbing, wishing he'd brought a polyethylene suit. He's gonna be filthy by the time he gets out. There's so much ancient crap lying on the floor in here. Chunks of papier mâché, torn lengths of canvas, remnants of previous sets.

His cell buzzes in his pocket. Ibanez. He answers.

'Johnny, please tell me you've not broken into Kingdom Pictures.'

'Nope. I'm at Dulli's Bar, Melrose and Highland. Want me to line you one up?'

'Johnny, I'm standing on Fountain and I'm parked right next to your car.'

Fuck.

'How come you always know where I'm gonna be?'

'Your little bit of speechifying earlier made it kind of obvious.'

'You find Crawford Nicholson yet?'

'No. But I did get access to his apartment.'

'You broke in?'

'No. I finessed that friendly neighbour. Told her about Mahoney, played the compassion card. Anyway, it turns out she and Nicholson have the combos to each other's key safes. Back-up in case either of them gets locked out.'

'What did you find?'

'I reckon he's blown town.'

'What makes you say that?'

'There's something I need to show you.'

'Okay, come on inside. The code is 5732.'

Johnny continues his climb, a tang of chemicals finding his nose. Paint most likely, maybe something from the workshops above.

He reaches a platform halfway up, a walkway between ladders that also allows access to the flats and lighting fixtures attached to the frame. It's like a gigantic wall stud.

Climbing again, he is reassured by the lack of movement as he ascends. He notes that the bases of the supporting piles are driven into the concrete, but he would have expected it to feel shakier the higher he got. Then he sees why. Above him, steel cables are keeping the structure steady, running from anchor points in the ceiling.

Johnny hears a vibration in the frame and a clattering somewhere below. Sounds like it came from the other end of the building.

81

He reaches the top of the structure. There isn't much in the way of headroom, certainly not enough to stand upright, but it's navigable. He plays his flashlight along the floor. Wooden boards are bolted down to form a platform, metal girders in between. He can see where the chandeliers are anchored, power lines lashed to the metal with zip-ties.

He feels another vibration and the unmistakable sound of thumping on metal.

'Johnny?' Ibanez calls.

'Up here.'

'How did you get in?'

'Told the security guard some bullshit. You speak to her?'

'No, but I think I saw somebody around the side of the building.'

'That'll be her.'

Ibanez starts to climb. He's annoyingly nimble, hauling himself up a lot faster than Johnny could.

'You find anything yet?' Ibanez asks.

Johnny trains his flashlight along the ceiling. He sees what looks like an access hatch, some kind of trapdoor. It ain't far enough along to be below the lighting storeroom, but at least he's got proof of concept. Johnny manoeuvres himself awkwardly forward, trying not to think of the state this suit is gonna be in. Then he feels a jolt: that minor earthquake shudder you get blasé about in LA, but not so much when you're someplace high and insubstantial.

'What did you just do?' asks Ibanez.

'I didn't do anything. That was your first tremor, Arizona. You'll get used to it.'

Johnny hears a dissonant metallic twang, like somebody just hit the world's biggest bass string and then rapidly detuned it. Then something crashes into the gantry nearby at the same time as a flash of light dazzles him. A weird effect of the sudden brightness is that the ceiling looks like it's buckling. Then Johnny's eyes readjust enough to see that one of the anchor cables has torn free, and that the ceiling *is* buckling because whatever is above it is on fire.

'Fire!' Johnny yells. 'We need to get down.'

As he starts to descend, he sees that the ballroom has begun to glow in a weird, swirling yellow. Then it suddenly collapses in on itself, moments before being consumed in flames.

Within seconds, it seems there's fire everywhere: the heat fierce, Johnny's nose picking up not just the smell of burning, but that chemical tang again. Accelerant. Fire above and fire below, started at the same time. Whoever Ibanez saw, it wasn't the security guard.

He hears more twanging and creaking, feels more jolts. The structure is starting to buckle.

Ibanez is waiting on that lower platform. Why the hell hasn't he gone down already, Johnny wonders, then sees the reason. Something is on fire directly below the ladder they first came up. The kid's staying in harm's way to make sure Johnny makes it down.

'There's another ladder at the other end,' Ibanez says. 'Come on.'

Johnny reaches the central platform. The smoke is starting to thicken. The flames are bringing plenty of light but only to show them the routes they can't take. Johnny pauses briefly to point his flashlight into the dark, picking out leather seats: the Formosa. That's their way out.

He feels the platform shift again, hears another grinding creak somewhere behind and above.

Then he feels hands on his shoulders.

83

'Look out, Johnny!'

Ibanez pushes him forward as a loose section of girder swings down on a cable. It misses Johnny's head by inches but catches Ibanez square in the chest and knocks him clean off the platform.

Johnny looks down and sees Ibanez land on his back next to a section of fake ballroom wall that is ablaze and threatening to collapse. He abandons the search for another ladder and ignores the blistering heat of the metal as he slides down one of the support beams.

He crouches next to the kid. Ibanez looks dazed but his eyes are open. He's conscious. Probably got a shitload of those little tweety birds going around his head, though.

Ordinarily the advice would be not to move him, but that's not an option. Sections of canvas and paper are falling aflame, landing on the tables and crashing into the days-old drinks. Johnny gets his arms around Ibanez's shoulders. He's finding it hard to breathe with the smoke and the intensity of the heat, but he doesn't stop until he has hauled his partner past the Formosa and into the relative safety of the corridor beyond.

Johnny lets himself breathe for just a moment before dragging Ibanez the last few yards. He makes it out of the building into the cool night air, laying Ibanez down on a patch of lawn.

Johnny calls in a code three, asking for immediate response. Officer down.

'You okay, partner?' he asks.

Ibanez doesn't say anything. His eyes are glazed but they're still open. Arms and legs look to be intact too. Kid got lucky. Amazing what you walk away from when you're young.

Ibanez reaches into his jacket and presses something into Johnny's hand. It's a car key.

'Just relax,' Johnny urges.

84

Ibanez's breathing don't sound right. Bloody foam is appearing at the edges of his mouth.

Oh no, Johnny thinks. Oh no no no no.

Ibanez is straining to speak. 'Ma . . . Ma . . .'

Christ. He wants his mother. He knows.

'Just take it easy, kid. Help is on the way.'

But Johnny already knows help will be too late. He understands what that foam means. Internal injuries. The girder smashed into his chest. Something has punctured his lungs: probably his own broken ribs.

'It's gonna be okay,' Johnny says, hoping Ibanez's glazed eyes can't make out the tears in his own. Because Johnny knows it's not gonna be okay.

The Corpse in
the Confessional

VIII

The crisp spring morning sun was sparkling off the oxbow lake and casting strange patterns around the living room at Silverbank Cottage, but Penny felt entirely at odds with the day. It might be bright and clear outdoors, but illumination and clarity were entirely missing inside her head.

With a sigh she put down her book, having tried to read the same paragraph four or five times. She was finding it difficult to settle or to concentrate. She placed the hardback volume on the table next to her teacup, and was momentarily startled by what she read on the cover. *Evil in a Quiet Glade* by Amanda Fraser, it said, when she was sure that was not what she had picked up.

The room swam briefly. Penny closed her eyes then took a sip from her cup. When she looked at the book again, it was the one she expected to see: Italo Calvino's *If On a Winter's Night a Traveller*. A feeling of reassurance warmed through her like the tea, but it was instantly undermined by the realisation that she could remember neither the title nor the author of the book she thought she had seen. Further confusing her, the sense of its familiarity lingered.

Penny sighed again. She knew that there would only be more mornings like these. This one was particularly bad because she had slept only fitfully.

Father Driver had been taken into custody. It was the talk of the village, and she couldn't help but worry what that talk might turn to when they learned about her role in it; if they hadn't assumed as much already. It had often been suggested that Penny would be famous had the murders she solved taken place somewhere better known, or closer to London. She would not have wanted that. Penny was happily anonymous, like Glen Cluthar itself, but around here her fondness for amateur investigations was common knowledge.

All night long, her restless mind had been recalculating her conclusions in the hope that for once she was wrong. Like everyone else in Glen Cluthar, she was not ready to accept what was being implied of Father Driver, and deeply troubled that she had been instrumental in implying it. Making it worse, she had the strangest, most unaccustomed feeling that she had missed something. When one's mind was not all it used to be, this was a particularly worrying thought.

She decided to give that Calvino paragraph another go. It was an intriguing but confounding novel in which each chapter seemed to belong to a completely different book. She had barely picked it up again when she saw Saeeda's car pull up outside. Her coming to the house meant something decisive.

'Mrs Gault called me not long after you and I last spoke,' Saeeda said, straight to business as she came through the door. 'She found a recording on her husband's phone. We had already been through his device to see who he had been in contact with, but found nothing to identify his lover. As an accomplished adulterer, there's probably a second phone we've yet to discover. But Mrs Gault found something we'd missed, and it wasn't about any mistress.'

Saeeda produced her own phone and placed it down on Penny's bureau.

'We believe this recording was made surreptitiously in the confessional booth. It's date-stamped from two weeks ago.'

She pressed play, and Penny listened carefully.

'I've come to hear your confession, Father.'

'Ehm, I'm afraid that's not how this works.'

'Not normally, but today I'm the one offering absolution. You know who I am, don't you, Father? You knew the minute you clapped eyes on me.'

'I know you threw me out of your shop and said some vile things. What are you doing here in my church? What do you want?'

'First let me tell you what I don't want. I don't want money. I don't want a scandal. What I do want is for you to apologise for what you did to me at St Serf's. And I want you to resign from the priesthood. Not retire, resign. You don't get to walk away and enjoy the trappings of respectability, of reverence, throughout a cosy retirement.'

'I have no idea why you have decided to persecute me, but I'm having none of it. I have no notion what you're talking about.'

Father Driver's voice was so familiar, his tone less so: brusque and dismissive in his adamant denials. Penny had known him for at least twenty years. She had known Brendan Gault barely at all, but of the two of them, she had no doubt which one she believed. Which one was lying. Which one had betrayed everybody.

'As I said, I don't want a scandal. I don't want the humiliation of

what was done to me becoming public knowledge. But if that's what it takes, I'd rather that than continue to suffer alone. And in silence.'

'Father Driver denied everything,' said Saeeda, turning off the recording. 'Even when we played him this. But this isn't all we had. When we looked on his computer, we found a deleted file, a draft letter he was writing to the diocese. It was a resignation letter. He doesn't confess outright, but reading between the lines, he's telling the bishop that he's taking one for the team. Stepping away because of "past failings that I do not wish to become public", as he put it. When we presented him with the letter, he copped to it all.'

'Really?' asked Penny, as the last flicker of hope that she might be wrong was snuffed out. 'Just like that?'

'That's how it goes sometimes. One little thing finally causes the dam to break.'

'But if he was planning to resign the priesthood, giving Mr Gault what he wanted, why would he . . .?' Penny let it hang, unwilling to name the deed.

'He said he invited Gault to the church on Saturday night to show him the letter and let him know his intentions. He was going to ask him for a couple of weeks' grace to make his preparations and say his goodbyes. But when Gault saw the letter, he snatched it and said he had decided to go public after all, and he would use this as proof. At which point Father Driver confessed that he just snapped. He strangled Gault with his silk scarf thing. What do you call it?'

'A stole,' Penny said, the image horrifying her in so many ways.

Penny felt something inside her deflate, the opposite of the exhilaration she normally enjoyed when she had solved a case.

'What of your intuition that the killer was a woman?' Penny

asked. It was not so much a straw to clutch as a straggly loose end she needed snipped.

'I think that must have been sparked by the detail about the ligature,' Saeeda replied. 'An image created by the idea that Gault hadn't been throttled by a man's bare hands.'

'Of course,' Penny said numbly. She glanced out of the window. It was turning into a beautiful day, but she could not countenance going outside. She wanted to hide herself away.

'Are you all right?' Saeeda asked.

'No,' she replied. She was aware that her eyes had filled with tears.

Everything seemed so squalid these days. Murder was always squalid, of course, the most squalid thing anyone could do. But the murders she had dealt with tended to be about passionate love triangles, rivalry for an inheritance or to cover up an ingenious embezzlement scheme. Not truly gut-wrenching atrocities like child abuse, and by the priest in her own parish.

This whole business felt like something that didn't belong in the world of Glen Cluthar. But perhaps Penny was the one who didn't belong here any more.

'I fear I no longer have the appetite for certain things,' she said. 'For many things.'

She thought of William's brochure. Of peace, of rest. It was a more enticing prospect than she liked to admit.

Saeeda picked up her mobile, noticing as she did so the invitation sitting on the bureau.

'I was going to ask what's next for you, but I see you're going to a wedding. No, scratch that, you're going to the *Stonebridge* wedding.'

Glancing at the invitation, Penny was suddenly in the throes of that occasional anxiety regarding matters unfinished: a hollow that needed to be filled, a crime that all of her skills and efforts had been unable to solve. It was something about her niece. Except that Penny didn't have a niece. Or did she simply not remember? The fragment of memory was gone, but the feeling itself endured. She felt a fire burn inside her. A fire that demanded more fuel.

'And at Crathie Hall, no less,' Saeeda added with undisguised envy.

'Yes,' Penny replied, finding herself smiling at the prospect. 'A change of scene is just what I need after this nasty business.'

'Have you been there before?'

'Oh, many times,' she replied, memories reassuringly flooding in. 'They do an excellent gin and tonic, and a good old-fashioned afternoon tea.'

Not to mention, on occasion, a good old-fashioned murder.

Everybody Dies Alone

Chapter Nine

Everybody shows up too late. And it really is everybody: fire, ambulance and police. Including Nimitz.

Johnny waves away the paramedics when they come to assist him, though he does accept a bottle of water. He's sitting on the steps of the office building on the other side of the parking lot, which is now dominated by fire trucks hosing water into the studio.

They had already pronounced Ibanez at the scene.

Nimitz comes across, just stands there awhile, watching the firefighters.

'How's your throat?' Nimitz asks.

'I can speak.'

'Good. Then you want to tell me what the fuck just happened? Because it looks to me like you managed to get your partner killed and burn Dominique King's studio to the ground within a few hours of me telling you to leave this thing alone.'

'I didn't burn shit,' Johnny says. 'Somebody else was in here. I heard them. Ibanez saw someone too.'

'Well, at least that gives us corroboration, because for a minute there I thought you had nothing. Let me just ask Ibanez if he's ready to write a statement. Oh, that's right, he can't, because you got him fucking killed.'

Johnny knows it's useless, but he's going to say it anyway.

'There *is* access to the storerooms from below. Someone was covering their tracks.'

'I don't want to hear it, Johnny. I don't want to even fucking look at you. What I do want is your gun and your badge.'

Johnny wants to laugh. Even amidst the hurt, maybe because of the hurt, he wants to laugh, because he can hear Ibanez's voice, picture his response.

Did he really just say that?

Christ. That was less than two hours ago.

Johnny places his ID and his gun down on the concrete of the step. Let Nimitz pick them up if he wants them.

He does.

'Now get the fuck out of town,' he adds.

As Johnny walks away, he feels this toxic cocktail of anger and regret. A voice inside is telling him he can be angry all he likes: he's just deflecting from the fact that he fucked up. That he was doing something he shouldn't.

As he makes his way to the street, Lori the rentacop is standing at the gate post.

'How did paying it forward work out for you?' she asks. Her tone indicates she now knows he was full of shit.

It worked out just like he deserved. Somebody killed his partner while trying to kill him. That same somebody, he's pretty sure, killed Jed Mahoney. But there's nothing he can do about that now. He's off the case, off the goddamn job.

He's walking along Fountain towards his ride. Fifty yards

ahead, a black SUV peels away at speed. Might have been a Bronco but he doesn't get a good enough look. His instincts tell him whoever was behind the wheel got a good enough look at him, but maybe he's clutching.

As he reaches his car, he notices a blue Mazda parked behind it.

I'm parked right next to your car.

Ibanez gave him a car key. Kid knew he was dying, why would he give him a car key?

Because he wasn't asking for his Ma. He was trying to say Mazda. On the phone, he said he'd found something at Crawford Nicholson's apartment. Something he needed to show him.

Johnny looks through the windshield. There's a manila folder on the passenger seat.

He unlocks the car and opens the passenger door. Lifts the folder. He brushes some crumbs from it. Ibanez must have been eating a sandwich. Inside is a single page. It's a print-out of an email to Crawford Nicholson, confirming travel plans and flight details. The name of a hotel. A flight that left around the same time Jed Mahoney's body was found. There's a couple of names scribbled on it, and a number too: 040381.

It's the only lead Johnny's got, and getting it to him was Ibanez's last act. The least he owes the kid is to follow it up.

Besides, Nimitz wants him out of town. He figures Crathie Hall, Perthshire, Scotland ought to be far enough.

PART TWO

PRIVATE INVESTIGATIONS: EDINBURGH

Rattigan saw her sitting in the corner of the bar, at a table looking out onto the dockside. Back to the wall, view of the whole room, strategically positioned to see who was coming and going: that was how he ID'd her.

She looked forties, medium height and build. There was a weariness to her features he could relate to, on a face that looked like it had taken some punches. He could relate to that too.

'Jenny, right?' he said.

'Large Hendrick's and tonic,' she replied. 'Cucumber, not lime.'

'What?'

She reached into a bag on the seat beside her and pulled out just the edge of a blue folder.

'You want this, you're buying.'

He wasn't arguing. Rattigan went to the bar and returned a few minutes later, placing the gin and tonic down alongside a pint of Guinness.

Jenny took the folder out and slid it across the table. There was a smirk on her face as she did so.

He opened the file and saw why. The contents were barely worth the slice of cucumber.

'This is it?' Rattigan asked. 'Do you know how far I've come for this?'

She looked defiantly unapologetic. It might even have been kind of sexy if he could afford to get messed around right now.

'My dad wasn't known for being fastidious in his record-keeping, or particularly methodological in his practices. Not on the investigation side of the business, anyway.'

'What other side is there?'

She ignored this.

'But further to our telephone conversation, I can confirm that he took the case, and the name of the client. Juliet Oswald.'

Rattigan looked again at the file. Just a page of scribbled notes. Three names, two addresses.

Toby Delamere. Andrew Delamere. Robert Carmichael.

'Do you know why he would have been talking to these people?'

She knocked back the gin and tonic pretty much in one go and got up.

'You now know as much as I do,' she said, then left.

Something Bloody, Something Blue

Chapter One

The plane is on final approach when Johnny comes to in his seat, his stomach lurching as the little turboprop is buffeted in the wind.

He's feeling woolly-headed, more than he would expect from mere sleep. He tries to recall how much he drank at the airport. It must have been a lot, because though he remembers getting on a 747 at LAX, he has no recollection of ever boarding this metal gnat. That ought to stick out, for the sheer terror. He ain't normally a nervous flyer, but he normally flies in actual airplanes. The only times he's previously travelled in vehicles this small, they've tended to have four wheels and no wings.

He's not quite sure if he is hungover or still drunk, which makes him wonder what kind of condition he must have been in when he landed in London, and how the hell he made his connection. It's amazing what an experienced drinker can accomplish on autopilot.

As the plane comes in ever lower, Johnny looks for the airport building and doesn't see one. He doesn't see any other aircraft either. No, wait, there is one more plane: a Cessna even smaller than this puddle-jumper. He figures it for a private airfield. This prompts a worry about how much damage this must have done to his bank balance, until he remembers the damage that had been done to Ibanez, and to Johnny's standing in the force. He urgently needs a way back into this case, no matter what it costs. Still, he could surely have flown to a regional airport and sprung for a rental car.

Which brings him to his next problem as he steps onto the tarmac. He doesn't know how he's gonna get to his destination from here. Then he spots a vehicle approaching the airfield, and with some relief sees that it's old and beat up enough to be a taxi. For a panicky moment he'd been worried he might also have sprung for a limousine if he'd already lost his mind enough to charter a plane.

The pilot is standing next to the aircraft, filling in some paperwork ahead of flying back to their point of origin.

'How far are we from the nearest major airport?' Johnny asks, thinking of cheaper ways to make his connection home.

'Glasgow's maybe about an hour and a half away.'

'By air?'

The pilot laughs. 'No, by car.'

An hour and a half, Johnny thinks. That's nothing. It could take him that long to get to LAX in bad traffic. So how the hell did he end up on that turboprop?

The taxi has reached the airfield, parking only yards away from the landing strip. An older guy gets out, early sixties, wisps of grey hair blowing in the cool breeze.

'Booking for Hawke?' he says, squinting at Johnny.

'That's me.'

The driver pops the trunk and Johnny slings his bag in there. He climbs into the back and the driver hits the gas.

'You American?' he asks.

'Yeah.'

'Most Yanks are here for the golf, but I didn't see any clubs. Of course, it costs more to take them on the plane than to hire a set, but some folk still prefer to have their own.'

'I'm not a golfer.'

'Then what brings you here?'

Johnny thinks about it.

The email print-out of Crawford Nicholson's travel plans had the words 'Deacon Gossard, Crathie Hall' scrawled in pen. That's all he has to go on. Johnny had searched for Deacon Gossard online and come up with nothing: not a person, not a company. He hopes it ain't a code-word, or a fuckin' anagram. He hates that shit.

'I don't have a rod with me either, but I guess you could call this a fishing trip.'

They drive along winding country lanes barely wide enough for two cars, and certainly not wide enough to overtake the tractor they get caught behind for a couple miles. When it turns left into a field, the driver hits the accelerator, but he's stepping hard on the brake as soon as they meet the next bend.

'Sugar,' he says.

Johnny wonders if a truck has shed its load, then he sees that sugar is not what's blocking the way. There's like a dozen sheep strayed onto the blacktop, wandering aimlessly and in no hurry. He figures the driver was reining in his language in front of a customer.

'Always a danger round here. Stupid flippin' animals. And the cows are worse. Had to get a side panel beaten last month because of one of those bandits.'

'Yeah, I could see how that would be a flippin' pain in the armpit,' Johnny says. 'But buddy, you don't need to keep the language PG on my account. I'm a fuckin' cop.'

Johnny sees the guy flinch in the rearview, face creasing into a disapproving frown. So he wasn't just being polite for the customer.

'Sorry,' Johnny says. 'Your cab, your rules.'

Murder by Invitation

I

Crathie Hall was located on a hillside on the outskirts of Ardfell, nestled high enough above the village to afford it a sumptuous view across the broad Perthshire glen. It was a hotel that had never been officially named as such: nobody in the know ever said they were going to stay at Crathie Hall Hotel, they said they were going to Crathie Hall. And though Penny lived less than thirty miles away, she was partial to a stay there herself.

It had been built in the 1830s as a health retreat, the austerity of its early Victorian architecture seemingly intended to impress upon its guests that while they might be there for their health, they were certainly not there to enjoy themselves.

Though the place had frequently been refurbished, it had in many respects never been modernised. The older she became, the more Penny found it comforting to be somewhere that looked neither briskly on-trend nor lingeringly dated, for both of those conditions underlined the passing of the years. To step into a place that gave the impression of having looked like this for almost two centuries gave a reassuring sense that certain things could endure. That certain things might always belong.

Penny presented herself at the reception desk with a mild degree of apprehension, conscious that this might be the moment when her invitation was revealed to be a mistake after all. However, the young woman behind the desk confirmed that there was indeed a room reserved for her, for two nights, as had been indicated on the back of the embossed card.

'You're here for the Stonebridge wedding?' the receptionist asked with breezy enthusiasm.

'I am indeed,' Penny confirmed.

It was not the first time she had heard it referred to as such. As was tradition, it was the bride's family who were formally extending the invitations, but clearly there was little question over who the occasion actually belonged to.

The receptionist handed her a key; an actual, metal key with a wooden fob that had been held by thousands of guests. Every time Penny came here, she feared their replacement with a plastic card, so she was pleased that this still hadn't happened. Even more gratifyingly, she was not asked to present a plastic card of her own, not even to cover extras.

'Who is picking up my bill?' she asked.

'We've been instructed in the interest of discretion not to disclose that.'

'Understood,' she said. And very much approved of. Penny had long ago learned to be suspicious of ostentatious largesse. Deliberately discreet largesse, however, indicated a touch of class. Nonetheless, this further piqued her curiosity regarding why she had been invited, and by whom.

It also further piqued her concern regarding how much she might have forgotten about them.

Something Bloody,
Something Blue

Chapter Two

The hotel looks like a castle, or maybe an asylum: craggy and imposing, with parapets and a bell tower. Johnny wonders if they used to ring it when somebody escaped. It also looks real pricey. Maybe he could submit all this as an expense claim to Nimitz, see if he pops an aneurysm.

The front is all glass, the reception area an extension built onto the front of the ancient building, with the original lobby beyond two archways through what used to be the outside walls.

Johnny approaches the reception desk just as a little old lady vacates it. She's dressed in a matching skirt and jacket in a kinda plaid pattern, which doesn't quite look like tartan. Is that what they call tweed? Either way, he feels like he's not just travelled a long distance, but maybe stepped back in time.

The young woman behind the counter gives him a brief glance then steps away with an apologetic wave, like she's got to go deal with something. He doesn't have to wait, though. Another woman steps out from the back office. Her name badge says Alison Innis, Hotel Manager.

'Good afternoon, sir. Checking in? What was the name?'

'Hawke. Johnny Hawke.'

She taps at her computer.

'We've got you down for two nights, is that correct?'

Johnny doesn't remember booking this either, but he knows he's been in a weird state of mind since Ibanez died. He knows why he's here, though. That part is clear as a bell.

'That's correct. Hey, before we do that, can I ask if Mr Nicholson checked in yet? Crawford Nicholson?'

'Let me check the system. No, I'm afraid we don't have a booking under that name.'

Dammit.

'Is he here for the wedding?' Innis asks. 'Some of the guests attending the evening reception tomorrow are not residents. He might be staying at one of the B&Bs down in the village.'

Johnny is trying to eyeball her computer screen, but it's angled away. He does notice a list on her side of the counter, headed 'Lilian Deacon–Sebastian Gossard Wedding'.

Holly golly.

Johnny didn't know anything about a wedding, but this indicates Nicholson must have been planning to attend *before* Jed Mahoney died. Johnny isn't sure how that changes the picture. Was it a happy coincidence that Nicholson already had someplace he was booked to go when he decided it would be wise to get out of Dodge? Or if he had something to do with the murder, had he timed it so that he would be on his way overseas when the body was discovered?

'How many B&Bs are there?' Johnny asks.

106

'Maybe a dozen. Twenty if you're talking about the whole glen.'

Johnny goes to his room and unpacks, grateful that he's brought a decent coat and tie. The wedding guests will be mingling with other residents, so if he looks smart enough he can blend in, let people make a few assumptions, and get them to talk. He had packed in a hurry back in LA, so he'll just have to hope he brought everything he might need.

He has a shower and reaches for a change of clothes, which is when it hits him that there is one thing he conspicuously hasn't brought: his gun.

It feels weird pulling on his jacket without the holster underneath. Good weird: like he's on vacation. People generally don't have guns here though, which is pretty fucked up. How are you supposed to murder all your co-workers when you've had a bad day?

He catches sight of himself in the mirror, pleasantly surprised by what he sees. He keeps expecting someone older, not sure why. Subconsciously worried the job is taking its toll, maybe. They say the mirror never lies, but what it says can be open to interpretation. He asks himself what description he would give if he was calling in a sighting. White male, forties, medium build, six feet. (Five-eleven on a wet day when the quiff has been dampened down.) Blue eyes, black hair, a few flecks of grey showing through.

That girl Shawna said he looked like Brad Pitt, but that was six beers down, and she did clarify that she meant 'Brad Pitt in *Fury* as opposed to Brad Pitt in *Thelma and Louise*. You know, almost handsome, kind of in a gnarly way.'

He pictures her in just a t-shirt that morning. Then he remembers what happened next. Ibanez showed up, no idea he was kindly collecting the asshole who was about to get him dead. In Johnny's bleary and jetlagged state, it's a jolt that reminds him why he's here.

He has a seat on the edge of the bed and picks his phone up from the nightstand. The mobile signal looks patchy, but the wi-fi is even worse. Must be the thickness of the walls. He has no option but to go back downstairs, figuring the public areas will have better bandwidth.

Taking a seat in the spacious glass-walled reception area, Johnny spends a tedious and unprofitable half hour methodically googling and phoning every bed-and-breakfast place in the district. There are a few who don't pick up, but so far nobody has a booking for Crawford Nicholson.

He glances across to the front desk, where the hotel manager is taking a call. It must have been important because she's on her walkie-talkie as soon as she hangs up, gesturing to the bell-boys and the concierge. Something's going down.

Alison Innis is the obvious person to ask about Lilian Deacon and Sebastian Gossard, but that won't work if he wants to pretend to her that he's part of the wedding. It's been a while since Johnny did any undercover work. He's rusty, but the principles are ingrained, and one of those is that every question you ask somebody tells them a little about you.

Johnny is trying one of the B&Bs a second time when he sees three black SUVs pull up in front of the hotel: identical models, tinted windows. Nobody gets out of the drivers' seats, indicating they're all chauffeur-driven. Primed by Innis, the hotel staff swoop in almost as soon as the vehicles are stationary.

Johnny looks at who does get out. First is a guy in his sixties with sandy hair swept back to his collar, almost certainly a dye job and possibly even a wig, because nature is seldom that generous. Even the guy's glasses look expensive, the frames picked out in a shade of grey to match his suit.

A woman gets out of the same SUV and stands alongside him. Johnny figures her for fifteen to twenty years younger, dressed in a warm quilted coat with fur trimming around the hood.

Johnny hears someone say 'Lord and Lady Stonebridge' with an urgency like it's the code-word for a drill.

He watches Innis greet them, going directly to the woman, who begins pointing at various things. Johnny can't see what: something in the gardens, out of his sightline. Innis is nodding, taking notes on an iPad.

Six more people get out of the other two vehicles, all looking like they're dressed more for business than for leisure. Four men, two women. They're mostly thirties apart from one woman who looks no more than twenty-five. One of the men is wearing shades even though it's not that bright outside.

They all make their way into the reception area, but weirdly, nobody goes to the desk. Instead, keys are handed directly to them, no paperwork, while their bags are whisked from the SUVs.

'If the weather holds, we will have the ceremony in the Sculpture Garden,' he hears Innis say, accompanying the older couple as they head past him through one of the archways into the lobby.

Johnny hasn't heard the names Deacon or Gossard, but unless there are two weddings taking place here, these people are running the show. He stands up and pretends to be browsing leaflets for tourist attractions so that he can watch them a little longer, while also moving into earshot of the remaining six. He notices that the guy with the shades has kept them on inside. Asshole.

Johnny pulls out a leaflet for someplace called Inveraray Jail. He's acting like he's reading it when through the arch he sees the elevator doors open and out walks Crawford fucking Nicholson.

Something Bloody, Something Blue

Chapter Three

Johnny has never seen Nicholson in the flesh, just a photo, but there's no question that's who it is. He's glad-handing Lord and Lady Stonebridge, who both look real happy to see him, all handshakes and air-kisses. It don't look like anybody's saying 'Sorry to hear about your friend eating his gun', but maybe they've already been through all the consolatory stuff on the phone.

Nicholson then turns to look in Johnny's direction and gives a wave. Johnny panics for a moment, thinking he's been made. Then he glances to his side and confirms Nicholson is actually waving at the other SUV passengers. They're waving back.

When Johnny looks round again, Nicholson is walking into an open elevator.

Shit.

Johnny fights the urge to take off after him. There's no need to be conspicuous. The guy's here: that's what matters. He must have just come down to say hi to the Stonebridges then gone back upstairs again. Saw them arrive out of his window, which means he does have a room here.

That being so, why would Innis say otherwise, Johnny wonders. He guesses an upscale place like this must be fastidious about privacy: they don't confirm something like that to any schmuck who walks in off the street.

The main thing is Nicholson ain't going anywhere and he doesn't know who Johnny is, so it's not like he's going to rabbit. Johnny can choose his moment; maybe get some context first, find out what Nicholson's connection is to Lord and Lady Bigwig.

It looks like the group in reception is starting to break up.

He hears someone say 'I'll see you all at dinner.'

Shades replies that he can't wait that long for a drink.

Copy that, Johnny thinks.

Johnny positions himself on a stool at the bar. The Laird's Lounge is a far cry from the dives he's used to scoping for intel: high ceilings, chandeliers, huge windows looking out onto lush lawns. It's barely a quarter full at this time of the afternoon, so Johnny could have sat anywhere, but he chose this spot for maximum passing traffic. He's hoping Nicholson shows up, but ideally he'd like a little context first.

He's taking the first sip of the beer he ordered when he sees Lady Stonebridge come in with two other women Johnny didn't see before. They walk to a table right by one of the big windows, and have barely taken their seats when a waitress swoops in. Johnny didn't see her before either. He hadn't noticed there was table service, though maybe there's only table service for one particular party.

He watches the waitress take their order then make her way across to the bar.

'Two Aperol spritz, one tonic,' she tells the bartender. 'Ice and lemon.'

'Two Aperol, one gin and tonic, got it.'

'*No,*' the waitress says. Not like she's merely correcting him, but like she's stopping the guy cutting the blue wire instead of the red. 'Lady Stonebridge,' she adds under her breath. 'Just tonic.'

Okay, Johnny thinks, taking note.

The bartender fixes the drinks and the waitress has just whisked them away on a tray when the guy with the shades shows up. He's still wearing them.

Shades orders a pint and tells the bartender to put it on his room.

'What's the name? the bartender asks.

'Brooks. Room 214.'

Johnny notes that too.

'Lighting too much for you, buddy?' Johnny says to him.

'Huh?'

Johnny points to his own eyes.

Shades smiles self-consciously. 'Just off an overnight flight from New York. A very delayed flight. Decided I'd rather look like a poser than like I've just been pepper-sprayed.'

He lifts the shades briefly to reveal tired-looking, bloodshot eyes.

'Guess there's a reason they call it the red-eye,' Johnny says, though he's noticed more than that going on. It's no crime to look tired, but that's not what Shades is afraid of revealing. By virtue of him making the bar his first destination, Johnny had already sussed the guy liked to party. But Johnny figures Shades will be looking for more than just a few brewskis tonight.

Shades lifts his pint, about to walk away.

'Hey, don't leave me hanging, man,' Johnny says, opening his arms. 'You don't remember me? Guess that's a sign we really tied one on. I barely made my flight home to LA the next day.'

Shades is desperately trying to place him and probably trying to work out whether he's important enough to pretend. The very fact that Johnny's here at the wedding means he must be somebody.

'London Book Fair? Frankfurt?' he tries.

'Frankfurt,' Johnny bluffs.

'Of course. The Hof. Where else.'

Johnny thinks of the name Shades gave the bartender.

'Brooksy, right?'

Shades lets out a chuckle. 'I really must have been in a state. I haven't been Brooksy since secondary school.'

'Well, you were Brooksy in Frankfurt. For one night, anyway.'

'Alan,' he says, shaking hands.

'Johnny. Johnny Hawke.'

'Cool name. You say you're based in LA? Remind me, who are you with?'

'Most recently, I've been working with Kingdom Pictures.'

Brooks looks impressed. The Hollywood card has come up trumps.

'So you're not in publishing. What's your remit, remind me. Are you a producer? Do you acquire options, IP?'

'IP is still king,' Johnny says. He'd seen that on a newsstand, a headline in *Variety*. It would be wise to change the subject, though. 'I've been working with Crawford Nicholson. You know Crawford?'

Brooks clearly doesn't.

'He's a scriptwriter. Kingdom Pictures bought a screenplay he co-wrote with his writing partner, Jed Mahoney. *Everybody Dies Alone.*'

Brooks lights up. Even behind the shades, Johnny can see the excitement in his eyes.

'How's that going?'

Clearly the guy hasn't heard anything about the suicide. Johnny will need to remember he isn't in La-La Land any more. An unknown screenwriter blowing his brains out in West Hollywood isn't gonna make *The Times* of London, is it?

'I'm sworn to secrecy,' Johnny says, smiling. 'Though a few more of these and I might get careless.'

'I hear that. So how come you're at the wedding? Are you friends with Sebastian? Lilian?'

'No. It's actually my man Crawford who knows them. He invited me because he knew I was gonna be in the UK and his buddy couldn't make it. How about you? And forgive me if I've forgotten. Like I said, Frankfurt was a blur.'

'I've kind of got a foot in both camps because I'm on Stonebridge Publishing's board, but I used to work for RoadMiles Press. Lilian and Miles Deacon founded it. Lilian is marrying Sebastian Gossard, Lord Stonebridge's son.'

'Gossard? Why is his name not Stonebridge?'

'Sebastian adopted his late mother's name after his parents divorced.'

'Messy?'

'You've no idea.'

Brooks looks up and gives someone a nod, saluting with his beer. Johnny turns around and sees another two of the SUV passengers: the older of the women and a man around the same age.

'Who's that?'

'Monica Stonebridge. Lord Stonebridge's eldest. The anointed.'

Johnny detects an edge to Brooks's voice as he says this.

'Along with her latest boyfriend. Steve, I think. He's nobody, and he'll be gone soon anyway.'

The younger of the SUV women comes in shortly after. She glances across at Brooks but continues into the room without acknowledging him. A definite diss.

'And her?'

'That's Lucy Stonebridge, the youngest of the three.'

'She on the board too?' Johnny asks, figuring she doesn't look old enough.

'Indeed.'

'What's her position?'

'One more scandal away from getting fired, usually. Oops. Did I say that out loud?'

Johnny raises his eyebrows. 'She doesn't strike me as a fan of yours either.'

'Yeah, well, everybody will be on their best behaviour this weekend. Maybe even her.'

'And what about Sebastian?'

'The man of the hour. The man of most hours, to be honest.'

Johnny sees that Lucy has made her way directly to the bar. She stands a few feet away, still blanking Brooks. She orders a bottle of champagne and starts chatting to the bartender. There's a huddle of customers between her and Johnny, so he can't hear all she's saying, but she seems to strike up an easy rapport, just the right side of flirty. Johnny is thinking about what Brooks said, and wonders what side of it she'll be after a few glasses of the fizz.

Brooks orders another pint, but he's seen someone else he knows, and is getting ready to make a move.

'There's someone I need to talk to, but good to meet you again, Johnny. I'm sure I'll remember better next time.'

'Yeah, Frankfurt's always carnage. Had a little help with my stamina over there, though,' Johnny adds, briefly touching under his nose.

That stops him, like he figured it would. Brooks leans in, speaks quietly.

'As I said, I'm just off a delayed flight from New York, so I didn't manage to pack everything I might need for this weekend, you know? I don't suppose . . .?'

Johnny hears the sweet sound of opportunity knocking. He slaps Brooks on the shoulder. 'Come find me later,' he tells him.

Brooks grins. 'Count on it.'

Brooks walks away to join the table where Monica-the-anointed is now sitting with half a dozen other expensively dressed people.

Johnny finishes his beer. He's feeling pretty satisfied with his half-hour's work until it hits him that he now has to score cocaine in Brigadoon.

Murder by Invitation

II

After dropping off her bag in her room, Penny proceeded downstairs with a singularity of purpose, having planned her journey so that she would arrive in time for afternoon tea. Her appetite had diminished as she got older, so she preferred a small meal in the afternoon and a light supper late in the evening to a big lunch or dinner. And as she had mentioned to Saeeda, Crathie Hall did a particularly good afternoon tea, one elevated almost to the level of a sacrament by where it was served.

The Winter Garden was a glass dome festooned with greenery, enjoying southerly views across the river snaking through the glen, to the pine-covered hillsides beyond. Guests were seated on two levels: a raised horseshoe of a terrace hugging the windows, with other tables below, dotted around the polished hardwood floor. Penny knew it was not an original feature, but it nonetheless evoked some imaginary belle époque. Odd how one did not need to have personally experienced a time in order to feel nostalgia for it.

She sat back in a firmly upholstered chair and took a look

around the room, luxuriating in being back here in the Winter Garden: the sights and sounds, but most of all the smells – the aroma of coffee mixed with freshly baked scones. So many memories, she thought, until her reverie was punctured by the realisation that she could not access any specific one. It struck her that what she had were merely memories of a feeling, rather than of particular occasions. She wondered, if she had to accept the loss of one, was it better to retain the feelings than the specifics? Her instinct said yes, but as a librarian and an archivist, she had prided herself upon her gift for recall, something that had been a factor in solving so many mysteries. What consolation would feelings be if all of that was gone?

A silver tray was placed delicately in front of her, the scent of tea immediately filling her nose. She looked up to thank the waitress, but that was not who had brought it.

'What a pleasure to welcome you back, Ms Coyne.'

Despite the familiarity of her words, Penny did not recognise the young woman who was standing before her. Her name badge said 'Alison Innis, Hotel Manager'.

It was too late for Penny to disguise her disappointment. As long as she had been coming here, the manager had been Morag Petrie, the person Penny most credited with maintaining Crathie Hall as an oasis of tranquil permanence from a world in a perpetual state of upheaval.

'You were expecting Morag, I'm sure. Unfortunately she is no longer with us.'

Penny registered shock. Morag must only have been in her sixties.

Ms Innis read her reaction. 'No, I mean she took early retirement. But she was very thorough in her briefings, especially about our most valued guests. So please be assured that I am here to serve.'

The young woman had a pleasant demeanour: friendly but not overly so. Penny's instincts were always set on edge by insincere familiarity. An unwelcome American import, as far as she was concerned.

'A great pleasure it is to be here, Ms Innis. Just what I needed, in fact.'

'Yes. I read about that awful business in Glen Cluthar. And Morag apprised me of the hotel's debt to your discretion in clearing up certain delicate matters over the years.'

'Did she indeed.'

Ms Innis's candour in discussing this conveyed a great deal – not least that Morag had trusted her with certain information, in itself an endorsement of Ms Innis's own discretion.

Ms Innis set the tea-strainer down upon its drip bowl like they were sacred objects.

'Are you here for the Deacon–Gossard wedding?' she asked.

This was truly the moment that Penny decided Ms Innis was a fitting successor to Morag, for she was the first person not to refer to it as the Stonebridge wedding. One of the things Penny liked about Morag was her unfailing sense of propriety. Like Penny, she paid attention to the small details because she knew that they mattered; or that they would matter were they *not* attended to.

'I wonder if whenever Mr and Mrs Deacon arrive you might point them out to me,' Penny said. 'I'd like to thank them for the invitation.'

There was just a momentary flash of confusion on Ms Innis's face. Long enough for Penny to see it, short enough for her to let Penny pretend otherwise, should that be her preference.

'You may well ask why they would invite me if I don't even know what they look like. Just between you and me, I'm asking myself the same question. That's why I'd like to speak to them.'

'It's a wedding,' Ms Innis replied. 'There are always mysteries to be uncovered in the guest list, the politics and diplomacy of which would confound the UN. But your timing is impeccable. Mr and Mrs Deacon have just sat themselves down. They're the couple to the right of the peace lilies.'

Penny glanced inconspicuously to the far side of the horseshoe, where she saw a middle-aged couple settling into their chairs and reaching for the menus.

'Thank you, Ms Innis.'

Penny enjoyed the tea at her leisure, casting the occasional glance across to Mr and Mrs Deacon. She was most grateful to Ms Innis for identifying them, for she would never have picked them out as being the hosts of such an auspicious event. There was little question as to why it was not being referred to as the Deacon wedding.

Once Penny had finished the last of her tea, she walked around the horseshoe terrace and stopped at their table.

'Mr and Mrs Deacon?' she asked.

They struck her as timorous in their response: unused to unsolicited attention but trying to appear relaxed in the face of it.

'Penelope Coyne. I wanted to congratulate you on the forthcoming happy occasion.'

It was Mrs Deacon who replied. 'That's very kind. I'm Catherine, by the way, and this is Martin.'

'Pleased to meet you,' Mr Deacon said, extending a hand. His fingers were faintly criss-crossed with fine lines, scratches and pockmarks embedded in layers of callused skin. These were hands that he worked with. Mrs Deacon's hands were smooth by comparison. To Penny's eye, she had the look of a school teacher.

'I also wished to thank you for the kind invitation.'

'Oh, you're most welcome,' Mrs Deacon said. 'Although to be perfectly honest, we know very few people on the list given to us by Lord Stonebridge.'

'It was quite a long list,' Mr Deacon added, as though concerned Penny might be offended at not being recognised.

They spoke in Dundonian accents, unpolished by living elsewhere.

'Nonetheless, I am hugely grateful.'

'That might be misplaced too,' said Mrs Deacon, colouring a little. 'Lord Stonebridge is picking up the bill for everything. We're very grateful. He's really pushing the boat out.'

This sounded like a sentiment Mrs Deacon was obliged to express rather than gratitude entirely felt.

'It's going to be a beautiful occasion,' Penny said, hoping to put them at ease. 'Such a magnificent setting. But then, we're very blessed here in this part of the world.'

'Oh, I know,' Mrs Deacon replied. She dropped her voice just a little. 'Though confidentially, part of me will be relieved when this is all over. I'm not used to being at the centre of such a fuss.'

'We're a wee bit overwhelmed by it all,' Mr Deacon confessed. 'I mean, we felt like we'd gone up in the world when we bought a house in Monifieth.'

Penny laughed, but Mr Deacon still had a point he wished to make.

'It's not just about the wedding. It's everything else as well. It feels like we're marrying off *both* our children.'

'What do you mean?'

The Deacons looked at each other, perhaps surprised Penny didn't know, or wondering whether they had said too much.

'Our children founded an independent publishing company,' he said. 'Well, Miles started it and Lilian made sure it got off the ground. Have you heard of RoadMiles Press?'

'Of course,' Penny replied, a few things falling into place. She had a vague notion of having read something about RoadMiles recently. Something very positive.

'I'm an English teacher,' said Mrs Deacon, to Penny's private satisfaction; her memory might be failing her, but her judgement was still keen. 'Lilian and Miles always had their heads in a book growing up.'

Before either of the Deacons could say anything more, their attention was drawn by a new arrival, and they became suddenly animated.

'Sebastian!' Mrs Deacon hailed, waving to a figure who had entered from the main lobby.

He acknowledged the wave and began making his way across the polished floor. Perhaps it was not so much the lightness of his gait as the warmth of his expression, but he seemed to convey himself across the room with a gliding grace that suggested, were he walking on sand, he would leave no footprints.

People often talked of someone whose presence lit up a room, but in Penny's experience those described were not always so much the source of light as adept at making themselves the focus of it, while everyone else basked in the reflected glow. In Sebastian Gossard, Penny recognised someone rather whose presence *lightened* a room, for she could sense the Deacons' stress levels reduce in response to his arrival. Whatever anxieties they held regarding the wedding itself, they had none about their daughter's betrothed.

He looked late twenties or early thirties, dressed in jeans and a polo neck that might have made someone else look like a beatnik, but on him almost seemed tailored. He was a handsome young fellow too, though Penny knew it was not her place to judge.

He addressed them both with easy familiarity.

'Catherine, Martin, what a relief to see you here. I'm taking it as a good omen that Lilian will show up too.'

The Deacons laughed. 'I'm making no promises,' said Mr Deacon.

Sebastian looked around the Winter Garden. 'It's such a stunning setting, isn't it? Antonia just fell in love with Crathie Hall when she visited a few years back. So much that she ended up buying the place.'

'Antonia?' asked Penny.

Sebastian turned to her, as though just realising she was there, having been caught up in the moment.

'Sorry, Lady Stonebridge. My stepmother, though I hate that word, feel like I'm in a fairy-tale. Or the eighteenth century at least. And where are my manners? Sebastian Gossard,' he said, extending a hand.

'Penelope Coyne.'

'Are you a friend of Catherine and Martin?'

'No. I believe I am on the groom's side of this occasion.'

Sebastian tried to disguise that he had no idea who she was, while clearly racking his brains in the hope that one might pop up.

'I used to work at Stonebridge Publishing, about a hundred years ago, in your grandfather's time. The late Arthur Stonebridge,' she explained to the Deacons.

'I'm jealous,' Sebastian said. 'I only have the vaguest recollection of him. He died when I was four.'

'Your father was there too, of course, though I'm surprised he remembers me, never mind inviting me to your wedding. I was closer to Arthur, and he and your father didn't always see eye to eye back then.'

'Hard relate,' Sebastian replied. There was a mischievous twinkle in his eye, but Penny could see the sincerity that lay beneath it. It might have sounded light-hearted, but clearly the sentiment was close to the surface.

'People become unusually sentimental at times like these, I'm learning,' Sebastian said. 'I have this strange desire to reconnect with people I used to know, just to tell them this amazing thing is happening to me. I think my father must be experiencing something similar, which says a lot about what he thinks of Lilian.'

'Or of RoadMiles,' said Mr Deacon. Like Sebastian's earlier remark, he tried to make it sound like a joke, but it betrayed more serious thoughts.

Penny caught the briefest flash in Sebastian's eye to indicate that he shared them, before he colluded in the common cover of laughter.

'Yes. He's not so much losing a son as gaining a publishing house,' Sebastian said.

He glanced across the room, something having caught his attention.

'Oh my goodness. Look, I'm embarrassed to love you and leave you, but my fear is that I inadvertently snub someone in a corridor here and the share price goes down five points. I'll be right back.'

'Not at all, not at all,' said Mrs Deacon.

Sebastian glided away across the Winter Garden towards the lobby, greeting an older couple who beamed warmly in response.

His sudden absence left an awkward void, as was often the case when someone so charismatic departed.

'You were telling me about your children's publishing house,' Penny said, to restart the conversation. 'I gather they've been doing rather well.'

'Aye,' said Mr Deacon. 'Of course, when Miles first set it up we were worried sick. Fortunately Lilian came on board too. Miles is a dreamer, whereas she's always had a sensible head on her shoulders. It was hand to mouth for a long time. Then, of course, along comes *The Cracked Mirror*.'

Ah, Penny thought. This was why she had read about RoadMiles.

'Suddenly not only have they got a bestseller on their hands,' he said, 'but a Hollywood movie deal as well. Now Stonebridge are buying them out, for serious money. Our heads are spinning. I mean, you heard Sebastian talking about Lady Stonebridge, Antonia. She liked this hotel, so she bought it. I worry it's an impulse purchase when I buy new work boots before the last pair has worn out.'

'It's what you want for your kids, though, isn't it?' Mrs Deacon said, addressing her husband as much as Penny. 'For them to have more than you had. To move in higher circles.'

Mr Deacon was nodding, but it sounded like they were both trying to convince themselves. Penny suspected they knew that, though those circles might be higher, it didn't mean they were a better place for their children. Or a safer one.

Something Bloody, Something Blue

Chapter Four

The irony of being occasionally fielded as a soldier in the war on drugs is that Johnny has learned how ubiquitous those drugs are and therefore how pointless the whole exercise. He's read somewhere that Scotland has, per capita, the highest cocaine use of any country on the planet. Consequently he figures that even in a rural backwater like Ardfell, there's gonna be at least one skeezy bar where he can hook up with a dealer.

He's reassessing this after sticking his head around the door of the first place he comes to, which has only a dozen people inside, almost all of them old guys watching golf on TV.

A hundred yards down the street he finds a better prospect in the Tully Vaults, which has a younger crowd, or at least a younger element. There is pop music coming through the speakers, not so loud that you can't hear a conversation, but loud enough that you can't hear *everybody's* conversation. Johnny buys a beer and scans the room. It takes him all of thirty seconds to identify six people as likely users and two as one hundred per cent, nailed-on cokeheads. One of those has just come out of the gents, walking with a certain swagger Johnny long ago learned to recognise. He's a skinny guy in his mid-twenties, dressed in some kind of blue sports shirt; maybe a soccer team, Johnny doesn't know.

Skinny rejoins his group, sniffing as he sits. Johnny picks up his beer and sits down at a table next to him. He gives it a minute, waits for a lull in the group's conversation. He leans over and speaks quietly.

'Hey, man, if a guy was looking to pick up some white goods round here, would you know who he could speak to?'

The guy looks him up and down with the requisite suspicion and a small, highly hypocritical element of feigned offence.

'How, you looking to buy a fridge, like?' he says with a smirk.

Johnny takes a fifty-pound note from his wallet, thinking how it looks fake, like foreign currency tends to for a while. He folds it and places it underneath his beer mat with the edge sticking out.

'You know any more now?'

Skinny looks at the money then at Johnny, sizing him up. Johnny's worried he's played it too fast. The problem with being a cop for so long is that some people can see it on you no matter what. Johnny's hoping the accent means the guy sees a tourist first and foremost.

Skinny pulls out his phone.

'I know a man who might be able to help,' he says. Then he pauses, doubt clouding his expression. 'Only thing is, is this gaunny be worth his while?'

Johnny gives him a reassuring grin. 'We're at the hotel for a wedding. There's a few of us looking to party all weekend.'

'And are you holding folding?'

It takes Johnny a moment to parse this.

'If you mean the weird plasticky notes you guys call cash, then yeah.'

'I'll no' be a minute.'

Skinny gets up and walks outside to make his call.

The dude comes back a few minutes later. Sits down, takes a drink from his pint without saying anything. It's like he's seen a YouTube video on 'acting casual'. Eventually he leans over. 'You're on.' He holds his hand out for the fifty. 'You give me that and I tell you where.'

Johnny slips him the note. He notices the guy is eyeing the barman as he takes it, checking it isn't noticed. The barman seems oblivious.

Skinny says nothing, takes another sip of his beer. Waits long enough for Johnny to worry the guy has played him and is gonna deny everything. Then he speaks again.

'Gents toilets. Fifteen minutes.'

Johnny glances at the barman and then at the bathroom door.

'What, your man's just gonna walk in here and go straight to the john?'

'No, are you daft? My connect doesnae want barred from the only other pub in town. The *public* toilets, Atholl Square, end of the Main Street.'

Johnny finishes his beer and heads out ten minutes later. On his way down Main Street he walks past a bookstore and is briefly pulled up by something in the window. The titles on display look to be largely curated towards local interest and the tourist market: books about golf, fishing, hill-walking and Scottish history. What stops Johnny is a promotional display for a novel called *The Cracked Mirror* by Alex Gillen. A poster is touting it as a number-one bestseller, nominated for several awards, but what catches Johnny's eye is that it's published by RoadMiles Press: Lilian and Miles Deacon's company. These guys are a bigger deal than he thought.

The public toilets are in an ugly concrete block near the entrance to the car park, one side of which is allocated to bays marked COACHES ONLY. There are no coaches at this time of the evening, and no cars either. Johnny walks through the door on the left, marked Gents, bracing himself for the public toilet smell of urine. Instead he gets fresh paint and a hint of bleach. No graffiti either, just framed posters: a local map, a testicular cancer check-up campaign, an ad for a stage play: *The Government Inspector* at Glen Cluthar Town Hall.

There is nobody else here. Yet.

Johnny doesn't want to wait around conspicuously. He takes a piss, goes to wash his hands. There's another framed poster above the sink, next to the mirror. It shows a cocky young white guy looking straight to camera, the caption encouraging the reader to intervene if his friend is being an asshole towards women on a night out.

Johnny lathers, rinses his hands. When he looks up, the poster has changed. There's now a boyish-looking Black teenager staring back at him. The caption reads: 'Justice for Jayden Freil.'

Johnny recoils from the sight of it, closing his eyes like he's been dazzled. When he opens them again, the poster shows the cocky white kid once more, the other face gone, as is his memory of it. This time, though, the name stays. Jayden Freil.

It don't mean anything to him. Johnny ain't got time to think about it now though, because there are two men walking into the bathroom.

One is the skinny guy he spoke to in the Tully Vaults. The

other is a stocky dude, maybe mid-thirties. Shaven head, neck tattoos, a boxer's nose and a scar on his cheek.

Johnny's hazard alarms are going off big time. He can tell right away that Tats here has done hard time, but that's not what's spooking him. It's the intuition that the guy hasn't done hard time for dealing drugs.

They stop a few feet in front of the door. Johnny clocks that they have positioned themselves to cut off the exit. It's looking more like a shakedown than a coke deal, but he might be wrong. He's from out of town, after all.

'I hear you're looking for chico,' says Tats.

'That's right.'

'Let's see the colour of your money.'

'No offence, dude, but I ain't showing you green until you show me some white.'

'How about I show you some red?' Tats says, pulling out a blade. Looks like a fishing knife, sturdy and sharp, serrated down one edge. Skinny produces a box-cutter, the retractable blade sticking out about an inch. Deep enough to cut the carotid artery without even applying much pressure.

Johnny feels an instinctive tingle in his hand in anticipation of reaching for a gun that isn't there. He decides to gauge how much stomach they have for it, or whether the weapons are just for show.

'And how about you guys put the blades away, so I don't need to fuck you both up so bad your mommies are crying the next time they see your faces?'

Skinny looks unsure, used to easier prey, but Tats brandishes his knife with a scowl.

'I'm not flipping joking,' he says. 'Get the money out, or we'll be giving you a wee souvenir to take back to America.'

Flipping? Johnny thinks, but he doesn't have time to dwell on it. He takes a rapid half step onto the balls of his feet, urging a response. Tats is game. He lunges forward, raising the knife, intent on plunging it downwards. Johnny blocks hard with a high left hand and sends his right into Tats's neck, crushing his windpipe. He grips Tats's right wrist with both hands while stepping and spinning beneath him. There's a crack as the wrist snaps and the knife hits the floor. Johnny kicks the knife away, sending it skidding into an open bathroom stall. Skinny swipes awkwardly with the box-cutter, encumbered by Tats sprawling in front of him and by the fact that he already knows he's fucked.

Johnny grips one of the sinks with both hands and uses it as a pivot to launch himself two-footed, catching Skinny simultaneously in the sternum and the face. The back of his head smashes hard against a vending machine and he drops to the floor unconscious. Unfortunately the box-cutter drops too, and skids to within six inches of where Tats has sprawled.

Tats picks it up with his one good hand and climbs to his feet, not as breathless as Johnny hoped. He thought he'd hit him hard enough but the guy must have a thick neck. He looks real pissed off, deranged fury in his eyes.

'I'm gaunny open you up like a packet of crisps,' Tats says, then makes his move.

Johnny grabs one of the framed notices as Tats slashes at him, using it to deflect the box-cutter while sending a full-force kick to the guy's balls. Tats doubles over but he keeps hold of his weapon. Johnny slams the framed poster down onto the back of the guy's hand, causing him to drop the blade. But Johnny ain't done with this motherflipper. He gets Tats's left arm twisted up his back and runs him full speed into a stall, crashing his

131

head off the tiles. Then Johnny lets him drop, like he just cut his strings.

The whole thing has taken about ten seconds, each of them a moment of pure exhilaration.

Johnny checks himself in the mirror. No cuts, no marks, no bloodstains. And looking damn fine.

Man, I love being Johnny Hawke, he thinks. *So much better than being . . .*

Being what? He doesn't know. Doesn't matter.

He goes through Tats's pockets. Like Johnny figures, he ain't a dealer, just an asshole. But he *is* holding for personal use. And so, it turns out, is Skinny. Johnny doesn't need enough for several people to party through the weekend. He just needs enough to get Brooks onside and talkative.

As he walks out of the building, he sees there is now a car parked way back, where the streetlights don't reach. Tats's ride, set for a quick getaway. He thinks he can make out somebody in the driver's seat. Too far and too dark to see a face. They can probably see his, though, and he figures he's not the one they were expecting to walk out of there first.

Murder by Invitation

III

The hubbub from the lounge bar carried along the lobby. Gales of laughter erupted above the piped-in music, mixed with other noisy outpourings: incredulity, exclamation, indignation, delight. It was almost half past nine, which would normally be approaching Penny's bedtime, but she had a mystery to solve: that of who had brought her here. To this end, she anticipated that the most judicious time to seek information would be after dinner, when people gathered in the bar, well-refreshed tongues thoroughly loosened.

She stopped just inside the Laird's Lounge, giving herself a moment to get the lie of the land. People were gathered mostly in groups, occasionally in couples; the former seated in cloistered horseshoes of couches and armchairs, the latter intently around small tables. There was one woman sitting on her own, and Penny wondered if she was also here unaccompanied, before noticing several empty glasses on the table in front of her. Her companion would be at the bar, or perhaps the toilet.

She spotted the Deacons sitting with another couple of around the same age. They were tucked away in a corner, as though hiding from the crowd, the four of them sharing a bottle of red. Mr Deacon acknowledged her with a wave, but not one that could be interpreted as an invitation to join them; nor would she wish to impose.

She noticed another individual whom she suspected was there alone, though it was not easy to tell whether he was merely standing on the periphery of a group. He was dressed smartly, if soberly, more like he was at work than attending a party, and he didn't appear to be paying close attention to the nearby group's conversation. Rather, his blue eyes seemed to be scanning the room, swiftly averted when he became aware that Penny had noticed. He was on the lookout for something, and clearly she wasn't it. In fact, she suspected she was at least forty years too old to be it.

Then she saw someone else she recognised, even though she had not encountered him in at least thirty years. Jonathan Stonebridge, as she had known him, was standing up from an armchair at one of the low tables, emerging from a group of people.

He edged his way out through a tight gap between chairs, then proceeded across the room, his face breaking into a smile as he approached Penny. She reciprocated, pleasantly surprised by the delight in his expression. She had known him as a rather restless and frequently rude young man. He had been over-eager to make an impression, sometimes ugly in the way he wielded what authority was granted to him. But many young men were restless until they could prove themselves, or understood enough to know that they did not need to prove anything.

Penny addressed him by his title, though they had been on first-name terms back when she had worked with him.

'Lord Stonebridge,' she said warmly.

Upon which his face creased into a look of consternation, sufficient for Penny to fear she had addressed the wrong man. That was before the true source of his confusion became clear.

She realised his smile had not been for her, but for a fellow who had entered the room at her back, and she had cut him off en route to making his greeting.

'Yes?' he replied, barely concealing his irritation.

'Penelope Coyne,' she offered.

She watched the wheels turning behind his eyes, searching for a resolution that did not arrive.

'We worked together at Stonebridge Publishing, back in . . .'

Still his expression remained blank. He forced a smile. 'Do forgive me. So many employees down the years, so many imprints, so many books. But what a charming coincidence that you're here. Are you a guest at the hotel?'

'I'm a guest . . . at the wedding,' she replied, her voice threatening to fail her.

'Oh. You're a friend of the Deacon family?'

'No, I, er . . .'

'Anyway, lovely to meet you again,' he said, brushing past before loudly hailing and embracing the gentleman he had originally been on his way towards.

Penny felt her cheeks burn in a way that took her back seventy years to schoolyard cruelties. As a woman in her eighties, she had grown used to being treated as invisible. Being dismissed as unremembered was something altogether different. And somewhere amidst the sting of humiliation, the question of who then *had* invited her took on a darker aspect. She wondered, in fact, whether it had been done with malevolent intentions.

'He made out he doesn't remember you,' said a woman's voice.

'He was probably lying, either as a power move, or because it's his default means of expression.'

Penny turned and saw that she was being addressed by the woman who was sitting alone.

'Can I get you a drink?' she said. 'I'm on my way to the bar.'

Penny's first instinct was to decline and retreat back to her room like some frightened little mouse. But a stronger instinct told her a drink would help her care considerably less about a stupid, awkward encounter.

'I'll have a gin and tonic, please. A large one, if you don't mind.'

'Oh, I don't mind at all. Ursula Bryant,' she said, extending a hand.

'Penelope Coyne. Penny to my friends.'

Ursula returned from the bar a few minutes later, carrying Penny's gin and two cocktails. She placed all three down on the table, already heaving with empties.

'Would you care to join me?' she asked, indicating the empty seat.

'That's very kind.'

'So you worked with *Lord* Stonebridge,' Ursula said, with sarcastic emphasis. Her speech sounded a little slurred, which was when Penny deduced Ursula was here alone but drinking for two.

'Yes, though he was simply Jonathan Stonebridge when I knew him. I worked for Stonebridge Publishing under his late father. How do you know him?'

'I run a typesetting firm. For now, at least.'

'What do you mean?'

'Stonebridge is trying to buy us out. Not so much a hostile takeover as a mugging. We're struggling to keep the lights on because he's been stalling on paying us: disputing invoices, pulling every dirty trick he knows.'

'It sounds dreadful,' said Penny.

Ursula downed the rest of her cocktail and reached for the next.

'He invited us to the wedding as another power move. Wanting us to bend the knee and act like everything's lovely. My husband wouldn't give him the satisfaction, but I'm drinking as much as I can stomach, because it's the closest I'll get to him paying . . .'

Ursula's attention drifted away from Penny, who looked up to see what had drawn her focus.

There was a striking young woman making her way through the lounge. She wore a pale blue dress that clung to her tall, thin frame, the material shimmering in the light. The word that came to Penny's mind was diaphanous, but she wore it like a suit of armour.

'The bride-to-be,' Ursula said under her breath. 'Lilian Deacon.'

She was trying to make her way towards her parents through a throng of people intent on wishing her good luck for tomorrow. Someone handed her a glass of champagne, which she initially refused before having second thoughts.

She was smiling but there was unquestionably a seriousness about her. Penny thought of what her father had said.

She's always had a sensible head on her shoulders.

It was a very beautiful head, if supported by rather skinny shoulders.

'She's gorgeous,' Penny said.

'Could do with some meat on her bones, though,' Ursula replied, her bitterness towards Lord Stonebridge begrudging a compliment to his son's betrothed. 'I've heard there's an eating disorder. There are mental-health rumours too. Bipolar, apparently.'

Ursula took another gulp of her latest cocktail as Lilian finally made it to her parents' table.

'I spoke to Mr and Mrs Deacon earlier,' Penny said. 'They seem very taken with Lilian's intended. I only met him briefly, but he was quite charming.'

'Sebastian *Gossard*,' Ursula replied, with further arch emphasis. 'He adopted his late mother's surname. I assume he got more of her nature too.'

Ursula stared intently at Penny, as though just remembering something.

'What was Stonebridge's father like?'

Penny cast her mind back. Details were, as ever, frustratingly scarce. Only a general feeling remained, but it was a strong one.

'A little cold, if I'm being honest. High-handed. Just from the little I have to go on, Sebastian strikes me as very different to both of them.'

'That family is a nest of vipers,' Ursula said, putting down her glass and leaning in. 'When I heard about Lilian and Sebastian being in a relationship, I hoped it might play out the other way round. If she drew him away from his family, that would be the best chance for both of them. But it turns out it's not just Sebastian that Lilian Deacon's getting into bed with.'

Something Bloody, Something Blue

Chapter Five

Johnny is searching the name 'Jayden Freil' on his phone as he walks back up the hill towards Crathie Hall. He's getting nothing. He doesn't remember it from a case, so why is it in his head? Could it be from a TV show? No. That would give a ton of search results. As would a character in a book. A really old case, maybe, from before digitised archiving, before everything was searchable? Possible, but it doesn't help.

As he approaches the entrance to the hotel, through the glass walls he sees Crawford Nicholson again. He's standing close to one of the archways, chatting to a tall, slim woman in a blue dress. In truth, it takes Johnny an extra second to notice Nicholson because the broad is such a looker. Turns out it's a second too long, because Nicholson leans in to hug and kiss her then walks away towards the lobby.

Johnny hastens his stride as he comes through the glass doors into reception, calls out: 'Hey, Crawford, wait up.'

The guy doesn't answer, doesn't look back. Reaches the lobby and turns left, out of sight.

When Johnny gets through the archway, Nicholson is nowhere to be seen. There's a group of people further down the corridor, near the entrance to the Laird's Lounge, but he can't see Nicholson among them. Couldn't have made it that far, anyways, surely.

He looks at the two elevators, sees they're already at the third and second floors, so he can't be in one of those. There's a staircase either side, going down to the gym and swimming pool on the right, climbing to the residential floors on the left. Johnny figures Nicholson took the elevator when he saw him earlier, so his room must be on a high floor.

He skips down the stairs, as fast as he can go without looking desperate. Doesn't see anybody when he reaches the bottom. There's a smell of chlorine mixed with body spray and perfume in the corridor. Johnny tries the changing room and finds it locked. A sign on the door says the facilities are open until eight.

Johnny runs back upstairs and looks again at the group gathered down the corridor. He now spots Nicholson among them, revealed when a big linebacker of a dude moves out of the way. Must have been there the whole time. He's shaking more hands, smiling. For somebody based in LA, Nicholson sure knows a lot of people here.

Johnny feels a rage kindling in him, watching the guy glad-handing friends. Like his writing partner wasn't just found with his brains blown out. Like Johnny's partner didn't die fifty feet from the same spot.

Nicholson breaks off from the group and heads into the bar. Johnny walks past the group at a leisurely pace, making eye contact. He gives them a smile and a nod like he knows them and they ought to know him, then saunters into the Laird's Lounge, which is now rammed and raucously noisy.

He can't see Nicholson. He's lost him in the crowd, but he's in here somewhere, and Johnny can be patient.

Johnny takes up position, though because the bar is a lot busier, he can't stand where he's in the way of folks queueing. He finds himself on the edge of a group, picking up snippets of conversation. People aren't just talking about a wedding. Seems Stonebridge Publishing is buying RoadMiles Press.

He scans the room, taking in the groupings. He sees Lord and Lady Stonebridge but still doesn't see Nicholson. He notices that little old lady in the tweed suit looking his way, worries for a second that she's about to mistake him for someone else, then she walks further inside, intercepting Lord Stonebridge as he gets up to go someplace.

Johnny hears a familiar voice ordering at the bar and sees Alan Brooks standing there, minus the shades. He's altogether less self-conscious and considerably more perky. Somebody else must have helped him out. Shit. There goes his leverage.

'Johnny, how you doing?'

'I'm good. Took a trip into town, picked up some supplies, if you know what I mean.'

Brooks acts like this don't mean shit. 'Hey, have you seen Sebastian?' he asks. In his now coked-up state he has forgotten that Johnny doesn't know what Sebastian even looks like, and nor does he care how clear it is who he'd rather be talking to.

'I don't think so.'

'Nah, me neither. Not since dinner. I think he's laying low, maybe just staying away from Lilian the night before in case he jinxes it or something.'

Brooks gets his drinks and takes off, leaving Johnny to keep scoping the room for the incredible vanishing man. He's been noting all the arrivals and departures, table swaps and trips to the bar, but still hasn't seen Nicholson. Maybe missed him when he turned around to talk to Brooks. One person he does see is Lilian Deacon – it transpires she's the knockout Nicholson was hugging in reception. She walks in and draws every eyeball in the room, Johnny picking up her name from the chat around him.

Though she's getting an A-lister response, she's not quite comfortable with the attention. There's an awkwardness to her body language at odds with her otherwise elegant appearance. She has to think about it when someone offers her a glass of champagne, like she's wondering what's the catch.

Johnny is watching her make slow progress across the room when he hears a voice in his ear.

'Hey, Johnny Hollywood.'

He turns around and finds Stonebridge's younger daughter, Lucy, standing beside him. She's in jeans, a t-shirt and a leather jacket, which he figures is some kind of statement when everyone else is in semi-formal attire. She's at the bar but she's gripping a bottle of single malt by the neck, and she looks like she's already done it some damage.

'I don't believe I've had the pleasure,' he says. 'But you got the Johnny part right. My name is Hawke.'

'I got the Hollywood part right too. I overheard you saying you work in the movie biz. I'm Lucy.'

'What can I do for you, Lucy?' he asks, as she clearly has an agenda.

'Are you carrying, Johnny?'

For a second he thinks she means a gun. He says nothing, keeps his expression blank.

'Where you work isn't the only thing I overheard. I wondered if you could help me out?'

Lucy doesn't look like she needs much help. She's not swaying drunk, but there's an edge to her. In Johnny's experience whisky can be a strange drink. Brings out a mean streak in certain people. She's smiling, but she's not happy. And misery loves company. Misery likes to talk.

'I could,' he says. 'But it would mean going someplace else and leaving all these lovely people.'

'Yeah, that would be a tragedy.'

Lucy leads him along a corridor, through a set of double doors and into a modern annexe at the rear of the building. He can smell the chlorine again, so they must be above the swimming pool.

She's asking him about the movie business. He bullshits vaguely then pivots to asking her if she knows Crawford Nicholson.

She shakes her head, her expression blank. The guy seems to know everybody except the people Johnny has been speaking to. His connection is definitely to the Deacon side of the wedding.

She takes a swig from the whisky bottle, then holds it out to Johnny.

'You want some? It's decent stuff. Springbank. It's okay, I haven't back-washed it.'

She thrusts it at him like a challenge.

'Yeah, but I might.'

He takes hold of the neck, has a mouthful. It burns real nice.

Lucy puts her lips to the bottle again as soon as he's done, like she's proving a point.

They come to a gallery overlooking two squash courts, empty and unlit beneath them. There are several sofas lined along the wall, tables in front of them. Lucy sits down at one of them, placing the whisky bottle on the floor at her feet. Johnny susses she wants to keep the table clear for something else. She looks at him expectantly.

Johnny produces the baggie he took from Tats, places it on the table with a gesture to help herself.

Lucy chops out two lines, does them both. She sits back in her seat, waiting for the hit. Johnny wonders how Tats's supply is going to measure up to what she's used to. She doesn't complain, but beggars can't be choosers. She eyes the baggie.

'You not having any?'

'I'm not as young as I used to be. Need to pace myself this weekend.'

Lucy takes another swig of whisky. 'Yeah, everybody's got to be on their best behaviour,' she says, sounding sarcastic. 'But that's the one consolation of being the family screw-up: it's hard to disappoint people when their expectations are down in the Precambrian sedimentary layer.'

'I'm from out of town,' Johnny reminds her. 'I don't know shit about you or your family. So this is your chance to give me your side before I've heard anyone else's. Who says you're a screw-up?'

'Everybody,' she replies with a giggle. It's mirthless though, like she's putting a brave face on hurt. 'It's my brand. They all think I'm a waste of space and call me a nepo-baby. But it's weird how they point to me and never Monica. She's the over-promoted mediocrity in this family. Dad knows she's not leader material, but she's the one being groomed to take over, because he can control her.'

'What about Sebastian?'

Lucy takes another swig from the bottle, eyes glazed, expression kinda wistful.

'You know how they talk about families having a madwoman in the attic? In our family, Sebastian is the sane man in the attic. He should run away, take his gifts elsewhere, but looks like it's too late for that.'

Lucy jolts out of whatever reverie had seized her. She chops out another two lines. Johnny's instinct is to tell her to slow down, but he doesn't want to risk the connection he's trying to build, and he's pretty sure it would be pointless anyway.

'You sure you don't want to partake?' she asks.

'I need my beauty sleep.'

Lucy eyes him up and down. 'You look beautiful enough as it is.' Her tone is coy, flirty. She puts a hand on one of Johnny's biceps and gives it a squeeze. 'I'm guessing you work out. I bet you have some staying power too.'

Johnny gently lifts her hand away and places it in her lap. It breaks a spell. For a moment he thinks she might get angry but instead she looks embarrassed. Tearful.

'I'm sorry,' she says. 'Told you I was a screw-up.'

Johnny hands her a tissue. She dabs her eyes and nose, then reaches for the bottle again. Johnny takes it from her, places it on the floor to his side.

'Take it easy,' he tells her.

Lucy nods. 'You're a good man,' she says. 'A decent man. You see someone in a vulnerable state and your instinct is to protect. My father sees vulnerability and he senses opportunity. Whether that be in business or anything else.'

'Anything else? You mean . . .?'

'I mean it's a miracle he's not been MeToo'd. Actually, there's no miracle. I know for a fact there's women who've been paid off because they'd rather take some money than risk going public and being destroyed.'

145

'Does Lady Stonebridge know about all this?'

Another mirthless laugh.

'My wicked stepmother? She's from money, so she understands how to play the game. And rule number one is stay on the side of the man who has the most.'

Lucy looks Johnny in the eyes. The bratty rich-kid act is gone. She seems older, suddenly. She smiles, but not like she's happy. Or if she is happy, it's not because she's picturing something good.

'My father collects enemies like other people collect antiques, showing them off because of what it says about him. But one day soon, he's going to need a friend, and discover he's fresh out.'

Murder by Invitation

IV

The gin and tonic had been a mistake, and a foolish one at that. Penny never over-indulged in alcohol, or at least hadn't for a very long time, so she was annoyed at herself for forgetting that these days, having a drink so late in the evening would mess with her sleep patterns.

Not long after leaving the lounge bar, she had felt suddenly tired and decided not to bother with supper. However, by the time she had undressed and brushed her teeth, the wave of alcohol-induced fatigue had passed, and she found herself lying there, unable to nod off. Making it worse, she was starting to feel naggingly peckish. Aware that the hotel didn't do twenty-four-hour room service, she tried to ignore it by reading a few more chapters of that book whose story kept changing into something else, but she was only becoming less sleepy, not more. With the clock approaching one, she pulled her clothes back on and decided to venture downstairs in search of a snack, even though she knew it might be a long shot.

Penny walked down one of the corridors that extended either

side of the main lobby, glancing at the framed photographs lining the walls. They mostly showed exteriors from different decades, evidencing a reassuring lack of change. One did stand out as different: a late-Victorian shot of the staff assembled before the building, standing in their starched white uniforms. She assumed it dated from Crathie Hall's sanatorium days, before the place reopened as a hotel. They looked a cheerless and intimidating lot, determined to restore your health even if it killed you.

She approached the reception desk and to her pleasant surprise found Alison Innis on night duty.

'Don't you ever sleep?' Penny asked.

'I might ask you the same question, especially as you're not the one paid to be awake right now.'

'But you've been working all day.'

'And yet,' she replied, smiling. 'How can I assist?'

'I don't suppose there's any chance of a roll and bacon at this hour?'

Her expression was apologetic. 'I'm afraid all the kitchen staff have gone home. I'd love to oblige you myself, but I don't have insurance certification for operating kitchen equipment. It's absurd, I know. I mean, I shouldn't need official clearance to stick some rashers under the grill, but . . .'

'No, not at all,' said Penny. 'I completely understand. And approve, to be honest, though I realise that puts me in a minority.'

'I do think there is a sufficient grey area for me to pop a slice of apple pie in the microwave, if that appeals. Definitely enough to boil a kettle.'

'Are you sure?'

'Yes, I'm feeling reckless. Maybe even enough to turn on a couple of lights in the Winter Garden at this hour, if you'd like to eat there.'

'Positively decadent,' Penny said. 'An illicit thrill of a midnight feast to rival the ones of my schooldays, back in the twelfth century.'

Ms Innis escorted Penny through the lobby to the Winter Garden's entrance. The moon and a few brighter stars were visible through the glass cupola, the potted plants and hanging vines looming as black shapes against the glass.

Penny watched Ms Innis dash ahead and briefly disappear, then heard the click of a light switch. She only turned on the sidelights, embedded in the floor and around the skirting. It was enough to see by, and pleasantly unobtrusive for the time of night. It was also enough to reveal that the Winter Garden was not empty.

Lilian Deacon looked up from where she was sitting in the semi-darkness, startled by the unexpected intrusion into her solitude. There was a bottle of champagne almost empty in front of her, but she did not look to be in a celebratory mood. She was heavy-eyed, but weary rather than drunk. Burdened.

'Ms Deacon, I was just about to fetch Ms Coyne some tea and a slice of apple pie,' said Ms Innis brightly, as though huddling in the dark was a perfectly normal activity for one of her guests to be pursuing. 'Can I get you anything?'

Lilian thought about it, looking at the champagne bottle for a moment before saying, 'Tea would be lovely.'

'I will be back presently,' Ms Innis stated, then hurried away with that skipping gait of hers.

Lilian looked up at Penny.

'Would you be *Penelope* Coyne?' she asked.

'Yes I am.'

'My parents mentioned you. Would you care to join me?'

'I would be delighted.'

149

Penny pulled out a chair and sat down opposite Lilian, feeling a slight chill from being so close to the glass. As she sat down, she noticed movement in the lobby and looked to see if Ms Innis had come back already, perhaps having forgotten to ask something. Instead she recognised the man she had noticed in the bar, the one she thought to be on his own. Whatever he was looking for, he hadn't found it. He peered inquisitively at the pair of them – as well he might, given the hour – then retreated unhurriedly.

'I gather you worked with Sebastian's grandfather,' Lilian said. She had a less broadly Dundonian accent than her parents, but it was still in there.

'I would say *for* rather than *with*,' Penny replied.

'Yes, I'm learning that's an important distinction.'

'What do you mean?'

Lilian gazed into the darkness again, disinclined to answer. A silence grew, interrupted by Ms Innis returning with a pot of tea and two slices of apple pie. She placed them down without fuss then absented herself again with consummate discretion.

Penny poured, nudging a cup closer to Lilian's side of the table.

'Won't your fiancé be wondering where you are?' she asked.

'We're in separate rooms tonight, just for, I don't know, the symbolism of it. He went off to bed early, demonstrating that he's a mature and sensible individual who understands his responsibilities.'

'Why, is there a suggestion otherwise?'

'Not from me. But I'm not the audience for the demonstration.'

Lilian let out a sigh and bowed her head momentarily.

'You should eat something,' Penny suggested. 'Settle your stomach so that you can get some sleep.'

'Will it do anything for the butterflies?'

Penny didn't reply, simply cut herself a piece of pie by way of example. Lilian did likewise, swallowing it down quickly, then having some more. Even in the dim light, Penny could see some colour return to her cheeks.

'I don't know, maybe it's just this place that's freaking me out. It's been giving me this weird feeling of constriction and confinement. I've been reading about its history, before it was a hotel.'

'A Victorian health retreat, I believe.'

'If that's a Victorian euphemism. It was the kind of place they sent women to cure them of hysteria. Everyone else is luxuriating in the timeless charm, all single malts and local venison. I'm seeing cold baths and straitjackets.'

Lilian was attacking her slice of pie now, guzzling it ravenously. Penny wondered if she'd had anything else all night, but drinking on an empty stomach was a symptom of what ailed her, not a cause.

'What was Sebastian's father like back then?' Lilian asked.

'You're the second person to ask me that tonight. And in both cases I suspect the purpose was not so much to gain insight into Jonathan as to gain insight into his son. Would I be right?'

Lilian nodded solemnly. 'Sebastian talks about how his family is a nightmare, but he's still part of it. They've been his whole life and so has the company. That's why I have concerns over which Sebastian I'm marrying: the one he is with me or the one he is when he's around his family.'

As Lilian said this, Penny briefly had the strangest sense of disassociation and déjà vu, like she was floating above herself and listening to a conversation she'd had before. She felt as though she knew Lilian, or had known her once, but that was impossible. She was grateful no one else was party to this. If

William knew, he would be having her carted off to that place in the brochure forthwith.

'Sebastian says he's playing a long game,' Lilian went on. 'That one day he'll be in charge and then he can do things his way. I'd like to believe that.'

'But you're not sure you do,' Penny prompted.

Lilian gazed at the champagne bottle, like she was thinking of having some more. She lifted her tea again instead, taking another slow gulp as she stared through the glass. There was nothing to see but her own faint reflection, a ghost-self sitting only feet away but impossible to reach.

'Sebastian initially planned to buy into RoadMiles independently, take a stake and help us expand. Then it turned out he couldn't raise the funds, and suddenly he's bringing Stonebridge into it after all. Lord S maintains we'll have autonomy within the company, but I don't know. Sebastian is being weird about it. I suspect his father is up to something, and I would very much like to find out what, preferably before this goes through.'

'Do you mean the merger or the wedding?' Penny asked.

'Both,' Lilian said.

Murder by Invitation

V

It was the day of the wedding, and a buffet lunch was being served in the Winter Garden. All of the guests were assembling there in their finery while awaiting a decision on whether the ceremony would take place outside in the Sculpture Garden as planned. If not, the Winter Garden itself would be used as an alternative.

Penny observed a pause in the preparation of the stage outside as the sky darkened and the wind threatened to pick up, a few droplets of rain carrying on the breeze to spray the windows.

Flutes of champagne were being handed round on wide salvers, but Penny was sticking strictly to tea. Alcohol made her sleepy in the afternoons at the best of times, and she was not feeling her brightest, having overslept as a result of her nocturnal interlude with the bride-to-be.

The ceremony was scheduled to commence at two p.m. and was to be conducted by a humanist celebrant. Though Penny's tastes ran to older traditions, on this occasion she was grateful not to be summoned into a chapel. The recent events involving

Father Driver and Mr Gault had left her disturbed by the pain some people were forced to carry around with them, and disturbed more by how far others might go to protect their reputation.

Ms Innis was in conference with Lady Stonebridge. It had just gone one-thirty and clearly a decision was required as to outside or in. Penny had spoken briefly to Ms Innis over breakfast, the hotel manager inquiring as to whether all was well with Lilian. Penny had been discreet, conveying merely that the young woman was a little intimidated by the scale of what was in front of her.

'Stage fright?' Ms Innis had asked.

'One might put it that way, yes.'

'And how are you this morning? Looking forward to the ceremony?'

'Quite. Though I must confide, I would be looking forward to it more if I knew whose guest I am.'

'What do you mean?'

'I still haven't been able to ascertain who invited me.'

Ms Innis seemed to find this amusing, and Penny realised she perhaps ought to see the funny side too. She recalled a typically humorous Robertson Davies novel in which someone maliciously placed a false intimation in the newspaper announcing the engagement of two scions of warring families. Nonetheless, until she had an answer, the possibility of a malevolent motive cast a shadow.

Shadows were also being cast in the Winter Garden, but happily this was because the clouds had lifted and the sun was out. Penny watched Lady Stonebridge give a satisfied nod, then Ms Innis opened the double doors. With a warm smile she announced that the ceremony would take place outside as planned, and invited the guests to take their seats.

Penny had never married. There had been lovers, of course, and even a couple of proposals: one ending in a change of heart and the other in tragedy. She had generally considered it a blessing to be happy in her own company, observing how many people seemed afraid they might fade from existence if their presence was not constantly acknowledged. However, attending a wedding, she found herself prey to an unaccustomed regret that she had no one to share these later years with. She had never feared being alone, believing she had memories enough to keep her company, but now that those memories seemed to be erasing themselves, she was beginning to feel vulnerable in a most unaccustomed way.

Penny made her way down to the Sculpture Garden, enjoying the serenity of the setting. It had been beautifully decorated, vibrant floral arrangements adorning the pergola beneath which the chairs had been arranged. Penny took a seat near the back, partly out of deference to those who definitely ought to be there, and partly so that she could observe all of the above.

She watched Ms Innis escort Mr and Mrs Deacon towards the pergola, the pair still evidently apprehensive as they took in the grandeur of it all. Having got them settled, Ms Innis glided back towards the hotel, but not before stopping to speak to Penny.

'Just FYI,' she said, 'I was copied into the email chain regarding the guest list. I had a look through the correspondence, and it appears your name was added by Miles Deacon.'

'Oh. Thank you,' Penny replied, endeavouring to conceal the extent of her surprise, and the fact that she had never met or spoken to Miles Deacon. Unless she had met him and simply could not remember. Either way, she was none the wiser.

As Ms Innis departed, Penny saw Ursula Bryant shuffling

sideways along the row to sit beside her. She looked perky and alert for someone who had put away so many cocktails last night; had Penny consumed half as much, she'd have been bed-bound for a month. They traded pleasantries about the setting and the sunshine, Ursula seemingly geared up for greater magnanimity than she displayed the previous evening.

That was until Lord Stonebridge appeared, making an ostentatiously regal progress to the front accompanied by his two daughters. Penny realised that Ursula's disdain last night had not been mere boozy bitchiness, because in relative sobriety and the brighter light of day, her true regard for him was considerably starker. She was radiating hatred, perhaps all the more so for watching him in his pomp, at the wedding of his storied son.

Given what she had heard about how the man did business, it struck Penny that Ursula might not be the only person who felt that way.

'Does Lord Stonebridge have some kind of security?' she asked.

'Good question,' Ursula replied. 'I'm hearing he's over-leveraged and vulnerable to a hostile takeover. Hence the urgency for acquisitions to drive up the share price.'

'Actually, I meant personal security.'

'Oh, I see. Not that I'm aware of. But he can afford the kind you're not *supposed* to be aware of.'

And with that, Penny realised she might have seen his security without realising it. That man she had observed first in the bar, then later in the Winter Garden. A man who didn't seem as though he belonged but was nonetheless inconspicuous because he carried himself like he'd every right to be there.

There he was now, in fact, sitting in the back row across the aisle: like Penny, choosing his position for maximum vantage.

Ms Innis reappeared, approaching the Deacons again. They rose from their seats and accompanied her back up the aisle and away from the pergola, where they joined Sebastian Gossard and Lady Stonebridge in hushed conversation. There was much checking of watches and glancing towards the Winter Garden.

'Trouble in paradise,' muttered Ursula with an undisguised note of relish.

The sense that something might be amiss began to pass through the gathering like a wave. Expensively millinered heads were turning, the atmosphere of reverent expectation trans-forming into something more agitated. Further wristwatches were consulted, phones glanced at for distraction.

Sebastian and the Deacons came and went from the building, Ms Innis shuttling back and forth also, speaking constantly into her mobile phone or her walkie-talkie.

As quarter past two became half past two, Penny's thoughts turned to her conversation with Lilian last night. She got up and approached Ms Innis, who intercepted her before she could reach the group hovering at the edge of the pergola. Lady Stonebridge had joined them, while her husband remained seated with his daughters at the front.

'We can't find the bride,' Ms Innis told Penny quietly. 'Nobody knows where she is, and she's not answering her mobile.'

'Can't someone do one of those find-my-phone things?'

'Sebastian already has. All it's telling us is the phone's still in the hotel, but I've had people searching high and low, from the bell tower to the swimming pool. Well, not actually the bell tower, as that's been locked up for about thirty years, but you get the gist. Frankly, even if we do track her down, I can't see this going ahead if it turns out that she's having second thoughts.'

'Is it possible she's still in her room?'

'Her parents have been up and knocked on the door. If she's in there, she's not answering.'

Penny had the most horrible feeling, one that oddly felt like an echo of something she had endured before. A fear that had grown and grown, only to meet its worst realisation.

'Surely you can check inside the room yourself,' Penny said, an urgency taking hold of her. 'You have a master key, don't you?'

'Yes. But if she didn't want to speak to her parents, she's hardly going to respond to me.'

'At least we'll know she's there.'

'True. Might she speak to you? I got the impression you had something of a heart-to-heart last night.'

'I'd hardly call it that, but I can certainly try.'

Ms Innis led her back into the hotel, Penny conscious of curious glances, not least from the Deacons and Lady Stonebridge. They took the lift to the third floor and followed the corridor to the Hunter Suite. Penny noted the absence of further doors down the corridor. She reasoned this must be the largest and most prestigious accommodation in Crathie Hall: effectively the honeymoon suite, but that appeared to be notional at this point.

Ms Innis knocked at the door. Gently at first and then a little louder.

'Ms Deacon? Lilian?'

There was no response.

'Let me try,' Penny said. She knocked again. 'Lilian, it's Penny. We spoke last night. Now, I'm not here to convince you of anything. But were you to open the door, it would put a great many people's minds at ease. Not least my own.'

There was nothing but silence.

Penny and Ms Innis shared a look, of what Penny could not quite say, but certainly agreement, acceptance, apprehension.

Ms Innis took out her key, placed it in the lock and turned. She opened the door slowly. Penny expected to hear sudden footsteps in response, but there was no sound. She sensed a bleak stillness that evoked a further echo of a remembered fear.

Ms Innis stepped into the suite, while Penny remained on the threshold, reluctant to enter where she had not been invited.

Then Ms Innis spoke.

'Ms Coyne, there's something I need you to look at.'

With growing trepidation Penny followed her into the room, bracing herself for what she might witness.

There was no gruesome or gory scene. It was a huge space, lit brightly by the dual aspect windows to the south and west. The Sculpture Garden with its waiting crowd was visible beneath them.

Ms Innis was standing at the foot of the suite's four-poster bed, upon which there sat two books and a single sheet of hotel notepaper. It bore only two words: 'I'm sorry.'

Ms Innis picked it up and turned it over, showing Penny that there was nothing on the reverse. She then indicated the books.

'You're a librarian, are you not? I can't think that these have been left here randomly.'

Penny took in the two volumes of fiction. On the left was *For Whom the Bell Tolls* and on the right *The Bell Jar*.

Penny looked out of the window at the bell tower, looming above the main building.

'They both have "bell" in the title,' Ms Innis observed.

'That's the smaller part of what's troubling me,' Penny confessed.

Ms Innis swallowed. 'What's the larger part?'

'That both Ernest Hemingway and Sylvia Plath committed suicide.'

Something Bloody, Something Blue

Chapter Six

It's become clear there's some kind of hold up. Johnny has noticed a lot of coming and going between the Sculpture Garden and the hotel, involving the hotel manager and the couple he now knows to be the bride's parents.

Johnny has wandered down and joined the wedding party, figuring it's not like anybody checks a guest list when it comes to the ceremony. Different if you're trying to gatecrash the parts involving free food. He reckons it's a stick-on that Nicholson will be here. He spotted him earlier but figured he would wait until he could buttonhole him someplace it would be hard to just up and walk away from.

He feels his phone vibrate and is surprised to find that it's a text from Nimitz, telling him two things: that Ibanez is being buried in Mesa in five days' time, and that Johnny is not welcome to attend.

It's a kick in the gut.

The desire to brace Nicholson suddenly becomes all the more

pressing, but the guy hasn't shown up yet, and it turns out he's not the only one. Johnny's seen Sebastian looking about as anxious as any groom ought to be, and in related news, there's no sign of Lilian Deacon.

Johnny has overheard people joking about her getting cold feet, but there's a growing sense that maybe that ain't so funny. This thing was supposed to kick off half an hour ago. People have started to get up from their seats, milling around the edges of the pergola; like they're not ready to abandon it and hit the bar, but they feel weird sitting there staring at an empty stage.

He sees Alan Brooks, who is evidently in the market for distraction, or possibly something else, as he's gravitating towards Johnny. The asshole couldn't get away from him fast enough last night.

'Johnny, my man. Where's your friend Crawford? I was hoping to be introduced.'

'That's a good question. He's supposed to be here. I'm feeling kinda stood up, but I'm guessing that don't exactly make me unique today. What do you reckon's going on?'

Brooks glances towards where Lord and Lady Stonebridge are now standing in agitated conference with Mr and Mrs Deacon. 'I don't know,' he says, 'but given that I haven't seen Miles either, I'm guessing he's been sent to engage Lilian in crisis talks.'

'I'm guessing they're pretty close, running a company together.'

'Yeah. They've always had a yin and yang thing going on.'

'How so?'

'Miles is ultra-positive and Lilian, well, not *ultra*-negative, but certainly the voice of caution.'

'They've sent Miles to talk to her because he's the one who tells her everything's gonna be alright?'

161

Brooks winces a little. 'Sebastian is the one who usually convinces her things will work out, so if she doesn't want to see him, we've got a problem. If Sebastian believes in something, you'll be believing in it too after talking to him for half an hour.'

'Did Miles and Sebastian meet through Lilian?'

Johnny's thinking about how he saw Nicholson with Miles's sister, and is curious about her circle of friends. Did she know Jed Mahoney too, he's wondering.

'All three of them met when they were at university. They went to St Andrews. Sebastian talked about going in with them when they first set up RoadMiles, but his father persuaded him to work for the family firm instead. Though I don't know how much persuading it took to start way up the ladder at a major publisher instead of battling in the indie trenches.'

Johnny looks towards the hotel. The Stonebridges are heading up there now. He doesn't take it as a promising sign.

'What's your read on this situation?' Johnny asks.

'My money says she's done a runner.'

'And will that have ramifications for the takeover deal?'

Brooks's eyebrows twitch. 'If she's bailing out of the wedding, I can't see her going ahead with selling RoadMiles. And that will *not* be good news for Stonebridge's share price.'

Johnny doesn't know him well enough to judge, but for somebody so high up in the company, Alan Brooks doesn't exactly look distraught at this prospect.

Murder by Invitation

VI

As the lift doors opened onto the lobby, Penny saw that Lord and Lady Stonebridge, Sebastian, his sister Monica and Mr and Mrs Deacon were gathered outside the Winter Garden. Sebastian had his phone held to his ear, then shook his head regretfully.

'We say nothing about what we just saw,' Ms Innis told Penny quietly. 'Not until we know more.'

'Of course.'

As they walked towards the group, all eyes turned expectantly towards Ms Innis.

'Any sign?' asked Mrs Deacon.

'She's definitely not in her room. I have a house key.'

Lord and Lady Stonebridge reacted with frustration, the Deacons and Sebastian with palpable anxiety. Monica exhibited a mixture of the two, like she had a foot in both camps – or wanted both camps to think that.

'Someone needs to make an announcement,' Lord Stonebridge said. 'We can't leave everyone just sitting out there.'

'I'll go,' said Sebastian.

'And say what?' asked Lady Stonebridge.

'That the ceremony is postponed, for the time being.'

'No, I'll do it,' insisted Monica, placing a hand on her brother's arm. 'You shouldn't have to face everybody right now.'

'I'll have to face them sooner or later,' he replied.

'Yes, but later would be better, when you know more. There's no need to put yourself through this. Besides, you're the one she's going to call when she's ready to talk, and you don't want to be standing in front of a crowd when that happens.'

Ms Innis excused herself, saying she was going to check in again with the staff she had sent to search. She led Penny into the office behind reception, where, rather than reach for her walkie-talkie, she began rifling through drawers.

'What are you doing?'

'We need to check the bell tower, and I don't know where to find the key. To be honest I don't even know if I've ever seen it.'

Ms Innis opened a large cupboard and was confronted by shelves upon shelves of boxes, concertina files and overstuffed plastic baskets.

She closed the cupboard again and picked up her phone instead.

'There's a locksmith in the village. He's bound to be here long before I find the needle in this haystack; even if he's got two other jobs on and one of them is in Edinburgh.'

The locksmith, a Mr Layton, did not have any other jobs on and arrived within ten minutes, Ms Innis intercepting him as soon as he set foot inside reception. She clearly wanted to ensure that his presence was not noted by anyone in the wedding party, but they had all departed from the lobby anyway.

The bell tower was at the western end of the building, jutting above the hotel's three floors by another thirty or forty feet and topped with a grilled cupola. Penny expected Ms Innis to lead them upstairs but instead they followed her along the main ground-floor corridor, then through a door marked 'Staff Only', which had to be unlocked. On the other side was a staircase leading down to a passage that was in stark contrast to the understated opulence of the hotel: crumbled plaster exposing bare brick walls either side of a cold stone floor, ancient strip-lights just about illuminating faded signage. They walked past a door marked FURNACE, long since disused, as was the equally redundant COAL CELLAR opposite. At the very end was a third door marked BELL TOWER.

Mr Layton tried the handle just in case. Penny heard the clunk of it echo, not just in the corridor but in an empty space beyond.

Mr Layton placed his toolbox on the ground with a rattle. He opened it and produced a torch, compact but powerful. He shone it into the keyhole for a moment then picked up a long, fine metallic implement, which he prodded into the opening. He gave a nod, as though confirming something to himself.

'Problem?' Ms Innis asked him.

'No. Don't want to jinx it, but I think we're in clover.'

'Why?'

'Because the key is in the other side of the lock.'

Penny and Ms Innis shared a look. What was good news to the locksmith was not so welcome to their ears. Someone had locked themselves in there.

Mr Layton gave a rueful chuckle. 'So many people keep a key half-turned in their lock overnight because they think that makes it hard for a burglar to pick it. In truth, with the right tools that just makes it easier, because you've already got something in there that's going to turn the tumblers for you.'

He picked up another device, one with a handle and a trigger, carefully sliding it into the lock. Penny watched him make some minor adjustments – pulling the trigger, turning it a little, pushing it minutely in and out, pulling the trigger again. Then he twisted his wrist and rotated the implement in a smooth, steady motion. Penny heard a clunk that echoed in the stillness of the corridor, before Mr Layton pushed open the door with a *voila* gesture.

Penny could see only darkness beyond. Ms Innis flipped a light switch on the corridor wall. Nothing happened. She produced her phone and used it as a torch.

'You might want to wait here,' she told Penny. 'It's a bit of a climb.'

Penny followed her inside the bell tower anyway. There was a musty smell, cut through with something more acrid. It reminded Penny of old telephone boxes, in the worst way.

Picked out in Ms Innis's beam, Penny could see the first flight of a staircase that zigzagged its way up one side of the shaft. Mr Layton came in behind her, pointing his torch as well.

Ms Innis had only just started to climb the wooden stairs when they heard the sound of a drip. She stopped on the spot and listened. About two seconds later there was another.

Ms Innis directed her torch into the centre of the shaft, towards the base of the tower. There was a puddle on the stone floor, the torch only bright enough to pick out a dark glistening.

Mr Layton pointed his torch too. It looked like blood, mixed with something else.

There was another drip.

Ms Innis and Mr Layton both trained their beams up into the shaft. Then they all saw it.

Twenty feet above them, Lilian's body was hanging from a noose, her head almost severed by the force of the drop.

PRIVATE INVESTIGATIONS:
ST ANDREWS

There was a strong wind coming off the water. To Rattigan it felt pretty cold for the time of year, but maybe that was normal for this part of the world.

The house was a couple of minutes from the sands. He had taken a walk around earlier to get a feel for the place and remembered seeing that shore in a movie way back when. *Chariots of Fire.* He knew the theme music would be stuck in his head all day now.

It was a neat little semi-detached house with trimmed lawns and colourful flower-beds. Rattigan read precision, attention to detail. It was always useful to surmise as much as you could before you spoke to someone, though half the time he was miles out. Manicured lawns could just mean a slipshod messy dirtbag with the money to pay a good gardener.

The doorbell was answered by a stooped little man, easily in his eighties. He was wearing a navy cardigan and a pale blue shirt, crisply pressed. Not a slipshod messy dirtbag then. There was a radio on somewhere in the house, sports commentary. Quiet stuff, not too agitated. Probably golf.

'Robert Carmichael?'

'Yes?' he answered. Curious rather than wary.

'My name is Dan Rattigan. I'm a private investigator. I need to talk to you about Toby Delamere.'

'Then you can get to fuck,' the old man said, and slammed the door.

Rattigan rang the bell a couple more times. He heard the radio get turned up.

He went around the side and hopped a fence, saw Carmichael standing in his kitchen. He was chopping onions, a knife in his hand and a pissed look on his face. Rattigan tapped on the window gently, not wanting to startle the guy too much when he had a blade in his hand.

'Get lost! Get off my property. I'll call the police.'

'Listen, sir, if you knew how far I'd come to ask you some questions, you'd realise that saying you don't want to talk is just going to make me more curious. Believe me, the quickest way to get rid of me is to open the window and let's chat.'

Carmichael thought about it. With a resigned sigh, he turned off the radio and a few moments later opened the back door.

He led Rattigan into the kitchen, gesturing to him to take a seat at the table. Rattigan was aware that he'd have his back to the worktop where that knife was sitting, but his instincts told him it was cool.

'Wait,' Carmichael said as Rattigan sat down. He went scuttling off in a hurry. Rattigan listened for the sound of the front door closing, in case the guy was running out and going for the cops. He heard only footsteps. Carmichael returned a few minutes later bearing a determined expression and an old cardboard document wallet, frayed at the edges.

The old guy opened it up and took out its contents, comprising

168

no more than a single A4 sheet inside a plastic wallet. He slapped it down on the table in front of Rattigan.

At the top it said: 'British Gas Landlord's Safety Certificate'.

'There. You can check the dates.'

Rattigan did. 'I understand,' he said.

'No, you don't. If you had any idea what my life was like after what happened. The accusations and the innuendo. People drawing their eyes off me in the street. Nobody would rent from me. Ended up having to sell the place. I always tried to be a reasonable landlord. Unlike some, I didn't hike my rent to soak the rich students, and I kept everything maintained to the highest standards.'

He tapped at the certificate, his expression both adamant and hurt.

'The boiler and all the appliances had been serviced and checked six weeks before. I have no idea why that heater malfunctioned. It was a tragedy that has haunted me ever since. But it wasn't my fault.'

Something Bloody, Something Blue

Chapter Seven

Decades as a cop had conditioned Johnny to read the early signs that something bad was going down. The sight of a police car at a hotel could mean many things, especially at a wedding, but that it was accompanied by an ambulance indicated a less fluid situation than drunk assholes getting out of hand.

He's standing in the lobby, where he sees the distraught looks on the faces of Mr and Mrs Deacon as they realise the two uniformed officers entering reception are walking specifically towards them. Johnny watches as a female officer guides them away from the lobby, out of sight. The male officer greets the hotel manager, who leads him off down a corridor. As they pass him, their expressions tell Johnny everything he needs to know. That cop is being taken to see a body, one that Innis has found.

The hotel enters a form of stasis. Other guests are still going about their business, regarding the emergency vehicles outside with mild curiosity, maybe thinking somebody's been taken ill at the wedding. But the wedding guests are in a state of suspended animation. Nobody knows what to do with themselves, still less what to say.

That's until the news comes down.

Nobody can really deal with it. Mere hours ago they were sitting waiting to watch this woman get married. Now they're trying to process the fact that she's dead.

It's always a moment of unreality, a basic human inability to accept that somebody can be alive one moment and dead the next. Johnny went through it only a couple days ago, looking at Ibanez's broken body lying before him less than five minutes after walking into the Kingdom soundstage.

More police have arrived. Johnny takes a walk around and sees one of them standing guard in front of a door that says STAFF ONLY. His instinct is to walk up and flash his badge until he remembers he doesn't have one and that he's about five thousand miles out of his jurisdiction. He just has to wait for information to filter down like an ordinary shmoe.

Back in the lobby he sees Mr and Mrs Deacon with Sebastian Gossard, huddled together on a sofa, a triptych of grief, desolation and pain on public display. Disaster and bereavement don't always allow for privacy, but Johnny figures it doesn't matter much who's watching when your world has just fallen apart.

Elsewhere he sees Lord Stonebridge sitting around a coffee table with his wife and older daughter. Monica looks tearful, Jonathan Stonebridge and his missus kinda confused, like they're just not used to unexpected bad shit happening in their perfect lives. The officer he saw going off with Innis is talking to them, laying out whatever he now knows.

Lord Stonebridge asks a lot of questions and doesn't look happy with the answers. He's on the phone before the cop is through, his face flushed with frustration. Somebody's boss is getting a call.

It strikes Johnny that Sebastian hasn't gone to be with the Deacons out of decorum or as a gesture of solidarity. These are the people he'd rather be with.

Johnny wanders through into the Winter Garden. People are hanging around in groups, like nobody wants to go back to their room in case it seems disrespectful or lacking in solidarity or whatever. Through the glass he sees Alan Brooks standing outside, unexpectedly in the company of Lucy Stonebridge. She's got her head on his shoulder, shock and grief apparently bridging the gaps of enmity.

Lucy looks up and notices that Johnny has seen her. She mutters something to Brooks and breaks away, heading in Johnny's direction. He meets her just inside the glass doors. Her eyes are red, her distress emphasised by smeared kohl.

'How you doing?' Johnny asks.

'Like my big brother's fiancée just killed herself on their wedding day. How you doing?'

'Yeah, I saw Sebastian with the Deacons. They're in pieces.'

She stands a little closer and drops her voice. 'Hey, have you got anything left? Because I really need something to get me through the next few hours.'

He sees the real reason she had sought out Brooks. It wasn't to bridge any kind of divide, though it *was* about seeking comfort; just not the kind of comfort Johnny assumed. She knows Brooks is a cokehead too, so she must have figured there was a chance he was holding. Evidently he wasn't. But Johnny is.

Conditioned by the job to see drug-taking as a criminal act, there is a part of Johnny that instinctively worries about the propriety of this, and the ethics of enabling it. But there's also the more human part that figures whatever gets you through; and that's the part that keeps him *doing* the job. If you've got a drug habit and you just got hit with something traumatic, then yeah, you're gonna need the thing you need most even more than usual.

But not without a quid pro quo.

Johnny palms the baggie, lets her see it, but when she reaches out, he takes hold of her hand, pulls her close, makes it look like he's comforting her.

'Maybe before you go off to the bathroom, you do me a solid. Tell me what you know.'

'What's it to you?' she asks, reminding Johnny who she thinks he is.

'I work with interested parties.'

She shrugs. 'I know as much as you.'

'Bullshit. I saw you sitting with your old man. What did the cops tell him?'

She eyes Johnny's closed hand where the baggie is, like she's watching a magician hiding a coin.

'They found her in the bell tower. She hanged herself.'

'And they're sure she didn't get some help with that?'

'The tower was locked from the inside. Nobody even knew where the key was. It's been out of use for years.'

'How did they find out where she was?'

'She left a note, kind of. It just said "I'm sorry." Along with a couple of books with "bell" in the title. Plath and Hemingway: writers who killed themselves.'

'That's not a suicide note. That's a scavenger hunt.'

'I'm only telling you what the police told us.'

Johnny loosens his grip and Lucy grabs the baggie, taking off in a hurry.

He watches her leave then looks up at the bell tower, which is when he gets this powerful feeling that he's seen this picture before, and he doesn't mean like these weird flashes he's been getting.

Just like Jed Mahoney, Lilian Deacon locked herself away to commit suicide. Just like Jed Mahoney, she had gone to some trouble to make it clear that nobody else was involved.

And in both cases, Crawford Nicholson had been on the premises at the time, then disappeared before the body was discovered.

Murder by Invitation

VII

There was a knock at the door of Penny's room, one that she was reluctant to answer. It had been several hours since the discovery, but she suspected it might be days before she regained her composure, and as for recovering a sense of equilibrium, well, that felt far from guaranteed.

Penny had observed dead bodies before, particularly those taken before their time. She had seen victims who had been shot, stabbed, strangled, bludgeoned, and at least two others who had been hanged. She recalled seeing neat wounds and very little blood, even when throats had been slit. Victims lying with their eyes closed, looking as though they could be sleeping. What she had witnessed in the tower was something altogether more gruesome: Lilian Deacon's head all but torn off, the rope shearing through to the bones of her spine. Blood drenching her dress from severed veins and arteries. Eyes bulging from their sockets, swollen tongue lolling, and she had emptied her bladder.

In addressing murder after murder, sifting through hatred and cruelty and deceit, Penny was sure she had seen the worst this world had to offer, but she had never been confronted with such explicit and vivid details.

She wanted to go home, retreat to the sanctuary of Silverbank Cottage and the cosy familiarity of Glen Cluthar, except that Glen Cluthar didn't seem as cosy or familiar as it used to. She thought of Father Driver concealing crimes she didn't wish to name. Everything was becoming more hideous. It didn't feel like her world any more.

'Penny? Are you in there? It's Saeeda.'

The sound of a friendly voice was a much-needed tonic, and it got better when she opened the door and saw that Saeeda was holding a tray of tea and scones.

'I'm from the government and I'm here to help,' Saeeda said, an old joke between them.

She walked in and placed the tray on the low table by the window.

'How are you?' she asked.

'I've been to better weddings.'

'It must have been a horrible shock. You poor thing. Shall I pour?'

'Please.'

Saeeda picked up the teapot and poured two cups.

'Are you in charge of the matter?' Penny asked.

'Oh heavens, no. With Lord Stonebridge involved, the brass were never going to entrust it to a humble DI. Chief Superintendent McLeod is downstairs.'

'So is this a social call to inquire after my general wellbeing, or . . .?'

'I am informed you spoke to the deceased late last night. I've been asked to ascertain her mental state.'

Penny felt torn, as though it would be some kind of betrayal to admit that Lilian Deacon had not been giddy with excitement at the prospect of her forthcoming nuptials.

'She admitted she was having doubts, regarding both the wedding and the takeover. In both cases it came down to a reluctance to become too involved with Sebastian's family.'

'Why?'

'I think she felt they made him unhappy. "Nightmare" was the word she used. Lilian suspected Lord Stonebridge was up to something regarding the takeover, and she seemed determined to find out more. She struck me as a woman with a purpose, not someone with an imminent desire to end her life.'

'Was she drinking?'

'Yes. But she wasn't blind drunk or anything. She was burdened, is how I would put it. She was under a lot of pressure, but everything can feel worse in the middle of the night. Did anyone notice how she was this morning?'

'According to witnesses, despite her late night, she was up early. She had breakfast alone, working on her laptop and making phone calls.'

'Again, these hardly sound like the actions of someone planning to take her own life the same day.'

Saeeda gave her an awkward, apologetic smile. 'It runs contrary to assumptions, but often those are precisely the actions of someone planning to take their own life. Once they have resolved to end things, the turmoil is gone, and they are calm and purposeful. Hence she could have been putting her affairs in order.'

Penny's expression must have betrayed her dissatisfaction.

'I understand how hard that is to accept,' Saeeda went on. 'We have to wait for the post-mortem, but so far there is nothing to indicate that we should treat the death as suspicious. There's no indication of a struggle, so it's impossible to envisage her going to the top of that tower anything other than voluntarily.'

'My question would be how she was able to find the key,' Penny said. 'Ms Innis, the hotel manager, didn't even know where it might be.'

'Perhaps Lilian knew the place better than we assume. Other witnesses mentioned that she had expressed an interest in the building's history.'

'She did talk about the hotel having been a place where women were once confined,' Penny acknowledged.

'But what makes it open and shut,' said Saeeda, 'is that it is literally open and shut. She locked herself inside a tower that has no other means of access. And she left the key on the inside to make it clear nobody else was involved. There's no mystery for you to solve on this occasion, Penny.'

Penny drank some more tea and nibbled on a scone, aware she had eaten almost nothing all day. She knew everything Saeeda said was true, and yet she felt an unexpected sense of obligation towards Lilian to resist it. She also had this nagging awareness of having noticed something out of place, but she could not remember what it was.

Penny lifted her cup and glanced again at the view of the Sculpture Garden through her window. That was when she saw it, or more specifically, him.

'I need to speak with Ms Innis,' she said to the young man on the reception desk.

'I'm afraid she's not available right now. Is there something I can help you with?'

'It's all right, Darren,' Ms Innis said, emerging from the office where she had been understandably taking respite. 'I am always

178

available to Ms Coyne. But perhaps we can deal with it through here.'

Ms Innis invited her behind the desk and into the office. She looked exhausted but was masking it behind a professional face.

'I need you to look into something,' Penny said. 'Does Lord Stonebridge have security?'

'Like bodyguards?'

'Yes.'

'Not that I'm aware. Certainly no added personnel that were checked in on his booking. Why?'

'I want to be absolutely sure that everything is as it seems with regard to today's tragedy. There is an individual I've seen acting suspiciously. I had thought he might be Lord Stonebridge's security, but you have confirmed otherwise. He appears to be here on his own.'

'Being alone at a wedding is not suspicious behaviour,' Ms Innis said patiently. '*You're* here alone.'

'There was something furtive about him,' Penny insisted. 'He always seemed to be on the lookout, hence my wondering if he was a bodyguard. He was seated at the back this morning, watching everyone assemble for the ceremony. But most importantly, I saw him last night. He came into the Winter Garden and stared at Lilian and me. I know it's probably nothing, but under the circumstances . . .'

Ms Innis nodded, understanding.

'Can you describe him?'

'Late forties, perhaps. Dark hair with a bit of grey. A rugged-looking sort, not someone you'd want to tangle with. I only overheard him briefly, but from his accent, I believe he might be American.'

Ms Innis's expression indicated that she recognised exactly who Penny was talking about.

'Just to put my mind at ease, Ms Innis, would you mind checking your email chain again, and please verify whether he is supposed to be here?'

Ms Innis considered it for a moment. Penny got the strong impression that on any other day, and under any other circumstances, she would have politely told her to sling her hook. On this day, however . . .

Something Bloody, Something Blue

Chapter Eight

There's a breeze picking up, a bite in the wind. The sky is a darkening blue; looks like it's gonna be a clear night, if a cold one. Johnny is standing outside, on the emergency exit on the third floor.

There's been an eerie atmosphere about the joint. The majority of the wedding party have checked out and left, as have a lot of the regular guests, maybe reckoning it was disrespectful to be wining and dining in the vicinity of what just happened.

Johnny has checked online for updates on the Jed Mahoney suicide. Nothing fresh, just a nib on the *Hollywood Reporter* website with a quote from Dominique King, saying how devastated everybody is, asking for privacy at this difficult time, blah blah blah.

He's surprised he hasn't seen reporters and photographers here. Surely the word is out. He guesses publishing ain't sexy enough for it to be news.

There's still been no sign of Nicholson since this morning,

and Johnny is none the wiser as to what the guy's connection is to Lilian Deacon. He saw him hug and kiss her, and not a Hollywood air-kiss either. They were close: personal close, not business close; or not *just* business close.

The police guard has gone from the corridor downstairs, but the door is still locked. He knows because he tried it.

Johnny was right about Lord Stonebridge making phone calls to the brass. He saw more cops show up earlier, led by a grey-haired dude with that unmistakable air of self-importance: somebody used to having his ass kissed when it wasn't stuck to a plush upholstered seat behind a big desk at headquarters. Johnny watched him go straight to Lord Stonebridge, shake his hand. Didn't look like he was introducing himself. Didn't look like he needed to.

Johnny has scoped the layout and picked his time carefully, making his move in the twilight. He doesn't want to risk being conspicuous, but he doesn't want to be climbing in the dark either.

He hauls himself over the fire-escape railing so that he's clinging to the outside of the iron frame. From there it's pretty straightforward, if a bit of a strain on the arms, to clamber onto the roof. This is the easy part though. The tower abuts the end of the building, rising another thirty feet above it. The only way up is via a drainpipe descending from the rain gutter that skirts the roof of the cupola.

Johnny scrambles across the rooftop on all fours, keeping one eye on the courtyard at the front of the hotel in case anybody is out there and happens to look up. He skids as a slate comes loose and slides its way down to the edge, fortunately jamming in the gutter. It gives his heart a jolt, and he likes it.

There's a thrill running through him as he reaches the

182

drainpipe and grips the metal. He pushes off with his right foot, getting traction with his left on the edge of some brickwork where the mortar is eroded. There's a part of him thinking how crazy dangerous this would be if . . . if what? The thought fades, incomplete. This *is* crazy dangerous: that's why it's fun.

He makes his way up that thing like a spider monkey, enjoying the sensation of danger, enjoying the strain in his muscles, from his fingers gripping the pipe to his legs driving him upwards.

He reaches the belfry. The wind feels stronger, the air that bit cooler up here. He's out of pipe but still holding on to the metal, his feet enjoying the relative security of a ledge. He's concerned about how he's getting through those wooden slats blocking the arches on all four sides, but it's not imperative that he gains access. He's just trying to suss whether someone *could* get out of there, having locked the door at the bottom. If it can't be done, then that tells him something valuable too.

The slats are there to keep out the elements, but angled to let out the sound of the bells. Up close he can see some of them are rotten. They haven't seen fresh paint in a very long time. Johnny takes his blackjack from his belt, gives the wood a prod. It's so soft he reckons he could bust through it, but first he tries to lever it at one end. He grips it with his fingers and the wood lifts right off the bracket, crumbling to the touch in places. He's able to climb through the gap he made and drop down onto the platform, where he turns on his flashlight.

The first thing he looks at is where he's just come in. He tries lifting another slat and finds it almost too easy. Most of them are barely being held in place, the wood so rotten the nails can barely grip. Like the storage room where Jed Mahoney was found, people have wrongly assumed there's only one way in or out.

Unfortunately, that's where the practicalities cease to support his hunch. Johnny looks at the staircase. You ain't getting nobody to the top of this thing unless they cooperate. That said, there are ways to persuade.

He plays his flashlight above him, along the beam supporting the bells. It picks out striped marks in the centre, where something has recently swept away dust and mould. This is where the rope was tied. He winces at the height of the drop. You wouldn't need a professional executioner's knot for an instant kill.

He imagines what Ibanez might be saying right now.

You've flown all this way in a state of disgrace and desperation, not to mention guilt. You're in search of something that would make what happened to me worth it. So maybe you're seeing something you need to see, rather than something that's there.

Yeah, kid, I'll give you that much, he concedes. But it's one motherfucker of a coincidence that two people connected to Crawford Nicholson should kill themselves in circumstances similarly designed to rule out foul play.

Johnny decides it's time to leave, starts psyching himself for the descent. He knows down is harder than up, though it can be considerably quicker, which is what he'd like to avoid. He lifts the same slat he came in through, trying not to leave any traceable damage.

He looks down, wanting to recce the route before he grabs that drainpipe again. It's got darker, but not so dark that he can't see the fire escape. Or the cop standing on it, looking his way.

There are two more cops at the base of the tower, both waving to him.

Shit.

Something Bloody,
Something Blue

Chapter Nine

'Would you care to tell us what you were doing in the bell tower, Mr Hawke?'

'Sleepwalking,' he says.

There's two of them, an Asian woman named Inspector Sattar, and a white dude: Chief Superintendent McLeod. He's the guy Johnny saw buddying up to Lord Stonebridge, which explains why somebody of that rank would be dirtying his hands with a suicide.

They haven't taken him to the station, so he figures that's a good sign. They're in an office in the hotel, and he's not under arrest. Yet.

'Let's try an easier one,' says McLeod. 'What are you doing here at the hotel?'

'Same as everybody. I was here for the wedding.'

Sattar has an iPad in front of her, which she has angled so that he can't see it.

'Your name does not appear on the list of invited guests,' she says. She stares at him, inviting a response. Johnny knows he doesn't have to tell them jack, but they ain't the only ones looking for info here.

'Yeah, it's awkward. I'm kind of a plus one. I'm here to meet up with a buddy of mine. He's the one who was invited.'

'What's his name?'

'Crawford Nicholson.'

Sattar looks at the iPad, runs her finger down it, looks up at Johnny again.

'That name does not appear on the list either. And nor is that name registered as a resident at the hotel: something you are aware of, because the manager informed you of this when you first checked in.'

'Alison Innis: is that who put you onto me?'

'We don't disclose details regarding witnesses,' Sattar replies.

'Why are you lying to us, Mr Hawke?' asks McLeod. He's tetchy, impatient. Johnny figures he's out of practice, hasn't conducted an interview in years. Sattar has more recent game-time. He wonders what she's thinking about being saddled with this show-pony.

'I'm not lying. I'm here to meet Crawford Nicholson. Why would I make something like that up?'

'Perhaps to attend a society event under false pretences,' McLeod suggests. 'Who are you working for?'

'I'm not working. I'm on vacation.'

'From what?' Sattar asks.

Johnny really doesn't want to answer that. If somebody puts in a call to Nimitz, he'll be in shit up to his neck. But he also doesn't want to lie, especially not to fellow cops. There are rules you need to break to get the job done, and rules you never break because otherwise what's the point of the job?

186

'I work in Hollywood.' Technically true.

'What do you do?'

'It's complicated. But mostly it involves finding the right people.'

'Have you been down to the village?'

Johnny guesses she's asking because she knows he has. CCTV maybe.

'Sure. I took a walk last night, had a drink.'

'Did you visit the public toilets on Atholl Square?'

'Why, is that like the big attraction round here? I figure most people come for the golf or for the fishing.'

McLeod bristles. Johnny can tell Sattar is suppressing a smile. She looks composed though. She's going someplace with this.

'There were officers there last night on routine observation, as the toilets are occasionally used for drug transactions.'

Johnny thinks of the car he saw. It wasn't Tats's ride after all. With some relief he remembers he gave the last of the coke to Lucy.

'They encountered two individuals, one of them well known to the authorities. Both of them had been assaulted.'

Sattar leaves it hanging there. Johnny is good with that.

'An individual matching your description was seen leaving the premises,' she says eventually.

'These guys gave a description that matched mine?' he asks. He is only half faking his incredulity. Johnny can't see those losers talking to the cops, especially not about how they lured some tourist with the promise of a drug deal then tried to roll him.

'No. They refused to answer any questions, in fact.'

He has to suppress a smile of his own, conscious Sattar will be looking for it.

Johnny's been on the other side of that table; he knows they got nothing. It's what they're looking for that interests him, though.

'What's the deal? Why are you wasting your time bracing me, given everything that's gone down today? You guys thinking maybe it wasn't a suicide?'

'We're not prepared to discuss today's tragic events,' McLeod says, sounding pompously self-righteous. 'The last thing we need is anyone engaging in unhelpful speculation at a difficult time for Lord Stonebridge and his family.'

'Kind of a difficult time for the Deacons too, I would have thought.'

McLeod flashes him a look of annoyance, but mainly he's pissed because he's given himself away. That type of cop always does.

'Understand me, Mr Hawke: I do not wish to hear of you harassing anyone involved in today's events, or conducting some amateur investigation on behalf of whatever agenda you're prosecuting. I get enough of that with you know who,' he mutters to Sattar.

Johnny says nothing. He's tempted to promise he'll comply, on the grounds that he has no intention of carrying out an amateur investigation. It will be a highly professional investigation, even if he's not getting paid for it.

'I'll ask you again,' McLeod says. 'Who are you working for?'

'And I'll say again, I ain't here working for nobody.'

Let the fucker decode the negatives in that one.

'Are you freelance, then?'

So, McLeod thinks he's a reporter or a photographer or even both. Maybe publishing is sexy after all, or perhaps it's the 'society' angle that's sexy. But what Johnny now knows for sure is why McLeod is sitting in on this. His agenda is the same as Nimitz's, or whoever is leaning on Nimitz from above: clear this shit up without it becoming a thing, because it involves rich people with powerful friends.

'Like I said, I'm on vacation. And so far it's been a shitload more stressful than I would have liked, so if you don't mind, I'd like to wrap this up.'

'We decide when we wrap this up,' says McLeod.

'No, you don't. Not unless you're gonna charge me with something.'

'How about breaking and entering, for starters,' Sattar says. 'Or trespassing on a crime scene. We caught you red-handed at the bell tower.'

'Yeah, except I can't be trespassing inside a hotel where I'm already a paying guest, and I didn't break nothing to enter that tower. But most importantly, we both know you ain't gonna book me for trespassing on a crime scene, because unless you're ruling this something other than suicide, there *is* no crime.'

That lands. He can see it on both their faces.

He can't lie: it feels good to tell someone like McLeod to eat shit. Feels like sticking it to the boss, even if he ain't Johnny's boss.

McLeod stands up, trying to reassert his authority, but in truth he's on his feet because Johnny is right and the interview is coming to an end.

'A family lost a daughter today,' he says, pitching for the high ground. 'They lost a sister. A friend. A colleague. She's not a story. *This* is not a story.'

And with that McLeod stomps off and shuts the door, leaving Johnny staring at Sattar.

'We good?' he asks. 'Can I go?'

Sattar doesn't answer for a moment, like she's weighing something up.

'If you've got reason to believe this was not a suicide,' she says, 'you should tell me what that is.'

'I'm figuring there's nothing I might say that would change your boss's mind, what with Lord Mucky-Muck being involved and all. But if you're really curious, maybe you should go ask the person who was meeting with Lilian Deacon at one o'clock this morning.'

'How do *you* know who she was meeting?'

'I saw the two of them in the Winter Garden. Lilian was talking to some old broad. It looked kind of intense.'

Sattar doesn't look that interested. Doesn't look that surprised either.

'You already know,' he surmises. 'Are you looking into it?'

'I'm looking into it right now. Reports of someone spying on Lilian Deacon in the middle of the night.'

Johnny sees it now. The old broad was the one who put the cops onto him.

'Wait, you're more interested in the guy who *saw* this late-night rendezvous than the meeting itself?'

'Only since the guy who saw it started breaking into places.'

Johnny can't believe this. 'You don't think it's at all suspicious?'

'No. Because the "old broad", as you call her, is a friend of mine. And down the years information she's provided has been instrumental in the apprehension of at least fifteen murder suspects around the village of Glen Cluthar.'

Johnny pauses to make sure he heard right.

'Did you say *fifteen*?'

'At least.'

'What kind of village is it: the village of the damned? Sounds more like South Central than north Perthshire. A place with that kind of attrition rate, you don't start to think she might be the common denominator? I mean, if I was working this murder, she'd be the first person I interviewed.'

'This is not a murder, Mr Hawke.'

'Yeah, but you say she helped finger the perp in fifteen cases that were. *I* don't have a clean-up rate like that.'

Now Johnny's the one who has given himself away. Difference is, he meant to.

Sattar looks at him for a long time. Something passes between them, a mutual understanding.

'What's your interest here?' she asks.

'That's a can of worms I'd be doing you a real favour not to open at this table. But seeing you're so relaxed about the old broad's involvement, how about you tell me what's *her* interest?'

Sattar thinks about it. Comes to a decision.

'Given Chief Superintendent McLeod's position on this case, it would be inappropriate to tell you that Ms Coyne has been frequently useful in researching angles that the police have neither the resources nor the inclination to pursue.'

'Inappropriate,' Johnny says. 'I read you.'

Loud and clear.

Murder by Invitation

VIII

'Did Mr Hawke tell you he was here for the wedding?' Penny asked.

'Not exactly,' Ms Innis replied. 'He claimed to be meeting up with another wedding guest by the name of Crawford Nicholson, who was not registered at the hotel. After you raised your questions, I checked my information, and it turns out he's not on the wedding list either.'

'I suspect Hawke might have made him up as a pretext.'

Ms Innis had convinced Penny to join her in a late supper. Penny had known her little more than a day, but a bond had been forged through the horrible experience they had gone through together. Certainly there was no one else in the hotel Penny could imagine sitting down with right now, and she suspected that Ms Innis felt the same way.

They were dining in the grand restaurant. Their table was in what Penny might have called a quiet corner, were it not that all its corners were quiet tonight, as were the spaces in between. The solemnity felt all the more conspicuous in a place where the chimes of crockery were often drowned beneath chatter, laughter and music. The pianist had been given the night off, and many guests had departed. Those few diners who had remained were finishing their meals amidst quiet conversation.

Among their number was the Stonebridge party, though they were in a private dining room, the end of their table just visible through an archway at one end of the restaurant. As many of them were based in London, they had remained at Crathie Hall for tonight.

With no such long-distance travel arrangements to consider, Penny could not quite say why she had also stayed. She might like to tell herself it was solidarity with Ms Innis, but in truth, what had held her was that feeling of restless curiosity. It was a compulsion further driven by her quite explicable feeling of connection with the deceased: her sense that she had known Lilian Deacon before, and thus felt the need to be her last advocate.

'Your suspicions were certainly vindicated,' Ms Innis said. 'You have remarkable instincts.'

'I think my instincts are similar to your own. Both of us understand the value of detail and decorum, which means we are quick to notice when something is slightly amiss.'

Penny had watched with some satisfaction as Saeeda led Mr Hawke out from the staff-only corridor with two officers flanking him.

'What details do you have on him?' Penny asked.

'I'm not strictly permitted to share all of those,' she said. 'He *is* American, though. His home address is in North Hollywood, Los Angeles.'

'I was wrong about him being a bodyguard, but there is certainly something about him that gives off, I don't know, an air of being dangerous.'

'That's one way of putting it.'

'Why, what would be another?'

'If he was twenty years younger, I could see myself taking a strong interest. I might even settle for ten years younger,' she added with a smile.

The sense of levity it brought felt like sunshine breaking through to remind Penny that there could still be fair weather; that there would be better days.

But for now, there were storm clouds nearby. Penny became aware of voices rising in the private dining room. Lord Stonebridge was angrily demanding confirmation of something, someone else muttering apologetically in response. She heard him shouting 'How dare they? How dare they?' each volley accompanied by a fist on the table. Then she heard a clatter and crash, the sound of something being knocked over and breaking.

Ms Innis gestured to her waiting staff, though they were already on their way to respond. Through the archway, Penny watched Monica Stonebridge fussing around them as they arrived, mostly getting in the way as they tried to mop up spilled red wine from the tablecloth. She looked like someone who wanted to be seen to be taking charge, probably because, like everyone else, she had been feeling useless all day.

Monica glanced towards Penny's table. Ms Innis rose to her feet in response, but before she could advance, Monica shook her head and signalled her to stay put. She began walking towards them instead, making placatory gestures towards the staff as she exited.

'I'm terribly sorry,' she told Ms Innis. 'My father's dreadfully upset.'

'No need to apologise. We all understand. Everyone's emotions are on a knife edge over what has happened.'

'Unfortunately it appears someone has added insult to injury by launching a hostile takeover bid for the company.'

'Now?' Ms Innis asked. 'After what happened today? That's hideous.'

Monica looked back to the private room, where a waiter was bringing her father a bottle of single malt.

'The intention was not quite as brutal as that,' she said. 'The news is just emerging, so I suspect the move was already in train, timed to commence while he was distracted with the wedding. But that was a low enough move on its own. Cowardly and underhand.'

'Do you know who's behind it?' Ms Innis asked.

There was a flash of thunder in Monica's expression, as though the question was impertinent, or perhaps the answer painful. 'We're still trying to ascertain that,' she said. She appeared to compose herself and turned to address Penny. 'Excuse my manners. I'm Monica Stonebridge.'

'Not at all. I am Ms Penelope—'

'Coyne,' she said, shaking Penny's hand. 'Yes, I know. Sebastian told me you used to work for our grandfather.'

'How is your brother?' Penny asked, anguish filling her heart on his behalf.

'He has driven Mr and Mrs Deacon back to Dundee. I imagine he'll stay with them overnight. They're going to need him. Especially as no one seems to know where Miles has disappeared to. I don't suppose either of you have seen him this evening?'

'I'm afraid I don't know what he looks like,' Penny replied apologetically.

Monica produced her phone and showed Penny a photo of herself standing next to a young man in this same restaurant;

last night, presumably. She could see the familial resemblance to Lilian, which renewed a lurching sense of loss.

'I did see him around the hotel yesterday,' Penny realised. 'But not since.'

She had hoped that Miles would look more familiar, so that she might have a clue as to why he had invited her.

Monica put her phone away. 'I saw you speaking with that policewoman,' she said. 'Inspector Sattar. I got the impression you know each other.'

'Saeeda is a friend, yes.'

'What did she tell you?'

Penny was struck by Monica's bluntness, but it was under-standable. Information was jealously craved in times of stress and hurt.

'I don't imagine she is party to anything that Chief Superintendent McLeod hasn't already passed on to your father.'

Monica wrinkled her nose. 'My father is seldom the best at sharing information. He likes being the one with the torch while everyone else labours in the dark. Country of the blind and all that. Do they think there's anything about what happened that is . . . not as it seems?'

'No. The police seem quite satisfied that it was suicide.'

'And what about you?'

Once again Monica was unsubtly direct, causing Penny to have second thoughts as to how much this was down to present circumstances. Perhaps it was how she conducted herself. Like her father, Monica seemed used to making demands.

'Something about it doesn't sit well,' Penny admitted. 'But maybe that's just because it's so difficult to accept, for all of us.'

'And this American fellow they've apprehended: what's his name?'

'Johnny Hawke,' said Ms Innis.

'I think I saw my sister talking to him. Dark hair, forties, looks like he could handle himself?'

'That's the one.'

'What's he doing here? Who's he with?'

Monica's curiosity seemed pointed. Penny wondered if her thoughts were primarily regarding Lilian or this hostile takeover.

'He claimed to be the guest of someone called Crawford Nicholson,' Ms Innis told her. 'But we're not sure such a person exists.'

'Oh, he most certainly does. Though I was not aware of him being invited to the wedding. Perhaps he was a guest of Miles.'

'You know him?'

'I know *of* him. He's a screenwriter. He's co-writing the film adaptation of *The Cracked Mirror.*'

'Johnny Hawke *is* from Hollywood,' Ms Innis pointed out.

'So this Nicholson chap might indeed have been present,' Penny observed.

'Might have been,' agreed Monica. 'Though I wouldn't know him to see. Can you look him up, find a picture?'

Ms Innis had already produced her iPad. Her fingers worked the screen, a troubled look clouding her face.

'No headshots?' Monica asked. 'Bloody writers. Half of them are narcissistic exhibitionists and the other half shrinking recluses.'

'No pictures, no,' Ms Innis said. 'But that's not the issue. The lead search result is a story from the *Hollywood Reporter.*'

She turned the iPad around.

'Crawford Nicholson's writing partner just killed himself.'

Something Bloody,
Something Blue

Chapter Ten

Johnny rolls over in his bed, opens one bleary eye and checks the clock on the nightstand. It's ten-thirty a.m. Dammit.

He's woken up later than he meant to. Same thing happened yesterday. It's the time difference, or maybe just the heaviness of the curtains. He slept great, though he did have weirdly vivid dreams, like segments of his own memories spliced up with someone else's.

Johnny pulls his clothes on and packs the rest of his shit. He's supposed to check out at eleven.

Alison Innis is on the front desk. He's wondering if she ever goes home, or if she even has one. She looks through his paperwork, processes his payment, hands him back his credit card.

'And was everything all right with your stay, Mr Hawke?' she asks. There's an edge to it, a hint of rebuke at his unauthorised exploration, plus just a glimmer of amusement at how it worked out. Johnny can't begrudge her that.

'I got no grounds for complaint,' he says, a mea culpa.

'Would you like me to call you a taxi?'

It's a good question. He doesn't know where he's gonna go. Crawford Nicholson is in the wind.

He remembers what Sattar said last night, that moment of solidarity they shared. If the old broad isn't buying that Lilian Deacon's death was a suicide, then there has to be a solid reason for that, and he wants to know what that is. Right now it's the closest thing he's got to a lead.

'Actually, could you put me through to one of your other guests, a Ms Coyne?'

Innis gives him a smile. Part of it is her professional demeanour and the rest is that she's happy to be saying 'I'm afraid Ms Coyne has already checked out.'

'How long ago?'

Innis pauses, like she's wondering how to answer, but as she does so she glances over his shoulder. Johnny turns and sees the lady in question climbing into a taxi. He runs for the door but it's already pulling away before he makes it outside.

Johnny goes back to the desk.

'Do you have a phone number or an address? I really need to speak to her.'

'I'm afraid I'm not allowed to give out that information. If you provide me with your details, then I can pass them on and ask her to get in touch.'

Johnny does that just to go through the motions, but he's already got a plan. He caught the name of the cab company.

He can't recall the name of the village, though. It was Glen something, but half of this country is Glen something. At least he knows she don't live far away, from what Sattar said. Which means for his idea to work, he'll need to leave it a while.

He remembers he's got signal down here. He takes a seat and

looks up Crawford Nicholson again. Still nothing new, just the same results. One of them is the IMDb link for *Everybody Dies Alone*, a movie nobody's made yet. He figures it's the closest he's gonna get to a list of known associates.

Nicholson is listed as co-writer alongside Jed Mahoney. But there's another name too, one he recognises now:

Alex Gillen (based on the novel by)

Johnny clicks on the name and confirms that the novel is *The Cracked Mirror*. There it is. Miles and Lilian's company publish the book and the adaptation gets written by Nicholson and Mahoney. They must have bought the option themselves, as the script was their property to sell.

Johnny doesn't recall hearing anyone mention Alex Gillen being at the wedding. He does an image search, in case it's a face he's seen around. He gets bupkis. There's a few Alex Gillens pop up but none of them is listed as a novelist. He does find a newspaper article, though: 'an exclusive interview with the publicity-shy author'. He follows the link. No photos, the interview done by email. Sounds like the screenplay has slightly diverged from the novel, though. *The Cracked Mirror* is about someone who steals a manuscript and passes it off as their own after killing the author. Confusingly, the stolen manuscript is also called *The Cracked Mirror*.

Johnny flashes back to when he was a kid and used to hold his mom's hand mirror up to the big one on her dresser, looking at the reflections bending away towards eternity.

He gives it an hour or so then phones the cab company.

'Yeah, I'm calling regarding a friend of mine. One of your drivers picked her up a while back and she should have been home by now, but she's not answering her phone. I just want to make sure she was dropped off okay. It was a Ms Coyne.'

'Glen Cluthar?' the despatcher asks.

'Yeah, that's right.'

'Aye, I think she was dropped off about twenty minutes ago.'

'Can you confirm where she was dropped off?'

The despatcher pauses. 'Who did you say you were, again?'

'A friend. I just want to be sure we're both talking about the right address.'

Another pause. Shit. He should have given a name. *A friend.* Fucking moron.

'Well, how aboot you tell me the address you're talkin' aboot, and I'll tell you if it's the right one.'

Johnny hangs up. He'll need to go to Glen Cluthar and ask around. He goes back to the desk and politely requests Innis call him a cab, figuring the despatcher will recognise his voice.

It arrives pretty quick. Turns out to be the same guy who picked him up from the airfield.

'How was the fishing?' he asks as Johnny gets in the back.

'I didn't catch anything. Yet.'

The trip takes about forty minutes, most of it along quiet roads between fields and woodland. It ought to be serene but the clouds look weird, a purple colour that seems wrong for the time of day.

'You ever seen a sky like that?' Johnny asks. 'Is that normal?'

'A sky like what?'

Johnny looks up again. The clouds are white, scattered against a blue sky. This jetlag really is messing him up.

The driver drops him off on Main Street, where Johnny feels like he's stepped into some new area of Disneyland. Everything's all neat and clean. The storefronts are colourful and pretty, and he can't see a single chain store or franchise.

He figures all these little independent businesses must be owned by the people who work there, because Glen Cluthar looks like the kind of place nobody on a regular shop-worker's wage could afford to live. And Sattar said this Coyne woman had helped solve fifteen murders here? He's not sure whether that undermines the liberals arguing poverty leads to crime, or the conservatives by proving rich people are naturally more homicidal.

He's wondering where to start, when just down the street he notices a red phone box. What's that still doing here? Could be it was in a movie or something, and they keep it for the tourists. *Local Hero*: was that filmed here? No, that place was by the sea. Or the old black-and-white one about a Scottish castle and a curse: *I Know Where I'm Going!*

Johnny doesn't know where he's going, but he just found a way to get there. Not only is there an actual payphone inside the box, but there's a phone book. An actual honest-to-God phone book. And her name is in it: Ms P Coyne, Silverbank Cottage, Birks Road.

Johnny gets out his cell and is relieved to see that it's still working. He'd been half expecting there to be no internet because it feels like he's stepped back in time. According to the app, Silverbank Cottage is a ten- or fifteen-minute walk.

He sets off along this unsettlingly perfect street, pulling up briefly as he walks past a business that looks to have shut down: a patisserie with the lights off. It feels weirdly reassuring, the sight of failed commerce. He was starting to think he really was in a theme park.

Johnny makes a left onto Marshall Street, immediately

noticing a contrast to the main drag. It's a neat row of terraced houses on one side with doors right onto the sidewalk, but there are no shops or cafés, and consequently no people. There's a grander building on the other side, the carved stonework elegant enough to be a church, but he already saw one of those at the end of Main Street, and this place doesn't have a spire or any religious insignia outside.

Then Johnny encounters something that is incongruous yet otherwise universal: a squeal of tyres, the sound of a car pulling away unnecessarily fast, driven by some asshole. It's a pimped-out compact with tinted windows, flame-detailing on the flanks, shitty music thumping on the inside.

As it accelerates along Marshall Street, Johnny allows himself a glance to confirm his prejudices. Sure enough, both the assholes in the front seats are wearing baseball caps. The passenger looks considerably older than Johnny would have assumed, but it's not him that catches Johnny's eye. It's the driver.

Johnny's lizard brain recognises Tats way before his cerebral cortex gets there. That's how he knows that the car is gonna mount the sidewalk a fraction of a second before it actually does.

Johnny dives to his left, grabbing hold of a bracket for a hanging basket as the vehicle scrapes the brickwork beneath his scrambling feet. The bracket comes loose in his hands and he falls to the ground moments after the car has passed.

It does a handbrake turn, fishtailing across the road. Tats is coming back for another try. Johnny looks through the approaching windshield. Tats is eyeballing him, but the passenger has his cap visor down low, like he's concerned he'd be recognised. Johnny only catches his jawline, maybe a bit of nose.

The tyres squeal again as he accelerates. Johnny tries the front door nearest him, finds it locked. He looks to the grand building opposite, starts running. Tats sees his plan, turns the wheel. It's gonna be close, and if this door's locked, he's street pizza.

The car is about half a second from impact when the door swings inwards. In disbelief he sees that it's none other than the old broad herself, but she's about to step out into the path of the dick-wagon.

'Get back,' Johnny shouts.

She stops more nimbly than he would have guessed and presses herself inside the doorframe as Johnny launches himself head-long through it.

The car shoots past on the sidewalk, Tats gunning the engine as it turns onto Main Street.

Murder by Invitation

IX

Penny was leafing through a well-thumbed copy of *The Name of the Rose* and wondering how many different readers had licked their fingers to turn its pages, when she was startled by a quite unnecessary screeching of tyres outside and the roar of an engine very close by. It was followed by a loud scraping, like the sound of impact but protracted.

She decided she ought to go and investigate, fearing someone might be injured, and pulled open the door just as a figure barrelled towards the library. He shouted as he bore down: something about getting out of the way, a redundant remark as Penny was already stepping clear of his charge.

As he dived through the doorway, she saw a car speed past, missing him by milliseconds. It was driving on the *pavement*, and not by accident.

He executed an impressively cushioned fall on the polished wood floor, given the momentum behind his approach. If Penny had tumbled at that speed, she'd have been spending the rest of the day at A&E with two broken wrists.

There was another screech as the car skidded into a left turn onto the Main Street, then a growl from its engine as it sped away.

It was when he righted himself into a crouch that she saw the fall had not been entirely cushioned, as the gentleman had a cut on his right temple. It was also when she saw precisely who he was.

'Mr Hawke. What on earth are you doing here?'

He dabbed at his head and examined his fingers.

'So far, bleeding, mostly.'

'Are you injured? That looks nasty.'

'It's nothing. Reopened an older cut. Are you okay?'

'I'm perfectly fine. Do you need to use the telephone?'

As she said this, Penny realised how anachronistic it sounded, but asking was a matter of habit.

'Thanks, I'm good,' he said, climbing to his feet.

'What happened? It looked like a deliberate hit and run.'

'Could have been my fault, being from the States.'

'What do you mean?'

'We have different words for things. What we call a sidewalk, you guys obviously call the road.'

She assumed he was joking but wondered why he would trivialise the incident.

'Come on inside. Can I get you a cup of tea?'

'Got anything stronger? Just kidding. Tea would be fine.'

She led him into the body of the library, where he stood taking in his surroundings. Penny always enjoyed the vicarious pleasure of imagining how this place looked to fresh eyes. Did they see a treasure trove, a palace of wisdom, or a ramshackle fire hazard? She didn't mind, as long as they didn't see a property development opportunity.

He stared up at the cupola. Few people noticed it first time, as few people looked directly up when they entered a room, but she got the impression Hawke was the kind of man who examined every angle.

'I'd advise against climbing it,' she said.

Hawke ignored her. 'What is this place?'

'A library. Don't they have those in America?'

'Only in blue states. Looks like somebody opened a second-hand bookstore in a church: a real "rag and bone shop of the heart" kinda deal. Where's the librarian?'

'I am the librarian,' Penny answered.

'Oh. I thought you were a retiree.'

'There are some things one never retires from.'

'Ain't that the truth.'

Penny filled the kettle at the sink in the cramped utility room behind the reception desk as Hawke continued to look around.

'Aren't you going to call the police?' she asked.

'I think I've bothered the local cops enough, don't you?'

Penny found this reluctance odd. 'It looked like attempted murder.'

'Yeah, but I figure no harm no foul.'

Another odd position to take. Penny worked something out.

'You know who they were, don't you?'

'I have a notion.'

'The police should be informed. It's your duty to report a crime. Why wouldn't you?'

'Because maybe I didn't enjoy my last encounter with the local cops. You know, when you got me apprehended.'

There was an edge to his tone that Penny did not care for.

'You got yourself apprehended,' she replied.

'Yeah, but they were only looking for me because someone told them I was acting suspiciously.'

She was belatedly starting to wonder what he was doing here, having initially been distracted by the dramatic manner of his arrival, and one vivid possibility was that he wished to settle a score. Her hand went to her pocket, checking her phone was there should she need to call the police herself.

As the kettle came to a boil, she considered that he wouldn't have accepted the offer of tea if he was that angry with her. Nonetheless, she was keen to take the heat out of their exchange.

'It was nothing personal,' she insisted. 'And whatever I said would have been neither here nor there had they not caught you climbing into the bell tower. What were you doing up there?'

'Why? What's it to you?'

'A young woman just died and you were snooping around the site of her death.'

'I wasn't rubbernecking, if that's what you're worried about.'

Penny popped teabags into two mugs.

'Why were you at Crathie Hall anyway? I know you weren't invited to the wedding.'

'As I explained to the cops, it's my friend who was the wedding guest.'

'And you were his plus one?'

'Something like that.'

'If he's that good a friend, how come you didn't know where he was staying? Ms Innis told me you had no idea.'

Hawke sighed, dabbing again at his cut with a tissue. 'It was a last-minute thing. Arrangements have been complicated.'

'Were they complicated because you don't actually know Crawford Nicholson, or was it last-minute because his writing partner just killed himself?'

Hawke paused mid-dab. Penny poured hot water into the mugs.

'How would you know about that? Oh, yeah. Sattar said you're some kind of amateur sleuth, solving murders here in Toytown.'

'And what kind of sleuth are you, Mr Hawke? I'm guessing a professional one. LAPD, perhaps. Or maybe ex-LAPD. Because if you were here in an official capacity, you wouldn't be skulking around. Milk and sugar?'

Hawke took time to respond. Presumably he was thinking about what she just said rather than how he took his tea, but one never knew with Americans. Tea often seemed exotic to them.

'Milk, one sugar,' he replied. 'Thank you.'

She passed him his mug and he took a sip, leaning against the desk.

'I am LAPD, but I'm investigating a case off the books. Officially it's gone down as a suicide but I'm not so sure. Is that a scenario you can relate to?'

Penny had been wondering why Saeeda would be so indiscreet as to be talking to Hawke about her, but now she understood. Saeeda evidently had more doubts than she had admitted to, and Hawke had suspicions of his own.

'Perhaps. What's your interest in Lilian Deacon?'

'I might ask you the same question. You're the one who was all huddled up with her the night before she found herself on the end of a rope.'

'It was a chance encounter, nothing more.'

'It looked like a real heart-to-heart from where I was standing.'

'From where you were skulking, anyway.'

Penny opened the cupboard where she kept the biscuits. Politeness dictated she at least put a couple of digestives onto a plate, but she wasn't breaking out the Tunnock's for this chancer.

'I'm guessing you were close,' he said.

'I only met her two days ago.'

'So why did I see the pair of you in the Winter Garden at one o'clock in the morning?'

'She confided in me because I used to work with her father, back when *his* father was running the company.'

Hawke looked around at the shelves. 'So you've always been in books?'

'One way or another, yes.'

'But you're not connected to RoadMiles?'

'No. It was the Stonebridge family Lilian wanted to talk about. She was worried about what she was getting into.'

'Yeah, from what I picked up they ain't exactly the Brady Bunch.'

'What do you know?'

'I spoke to Lucy, the youngest. She made out her father is some kind of sexual predator: victims paid off, corporate complicity, the whole enchilada.'

'She just told you this?'

Hawke offered a wolfish smile.

'The coke I gave her might have loosened her tongue.'

Penny almost choked on her tea. 'You gave her drugs?'

'I needed to get her confidence. Different people respond to different things.'

'Yes, but that's as unethical as it is illegal. What kind of policeman are you?'

'One who does what it takes to get the job done. If the good guys don't slip the leash sometimes, it's the monsters who get to roam free.'

'The rules apply to everybody or they apply to no one,' Penny insisted. 'I've heard all manner of self-justification down the years, and it's never once shifted the line between right and wrong.'

'Look, we're getting off track,' Hawke said, lifting a digestive. 'The point is she painted a vivid picture, one I'm voluntarily sharing with you now. How's about a quid pro quo?'

Penny had to swallow her disapproval along with her tea. Dealing with unpleasant people was often a necessary part of gathering information. The trick was not to find oneself tacitly condoning them, or worse, complicit.

'Lilian was worried that Lord Stonebridge was up to something, regarding the buyout. I'm told she was up early yesterday morning, making calls and sending emails.'

'That doesn't seem like the actions of someone on the verge of despair. Unless one of those calls or emails contained earth-shattering news.'

As he said this it struck Penny that, while not earth shattering, something significant was indeed being set in motion around the same time.

'According to Monica, a hostile takeover bid was launched for Stonebridge Publishing yesterday.'

'I thought it was a family firm.'

'No, it's public, though I assume the family controls most of the stock.'

'Surely nobody would launch a takeover bid unless they had reason to believe someone on the inside was willing to sell,' he said.

'I don't know. That sort of thing is mystifying to me.'

'I'm just wondering where Lilian Deacon might have fitted into this.'

'What about your Mr Nicholson – where does he fit in?'

Hawke finished his biscuit and wiped the crumbs from the corner of his mouth. He was clean-shaven and he was dressed in a suit, but she detected an inner scruffiness being barely covered up.

'He and his partner bought the movie rights to *The Cracked Mirror* and were in the process of selling their script. It was a hot property, and a big movie clearly makes RoadMiles a more valuable entity. Drives up the purchase price, for sure.'

'So Mr Nicholson has a business relationship with Lilian and Miles? That's why he was at the wedding?'

Hawke frowned. 'I think it was more than just business. I saw him kissing Lilian.'

Penny gaped. A multiplicity of implications ran rapidly through her mind before Hawke dispersed them with a shake of his head.

'Not like that. Maybe I should have said "embracing". It was affectionate but . . . chaste, shall we say. Did Lilian talk to you about him?'

'No.'

'And you didn't happen to speak to him at any point? Maybe at the bar that first night?'

Penny thought of the many exchanges she had had over the past two days. Very few were memorable, and none had risen beyond polite small talk.

'If we spoke, I certainly wasn't introduced. Have you got a photograph of him?'

'Sure,' Hawke said, fishing a mobile phone from his jacket and thumbing the screen. 'There you go.'

He was showing her the wrong picture.

'That's not him,' she said.

Hawke briefly turned the phone around to check. 'What do you mean it's not him? You just said you don't know what he looks like.'

'I don't know what he looks like, but I know that's the wrong picture.'

Frowning, he presented it to Penny once more. Same picture, still wrong.

'Have you seen this guy or not?'

How could a detective be so obtuse?

'Of course I have, which is how I know it's not Crawford Nicholson. That's a photograph of Miles Deacon.'

Penny and Hawke looked at the phone, then at each other.

'Goodness,' said Penny.

'Holly golly,' said Hawke.

Something Bloody, Something Blue

Chapter Eleven

Johnny knows he took a pretty good bang to the head. He's not sure if it was when he scrambled up the wall or when he dived through the doorway, but he knows he didn't get hit so hard that he's confused as to what Crawford Nicholson looks like.

He's not been introduced, but he's seen the guy around the hotel. Saw him greeting Lord and Lady Stonebridge. Saw him kissing Lilian Deacon. And now that makes sense: *kissing her like she was his sister.*

'Miles Deacon has an alias,' he says.

'Not uncommon in the world of publishing,' Coyne replies.

'Not uncommon in the world of criminals either. We're talking about more than a nom de plume. This guy has an apartment in LA. I've been there. He's got people who only know him as Crawford Nicholson.'

It occurs to Johnny that if Deacon and Nicholson are the same person, then the code scribbled on Nicholson's travel plans would be common to both of them.

'Does the number 040381 mean anything to you? Or the date, April 3rd 1981?'

'Don't you mean 4th March 1981?'

Of course. Brits put the day first.

'Either.'

She thinks about it.

'Afraid not.'

Johnny hears the sound of a vehicle stopping outside. He glances up, sees a black SUV with tinted windows. Different model from the ones the Stonebridge party arrived at the hotel in. The front passenger door opens and Chief Superintendent McLeod gets out, wearing his dress uniform. Got one of those flat hats with the black-and-white trim.

'Looks like the police have found out about the hit and run anyway,' Coyne says with demonstrable satisfaction. 'There is little goes unreported in this village.'

McLeod bows his head momentarily, leaning in to talk to whoever's in the driver's seat. With the visor of his hat tipped, Johnny sees just his jawline and a little bit of nose.

Maybe that bang on the head was harder than he thought, and he's starting to imagine things. Because it could *not* have been McLeod in the passenger seat of that souped-up dick-wagon, sitting next to Tats.

The SUV doors open. Out of it emerge three guys in full tactical gear carrying HK-G36s. An armed response unit to a report of a hit and run? Something here feels off.

Johnny looks down the aisle between two rows of ancient and rickety bookshelves towards the front door. It's still wedged open.

'Is there a back way out of here?'

'Mr Hawke, I would remind you that in this instance, you were the victim, not the offender.'

'Either way, I'm not convinced these guys are here to protect and serve.'

He sees McLeod make a gesture, executing a command.

Two of the armed officers take up cover positions behind the SUV as the point man heads for the library's front door.

Johnny is looking for rational explanations, running through every scenario of police procedure that might cover this. Not only is he coming up short, but all of his instincts are telling him this is very wrong. Like mortal-danger wrong.

Johnny needs a weapon. The closest he can find is a fire extinguisher and a leather-bound volume of the *Chambers Dictionary*.

He runs down the aisle and slips behind the open front door. He hears the point man approaching, boots on concrete. The guy doesn't say 'armed police', doesn't announce himself at all. Also not good. But if he's gonna do this, he needs to be sure.

Johnny launches the fire extinguisher, arcing it through the air so that it lands about ten yards back down the aisle.

The point man opens fire immediately, a short, controlled burst.

Yeah, he's not here to make an arrest.

Johnny sees the muzzle come through, passing the edge of the door. He swings two-handed with the dictionary, upwards into the barrel of the weapon, driving metal into the guy's face. Johnny then twists the gun from his grip while sending a kick to his midriff that slams him into the wall. As he sways on unsteady feet, Johnny cracks him in the temple with the butt of the HK, sending him sprawling out the door, which he slams closed and locks.

He sees Coyne walking towards him, her expression as confused as it is appalled. She's looking the wrong way, though.

Looking at him rather than at what's going on through the windows, at McLeod making another gesture.

'Get down!' Johnny shouts.

'What, or you're going to shoot me?'

Stubborn old mule stands her ground, looking defiant even as he bears down on her. He doesn't have time to argue. He pulls her to the floor and behind a row of bookcases just as all the windows explode. A hail of bullets rips into the books above them, dust and fragments of paper exploding from a hundred broken spines.

There is a lull of sorts, half a second before the shooting recommences, except now they're concentrating their fire on the front door. It's an ancient-looking heavy oak construction but it's taking a lot of punishment and it's not going to last.

Johnny stands up and sends a burst from the HK through one of the shattered windows into the side of the SUV. They return fire, bullets ripping through another hundred books.

Coyne looks as tearful at the destruction as she is afraid.

'I ask you again,' he shouts, 'is there a back way out of here?'

'I won't be your hostage,' she replies. 'Why don't you give yourself up before they destroy everything?'

Jesus H. Candlesticks. What does she think he is?

'I'm not taking you hostage. And *they're* not taking prisoners. Don't you understand? They're here to kill me. And they'll kill you too, as a witness, or so they can say I shot you and that was why they had to off me.'

Coyne doesn't look convinced, but she points back and to her left. 'Between sci-fi and romance. It leads to the car park, such as it is.'

'Please tell me you have a car.'

She holds up a set of keys. There's a plastic fob on the ring.

'When I say run, you run,' he tells her. 'But stay low.'

He ain't even sure she *can* run, but it's the message that matters.

Johnny holds the HK as high as he dares and fires through the empty window frames, over the heads of the gunmen but enough to keep them down.

He urges Coyne to run. She doesn't exactly duck, though she's short to begin with; doesn't exactly run either, but she's a little more spry than he was fearing. She hastens between the rows of bookcases. Johnny follows, walking backwards so that he can keep firing, keeping the bursts short but regular.

He turns his head and sees Coyne already at the back door, pulling her keys from the lock.

The rifle jams. The clip is empty.

He watches her slip through the gap and disappear, the door closing again under its own weight. He realises she can lock him in here.

There's a weird silence, an expectant moment like that beat after the orchestra finishes tuning but before they start to play.

Johnny hears something go clunk – the sound of a lock, most def – just before the shooting resumes, bullets thudding into the walls and ceiling.

He reaches the door, tries the handle. It opens. He steps into the light of a small courtyard. Realises the clunk was the central locking system of her car. That's the good news. The bad is that Coyne is pulling open the driver's door of an ancient Fiat Panda.

'Is this it?'

Coyne glares. 'You're welcome to ask someone else for a lift. Perhaps you can flag them down with your machine gun.'

'At least let me drive,' Johnny says.

She doesn't argue.

Johnny puts the key in the ignition, slinging the HK into the back. Hears the engine kick in with a level of horsepower he had previously only associated with lawnmowers. He reverses from the parking space, sticks it in first and drives out of the lot just as a gunman comes around from the front of the building, dropping to a crouch.

Johnny hauls at the wheel and floors it, mounting the sidewalk and driving straight at him. The guy doesn't like his chances, throws himself clear against the wall. Johnny can see the other cops getting into the SUV. They know he's mobile.

Johnny executes a handbrake turn to pull a one-eighty. The handbrake comes away in his hand. He's left holding a lump of metal with a torn strip of leather at the base as the car continues its skid, the back end bouncing off a lamp-post. The engine is still running though.

He goes up the gears, the engine screaming in protest at the revs he's asking for. Checks his mirror and counts in his head: one Mississippi, two Mississippi. After about fifteen, the SUV is in his rearview.

'Fuck me. I gotta be running from gunmen on the day I get into the slowest car I ever drove in my life.'

'I don't care for your language,' Coyne scolds. 'And believe me, you're lucky to have this. I don't normally take my car to the library.'

'Well, I'm glad you're not so shook that you can't still care about cuss-words. Or maybe you're in shock and you don't realise what's going on. That was a professional hit back there. This *is* a hit. Why else would they turn up armed to a library?'

'I don't know, but it looked to me like they opened fire because you assaulted one of their officers.'

'He opened fire without identifying himself, without calling out any warning. He wasn't there to arrest anybody.'

The road is frustratingly straight, keeping the Panda in the gaining SUV's sights. Johnny passes a sign warning of deer. He checks the mirror, counts until the SUV reaches it. Twelve, maybe thirteen Mississippis. They're gaining.

Finally there is a bend, trees rising on the right-hand side. A couple of hundred yards after he hits it, he sees a junction on the right, veering into woodland. He'll have to take it pretty hot because he can't afford to slow down, and he can't use the handbrake because it's currently sitting in the rear footwell.

'Hold on tight, lady.'

The little car threatens to tip as he hits the ninety-degree turn. He glances to his side and sees the SUV come into view before the Panda can disappear.

Shit.

Johnny counts again until he sees the SUV make the turn. Ten Mississippi.

About fifty yards further on, the road bends then starts to climb, leaving the last junction out of sight. There are trees to his left where the slope is rising, while on his right the ground drops away steeply. Johnny can't see how far it goes, just a blur of scrub.

The road is distressingly straight as far as he can see now, but there's a T-junction ahead. Cars going past. Witnesses. If he can reach that, they've got a chance.

Johnny's foot is to the floor but the slope is steepening and the revs are maxed out.

He checks the mirror, counts down looking at the last bend. Seven Mississippis. The SUV appears.

He looks towards the junction. It has to be quarter of a mile, straight line all the way.

The SUV stops. Why would they stop?

He looks in the rearview again. Gunmen are exiting the vehicle either side, taking positions and raising their weapons.

They've got perfect line of sight: no bend, no cover.

No choice.

Johnny turns the wheel hard to the right, sending the Panda off the carriageway as twin volleys of bullets are loosed.

The Panda is crashing through bracken and ferns, hurtling down a slope that just keeps getting steeper all the way to the bottom, where a river runs black and wide.

Johnny fights the wheel. Can't hold it as the car bucks from the impact of rocks and scrub on the underside. He sees black below, blue above, green left and right. Feels the moment the axle breaks. Then the sickening lurch and the sense of weightlessness as the car flips. Black above, green below, blue left and right. Bands of colour wheeling and blurring.

Then there is only black.

Murder by Invitation

X

Penny didn't know how long she had been unconscious. It could have been a minute, could have been a few seconds. She knew only that there had been a period of oblivion, during which her situation had not improved.

Her car was in the river, facing upstream, moving slowly backwards. It had taken her until this moment in her life to understand that floating and sinking were not opposites but increments. The top six inches of the windscreen remained above the water, enough to see how near she was to the bank. Below that rising line, despite the water's coppery opacity, she could see boulders and reeds and fish. These were not things you generally wished to see through the windows of a Fiat Panda.

At least the vehicle was sitting the right way up, though she wasn't sure how that had happened. The last thing she remembered had been a sense of weightlessness and of being upside down. The final drop into the water must have been longer than she expected, because the Panda had evidently flipped a full 360 degrees, or at least enough to tip and right itself.

There was water coming in, leaking from a dozen different places in a constant white-noise hiss, pooling at her feet and already ankle-deep. It was freezing.

She glanced to the driver's side. Hawke looked momentarily groggy, then his eyes widened in sharp alertness as he took in their predicament.

'You okay?' he asked.

Penny simply glared by way of response to this monumentally stupid question.

She released her seatbelt, keeping a light grip on the fabric so that it didn't snap back too quickly. It was a habit she had never got out of since an overtightened spring on a previous car had whipped the buckle back so fast that it cracked the window.

'What are you doing?' Hawke asked, his tone more of admonition than inquiry.

'It's not far to the bank. I go wild swimming twice a month,' she added, aware he probably thought she was some hapless old crumble.

'Put your seatbelt back on. Swimming is not the challenge here. It's getting out of the car.'

'How so?'

'For one, you're not gonna be able to open the door with all that water holding it closed.'

'I can climb through the window,' she replied, reaching for the button.

'DON'T!' Hawke shouted, but she had already pressed it.

Nothing happened. She pressed it again. Still no response.

Hawke sighed with genuine relief. 'The electrics are fried. Thank God.'

'And why would that be a good thing? You're saying we can't

open the doors and the water outside is almost over our heads.'

'I'll tell you, but first of all I need you to put your goddamn seatbelt back on.'

'Are we about to drive somewhere? I wasn't aware this was a Lotus Esprit, because you're definitely not James Bond.'

Penny knew she was being needlessly facetious, but she was frightened and nothing Hawke said was helping. He seemed to sense this. When he spoke again, his tone was gentler.

'To get the door open, we need to equalise the pressure. Which is a less disturbing way of saying we need this car to be completely full of water. To do that, I'm gonna have to break the window, and when that happens it's gonna get rough in here if you are not strapped to your seat. Understand?'

'Why can't we just wait for the car to fill up? It's coming in from all sides.'

'Because these windows could shatter at any second, and I'd rather be in control of when that happens.'

Penny nodded. The prospect he had outlined sounded unutterably awful, but at least he had a clear plan.

'How do you know all this stuff?'

'There's a police cruiser sitting ten yards west of a pier off Long Beach that is a permanent underwater monument to the day I learned it the hard way.'

The car was completely submerged now. It was like being in one of those aquariums with tunnels running through them, except she was accompanied by a deranged tourist who was about to break the glass.

Penny reached for her seatbelt, but confoundingly he stopped her.

'First you gotta take off any items that could catch on something or cause drag.'

Penny shucked her jacket and slipped off her shoes, which were submerged anyway. Hawke did the same.

'Now jam them under the seat so they don't end up floating around and getting in the way.'

Penny complied, then finally fastened her seatbelt again.

The car stopped moving, coming to rest with a grinding sensation to her right. She looked up through the windscreen, and saw that the surface was only a few inches above it. So near and yet so far. But as Hawke said, swimming was not the challenge.

'Do you have anything to eat, like a packet of potato chips or a bag of cookies?'

Penny couldn't believe anyone could be hungry at a time like this, but she estimated she had already asked too many stupid questions. She opened the glove compartment and pulled out a bag of Pan Drops.

'I think these might have been in there since the nineties, so I can't vouch for their comestibility.'

Hawke very carefully opened the packet, then very carelessly dumped the contents back in the glove compartment before closing it.

'Give me your phone,' he said.

Penny handed him her mobile. He placed the device alongside his own inside the plastic bag.

'I don't have anything to create a seal but it's better than nothing.'

He slipped the package into his right trouser pocket, where it bulged on his thigh. She saw him take his passport and place it in the left one. That was when she remembered her handbag was back at the library. Her passport wasn't in it, but just about everything else was.

'Okay, are you ready to do this?' Hawke asked.

225

'No, I thought we might sit and enjoy the view a little longer.'

'Hey, don't get snarky with me, lady. I'm the one who's trying to save your life here.'

'You're the one who has endangered my life. Repeatedly.'

'Well, he giveth and he taketh away. And if you don't want it endangered further, cover your face with your hands, because there's gonna be ten thousand fragments of glass coming at you, pushed by the level of pressure that results when an entire river is trying to enter a single car window.'

Penny closed her eyes tight, raised her hands and tilted her face away from Hawke.

'You're gonna want to start taking deep slow breaths.'

She understood. It was to slow her breathing in advance of the big one.

Hawke lifted the rifle from the rear footwell.

'Now, I want you to take that last big deep breath on three. You good?'

Penny bit back several unhelpful responses. 'I'm ready.'

'Okay. One, two, THREE.'

Penny inhaled to her vital capacity as Hawke drove the butt of the rifle against his window with a dull thud.

Nothing happened.

'Okay, this might take a few shots. Breathe out. Ready? On three again. One—'

The window imploded as a terrible force was unleashed inside the car. Hawke was taking the brunt of it, but she was grateful for his insistence regarding the seatbelt. She would have been thrown against the door, possibly knocked unconscious or worse.

The car did not fill instantly, and Penny was in the unexpected position of wishing it would flood faster, because with the water thundering in all around her, jetting and rebounding from all sides and angles, she was unable to take a breath.

After a very long two seconds, the car was not quite full, but the water was now above her head. At least the level of violence had abated enough for her to move her arms. She ran her hand down her seatbelt and felt for the release. She pressed the button.

Nothing happened.

Her heart surged in panic. She pressed again and it released, sluggishly, but she had come very close to an involuntary exhale, which could have been fatal.

Free of the seatbelt, with her eyes still closed she reached for the door handle, pulling it inwards and feeling the clunk as it released. She pushed against it. The door would not open. She dug her foot into the floor and shouldered it. It was stuck fast. Something was in the way: a boulder or part of the riverbed.

The car was completely full now. Penny opened her eyes. It stung but she could see. On the driver's side, Hawke was struggling to open his door too, but he was only fighting against the weight of water and the force of the current. He forced a gap. She feared the water would drive it closed again once he slipped through it, and she didn't have his strength.

Panic threatened to consume her, then she saw that Hawke was holding the door open. She pulled herself across the seats, and two seconds after squeezing through the gap she was breaking the surface.

Penny rattled her knee off something, realised it was the bonnet. She climbed onto it and half scrambled, half waded across the metal. That left her only a few yards to swim. The current was strong, but so was her stroke. She made it to the edge and dragged herself onto a partially submerged table of rock, not quite dry land but safe enough until she caught her breath.

The water lapped gently at the riverbank, flanked closely by trees. She felt her heart pounding like a pile-driver. A few yards of swimming didn't normally do that.

Hawke emerged alongside her, climbing out like it was the public baths.

'You okay, lady?'

Penny needed another few seconds before she could breathe enough to respond.

'I'm doing as well as can be expected. And stop calling me lady. I'm not a dog.'

'What do I call you then? Ms Coyne seems kind of formal given all we've been through.'

'We've been in each other's company about half an hour, Mr Hawke.'

'Yeah, but it's quality, not quantity that counts.' He extended a hand to help her up. 'Call me Johnny.'

Penny looked at his hand, reluctant to accept, concerned about what complicity he might infer. But equally if she wanted to find out what this man was really up to, it would help to feign a degree of harmony at least.

'My name is Penelope. But people call me Penny.'

He gave her a look she had seen many hundreds of times.

'Your name is Penny Coyne?'

'Yes,' she stated through gritted teeth. 'Please deal with it quickly.'

'I'm dealing with enough.'

She looked up the slope on the far side of the water. With the incline and the vegetation, the road was not visible from down here, but she could hear engines and saw the top of a van as it passed.

She began waving both arms and calling out to attract attention.

'What are you doing?'

'We need help.'

'Did you take a bang on the head? We need to get into the trees and out of sight, that's what we need. They're gonna be looking for us.'

'Looking for you, you mean. You're the one they're after.'

Penny replayed the destruction of her library in her head. The police arriving, armed, clearly regarding Hawke as dangerous. He had ambushed one of them, and they had opened fire because they now knew for sure he had a gun: *their* gun. She saw now that in the violence and chaos he had taken advantage of her fear, coercing her into an unwitting and unwise course of action.

'I'm just your hostage,' she told him. 'Or maybe your human shield.'

'You ain't worth much as a human shield if they're willing to shoot you to get to me. But here's the thing: soon as I disarmed that first guy, they opened fire, knowing you were in there too. So how do you know they weren't willing to kill *me* to get to *you*?'

'Why would they want to kill me?'

Penny meant this to sound absurd, but even as she said it, she wasn't so sure.

'That's what we need to find out. Come on.'

'Where?'

'You always ask so many questions?'

'Not always. But often.'

'Then I've got one for you. What's blue and fucks old ladies?'

Penny stared blankly, trying not to rise to the vulgarity. Hawke didn't wait for an answer.

'Hypothermia,' he said. 'Come on. I think I see a house through the trees. Let's see if Hansel and Gretel ain't home.'

She knew he was right. The cold had started to bite now that she was out of the water. She was conscious of the danger of after-drop: the body reduced circulation when it was submerged, which helped tolerate the temperature, but the process continued even after leaving the water. She needed to get into dry clothes.

Hawke began walking into the trees in his bare feet. Penny looked down at her own and set off gingerly behind him. Fortunately the ground was soft, mostly grass and compacted earth.

There was indeed a small cottage up ahead, though Hawke must have good vision to spot it through the trees. As she got closer Penny realised that she recognised it. She had walked past here on occasion, as it was only a few miles from her home. The house was at the end of a single-track road, which narrowed to a footpath leading to the river.

Penny walked as fast as she dared in her stocking soles, careful with every stride lest she step on something jagged. They reached the path, which was harder underfoot but easier to spot stray stones and other hazards. She could feel the first shudders that would soon turn to shivering if she didn't get warmed up soon. At least being in the woods sheltered her from the wind.

It took them a few minutes to reach the cottage; she wasn't sure exactly how many, as her watch had stopped. There was no car outside, and no lights on. She was not hopeful as she approached the door, and no more optimistic as she heard the bell reverberate from within. There was often a stillness, an emptiness about a house when it was unoccupied, and whenever she sensed it, Penny had seldom found anyone home.

As expected, there was no response.

'Let's see if they left a key under a plant pot,' Hawke muttered, striding off around the side of the building. Penny thought this extremely unlikely. It was a weekend bolthole, a holiday cottage probably owned by people who lived in Glasgow or Edinburgh. She remained at the front door, wrapping her arms around herself and hopping from foot to foot. With the cold really starting to bite, though she knew it was pointless, she rang the bell again anyway.

To her delight and astonishment, she heard footsteps from within, then the sound of a Yale lock being unsnibbed. Someone was home after all. And with Hawke gone, this was her chance. She was already beseeching her saviour as the door opened.

'Oh, thank goodness. You need to help me, I've been abdu—'

She saw that it was Hawke standing in the dim front hall, holding the door open for her. Penny had a sudden flash of him holding another door open, helping her escape from the flooded car. She felt a kernel of shame.

'At what point are you gonna accept that I'm on your side?'

'You'll be among the first to know. How did you get in here?'

'Bathroom window. There's towels and a robe. You should have a shower, warm yourself up. I'm gonna go look for some threads.'

Penny's instinct was to refuse, as she felt most uncomfortable being in someone's house without their permission. However, she felt even more uncomfortable being soaked to the skin and frozen, with her blouse sticking to her and her feet filthy.

She had a gloriously welcome shower, lukewarm at first then gradually hotter. Feeling restored, she dried off and pulled on the fluffy bathrobe, fastening the cord tight around her middle.

She walked into the main body of the cottage, an open-plan living room and kitchen, her wet garments bunched in her hands. She was hoping there would be a tumble drier.

'I found some clothes,' Hawke said.

There was a navy-blue dress laid over the back of a chair. It looked five sizes too big for her, but she wasn't going out to dinner in it. Hawke had evidently found himself a pair of jeans and a t-shirt. The trousers were rolled up at the bottom and barely held around his middle by a belt tightened to its last notch. The t-shirt was too big for him too, but he had filled it across the shoulders. Even in a jacket it had been his build that made her think he was a bodyguard.

He was standing at the kitchen table, looking at a tablet. He glanced down at his oversize clothing by way of acknowledgement. 'I dunno whose place we broke into, but I hear "Fee fi fo fum" and I'm outta here.'

'*You* broke into,' she reminded him.

'Found an antique iPad,' he said, ignoring her. 'Wiped to factory settings, so no password. Wi-fi is pretty decent too.'

'What are you looking for?'

'Us. Nothing so far.'

Hawke turned on the radio, a digital model that identified the channels on a little screen in the middle. He was clicking through stations, stopping when he got to a local one. Pop music began playing. Hawke glanced at the clock on the wall. It was a few minutes before three p.m.

'No matter where you are in the world, top of the hour is when radio goes to the news,' he said.

Penny noticed that both their phones were sitting on a worktop, the backs open and batteries removed.

'Are you drying those out? Are they broken?'

'They're working, but they're traceable. I want them thinking we're at the bottom of the river. For now, at least.'

Penny frowned. 'You seem considerably better versed in being a fugitive than I would have expected for a police officer.'

'Every day spent knowing how to work as a cop is also a day learning how the bad guys operate.'

'Yes, but you're not supposed to imitate them. Just how many laws are you planning to break today?'

'As many as it takes to get out of this shit alive.'

Penny was forming a riposte when Hawke turned up the volume on the radio. The clock showed it wasn't quite three.

'Just ahead of the hourly bulletin, we have an update on those earlier reports of a gunman opening fire at Glen Cluthar Library and a serious incident on the Tayview Road, involving a vehicle leaving the carriageway. Police are now saying they were in pursuit of the vehicle following the abduction by the gunman of a local woman. It is understood that the gunman lost control of the car while firing at police, causing it to plunge down the bank into the river.'

Penny was disturbed by what she was listening to. It had been the police who opened fire, not only on the library with her in it, but at the car too. And the car had not gone out of control: the police had been shooting machine guns at it.

Penny felt unmoored. In her world, the police did not lie like this. They could be bumbling incompetents and over-officious jobsworths, but they were honest, truthful and a force for good. And in her world, the police most certainly did not open up indiscriminately with automatic weapons. Nobody did.

'Police are at the scene now. They are awaiting divers and have officers searching the riverbank, but a spokesman admitted that the longer it goes on, the less hopeful they are of finding survivors.'

'That asshole McLeod is laying down a narrative that allows them to disappear us.'

'I just can't comprehend it,' she said. 'I've known McLeod for years. He can be arrogant and boneheaded but if I hadn't seen it with my own eyes, I wouldn't believe he could be involved in

233

something like this. It's so completely and inexplicably out of character.'

'Has he got family? Maybe someone's got hold of whoever he cares most about. But either way—'

Hawke froze in response to something. He switched off the radio, allowing Penny to hear the sound of a vehicle. They looked out of the front window and saw the black SUV approaching through the trees.

'Get down,' Hawke commanded.

Penny ducked behind a sofa, making sure she was out of sight. She could hear Hawke closing the window he had forced open. Moments later he appeared behind the sofa too, clutching the dress and the phones. She shuffled along to make room. It felt like the world's most high-stakes game of sardines.

She could hear the vehicle's doors open, then footsteps.

The doorbell rang, loud and rattly. Her heart began to thump.

Hawke whispered to her, 'This is your chance. You can answer the door if you want, walk away, leave me to them. I won't stop you. But either way, this is when we both find out who you really trust.'

Penny stayed where she was, her breath held as tightly as when the car was underwater. She heard more footsteps, someone walking around the house to check the rear.

There was a voice from outside. 'Nah, it's empty and secure. All locked up, no sign of life.'

A few seconds later she heard the SUV's doors close again, followed by the sound of the vehicle driving off. She breathed out.

'This doesn't mean I trust you,' she said. 'It just means I trust them less.'

Something Bloody,
Something Blue

Chapter Twelve

Johnny breathes again as he watches the SUV retreat. He hadn't been a hundred per cent certain which side the old broad would come down. By her own testimony she had known McLeod a lot longer than she had known Johnny, and he got the impression hers wasn't a morally grey world where cops could be dirty. But she wasn't naive or stupid either. Even allowing for the fog of war, she knew who shot first. Mainly he'd been anxious because if he was in her shoes, he wouldn't trust him either.

With that thought he remembers she isn't in any shoes, and neither is he. That's just the first problem about getting out of here.

'That was close,' Penny says, tugging nervously on the cord of her robe.

Johnny's still dealing with the fact that her name's Penny Coyne, trying not to be a dick about it. It's tough because it's just hanging out there, begging. Figures she's Miss Penelope too. He'll save that one for a better moment.

'Should have been closer,' Johnny replies. 'If that had been me searching, I'd have been more thorough. My read is they're just checking where they can while they wait for divers to confirm what they already believe, which is that nobody escaped from that car.'

'Wouldn't they have seen us climb out?'

'The river was well screened from the road, and we must have travelled a distance before we fully sank. They're working on the presumption that we didn't make it. That gives us a window.'

'To do what?'

'We're vulnerable while we don't know where the threat is coming from. We need to find out who wants us dead, and why. The obvious answer is that we're the only two people unconvinced that Lilian Deacon killed herself, but why someone would want her dead is a whole other thing.'

'The most obvious answer to who wants us dead is Chief Superintendent McLeod,' says Penny, 'as he was the one conducting operations. But as I said, I simply cannot equate his conduct with his previous behaviour.'

'He has to be working for someone else. My first guess would be Stonebridge. I saw them talking at the hotel.'

'Why wouldn't they have been talking at the hotel? McLeod was there because Stonebridge's prospective daughter-in-law had just been found dead.'

'They already knew each other. I saw McLeod walk in: there were no introductions.'

'But what motive could he possibly have?'

'Lucy Stonebridge told me her father's a serial predator. Lilian Deacon told you she intended to find out more about what Stonebridge might be up to. The next morning she was seen checking emails, making phone calls. What if she uncovered something?'

236

'But how would he know she had uncovered anything? Unless she confronted him . . .'

'Did you see him yesterday morning? Was he acting weird, agitated?'

'No. I did see him get terribly upset at dinner last night, but that was because he'd learned about the takeover bid.'

'Says a lot if that's the thing he loses his shit over on the day his son's fiancée dies. But maybe it was just the last straw. I don't know. There's an angle we're not seeing here.'

Penny walks to the window and looks out, like she's not convinced they ain't coming back. Neither is he.

'I accept Stonebridge has a link to McLeod,' she says, turning to face Johnny. 'But can we think for a moment about the rather more substantial link between Miles Deacon and Crawford Nicholson? That surely has to be at the heart of this. His writing partner was found dead a few days ago, is that right?'

'Jed Mahoney.'

'Did he know who Nicholson really was?'

'No idea.'

'Or did he find out and that became a problem? Did Lilian know her brother was moonlighting as a scriptwriter? Did she know he had pseudonymously acquired the film rights to a book *they* published? Is it possible she and Jed both died to cover this up?'

'I just got a whole bunch of don't knows,' Johnny replies.

'I know precious little about Hollywood. Is this film a big deal?'

'The script was hot property. The majors were interested, but Nicholson and Mahoney went with Kingdom Pictures: not exactly a scrappy little indie but not Warner Brothers either.'

'Why?'

'Kingdom were offering more control, as well as a longer-term deal. But another factor has to be that Jed was engaged to one of Kingdom's executives, a woman called Blake Astor. I guess it helps if there's a personal connection, but Lilian Deacon might tell you that's a double-edged sword. I heard Jed was having doubts about the deal. Just like Lilian, he was the cautious one.'

'Tell me about the suicide. How did you get involved?'

Johnny has to pause for a moment. Not because he's having trouble remembering, but because he feels like he glimpsed something in his head and he doesn't want to look elsewhere just yet. It's gone again, though.

He picks up the old iPad and runs a search, hands the device to Penny. The lead result is now a story in the *LA Times*. Dominique King has given them some fresh quotes now that the coroner's ruling is official.

'It happened at a wrap party inside Kingdom Pictures,' Johnny says. 'At some point during the evening, Jed disappears. Next morning he's found to have shot himself in a storeroom padlocked from the inside. I was dispatched to investigate.'

Penny is scrolling down the story as he speaks. She looks up. 'So why are you here in Scotland?'

'Because Crawford Nicholson disappeared from the party too. He was on a plane by the time Jed was found. I discovered this was where he was headed.'

Penny stares at him with a stern expression. It reminds him of Mrs Watt, his fourth-grade teacher. He learned the hard way that she was smarter than him.

'Crawford Nicholson is who you're *looking for* in Scotland, not why you're here. Absurdly well funded as the LAPD might be, I don't imagine they would disburse the resources to send you overseas when they could easily get the Scottish police to apprehend him.'

Johnny sighs. He didn't realise quite how much it would hurt to talk about this, but that's all on him. He looks out the window again, acting like he's scoping for danger, but in truth he's buying himself a beat before he has to answer.

'You're right. I'm off the case and on suspension.'

'Why?'

'Because when I investigated, I didn't come to the conclusions certain people wanted me to. Kingdom Pictures is run by Dominique King, who is very well connected.'

He sees that thing again. Then once more it's gone. He shakes it off.

'But you weren't suspended merely for raising doubts,' Penny says.

Johnny knows he ain't gonna be able to fudge his way past her. He braces himself. He needs to say it aloud, get it out there. Catharsis. Maybe that will make him feel better.

'I went back to Kingdom Pictures and conducted a search. Without permission and without a warrant. I roped my new partner into joining me. There was a fire. My partner was killed. His name was Alessandro Ibanez. He was twenty-eight.'

Johnny feels something drain from him. He's said it aloud, got it out there. Catharsis.

He doesn't feel better.

There's a growing silence. He's not sure he's got the energy to fill it.

'That's a lot to carry,' Penny says. Her voice is real quiet.

'Yeah,' he manages, throat dry.

He grabs a glass and goes to the sink but he's not sure it's because he needs a drink of water or because he needs to be alone for a moment.

Penny reads aloud from the piece. 'King says, "We were looking forward to welcoming Jed into our family." Is that her just being all Hollywood?'

'No. Blake Astor is Dominique King's daughter.'

'Ah, yes, I see. "Astor, who last year divorced music promoter Tony Astor, is King's daughter from her previous marriage to movie producer Alvin Lennox." A family affair indeed. "The couple's elder son, Tom Lennox, is Kingdom Pictures' senior vice president in charge of production, while younger son Damien Lennox is vice president of marketing."'

Johnny almost chokes on the water. 'Wait, what? Those two are King's kids too?'

'You didn't know this?'

'I never got time to dig deep. I had barely scratched the surface before I . . . Holly golly.'

'Holly who?'

The thing he was glimpsing is now staring him in the face. He realises it's been there all along but he's been refusing to see it because it makes no goddamn sense.

'Blake Astor is Dominique King's daughter,' he says. 'She and her siblings all have senior positions with the family firm. She's regarded as the brightest talent. She's engaged to Jed, someone her family are about to do a deal with. Jed's business partner is Crawford Nicholson.'

'So?'

'Sebastian Gossard is the brightest talent of three siblings on the board of *his* family's firm. He is engaged to Lilian Deacon, who is also about to enter into a business deal with his family. Lilian's business partner is Miles Deacon, who we know is also Crawford Nicholson. Lilian and Jed both express reservations regarding what they might be getting into. Then before the deal can be inked, they each take themselves off to a locked room where they apparently kill themselves.'

'Yes, there is a certain similarity to the circumstances,' Penny says impatiently. 'So what?'

Johnny splutters. 'Don't you see? It's not just the same circumstances. It's the same goddamn murder.'

'What do you mean, the same murder?'

'I mean *everything* about it is the same. The story is the same. The dramatis personae are the same. Okay, some fine details are different and there's a few gender flips, but it's like if one of these was the book and the other was the movie.'

His fourth-grade teacher is back in the room. Mrs Watt is not impressed.

'I will not deny that there are strange parallels,' she says. 'But unless you can suggest why they might be relevant, I'd advise you not to become so distracted by what is strange that you lose sight of what is plain and factual.'

Johnny's been a detective long enough to know she's right. Weird coincidences can seem significant simply because they're weird, and then you start imposing meanings on them, like seeing faces in the clouds. That's why he's living in a world full of assholes believing in chemtrails and the Illuminati.

'When you went back to Kingdom Pictures,' Penny says, 'you found a way out of that storeroom, didn't you?'

'How do you know that?'

'You wouldn't be here otherwise.'

'Yeah. There was a trapdoor onto a rigging platform underneath.'

'And you found a way out of the bell tower too.'

'Same way I got in. Climbed the pipe.'

Penny nods, taking this in.

'These deaths are undoubtedly connected,' she says. 'But there is only one aspect of this that could truly be said to constitute two iterations of the same thing.'

'Crawford Nicholson and Miles Deacon.'

'I found it difficult to believe Lilian would kill herself, but at the same time I didn't see how anyone could get her to the top of that tower against her will. I understand now that the same question applies to Jed, and in both cases, we have the same answer. They were each persuaded to go there by someone they trusted. A confidant. A creative partner. A best friend. A brother.'

Murder by Invitation

XI

'We need to find Nicholson,' Hawke said. 'He's the alpha and the omega in all this.'

'We need to find some shoes first,' Penny reminded him. 'We can't stay here, though we're not going to get far on foot, shod or unshod.'

'You got something in mind?'

Penny was trying not to think about how the car that had served her uncomplainingly for so long was now lodged at the bottom of the river. The knowledge that her own home was only a few miles away was tantalising, to say the least. She could do with feeling its comfort and security around her, not to mention fresh clothes.

'We could call a taxi,' she suggested.

'And have the driver say, yeah, an American guy and the local librarian, sure. They're alive and well. Here's where I picked 'em up and here's where I dropped 'em off.'

Hawke had a number of unlikeable facets, but Penny was fast discovering that he was at his most annoying when he was right.

Partly it was that he did not express it delicately, but mostly it was that he tended to be right about things that she really wished were wrong.

'Besides,' he added, 'we don't know where we should be headed. First off, we need to find out where Miles Deacon lives.'

Penny had a notion how they might go about that, but he wasn't going to like it much either.

'I could call Saeeda Sattar.'

'Absolutely not. Are you nuts? McLeod is her boss.'

'A little while ago you asked me to trust you. Now I'm asking you to trust me.'

'Yeah, and you said you *didn't* trust me.'

'I trust her, though. We need an ally. I've known Saeeda a long time. I've babysat her son. She would never let any harm come to me.'

'And that's exactly why you can't trust her today. You phone up and tell her all this crazy-sounding stuff, she's gonna think you're being forced to say it. She'll rat you out because she'll think she's saving you from me.'

Again, very annoyingly, he was right.

'Who do you know around here who can keep their mouth shut?'

Penny thought about it, though not for long. In the village of Glen Cluthar it was not so much a shortlist as a blank sheet of paper. It was a village where discretion was seldom prized at the best of times, and with the place doubtless abuzz with reports of Penny's abduction, she could think of no one who would not call the police as a matter of instinctual civic duty, no matter how she pleaded with them to refrain. Just like Saeeda, they would doom Penny with the best of intentions. Equally, given the violence and destruction that had already been unleashed,

244

she did not wish to doom any of them either by dragging them into this.

Then she remembered the one person who was already in it. They were bound by shared trauma, one might even say bonded by blood, albeit someone else's. And it was an individual who also happened to be in possession of Miles Deacon's personal details.

Murder by Invitation

XII

It was getting dark when Ms Innis drove up to the cottage. She flashed her headlights in a pre-agreed signal: one long, one short, one long. If it was two short, one long, two short, that meant she was compromised. Hawke admitted he hadn't thought this likely, but he wasn't taking chances, and Penny approved of that.

Ms Innis had taken surprisingly little persuading to come to their aid, sounding almost tearful in her relief that Penny wasn't dead.

Penny got dressed again as soon as she saw the lights, having put her clothes over a radiator. They were not quite dry, but they would do, and were vastly preferable to the oversized dress.

Hawke got back into his slightly damp clothes too. At his suggestion, they put back the garments he had borrowed, as well as the towels and bathrobe, leaving the house as they found it. Penny was as surprised as she was pleased with this act of propriety, until Hawke mentioned the real reason he was doing it. 'We gotta make sure the owners don't notice anything amiss.

If the cops get a report of a break-in here, they'll know we made it out of the car.'

Ms Innis was sitting behind the wheel of a Mazda hatchback. It was too dark to make out the colour. Black or blue, perhaps. Hawke opened one of the rear doors for Penny.

'Keep your head down until we're on the freeway. You're way too recognisable round here.'

'I cannot begin to express my gratitude,' she told Ms Innis, sitting down.

Ms Innis turned around in the driver's seat to greet her. She was looking a little more flushed and less phlegmatic than usual.

'Are you quite well, dear?' Penny asked her.

'It's my first time aiding and abetting fugitives.'

'*A* fugitive, surely.'

'Yes, sorry,' she clarified. 'One fugitive and one hostage.'

'She's not my hostage,' Hawke said.

'Hostage to fortune, then,' Ms Innis corrected.

Hawke climbed into the passenger seat, wiping something from the upholstery as he sat down. 'Crumbs,' he said. He looked at his fingers as though they had touched paint or glitter.

'Yes, sorry about the mess. I came as soon as I could. Grabbed some wedding cake by way of dinner. We divided it up among the staff rather than let it go to waste.'

She put the car into gear.

'So, Edinburgh, then?'

'Via Silverbank Cottage,' Penny said.

Hawke turned around. 'I thought we'd been over this.'

'We have. We just didn't come to the agreement you wanted.'

'It's an unnecessary risk. I thought you didn't like those.'

'Having my own shoes and a jacket is entirely necessary. To say nothing of a good handbag.'

'All of which we can buy.'

Penny glanced in the rearview mirror and found Ms Innis looking back wearing an expression of solidarity. They would be stopping off at Silverbank Cottage.

They arrived at Penny's home only a few minutes later. She was relieved to see there were no lights on at Mrs Houston's house, and no cars parked in the vicinity. Penny had always believed there were many advantages to living outside rather than in the village. She had never anticipated that one would be the ability to gauge whether her home was under surveillance by armed malefactors.

As she promised Hawke, she was only inside for two minutes: long enough for a change of clothes and to grab a trusted pair of shoes. She also grabbed an equally trusted handbag, the one she'd taken on her recent cruise. She could swear there was still a smell of salt, but maybe that was her imagination.

She stopped briefly at the front door, assailed by an unexpected sadness, an unaccustomed feeling that after she left this place tonight, she would never see it again. She remembered painting the door that cornflower blue, erasing the previous owner's ill-judged orange. Making the place her own. Making the place her home. But still another part of her accepted that perhaps it was time; that she had spent long enough here.

She got back into the Mazda, keeping her head out of sight as Hawke advised. It was an unusual perspective, her face sideways on the leather, looking up through the side window and seeing only streetlights and trees. It reminded her of childhood, journeys in her father's car, sharing the space with her brother and sister.

Her sister.

Penny felt a crushing sense of loss and regret, then the memory was swept away.

She sat up straight once she felt the surge of speed that meant they must be on the A9.

'I said once we're on the freeway,' said Hawke.

'This is as close as you're going to get,' Ms Innis replied.

The road widened to a dual carriageway south of Dunkeld, and she accelerated some more.

'Keep it under seventy,' Johnny warned.

'Oh, *now* you're worried about breaking the law.'

'We don't want to be pulled over,' he explained, annoyingly right again, but mostly just annoying.

They were southbound, heading for Miles Deacon's address in Edinburgh, which Ms Innis had supplied.

'I should warn you that nobody's been able to reach him,' she said. 'I'm told Sebastian Gossard even went to his place earlier today, but there was nobody home. He's not answering his mobile either.'

'Yeah, it was the same in the movie version,' Hawke muttered.

'What?'

'Nothing,' said Penny. They had already filled Ms Innis in on Miles Deacon and Crawford Nicholson being the same person. There was no need to burden her with Hawke's more outré thinking.

'I just mean Nicholson flew the coop and went incommunicado,' Hawke said. 'So it figures his alter ego would too.'

That was probably for the best, Penny thought. If they were right about all this, then confronting him might be extremely dangerous.

'Given that there's likely to be nobody home,' Ms Innis said, 'what are you going to do when we get there?'

'I'm planning to conduct a search of the suspect's property,' said Hawke.

'You mean break in?' asked Ms Innis.

'I may have to gain unauthorised access, yes.'

'I assumed so,' she replied. 'It's just that I need to know your preferred footwear for the job.'

'Good point. Best make it sneakers. In a ten. Or whatever's the UK equivalent.'

Ms Innis turned off the motorway and into the big twenty-four-hour Tesco on the outskirts of Perth. She stopped near the back of the car park, so that her passengers wouldn't be closely visible to the shoppers coming in and out.

'I'll square with you once this is all over,' Hawke told her. 'I'm good for it.'

'I trust you,' Ms Innis replied.

Hawke turned to Penny with a smug expression. 'See how easy it is?'

Penny tutted.

'Now, no fighting, you two,' Ms Innis said as she got out and closed the door.

Penny watched her walk towards the ugly, hangar-like building. She was missing Glen Cluthar Main Street already.

'I wasn't kidding about the movie version,' Hawke said.

'What?' Penny retorted. She knew fine what he meant, she simply wished to convey that she wasn't entertaining it.

'Just saying. It's another element that fits the template. Seriously, don't you think there's something weird going on?'

Penny didn't want Hawke thinking she subscribed to his crazy idea, but she could not deny that things had felt . . . *different*, of late. As though her world had turned, and not in a good way. In the past, the cases she dealt with did not involve child abuse and murderous priests. The victims were not left bloody and near beheaded. There were no car chases or machine guns. And her fate was not bound up with men like Johnny Hawke.

'I do have to ask what manner of policeman you are,' she said.

'Lieutenant. Robbery–Homicide.'

'No, I mean what manner of policeman you are that you care so little about the law. Or is it only the laws of countries you're visiting that you disdain?'

'Is this about breaking into Deacon's place? Because if you've an alternative suggestion, I'm wide open here.'

'I mean in general. You supplied drugs to Lucy Stonebridge. You broke into the bell tower. Broke into that cottage.'

'You think McLeod and his goons were acting within the law?'

'Two wrongs don't make a right. As a policeman, you have to be better than the criminals, otherwise what is the point of you?'

'So you're admitting McLeod and his stooges are criminals?'

Penny sighed, betraying that she did not have a riposte. He was a truly infuriating man.

'I'm all about the law,' he went on. 'But there's the law and then there's rules. If somebody's breaking the law and there's a rule stopping me from bringing them to justice, which one should I respect: the law or the rule?'

'In my experience, when rules get broken, bad things happen. If a rule is getting in the way of an investigation, a more resourceful officer would find a way of doing their job *without* breaking that rule.'

'Yeah, sure, and while he's taking the long way round, the bad guy's in the wind. I've had too many cases go south because everybody got tied up in red tape that serves no purpose.'

'Are you familiar with G. K. Chesterton?' Penny asked him.

'No.'

'He wrote the Father Brown mysteries, back in the 1920s.'

'Wait, were you *in* the Father Brown mysteries?'

251

Penny ignored this. 'He once postulated that when you find a fence blocking your way, you shouldn't remove it unless you understand why it is there.'

'Yeah, but life is short, and there's a lot of fences. Who wants to waste it wading through pointless bureaucracy, creating a hundred contingencies against things that might never happen?'

'Life is indeed short,' Penny countered. 'We are clinging to this one life, an accident of cosmology and evolution. Thus we ought to take every precaution that reduces the chance of it being cut even shorter.'

'You gotta die of something,' Hawke said glibly.

Penny felt a sudden anger kindle inside her.

'But it's not only about you, is it? That's the point. That's why we need those hundred contingencies, why we need rules that might seem pointless to you: because they might mean life or death to someone else. If you lost someone dear to you, how many inconveniences would you tolerate if it could bring them back? How much bureaucracy would you endure if it was the price of undoing what happened to your partner?'

Hawke glared, a shot across her bows. His lower lip was trembling, though. It was brief and minute, but it happened. He swallowed, his voice threatening to catch as he spoke.

'Fuck you.'

Penny might have bridled at the profanity, or seized upon it as an admission that she had won the argument, but she saw the hurt in his eyes. Even as it had come to mind, she knew it was a low blow, but she had dealt it anyway. Now she felt ashamed, though not quite enough to say sorry.

Something Bloody, Something Blue

Chapter Thirteen

He shouldn't have sworn at her. A wounded part of him still thinks she shouldn't have gone there, but he knows the wound is only raw because he's got a guilty conscience.

His response was defensive, a reflex. He's been telling himself that what happened to Ibanez wasn't his fault. He didn't force Ibanez to follow him into that movie studio. But if he really believed that, why would he be so aggravated by what Penny said?

How much bureaucracy would you endure if it was the price of undoing what happened to your partner?

And not just to your partner, he thinks.

Wait, what?

There's a gas station on the edge of the supermarket parking lot. The sign lists prices for unleaded and diesel. Johnny blinks and it says: 'Justice for Jayden Freil'.

He blinks again, knowing that it will revert to the gas prices, and it does, but the damage is done. Problem is, he doesn't know where the damage is coming from.

253

Why can't he remember who Jayden Freil is? And why does the name spark so much shame and regret?

'I'm sorry,' Johnny tells her.

Penny places a hand on his shoulder.

'I'm sorry too,' she says, and she sounds like she means it. 'But mind your language in future.'

'Yes, ma'am.'

Innis comes back carrying a plastic bag.

'These are all they had in your size.'

She hands over a pair of black sneakers and a navy-blue waterproof jacket.

'Appreciate it,' Johnny replies. They're not exactly his speed but at least they ain't white. Worn with tailored trousers and that waterproof, white sneakers would have made him look like a bum.

He pulls on the shoes as Innis gets the car moving again. They're a decent fit, as is the jacket. Johnny puts his passport and phone into a zip pocket either side.

They reach Edinburgh inside an hour. Traffic's light, as it's close to midnight. The buildings all around are beautiful but weirdly uniform, which he doesn't associate with old places. Even in New York, there's modern tower blocks next to brownstones. It's a reminder that he's a stranger in a strange land.

'Ms Coyne, did you ever find out why Deacon invited you to the wedding?' Innis asks.

'Wait, Miles Deacon is the one who invited you?' This is new information. 'You *know* him?'

'No, I do not know him. And nor do I know why he invited me. I can only assume it was for the same reason Lilian sought me out. They knew I had experience of the Stonebridge family and the Stonebridge firm. But unlike Lilian, he never introduced himself.'

'Yeah, still: both of us ended up at that wedding because of the same guy. That's gotta mean something.'

'And nothing good, I fear,' Penny says.

They're driving on cobbles right now. Actual cobbles. There's a semi-circular terrace of houses to his left that he's expecting Helena Bonham Carter to step out of any second.

'This Gloucester Lane where Deacon lives,' Johnny says. 'What kind of neighbourhood is that?'

'It's in the New Town,' says Innis.

'Pretty modern then? Are we talking a hip vibe?'

'Pretty modern for the late eighteenth century,' says Penny. 'This *is* the New Town.'

'I'm just trying to suss how busy it will be in terms of witnesses.'

'It's a lane,' says Innis. 'Probably a mews.'

'What's a mews?'

'Somewhere quiet and secluded.'

'Quiet and secluded is good.'

Truth is, Johnny ain't exactly sure how he's planning to get into this place. Quiet and secluded it might be, but it won't be another cottage in the woods. Maybe he can do like Ibanez did and sweet-talk a neighbour. That's a lot easier when you've got your police badge and a reason to be there, though.

With that thought he remembers that the neighbour gave Ibanez the code for Nicholson's key safe. Maybe that's the number he wrote down. There could be a key safe here too; if Deacon's got places on two continents, he's not gonna want to remember a different code when he's just off an eleven-hour flight. Could be there's even a keypad instead of a lock. He's seen people install those so they don't need to carry keys. That would apply double if you're living as an alias.

Jeez, this sounds desperate even to himself.

'Have you got a screwdriver?' he asks Innis.

'There's a toolbox in the boot.'

'You carry a toolbox with you everywhere?' says Penny.

'I'm here to serve.'

The Mazda is approaching a junction on the left. Johnny sees the sign identifying it as Gloucester Lane. There are red No Entry signs either side of it.

'The lane is one-way,' Innis says. 'I just need to loop around and come up from the other end.'

'No, pull over,' says Johnny. 'Best not to stop right in front of it, in case somebody sees something suspicious and writes down your plate.'

'I'll park here on Heriot Row, then.'

She pulls over on the other side, past the junction. There's a free space under some trees.

Johnny turns to face Penny.

'Would you rather I handled this alone?' he asks. He knows that if he walks off leaving her in the car, she could get Innis to drive them both away. He wouldn't blame either of them.

'No, I'll come with you.'

'I'm off to commit another crime, remember?'

'*You're* committing a crime. I'm investigating one.'

'Whatever gets you through the night.'

'I'll come too,' says Innis.

'No,' Penny tells her. 'We've dragged you into this deep enough.'

'I'll stay here, then. Keep the car running.'

'You do that,' says Johnny. 'What the eye don't see, the mouth don't have to lie about under oath.'

He gets out of the car and Innis pops the trunk for him. There is indeed a small toolbox in the back. He grabs a flathead screwdriver and a claw hammer.

Deacon's place is a third of the way down the lane. He doesn't see any lights on in any of the adjacent properties his side of the street. On the other side there is a blank wall, beyond which are gardens and the backs of a terraced building. There's another tall, terraced building parallel to the lane on Deacon's side too. 'Mews' turns out to be a fancy word for converted garages, or maybe stables, given the age of the buildings.

When he gets within ten yards, Johnny can see he won't need the tools. Somebody already broke in. The door is leaning to, not quite closed. There's damage around the handle and part of the frame.

Johnny tells Penny to stay back, keeping his voice low. He approaches the door slowly, gripping the screwdriver in one hand, the hammer in the other. Enough to give him the edge on any asshole who gets the jump on him, but not much good if it's McLeod and his men holding HKs.

He nudges the door open. The place is in darkness, still and silent. Johnny flips a light switch, braces for action. This is the moment the roaches will scatter.

There's no movement though. Whatever happened here is over.

It's a tiny apartment, indicating how expensive real estate must be around here as it's essentially a converted lock-up. There's a combined kitchen and living room on the ground floor, bedroom and bathroom upstairs, presumably. Architects and interior designers often do cute things with perspective to give the impression of greater space, but weirdly, this place seems smaller on the inside than it looked from the lane.

It's not cluttered, but he can hear some LA feng-shui expert having conniptions over the fact that much of the back wall is taken up floor to ceiling with an overstuffed bookcase. There are rows upon rows of spines facing out, and in front of some are further stacks of volumes, haphazardly piled on their sides. Many of the spines are identical, multiple copies of titles published by RoadMiles. However, there is one section of a single shelf where several hardcovers have been afforded pride of place: face-out and plastic-wrapped. One of them is *The Cracked Mirror*.

There's a workspace in front of the bookshelf. A wooden desk with a laptop sitting on it.

He returns to the door and beckons Penny inside, then heads upstairs. The upper floor seems more spacious, maybe because there's a window looking out onto the back gardens of the terrace behind.

The bedroom has been turned over. There are drawers half shut, wardrobe doors ajar. Through in the bathroom the cupboard has been cleared out.

Johnny walks back downstairs, where he finds Penny standing between the desk and the bookcase.

'Whoever broke in, I don't think they were here to rob the place,' she says. 'They surely wouldn't have left a computer sitting there.'

'To be honest, if the front door wasn't busted, I might think Deacon came back here and packed in a hurry: blew town like he left LA after Jed's death. Except that in LA there was no hurry. He had already planned to leave for the wedding.'

'And the front door *is* broken,' says Penny. 'He didn't break into his own flat, did he?'

'It's possible. Anybody can lose their keys, especially if they got cribs on two continents.'

Johnny wonders how far Miles Deacon took his alias. There would be implications over getting paid for the script deal. Like Penny asked, how much did Jed know?

'But I agree,' he says. 'Somebody broke in here, and they were looking for something.'

'Maybe they found it,' says Penny, her hand on the laptop. 'This is still warm.'

Johnny flips up the screen and it wakes from sleep mode. It's asking for a password.

He keys in the number Ibanez wrote down.

'Incorrect pin or password', it tells him with a rebuking bleep. 'Shoot.'

He really thought that would turn out to be something.

Penny stares at the bookcase, an irritated frown on her face.

'What are we actually looking for here?' she asks.

It's an aggravatingly good question. She's got a gift for those.

'Not sure. But some hard proof that Miles Deacon is Crawford Nicholson would be a good start.'

He tries the desk drawer, which opens easily. Not a promising sign. He finds instruction manuals and warranty documents for the laptop, TV and printer.

Penny is still staring at the bookcase.

'What was that date you asked me about?' she says.

'March 4th 1981. Or April 3rd.'

'Was it definitely *1981*?'

'No. The number was 040381. Why?'

'Because if it's 4th March 1881, then that's the date Watson records Sherlock Holmes commencing his first case, in *A Study in Scarlet*.'

Penny points to the shelf. The book she just named is one of the film-wrapped hardcovers sitting face-out.

Johnny carefully lifts the volume.

'Holly golly.'

Behind it there's a ten-digit keypad embedded in the wood.

Johnny enters the numbers Ibanez wrote down. He hears something go click. A gap appears, wide enough to get his fingers around. He pulls and a section of the bookcase the size of a door swings outwards on a hinge.

There's a hidden space behind it, a secret cupboard. The room *is* deeper than it looks.

'Goodness,' says Penny.

The wall behind is bare brick above more shelves. There's some kind of decal painted on it, a stoned-looking dopey fish, underneath which is printed: 'Congratulations, you have unlocked a secret level.'

'What does that mean?' asks Penny.

'It means Deacon is some kind of games geek, or else he bought this place from a games geek.'

There are more books back here: film-wrapped hardcovers.

'First editions,' says Penny. 'Valuable ones.'

But Johnny is more interested in the tray of documents on a lower shelf. He pulls out the topmost one. It is four or five pages clipped together, a print-out of a corporate memo, the strapline of which expressly prohibits it being printed out. It's a top-level discussion document from a company called Sea Monster Software, concerning a proposed takeover by another firm, Pierpont Digital. The primary driver behind the purchase appears to be the acquisition of some kind of proprietary new technology, referred to as 'Diegesis'.

Underneath the memo is a glossier item, an embossed wrap-around folder. Whatever was in it is gone, but according to the text on the front, it's an 'accreditation and orientation pack' for something called Electronicon Thirty, taking place near Santa Barbara.

'The pattern is repeating,' Johnny says, holding out the

documents. 'Someone close to him dies and Deacon disappears before the body is cold. He gets out of the country in time to attend a major event a couple days later, and once again there's both a business deal and a gathering.'

'What is Electronicon?' asks Penny.

Johnny turns over the folder. There's more information on the back. '"America's premier games-industry showcase celebrates its thirtieth year, with a special focus on the evolution of digital storytelling."'

Underneath that, the pack boasts a list of special guests. None of the names mean shit to Johnny, but according to the copy, one is from Pierpont Digital and one from Sea Monster. The name of the guy from Sea Monster has been circled.

'Check it out.'

'Wesley Oswald,' says Penny. 'Am I supposed to know that name?'

'No, but we best acquaint ourselves with it.'

'You think that's his next alias?'

'Or his next victim.'

Murder by Invitation

XIII

Penny watched him wipe down everything they had touched. She was gratified to see him taking particular care over the Conan Doyle, until she realised that this was due to the plastic wrapping being a particularly adherent surface for fingerprints.

Hawke was not like any policeman she had ever known. There had been good ones, loyal ones, stupid ones and inflexibly bureaucratic ones. But she had never encountered one so comfortable shifting between law and criminality, recklessness and prudence, respect and disdain. And though his habitat was a crepuscular world between sunshine and shadow, the more she saw of him, the more she understood that he found no such twilight between right and wrong.

He was rude, uncouth, vulgar and dangerous. But were it not for him, she knew she would surely be dead by now, several times over.

'Let's book,' he said. 'Don't want to push our luck here.'

He checked the lane before stepping out, satisfying himself that their route was clear. They strode wordlessly along the cobbles, south towards Heriot Row. Penny had visited the New Town on a case years before: a vengeful lawyer who had murdered an estate agent over a property deal. She recalled the lawyer having a stuffed badger in his office, inside a glass case. Why did her brain offer up useless details like that while whole periods of her life remained inaccessible?

When they reached the junction, she saw with some relief that the Mazda was still there, and so was Ms Innis, her head resting on the wheel. The sight reminded Penny that it was after midnight: well past her normal bedtime, and she'd had quite a day.

They crossed the road, where Hawke held the rear door open for her then climbed into the passenger seat. Ms Innis didn't respond, poor thing, but unfortunately Penny knew they couldn't let her sleep.

Hawke gave her shoulder a nudge.

She failed to rouse.

Penny heard a drip.

Then there was silence. Not even breath.

'Eyes down, Penny,' Hawke said.

'What?'

'Eyes down. I don't want you to see this.'

But she was already looking in the rearview mirror in response.

She only caught a glimpse, but even in the half-light it was enough. Hell was empty, and all the devils were here.

Ms Innis's throat had been cut. She was dead. Ms Innis was dead.

Penny felt like she was alone at the bottom of some oubliette, trapped and abandoned. Then she heard a voice, seemingly from far away.

'I don't care how much you're gonna hate me for it, but I need you to park what you're feeling and hold it together.' Hawke's

263

register was low but stern, commanding. 'We got out of the last car, and we're gonna get out of this one the same way: on three. One, two, three.'

Penny felt like a marionette or an automaton, moving almost involuntarily as she opened the door and stepped onto the pavement. Hawke emerged simultaneously, though he was scanning his surroundings while Penny struggled to even focus.

'Look.'

'What?'

He pointed across the street. 'CCTV. There's a camera on that building.'

'Then they'll have captured what happened,' she suggested numbly, grasping the crumb of consolation he was offering.

Except he wasn't.

'No. They'll have captured *us* getting in and out of the car. But my worry is that whoever did this knew we were here, and knew we'd be back. They could have come up on the blind side of the camera, and clearly they managed to get in the car without Innis freaking out and running. McLeod maybe. Or Miles Deacon himself. Come on.'

Hawke took her by the arm and led her up Wemyss Place towards Queen Street. Her legs felt like rubber. Rubber that was melting.

'I need to sit,' Penny said.

'We have to keep going.'

'I need to *sit*,' she insisted. 'Just for a moment.'

'Okay.'

Penny sat on the edge of the low wall abutting Queen Street Gardens, shrouded in near-darkness beneath a canopy of leaves. The initial wave of shock was passing, but it was transmuting into something equally debilitating: guilt.

'I got her killed,' she said. 'I brought her into this without considering the risks. She died because of my negligence. It's just like before.'

Penny felt her grief not so much well up as erupt. She broke down in sobs.

Hawke sat beside her and pulled her head onto his shoulder. It was warm and firm.

'That's crazy talk,' he said. 'But it's talk I've heard a dozen times after a murder. Folks always think there's something they should have done, something they shouldn't have done. They're so messed up that they lose sight of who's to blame. Who's to blame is the fucker who did this. And we need to focus on that, because they're coming for us.'

From the throes of her torment, Penny's self-preservation instinct grabbed the whip hand. Hawke was right, but this brought its own perplexing questions.

'If they knew we were here, why *didn't* they come for us?' she asked,

'If I had to guess, it's because they figured we must have told her stuff, so we're all a threat. Killing you and me hasn't proven easy. Killing Innis and framing us for it takes all three out of the picture. But that's just the best-case scenario.'

Penny barely dared ask, but knew she had to.

'What's the worst-case?'

'That they're covering all bases until they can choose their moment.'

She nodded. He was right.

'What are we going to do?' she asked.

Hawke gazed up into the night sky.

'I think this is where we have to part ways. If you go to the cops here in Edinburgh, you can get ahead of the story. There's a greater chance they'll believe you on your own. You can lean into the abduction narrative, pin as much of it on me as you need to. You gotta put yourself out of danger.'

'What about you?'

'I'm gonna have to take my chances, get out of the country. Follow Deacon to Santa Barbara.'

'No,' Penny told him. She fished in her handbag, heart in mouth until she confirmed it was there. Her passport. She held it up.

'I'm coming with you. I've seen what these people can do, twice now. I won't take my chances with the Edinburgh constabulary any more than with McLeod or even Saeeda Sattar. At this moment, you're the only policeman I can trust. We're a team now, Johnny, for better or worse.'

Penny put out a hand. It looked so tiny, pale and shrivelled next to his.

He looked at it for a moment, considering. Then he nodded to himself minutely before grasping it.

'Okay,' he said, standing up. 'But full disclosure, this might not be the safer option. People who work with me tend to wind up dead.'

Penny managed a tearful smile.

'As a wise man once told me, you've got to die of something.'

PRIVATE INVESTIGATIONS: KIRRIEMUIR

Going in, Rattigan had thought this one would be the hardest, and it might yet, but when he showed up and said what he wanted to talk about, Andrew Delamere offered no resistance. Quite the opposite, in fact, like he was glad to have company, or maybe glad of the opportunity to discuss his late son.

'Last time I saw him, he was as happy as he'd ever been,' he said.

They were drinking coffee in the afternoon sunshine, his back garden looking onto fields that stretched into the distance. The place was in the middle of nowhere, but the weather was better here than it had been in St Andrews. Maybe it was just the lack of that sea breeze.

From his accent, even Rattigan knew Delamere wasn't local. They moved up from London in the late seventies, he explained. He and his late wife were teachers. Decided they'd try a change of pace and never looked back.

'Toby could be very obsessive, very single-minded,' Andrew said. 'He would lock himself away when he was working on something. Larval mode, he used to call it.'

As he said this, Andrew let out a fond chuckle tinged with sadness: more than three decades of regret, and of missing.

'I worried that he would be a bit reclusive when he went off to university, but he seemed happy, and he even had a girlfriend. Though he might have been exaggerating about that. A friend who was a girl, at least, but that was news in itself.'

'A bit of a computer geek,' Rattigan suggested.

Andrew nodded, looking away across the expanse of corn beyond his garden.

'You'll be wanting to see his files,' he said.

Rattigan's expression gave away his surprise.

'How did you know?'

'The other fellow who came here inquiring after Toby. That's what he was interested in.'

'When was this?' Rattigan asked, needing to make sure there wasn't someone else, more recent.

'About twenty years ago. Another investigator like yourself. Jim something. Weird surname I can't quite recall.'

'Based out of Edinburgh.'

'Yes. You know him? You've not spoken to him already?'

'He's no longer with us.'

'Retired?'

'No, I mean . . .'

'Oh. I see. Well, let me show you.'

He led Rattigan through to a small bedroom at the back of the house. There was a very old computer and monitor sitting on a desk, alongside some cardboard boxes full of yellowing magazines.

'I didn't want to create some sad little shrine, but it gave me and Cathy a lot of comfort to still have the things he loved. And I must confess that every so often, when I knew she wasn't home, I used to boot this up again just to see the images and hear the noises. It would always make me sad, and I would feel the loss all over again, but it was the closest I got to feeling near him. Do you know what I mean?'

'Yeah,' Rattigan said, a well-meant gentle lie. The only people of significance he had lost were a father who walked out when he was seven and a wife who walked out when he was in Vegas. He didn't want to feel either of them near him again.

'The computer died a long time ago. We hung on to it, though. Couldn't bear to let it go. And the disks. Even the ones he'd only just bought.'

'Even? As opposed to what?'

'As opposed to the programs he'd created himself.'

'What kind of programs?'

PART THREE

The Silence Forever Echoes

Chapter One

Johnny squints as the morning light finds him, but today the LA sunshine is a warm glow, a reassuring presence in the room telling him he's home. For a moment he's surprised by his surroundings, like he expected home to be someplace else, but the familiarity seeps in as consciousness becomes clearer. There's no bottle on the nightstand. That's a good sign. No woman in the bed either, so no mutual-validation-seeking, end-of-the-night, fuck-it-you'll-do sex to regret before coffee.

The immediate past is hazy, and for a blissful moment he thinks it must have been a dream, the only way that shit could possibly make sense. Then he hears her voice at the door.

'Mr Hawke?'

Penny fuckin' Coyne. Miss Penelope. It's all real.

'Mr Hawke, are you awake?'

'I sure am now.'

'I can't find any tea and I can't work out how to operate your coffee machine.'

'That's not a coffee machine, it's a kitchen ornament. The

coffee machine is at the Blackwing Diner on Sunset and Franklin, and the way you operate it is you get in a car and drive there.'

'Well, can we expedite that operation? My need of tea is becoming pressing.'

And my need of coffee just became critical, Johnny thinks.

They get their coffees to go. Blackwing is crazy busy this morning and he doesn't want to wait for a table. This early bird got a very slippery worm to catch.

'It must be the jetlag,' says Penny. 'I feel so woolly-headed. I tried to sleep on the flight, but every time I closed my eyes I saw Ms Innis in that car.'

Her eyes are bloodshot, but it's not from jetlag. He can tell she's been crying. He worries for a moment that she's going to break down again, but she holds it together.

'I hear you,' he says.

'Has there been anything about it on the internet? Or about us?'

'Nothing so far.'

They are headed westbound on the Santa Monica Freeway. There's a sign for Santa Barbara, but Johnny doesn't take the turnoff. Figures she won't notice.

She notices.

'Aren't we going to Santa Barbara?'

'Yeah. Via Marina del Rey.'

'What's there?'

'With a little luck, an unsuspecting Miles Deacon.'

They had tried searching the internet for information on the name Wesley Oswald and found one potential connection to Miles Deacon, in that they both went to St Andrews. Beyond that, the results were sparse: no photos, and very little

274

information beyond Oswald being the founder of Sea Monster Software. Johnny suspects the guy's name has been Google-washed, to a high and expensive degree.

As always, he feels happier at the sight of the ocean, but as they turn onto Pershing Drive it is tempered by the memory of his last visit here. It feels so long ago, when in fact it was only a matter of days. He came here with a new partner. It felt like the beginning of something, but then first days with a new partner always do.

They pull over in front of the building and Johnny steps out of the car. He gets a weird vibe, like something feels off. He looks up. He's pretty sure the blinds don't look the same as he remembers. It's not just Nicholson's apartment either. It's the whole place.

They walk up the stairs together and he rings Nicholson's doorbell. He can tell right away there's nobody home.

Johnny remembers the key safe. He looks at the walls either side of the front door, but he can't see one. Then he notices the large pebbles surrounding the stalk of a peace lily sitting in a planter in the middle of the landing, where the balcony overlooks the street. He picks one up and turns it over, examining it.

'Have you developed a sudden interest in geology?' asks Penny.

'I'm looking for a disguised key safe. A rock that's not a rock.'

'I see,' she says, like he's just told her he's also planning to eat the plant.

Ignoring her, he starts working through the others. As he discards the fourth or fifth pebble, he hears a door open across the landing and looks up to see a bottle-blonde woman with sunglasses perched on her head and an iPhone clutched in her hand.

It's not the neighbour he and Ibanez met. Maybe it's her roommate.

'Hi,' he says. 'We were looking for your neighbour, Crawford Nicholson.'

'Who?'

'Guy who lives in this apartment? Screenwriter?'

She wrinkles her nose. 'Nobody lives there. As far as I know it's been vacant for about two months. Before that it was a woman called Draper. A chiropractor, I think she was. Or was it chiropodist? I get those confused.'

What the hell?

'Wait, nobody was subletting, maybe?'

'I wouldn't know about that. But I haven't seen anybody in there for weeks.'

'What about your roommate. Would she know?'

'I don't have a roommate. I live here with my boyfriend. Look, I gotta be somewhere. I got a nine o'clock.'

Johnny watches her leave, then looks at Penny, unsure what to say.

'Are you sure you've got the right place?' she asks. 'A lot of these streets look the same.'

'Forget it,' he replies, heading back to the car. He figures if he's being asked if he's in the right place by an octogenarian with jetlag, it's a sign he's not only in the wrong place, but in a bad place.

He's starting to wonder how much he might have misremembered, or simply imagined. But no: he came here with Ibanez, and Ibanez came back and gained entry. That's how he found out where Nicholson had gone. It was also how they got the code that opened the secret room.

He starts constructing crazy explanations, like maybe the whole building is owned by Deacon and he has paid someone to pretend he's not her neighbour. He tries to shake it off as they head up

276

the coast, but it's in his head that Deacon is this Russian doll and he's wondering how many more layers there are.

Electronicon Thirty is taking place at the Oyster Catcher Inn, about ten miles north of Santa Barbara. The name makes it sound like some kind of nineteenth-century coaching stop, but as Johnny turns off the highway and sees it looming before him, he figures he'd need to go to Vegas to find a starker contrast in tone and scale to Crathie Hall.

Driving up the winding avenue through its acres of ocean-facing real estate, he can see that it not only has its own golf course, but also its own pier and marina. There's no greater testament to its sprawl than the fact they have golf carts running people from the parking lot to the reception lobby. But it's not just the opulence of the hotel that is setting down a marker. The scale of the branding, with twenty-foot electronic marquee signs erected just for this event, lets him know that Electronicon is a major deal. This isn't some regional trade show. These are major names, and that probably means major security.

A kid in a branded polo shirt approaches on a golf cart as they climb out of Johnny's car. Having checked the weather forecast, Penny has swapped the tweed jacket and skirt combo for a linen suit, but she still looks like she stepped out of the 1950s. Still smells like it too, some perfume he's convinced they stopped making decades ago.

'Do you require a lift, ma'am?' he asks.

'No thank you, young man,' Penny answers. 'It would be a sin not to enjoy the walk on such a beautiful morning.'

The kid beams at her accent and her manner. He maybe even figures her for royalty, Johnny thinks, until he remembers that the kid saw her getting out of his Cobra.

She gawps at the electronic signage bolted onto the exterior of the main building. It's like a corporate pissing contest, the logo of Pierpont Digital probably visible from Santa Barbara. As they get closer, it's clear that there's just as much signage inside.

Johnny is bracing himself for noise as they come through the automatic glass doors, but it's quiet in the high-ceilinged lobby. He quickly grasps that this is because it's just a vestibule. Everything is happening someplace beyond here: on the other side of several doors manned by greeters scanning codes, as well as security personnel with earpieces and sidearms.

'How are we going to get into this thing?' Penny asks.

Johnny doesn't have a plan. Yet. But whatever he comes up with, it can't go worse than back at Marina del Rey. At least this time he's definitely in the right place.

'I need you to understand that this is my world we're in now,' he tells her. 'There's rentacops, people checking passes, state-of-the-art digital security.'

'Yes, I can see that. Hence my question. Does your being an LAPD officer help us here?'

'Not up the coast. And not while I'm under suspension. So I need you to understand that we might have to break a few rules. This could involve theft, fraud, trespass or all three. But the point is, we're not gonna get anywhere with tea and cake and polite inquiries. We'll scope out the access to whatever parts of the hotel aren't restricted, then maybe take a walk outside and see how well the emergency exits are guarded.'

'Hmm,' Penny says, in a way Johnny doesn't like.

She strides off towards the main orientation desk, which is sited beneath a huge banner bearing the Electronicon logo and the legend *Story drives the experience. Experience drives the story.*

The desk has only two staff on it right now, though there are laptops and seats for nine. Johnny figures most people registered yesterday or earlier this morning, hence the lobby being so quiet. A smartly dressed young woman with a headset and an iPad perks up at the sight of someone approaching, though it's possible she's anticipating telling Penny she's in the wrong place, as she looks even less like a tech-industry player than Johnny.

'Good morning and welcome to Electronicon Thirty. I'm Tanya. Do you need help with registration?'

'Mm, possibly,' says Penny. 'My name is Penelope Coyne. I have come all the way from Scotland to speak to someone by the name of Wesley Oswald, so if you could let him know I've arrived, I would be most grateful.'

Johnny has to hide his disdain at the lameness of this doomed sincerity so that Tanya doesn't clock it. Tanya's busy trying not to sound too surprised at who Penny just asked to speak to.

'Wesley Os— Okay, well, first of all let's get your accreditation sorted out.'

Maybe her plan is to get the girl to open up the accreditation system then pull some kind of distraction, but he doesn't see that as a Penny kind of move.

'What did you say your name was again?'

'Penelope Coyne. C. O. Y. N. E.'

'And who do you work for?'

'I am retired. But my background is in literature. St Andrews University. I believe Mr Oswald went there too. That is perhaps why he would be interested in speaking to me.'

Tanya frowns, looking flustered. 'I'm sorry, I don't appear to have a listing for you.'

'No need to apologise,' Penny says warmly. 'I'm sure it's nobody's fault. I wasn't sure if it was being organised through

279

Electronicon or through Mr Oswald's company, and that's how things slip through the cracks. This is my assistant, Jonathan Hawke. He is an expert in both crime and fiction.'

Burn, Johnny thinks, though he'd be feeling more magnanimous if he could see how this shit might get them anywhere.

'We're both feeling rather jetlagged,' Penny tells her. 'And as I say, we have travelled a long way, so if you could get to the bottom of it quickly, we would be much obliged.'

'Why don't you take a seat and let me look into this,' Tanya replies, gesturing towards a couple of sofas just beyond the desks. 'Can we get you something while you wait?'

'Yes, I'd love some tea.'

Johnny says nothing. He's still trying to work out Penny's angle.

Tanya signals to the other staffer. 'Josie, can you get Ms Coyne and her assistant some tea?'

Tanya walks away to another part of the lobby so that they can't hear whatever she's saying into her headset, while Josie disappears off in search of the refreshments. Johnny notes that the desk is now unmanned. So that *was* the plan.

'Well played,' he says quietly.

'What?'

'Let me know when she's coming back. I'll see if I can print off some credentials.'

'You'll do nothing of the sort,' Penny tells him, in a tone he ain't got the stones to defy.

There isn't the time anyway. Johnny can see someone coming out of the elevators and walking towards Tanya, who glances back, indicating Penny and Johnny. It's another smartly dressed young woman, but from Tanya's deferential manner, he can tell she has weight here.

Tanya escorts her to where they are sitting.

'I'm Audrey Ireland. I'm Wesley's personal assistant. I'm afraid I don't have a record of an appointment, but Wesley says he would be thrilled to speak with someone from his alma mater. You're from the University of St Andrews, right?'

'That's what it says on my certificates,' Penny replies with a chuckle. 'Is Wesley available just now?'

'I'm afraid he's not free at the moment. I'll let you know as soon as he has a window. In the meantime, Tanya here can take a couple of quick headshots and issue your accreditation, so you can both explore Electronicon to your hearts' content.'

'That is most obliging of you.'

'I'm here to serve.'

Johnny gets a shudder when she says this, a flashback to Ibanez saying the same thing. He thinks about the funeral he's not welcome to attend. It stings, but he's got another way to pay his respects, and he's doing it right now.

Tanya grabs her iPad and snaps first Penny then Johnny. She then heads over to the desk, returning a minute later to hand them laminated passes bearing their names and photos.

'You can attend any session with these,' Tanya says. 'It's pretty much access all areas.'

'Is there a meal plan?' Johnny asks.

'Don't push it,' Penny mutters.

Just then Josie arrives bearing a tray, which she places before them on a low table. There is a teapot, two cups and a selection of patisserie.

Penny thanks her then turns to Johnny.

'See? Tea and cakes, and a polite inquiry.'

The Silence Forever Echoes

Chapter Two

Johnny can't believe Wesley's PA rolled out the red carpet just because Penny implied she works at Oswald's old university. He's wary that this is too good to be true, that there's a danger here he's missing, but maybe he's just sore because Penny's play worked better than anything he might have come up with. He's not looking a gift horse in the mouth, though.

Their passes are scanned and they go through a quadruple set of doors into a broad corridor, from which they emerge onto a gallery overlooking the main exhibition hall one floor below. It's like a cross between a village and an airport. There are exhibitor stands the size of houses, each probably pulling more power from the grid than Johnny's apartment building. Look like they cost more to construct too.

On the mezzanine floor where he and Penny are standing, there are colour-coded signs indicating lecture theatres, seminars, break-out rooms and meeting suites.

For something called Electronicon, Johnny is surprised to find himself surrounded by books. It's not merely the scrolling digital displays of covers, the animations of illustrated pages, but physical books too, lining wall space and sitting in dump-bins, evidently free to take. Johnny doesn't read too much into it. He figures if the theme was sports, there would be baseballs and team jerseys.

One of the screens close by changes from the cover of *The Hobbit* to showing someone holding the book, a middle-aged man with short grey hair and a *Doom* t-shirt. Looks like one of those coder geeks who doesn't go into the big room with the yellow light very often.

'When I got my first ZX Spectrum I wanted to play games,' he says. He speaks in a weird accent, part of which Johnny can now identify as Scottish, the rest American. 'Back in the eighties, those little cassettes in their boxes were treasured objects. I was excited just to hold them. I felt about them the same way I felt about books: they were things that could transport me. In fact, on the high street, the places you bought them primarily sold books and magazines. I quickly understood that this technology was actually a new way to experience narrative, to be immersed in stories.'

As he finishes speaking, the image freezes on a flattering frame, and a caption appears: *Wesley Oswald, founder of Sea Monster Software.*

'We can discount the notion that he is Miles Deacon's new alias,' Penny says.

'Not unless he's some kind of genius with latex and make-up,' Johnny agrees. 'That guy's gotta be twenty years too old.'

They walk part of the way around the gallery until they reach a helpdesk, staffed by a peppy adolescent in an Electronicon-branded polo shirt.

'Hey, can you tell me, is there a Miles Deacon registered as a participant?' Johnny asks.

'Let me just check that for you,' the kid says, sounding grateful for something to do. He checks his iPad and it takes about two seconds for him to report back in the negative.

'What about Crawford Nicholson?'

Another eager tap at the iPad.

'No, sir. Nobody of that name either. But all the delegates and their contact details are in the E30 app. You can download it here,' he adds, presenting a QR code on his iPad.

Johnny scans it. While he has his phone out, he pulls up the headshot of Nicholson. 'Does this guy look familiar to you? You seen him around?'

Kid takes a look. No bells are rung.

'No, sir, but you will find everybody's profiles, pictures and pronouns in the app. We ask that you send meeting requests and coordinate your convention diaries through it too, so that we can help facilitate anything you might need.'

Johnny watches the E30 app open with an animated splash-screen. He looks up Sea Monster and cross-references the recipients of the memo he found in Edinburgh. Including Wesley, four of them are listed as attendees. Johnny notes the names and scrutinises the headshots, committing certain features to memory. It's an industry showcase, not a public exhibition, so though he'll be looking for faces in the crowd, the crowd isn't gonna be in the thousands.

He then looks up Pierpont Digital, which appears to be a family affair. The principal attendees are listed as Lawrence Pierpont, Saskia Pierpont, Caleb Pierpont, Zoe Pierpont and Tony Grant. The video-games biz is not Johnny's wheelhouse, but from what he's reading on the app, Pierpont is an industry behemoth. That said, it appears Sea Monster ain't exactly a scrappy little start-up either. That video he just saw framed Wesley Oswald with something close to religious reverence.

'I reckon the LAPD should consider something like this,' he tells Penny, as they continue to walk the gallery. 'A digital directory of scumbags you can instantly message. "Yeah, I'd like to talk to you about your parole violation and multiple witness accounts of you being involved in a convenience-store robbery last night. Can we jump on a Zoom call, or is there maybe someplace we can meet up and exchange gunfire?"'

They're passing one of the hotel's six restaurants. Johnny takes a look at the menu to check the prices, gauge how damaging lunch here is gonna be. Glancing inside, he's pulled up by the sight of one particular diner, eating alone in a booth. He's pretty sure it's one of the Sea Monster faces.

Johnny pulls up the E30 app and checks the image, shows it to Penny.

'Can't always tell from a thumbnail, but does that look like this guy?'

She has a look. 'Quite definitely.'

'Okay, I'm gonna brace him, but I think I'd best do it alone.'

Penny looks at the phone again. Nods her agreement. 'As long as you do it politely.'

'Is lying polite? Because I saw how you operated back there and now I'm a little fuzzy on your rules.'

'How dare you. I said absolutely nothing untrue. It's not my fault if Tanya and Audrey wrongly inferred certain things.'

Johnny is playing back the discussion in his head. Realises she's right: she was subtly disingenuous but she never flat-out lied.

'Gotta be quite the tightrope you walk so you can keep telling yourself you're on the side of the angels.'

'The truth is seldom a hard line to stay the right side of,' she replies. 'I'm off to explore, as Audrey suggested.'

'And I'mma see if I can't find out more about Wesley Oswald and why Miles Deacon might be throwing him a suicide.'

'Best of luck. Try not to get us thrown out.'

The Silence Forever Echoes

Chapter Three

As Johnny walks into the restaurant, he glances down at the lanyard Tanya gave him and notices he's named as 'Jonathan Hock'. He figures it's maybe not a bad thing. He doesn't imagine he's gonna run into anyone around here who might be familiar with his name, but you never know.

Vikram Chaudhuri is sitting at a booth on his own, working on a laptop. There are two phones sitting on the table along with a plate of salad and some horrific-looking green smoothie. Johnny doesn't reckon he's gonna be able to pull the same shit he did with Alan Brooks. 'Hey, dude, remember me? We got wasted together. No, of course you don't remember – we were too wasted.' These goddamn tech types with their healthy lifestyles. Fuckers seriously thought they were gonna live to be two hundred, or long enough until the tech would let them replace all their organic materials and push on for eternity. At least in Hollywood they only got abstemious out of shallow narcissism. It had been reassuring to encounter book-industry people and find a tribe who still had weaknesses he could relate to. But

Johnny knows tech guys have their own vices. He's never met one who isn't addicted to information, and Johnny is holding.

He approaches the table and the guy looks up.

'Hey, Vikram. You probably don't remember me.'

'No, I don't, mate,' he says frostily. It's not a local accent. Johnny figures him for Australian. He looks at Johnny's laminate. It says University of St Andrews, which puts him in a certain context. Fortunately it doesn't say anything about crime or literature.

'Look, ordinarily I wouldn't buttonhole you like this but I'd like to talk to you about security.'

'All meetings have to be scheduled through the E30 app,' Vikram says dismissively. 'And sorry, but I'm slammed from soup to nuts.'

'Could you find a window if I said that it was to do with the Pierpont proposal to buy out Sea Monster?'

The offhand demeanour drops rapidly.

'How the fuck do you know about that?'

'I've seen the memo. That's why we oughtta talk.'

Vikram's eyes bulge. It's like Johnny just told him he's seen the guy's sex tape.

Johnny slides into the seat opposite without being asked. Vikram's anxious expression is invitation enough.

'Seriously, mate, how did you get that memo? Because you could be looking at jail time for being in unauthorised possession of that info.'

'It's not my possession of it that should be worrying you. It's who I got it from.'

That's got him even more edgy.

'Who did you get it from?'

'How about you answer some of my questions first.'

'No, you're talking about a proposed takeover only a handful of people are supposed to know about. If I'm caught blabbing, it could be a matter for the Securities and Exchange Commission.'

'Good thing I'm real discreet. But what's got me intrigued is that Sea Monster's turnover last year was $140 million. Pierpont are tabling almost four *bill*. It wouldn't be telling tales out of school to acknowledge the bid's surprisingly high.'

Vikram considers this. 'That's not a purchase price. It's mostly for investment in R&D.'

'Primarily for a project called Diegesis, yeah. I've read the memo, remember. Everybody's very excited about it, and Pierpont Digital clearly thinks it's a game-changer.'

'If you've read the memo, what else do you need to know?'

'Which way the wind's blowing.'

'Piss off,' Vikram says, getting indignant. 'You're asking for market-sensitive information.'

'Don't get your panties all in a bunch. My interest ain't to do with anything that's gonna sic the SEC on our asses.'

'What *is* your interest? I don't do one-way transactions, mate. Who'd you get the memo from? Are you a private investigator?' Vikram looks again at Johnny's lanyard. 'Because I'm not buying that you're any kind of academic.'

Johnny takes a beat, makes a calculation. Vikram's made it clear he doesn't want to be on the wrong side of the law.

'Correct, I'm not an academic. I'm a cop working two homicides and I think there might be a material threat to Wesley Oswald.'

Vikram stiffens momentarily. He wasn't expecting to hear that, and yet evidently it wasn't totally outlandish.

'So did somebody leak you the memo?' he asks.

Johnny ignores the question, keeping Vikram jonesing for his info hit.

289

'I need to know, is the deal likely to happen? Does everybody like the numbers?'

Vikram takes a sip of his horrible green drink. Looks back and forth like he's afraid somebody's listening in.

'Bloody oath,' he says quietly. 'Everybody likes the numbers. But that's not the issue. The sticking point is that Wesley doesn't wanna sell, at any price. He's on his own, though. He founded the company, but he doesn't have a controlling interest any more, and the rest of us are keen to accept. As well as the colossal moolah, selling to Pierpont gives us the opportunity to wrestle his hands off the helm. He's a genius but he can be a drongo too.'

'A what?'

'You never know where his head'll be at any given moment. He acts like he's still running a start-up from his garage sometimes. Like that bloody court case: it's typical he was diverting bandwidth elsewhere right when we're on the cusp of something huge.'

'What court case?'

'I don't know the details. Some contested power-of-attorney thing over a relly. End-of-life care and such. There's talk he hired a private investigator, which is why I thought it might be you.'

Johnny leans forward, drops his voice too.

'Real talk. If the board is against Wesley, the sale is a shoo-in?'

Vikram makes an awkward face, like his drink is giving him gas.

'It's not a slam dunk. Wesley can't stop the sale without convincing some more of us to say no, but I wouldn't entirely rule that out. Wesley still has heaps of clout. If he can convince the board that they might get similar investment with a partner more to his liking, they could still turn Pierpont down. Which, if you ask me, would be a mistake. This is a very big bird in the hand.'

'That being the case, wouldn't it remove all potential obstacles if someone took Wesley out?'

Vikram almost laughs. 'Yeah, mate, it would remove all obstacles while also removing the main thing that makes Sea Monster worth buying.'

'I get you,' Johnny says. 'I guess you can tell this ain't my regular turf.'

'I'm just saying, if you're chasing a threat, I wouldn't make any assumptions regarding which direction the threat is coming from.'

'What do you mean?'

'I mean Wesley Oswald built his fortune constructing mind-bending games, and he's playing the biggest one of his life right now to keep control of his company.'

As Johnny processes this, Vikram takes a forkful of beans and washes them down with the last of his liquefied lawn. He sits back in his seat and looks Johnny in the eye.

'Now, I think I've been pretty forthcoming, Mr Hock. You gonna front up your end now?'

'Sure,' Johnny says. 'Does the name Crawford Nicholson mean anything to you?'

'No.'

'What about Miles Deacon?'

'Also no.'

'They're both aliases of the same guy. He was in possession of your discussion memo. How he got it, I don't know. But how about if either of us finds out, we hit the other up.'

Vikram thinks about it. Johnny hasn't given him much, but

291

the involvement of police has the guy intrigued, sniffing something he might be able to use.

'No worries, mate.'

'One last question. Why doesn't Wesley want to sell?'

Vikram's brow twitches. 'It's not that he doesn't want to sell. He just doesn't want to sell to Pierpont.'

'Why not?'

Vikram looks incredulous, almost amused. 'He's *kind* of got a *little* history there.'

The sarcastic double emphasis is lost on Johnny.

'What history does he have that he's not prepared to make it water under the bridge for four billion dollars?'

'Seriously? You really don't know?'

'Like I said, this ain't my regular turf. I'd never heard of Wesley Oswald two days ago.'

So Vikram tells him.

'Holly golly,' Johnny says.

Death Is But the Overture

I

Penny descended a Perspex staircase, perhaps intended to give the illusion of walking on air but rather giving the impression of walking on other people's suspended dusty footprints. It took her down onto the main concourse, all of which seemed so much larger and more intimidating than it had from above.

The application on her phone included a map tracking her location and helpfully identifying all of the stalls and exhibits around her. It proved particularly useful in that Sea Monster's logo had been clearly visible from the mezzanine, but down here it was lost among the far larger installations of, she presumed, far larger companies. She navigated her way there, feeling somewhat assailed by the animated imagery on all sides. She had never played a video game, seeing little need while there were still books to transport her into more vivid alternate realms.

As she approached the Sea Monster stand, she saw Audrey Ireland chatting to a trio of businesswomen. She appeared to conclude her discussion with them as she noticed Penny approach, then strode across to greet her. She was struck by the level of attention this woman was extending. One would have thought Penny was some kind of VIP. She just hoped Audrey hadn't cut her previous conversation short. Deference was one thing, but Penny considered pecking orders discourteous.

'Ms Coyne, I'm glad to see you've found us. I'm afraid I have no word on Wesley's availability yet.'

'That's quite all right. I was hoping to find out a little more about him and his company, though.'

Audrey beamed. 'Step right this way.'

She led Penny to a cube-like enclosure, a white-walled space that was striking in its blank emptiness in an environment otherwise hyperactively overstuffed with visual information. Audrey lifted a headset and a pair of gloves from an inset in one of the walls.

'I can only give you the Cliffs Notes. In here you'll find the complete works.'

'I'm really not so sure about this,' Penny told her, tentatively pulling on the gloves. 'I've never been in a virtual-reality thingy. I've heard it can make you ill.'

'You'll be amazed how quickly you get used to it,' Audrey assured her, gently lowering the device onto Penny's head. 'You can forget you're not in a real place. Just don't stray beyond the visual boundaries or you'll walk into a wall.'

Strangely, once the headset was affixed, it was as though she had donned a transparent visor. Penny was looking at the same space, at Audrey standing before her. Then her surroundings dissolved into shimmering dust, which reassembled into somewhere altogether different yet entirely familiar.

The Tay Bridge was to her right, the V&A to her left. She was looking south towards Fife. She had come all the way to California merely to find herself in a digital Dundee.

A gentleman was walking towards her, one she recognised from a video screen she had seen earlier. He was dressed more like the tea boy than the head of a company.

'I'm Wesley Oswald,' he said, smiling but awkward in his manner.

'Pleased to meet you,' she replied. Then she felt rather embarrassed to realise that this was a recording and not some virtual conference technology.

'This was where it all started for me,' he said. 'Where it all started for a whole industry, you could say.'

The background reassembled itself again. Penny was still in Dundee, but now a black-and-white one, outside the old Timex factory.

'This is where Sir Clive Sinclair built his ZX series of home computers. But maybe I should let a friend take it from here.'

Wesley vanished and Penny's surroundings transformed again. She found herself in a cartoonish environment, where a pixelated purple creature appeared before her. It resembled a child's drawing come to life: a box-like head with arms emerging from each side and feet extending from below.

'I'm Qubo,' it said cheerfully, in a saccharine male American accent. 'I made my first appearance in 1985 in *Qubo's Quest*, which Wesley Oswald wrote and published himself at the age of just fourteen.'

A gilded picture frame then appeared, the image inside showing a teenage Wesley inside a garage. He was sitting behind a desk upon which sat a huge stack of cassette cases. The picture was life-size, large enough for Penny to recognise Qubo on the covers.

'Wesley started selling *Qubo's Quest* by mail order through computer magazines. I first dropped through people's doors in the form of an audio cassette in a run of just five hundred units. Now the Qubo titles have sold upwards of ninety million copies, and these days you don't need to wait two weeks for the postman to deliver them.'

Penny removed the headset and was relieved to see Audrey still standing nearby.

'Is there a way to fast-forward this thing? I've had quite enough of Qubo.'

Audrey laughed. 'That's just the Sea Monster welcome package you're viewing. If you click your fingers you can pull up the menu and access materials on every company here.'

Penny put the headset back on and clicked her fingers. It felt awkward in the gloves, but prompted a resounding snap in her ears as an index manifested before her eyes. She scrolled through it, experiencing a feeling of contact in the glove though she knew she wasn't touching anything. It was surprising at first, but as Audrey suggested, she quickly became accustomed to it. In fact, though it was a technologically impressive illusion, Penny felt that the more it tried to fabricate a tangible reality, the more it emphasised its falseness.

She tapped the name 'Sea Monster', causing several branches to extend from the panel, each listing sub-topics: from the welcome package she had just paused, to 'About Us', 'Our History', 'People', and 'Our Games'.

She quickly ascertained that Wesley Oswald had been the prototypical 1980s computer whizz-kid; brilliant but reclusive, and clearly a control freak, though this was euphemistically described as 'fiercely independent'.

It was put less euphemistically in a *Wired* magazine profile that popped out at the prompting of Penny's finger, a pull-quote catching her eye: 'Sea Monster would be among the biggest names in the industry if Wesley wasn't so afraid to loosen his grip. What should have been a major company has remained a kind of permanent super-indie instead.'

Penny noted that the source of these candid words was Caleb Pierpont, head of marketing at the company currently proposing to buy Sea Monster. She couldn't tell if his sentiment conveyed a note of concerned regret or sour grapes, but she didn't have the time to discern further.

Penny returned to the main index, where scrolling down she noticed that one of the topics was 'Seahorse Neuroscience', which seemed incongruous against all this fiction and frivolity. Tapping it, she read that as Wesley's company grew, he had channelled much of his personal fortune into neuroscientific research. 'His interest in the field followed the death of his semi-identical twin sister, Juliet, who had been a gifted neurosurgeon.'

Penny felt an unexpected surge of emotion, then it faded.

Wincing at the pseudo-sensation of the haptic feedback, she typed the name Juliet Oswald into the index's search field. It brought up only two results. One was a link to the *Wired* article, and the other stated simply: 'Juliet Oswald Foundation'.

She tapped on the name and was taken to a new environment, a warm and welcoming room, rather like a well-appointed academic study or perhaps a counselling suite. A woman in a smart trouser suit welcomed her to the Juliet Oswald Foundation, explaining that its purpose was to raise awareness of mental-health issues, to encourage greater openness in people's everyday discussion of their emotions, and to offer support to those bereaved after suicide.

A sub-menu appeared, offering several categories for further information. The one at the bottom was 'Trustees and Benefactors'. Penny tapped it. At the head of the list was its founder, who to her surprise was not Wesley Oswald, but Caleb Pierpont.

Something started to eat at her. Something cold. Something impossible. Frantically, Penny found her way back to the *Wired* profile that had quoted Caleb. It opened before her, floating in the air of the study.

Wesley first met Caleb when they were both students at St Andrews University in Scotland. Caleb and his older sister, Saskia, were sent there by their father, Lawrence, a man more interested in the town's golfing history than its academic credentials. Wesley and Caleb bonded not only over their love of playing video games, but of creating them. Even as an undergrad, Wesley was already something of a legend, having published several of his own self-coded *Qubo* games. But Caleb caught Wesley's attention too, showing him the project that he was working on each night in his dorm room: the medieval combat game we now all know as *Last Knight*.

This meeting of minds was to change the direction of the company Lawrence Pierpont had inherited from his own father. Primarily a manufacturer of two-way radios, Pierpont Electronics was struggling after enjoying a short-lived uptick during the late-seventies CB craze. Caleb convinced Lawrence to make a tentative move into publishing computer software, and thus began its journey to becoming an industry titan.

Having remained friends as they each forged their own paths through the burgeoning nineties video-game landscape, it looked like Caleb and Wesley would formally combine forces in 2002, with Caleb helping to broker a deal for Pierpont Digital to buy Sea Monster. Around this time, Caleb was also forging a growing bond with Wesley's twin sister, Juliet, with the couple setting a date to get married.

Penny felt herself stiffen, her insides turning to ice as she read on, somehow already knowing what the words would say.

Then tragedy struck, in a manner neither of them could have anticipated. Juliet, who was believed to have been concealing mental-health problems, slipped away from wedding preparations at the Pierpont family estate on the California coast. She was found dead on rocks beneath the property's century-old lighthouse, where staff had to break the door down to gain entry following a desperate, hours-long search. It is believed she threw herself from the gallery deck.

Reeling, Penny began walking towards one of the sofas in the study, then a flashing boundary reminded her of where she really was. She took off the headset and placed a hand on the wall to steady herself.

She had found another death by suicide that fitted the model, but it was one that had happened more than two decades ago.

The Silence Forever Echoes

Chapter Four

'I've been a detective more than twenty years,' Johnny says. 'Built cases from evidence and rational thinking all my career. But you can't be telling me there's nothing weird going on with this.'

They are down on the concourse, following signs for the Gripp Auditorium, where Pierpont Digital are doing their big expo presentation. The session is entitled 'Old Stories About the Future'. The signs are redundant in this instance, as it looks like everybody is headed to the same place, so they can just follow the crowd.

'In *The Sign of the Four*,' Penny replies, 'Sherlock Holmes says that when you have eliminated the impossible, whatever remains, however improbable, must be the truth.'

'Yeah, and Dirk Gently said he preferred not to eliminate the impossible. I'm starting to see why.'

'You've read Douglas Adams?'

'I'm trying to work out whether your tone of incredulity is at me having read that particular writer or having read a book period.'

He notices that she doesn't clarify.

'I would warn you again to be wary of strange coincidences,' she says. 'Furthermore, even when a coincidence is not a coincidence, make no assumptions in what you infer from it. Is history repeating itself or is someone taking inspiration from history and recreating it? If so, to what purpose? If Miles Deacon has taken his inspiration from events twenty years ago, we need to find out why and we need to find out more about those events.'

Johnny searches 'Juliet Oswald death' as they approach the auditorium, filtering the results to show the oldest first, looking for first-hand or at least contemporary accounts. It's slim pickings. The only result is from the website of a local newspaper, a page archived from more than two decades back. The website looks weirdly lo-fi, light on images, with some elements not loading at all.

'"Sheriff's Office says no suspicious circumstances",' Johnny reads aloud. '"Pierpont's fiancée suffered from mental-health problems. Family asking for privacy." Nothing we didn't already know.'

'There are no other articles?'

The more recent results are all related to Wesley and Caleb, predominantly the latter, as he has been vocal about it in public. Wesley, it appears, doesn't give interviews.

'Not from back then,' he tells her, keeping his voice low, conscious that they are within earshot of other delegates. 'The Pierponts were rich and getting richer, but at that time not rich enough for it to be a story beyond their own backyard. And suicide ain't never much of a story unless it's someone famous.'

The theatre is filling rapidly, though it looks way too big for the numbers likely to show up. Everyone attending the expo could fit in here at least twice over.

The stage is dominated by a bank of interlinked monitors suspended from a rig, with multiple screens flanking the hall.

He notices nobody is scanning passes or checking names. Clearly they reckon if you got this far, you're supposed to be here. There are security personnel, though: incognito but visible to those who know what they're looking for. Because despite what was said about their passes, there's no such thing as access all areas. There are always restrictions, whether that's spaces you can't go into or people you can't approach. And in Johnny's experience, those are often where the answers lie.

Johnny and Penny take their seats, leaving a gap between them and the next people in the row. Two men sidle in and sit down directly behind them, each clutching an oversize cup of take-out coffee, both chuckling about something. Johnny's mind goes back to the pandemic, the weird sense of defensiveness whenever anybody sat closer than he felt they ought.

The lights go down and there is a video ident on all the screens. It looks expensively understated, like it's Pierpont Digital telling the industry they can afford to spend a shit-ton of money just to emphasise that they don't need to be flash.

Then a woman takes the stage, identified on-screen as 'Saskia Pierpont, Head of Product Development'. She is in her fifties, tall and immaculately presented in a suit that looks bespoke. Between that and her title, Johnny reckons she ought to be an imposing presence, but there's something shy and under-confident about her.

She thanks everybody for coming, runs through all the usual platitudes. Her tone is not so much like she's reading from an autocue as from a card being held up by her captors.

'On behalf of the board, and on behalf of my family, I'd first like to acknowledge an absence. My father, Lawrence Pierpont,

302

will not be joining us on-stage today. He still holds the title of company president, but his doctors have convinced him to scale back his commitments. Any of you who know him will understand how compelling those doctors must have been, because he has always had a hands-on approach, even in the early days of navigating a new industry he didn't quite trust or understand.'

Johnny hears one of the guys in the row behind mutter to his buddy under his breath, 'A hands-on approach. Yeah, just ask the women he paid off.'

Penny hears it too. They trade a look.

Saskia moves on to introducing a video, a large-scale affair showcasing their big releases over the next twelve months. It's bright and noisy, but still aimed more at impressing industry peers than selling the product to consumers.

Saskia looks more relaxed as soon as it finishes, and Johnny figures this is because she knows her ordeal is almost over. Her final task is to introduce her brother, and it's the one time she looks genuinely happy to be there.

Caleb Pierpont walks out onto the stage and Johnny can feel the room light up. At first he thought Saskia was gazing adoringly at him because he was her brother, or just her relief, but Johnny notices that most people in the room are looking at him the same way.

Caleb is a middle-aged guy in chinos and a grey t-shirt; average height, passably handsome, albeit with evidence of work done. You wouldn't look twice at him if he passed by on the street, but in here he's clearly a god.

Charisma is a hard thing to define. It's not even that you know it when you see it: you need to *feel* it. Johnny never got the Steve Jobs thing. He had seen plenty of clips and just saw a businessman in a turtleneck instead of a shirt and tie. But as he sits in that auditorium, he understands: it's different when you're in the room. Even the cynical-sounding guys in the row behind sit upright, eyes brightly focused like they're afraid they might miss something.

Caleb waits for the applause to die down then walks to the front of the stage, ignoring the podium Saskia had been hiding behind. He's got this little chain around his neck, something Penny had read about in the profiles. When they were engaged, Caleb and Juliet both got these pendants made containing a few drops of each other's blood. The guy still wears his every day. Says it brings him comfort. Johnny finds it creepy, but whatever gets you through.

'Hey, everybody,' Caleb says. 'Thanks for coming, and I hope you enjoyed Saskia's video about what great shape we're in and what we've got coming down the pipe. Those new games – *Sacred Reign VR, Starfire Episode Seven, Neon City Revolution* – they're as good as it gets. Am I right?'

There is more applause.

'Of course I'm right, and that's the challenge we're facing. These games *are* as good as it gets, because the technology has plateaued and we're all reaching the limits of what we can do with it. Who remembers first playing *Doom*, or seeing what could be done with dedicated graphics chips? How that made you feel, the possibilities it opened up? Now we're spending millions just to make a character's hair move more realistically. The days of huge leaps are twenty years behind us. I mean, for a while there we all got excited about VR. But do you know what's wrong with it?'

There is a pause while people figure whether this is a rhetorical question Caleb is about to answer for himself. The audience seems kind of intimidated, but somebody calls out, 'Motion sickness.'

Caleb nods, in tune with general assent in the room.

'Can't see your feet,' calls out someone else, prompting laughter from the crowd and a smile from Caleb, but he clearly hasn't heard the answer he's looking for.

To Johnny's astonishment, Penny puts her hand up.

'Yes, ma'am,' Caleb prompts.

Suddenly Penny's face is on the screens, picked out by cameras Johnny can't see. More than that, she is captioned with her name and 'University of St Andrews'. So maybe he was wrong about not being scanned. Evidently there were subtler, if creepier ways of doing it.

'It's just a toy,' says Penny. 'A high-tech zoetrope, the latest heir to the magic lantern.'

There are murmurings of displeasure, like she cursed in their church. Caleb is scrutinising her though, a mercurial expression on his face.

'And what's wrong with that?' he asks.

'Nothing. It makes you feel like you're somewhere else, which is charming, but it's a mere spectacle. Virtual reality changes where you feel you are. But I prefer novels, because when you're truly immersed in a story, that can change *who* you feel you are.'

'Wow,' says Caleb. 'Penelope Coyne, everybody, from the University of St Andrews. My and Saskia's alma mater.'

He makes a gesture to an assistant, who gives him a thumbs-up acknowledgement. Some unspoken transaction between them.

'She's absolutely right,' Caleb tells the room. 'My old friend Wesley Oswald first created narrative adventures on a 16K ZX Spectrum. Even back in the eighties, he understood that while everyone was getting excited about computer graphics, it was the player's imagination that truly created the worlds they would inhabit.'

305

Caleb taps his head.

'The processor we need to be building the next generation of games for is in here. Which is why we need to think differently. The brain creates a model of our environment based on the data it receives. We might call it a picture, because it uses information from our eyes to construct that model. But think of creatures with poor vision and super-acute hearing, or super-acute smell. We imagine those animals seeing only a blurry fog and we can't relate to how they navigate their environment. But the model of the world created by their brains might seem similar to ours if we could experience it.'

Caleb raises his hands, almost like a priest.

'I want you all to close your eyes and think of your last vacation,' he says.

Johnny looks around at the near-universal compliance, then complies himself. He's picturing Crathie Hall, but he's not sure if that counts.

'When we close our eyes and dream, when we imagine, when we remember, there are no signals coming from our eyes, and yet we create a vivid world inside our minds. You might say we are picturing it, but it's not a picture. It's a model created by our brain from stored information. If we as game-makers truly want to create realms of the imagination, then we've been going about it the wrong way.'

Johnny's no tech-head, but he can grasp the concept. Then he realises that the concept already has a name.

Diegesis.

In the memo it was clouded in mystery but described as the future of the industry. Pierpont Digital are interested in acquiring Sea Monster entirely because of it, and according to Vikram they are prepared to pump around four billion into research and development. Caleb is already preparing the ground for his pitch before the product is even his to sell. A product that could be years from being viable.

Johnny has to hand it to the guy: Caleb is such a compelling orator that you don't just feel captivated by his enthusiasm, you feel an enthusiasm of your own. But as Caleb continues talking, it's Alan Brooks's voice he hears, and it sends a chill right through him.

If Sebastian believes in something, you'll be believing in it too after talking to him for half an hour.

The brightest talent. The golden child. Sebastian Gossard. Caleb Pierpont. Blake Astor.

Next he recalls Lucy talking about her big sister.

Dad knows she's not leader material, but she's the one being groomed to take over, because he can control her.

The first-born. The reluctant anointed. Monica Stonebridge. Saskia Pierpont. Tom Lennox.

A hands-on approach. Yeah, just ask the women he paid off.

The head of the family: powerful, manipulative and hiding a scandal. Jonathan Stonebridge. Lawrence Pierpont. Johnny hasn't heard about any impropriety involving Dominique King, but she sure went out of her way to stop him sniffing around.

It all lines up, no matter what Penny says. If Stonebridge Publishing is the book and Kingdom Pictures is the gender-flipped movie version, then Pierpont Enterprises is the video game.

But it's all the same story.

Death Is But the Overture

II

Penny had been given the impression that the Pierpont Digital garden party was *the* social highlight of the expo, but as she took her first look around, she felt like she had stepped into a theme park. All about the grounds there were people dressed in outsize and elaborate character costumes, but though she might have recognised Mickey Mouse or Donald Duck, or even Asterix the Gaul, the only one of these brightly coloured figures that meant anything to her was that wretched Qubo creature.

Mercifully, the gathering being outside, there was considerably less in the way of glaring and attention-guzzling video screens. She and Johnny were standing among immaculately tended lawns overlooking the adjacent marina. It was late afternoon, but still hot and sunny enough that most people were convening beneath the central pergola or seeking the shade of various gazebos and enclosures.

She could see Caleb across an expanse of lawn, seated beneath a canopy on the side closest to the ocean. He was surrounded by a small host in a state of rapt attention. Saskia was standing at his side, though her focus was more on her phone than on her brother or his courtiers. Nonetheless there seemed something vigilant about her presence.

'How are you finding everything?' said a voice, quite startling Penny from her scrutiny of the distant scene. She wondered whether her staring had been conspicuous. She turned to find Audrey Ireland standing beside her. She was smiling warmly, though her earpiece was a reminder that Penny and Johnny were unlikely to have her full attention. There was something effortless and graceful about Audrey's solicitude that briefly made Penny think of Ms Innis, a warming thought that instantly curdled into a darker memory. Would Penny ever again be able to picture her without that?

'We're finding everything except your boss,' said Johnny.

'Yes, my apologies. I won't lie, I'm afraid Wesley has been and gone again. There's a lot happening at the moment.'

'Yeah, I can imagine. I gather there's been a court case taking up his attention. What's that about?'

'I'm afraid I can't say. Wesley's private affairs are not really my remit, or my business.'

Audrey's tone was breezy, but there was a firmness behind it, and Penny inferred that she strongly wished them to understand it was not their business either.

'Of course,' Johnny replied. 'But workwise, I'm guessing he's crazy busy with Diegesis.'

Earpiece or not, Penny was now sure that they *did* have Audrey's full attention. She stiffened, her smile faltering.

'How do you know about that?'

'An occasion such as this is a ferment of gossip,' Penny replied. 'We're hearing it's some new technology that's going to revolutionise the industry. What can you tell us about it?'

'Not a great deal, but sharing what little I do know might be enough to get me fired.'

'Diegesis is what Caleb was alluding to during his talk, isn't it?' asked Johnny.

Audrey had regained her composure. She glanced towards Caleb, something wry in her expression.

'You'd think that, wouldn't you. Caleb is very skilled at inviting people to fill in the blanks using their own imaginations, something that has always served him well.'

Penny had the sense Audrey had been intentionally indiscreet.

Audrey glanced at her phone. 'Sorry. Incoming,' she said. 'Please excuse me.'

And as suddenly as she had appeared, she was gone.

'She knows as much about that court case as she does about Diegesis,' said Johnny. 'And my money says she knows plenty about Diegesis.'

'Quite. But unfortunately she strikes me as fervently loyal. She appears happy to chat as long as the subject is the wonder of Wesley, but anything else is off-limits.'

Penny and Johnny weren't left standing alone for long. Penny had just accepted a glass of fizz from a passing waiter when they were approached by a petite woman with strikingly polished teeth and huge sunglasses.

'Professor Coyne? It's a pleasure to meet you. I've been despatched to say that my brother would love to talk when you've got a minute.'

Penny was taken aback by being given this unmerited title, and reeled just long enough to decide that there was no good reason to correct it.

'Your brother?'

'Yes, sorry: my name is Zoe Grant, vice president of publicity at Pierpont Digital. I'm Caleb's younger sister.'

She offered her hand warmly to Penny, then rather cursorily to Johnny, who was definitely being regarded as her plus one.

'As you know, he was quite taken with your contribution from the floor, but when he found out you were a professor at St Andrews, he decided he just had to meet you. Honestly, mention that place to him and suddenly it's *Brideshead Revisited*. There's no rush. Just once you guys are settled.'

Penny refrained from raising an eyebrow at the literary reference. It was not what she was expecting from Zoe's appearance and manner, but maybe that was her own prejudices showing. If Johnny had read Douglas Adams, then why couldn't a bubbly Californian have read Evelyn Waugh?

Zoe all but skipped away, light on her feet as befitting someone so dainty. She carried herself in a girlish manner, though she must have been late forties.

Penny turned back to Johnny. He was already staring meaningfully at her, and she knew why.

'Zoe, she said her name was? Weird. I've met her before, except she was twenty years younger and her name was Lucy. The flibbertigibbet youngest sibling.'

Penny made a noncommittal noise, not wishing to engage in a subject that was causing her such unease.

'You're not telling me you don't see it,' Johnny pressed.

'I do see it,' she admitted. 'I just don't know what I can possibly do with it. This is all making me feel quite remote from my natural habitat. Murder, deceit and intractable mystery provoke no qualms, but I am altogether less compatible with the surreal and the scientifically impossible.'

Johnny waved at the scene before them. 'What are you talking about? Soliciting information through conversations with rich people over drinks in salubrious surroundings is *totally* your natural habitat.'

Penny took a sip of her fizz.

'It's a fair point,' she conceded. 'Let's go to work.'

Death Is But the Overture

III

Slaloming between the almost punchably ubiquitous Qubo and some kind of blocky cartoon knight as they crossed a stretch of lawn, Penny noted that even an exclusive corporate gathering could have a *more* exclusive VIP area. Two men in sunglasses and sharp suits were projecting an invisible cordon around a nearby shaded terrace where an older man in deck shorts and an open-necked shirt was holding court.

Standing next to him was a woman undoubtedly younger, but by quite how many years remained indeterminate due to plastic surgery of a quality that Penny guessed must have been more expensive than her jewellery and wardrobe combined.

'Lawrence Pierpont,' said Johnny as they drew closer. 'The patriarch. And his second wife, Viola.'

Penny was proceeding towards Caleb's gazebo when Johnny put a hand on her arm.

'Wait.'

'What?'

'I just wanna put something to the test.'

He indicated a waitress making her way towards the VIP terrace. She was carrying a tray of champagne flutes, presenting them to each of the guests in turn.

'What are we testing?' Penny asked.

'Whether Viola takes a drink.'

Penny was about to inquire as to the relevance of this when she remembered Johnny telling her that Lady Stonebridge was teetotal. He was trying to stand up his theory. She watched the waitress pivot away without offering a glass to Viola, while another member of the waiting staff swooped in to present her with an identical flute containing soda water.

Penny resumed her progress, not wishing to meet Johnny's knowing look. They continued across the lawn, where they encountered the two gentlemen who had been sitting behind them during the presentation. They were hovering conspicuously close to Caleb's gazebo, like devotees at the entrance to the temple.

'Hey, I enjoyed your take,' one of them said, recognising Penny from the presentation.

'Thank you.'

'I'm Jonas. This is Ari. We're with Softwave. You're academics, right?'

'Something like that,' said Johnny.

'Yeah, you and Caleb sure seemed to hit it off,' said Jonas. 'Don't suppose you got any inside skinny on what this new tech is? He's clearly talking about something specific.'

'I was about to ask you the same thing,' Penny replied. 'It sounds very exciting, though.'

'Yeah, I get the sense something big is going down. Caleb seems more animated than usual, and that's starting from a high baseline.'

'What's your take on Saskia as CEO?' asked Johnny. 'I've heard she didn't want it, even though she was Lawrence's preferred choice.'

More testing, Penny realised. Monica Stonebridge was *her* father's preferred choice.

'Yeah, that's no secret,' Jonas replied. 'It's the right role for her, though. She isn't a rock star like Caleb, but you don't need two rock stars. You need a salesman and you need a strategist. Word is there's *nothing* she doesn't know about what's going on inside the company.'

'She's a machine,' said Ari. 'The joke doing the rounds is that if an optimist says a glass is half full and a pessimist that it's half empty, Saskia would say the glass is twice as big as it needs to be. She's an engineer: she sees things in pragmatic terms and she values elegant solutions. Word is she was a bit of a hacker in her youth, and it's no secret she cleaned up Caleb's code back in the early days. Some even say she's the one who really wrote *Last Knight.*'

A passing waiter stopped and offered his tray for Penny's empty champagne glass. She and Johnny took the interruption as an opportunity to extricate themselves and proceeded beneath the gazebo.

Caleb noticed their approach. He interrupted himself mid-flow and muttered something to Saskia, who in turn gestured to the gathered devotees. They obediently dispersed into smaller groups, leaving Penny and Johnny with the two elder Pierpont siblings.

Caleb got up and extended a hand to Penny.

'Professor, thank you for coming.'

'Thank you for the invitation.'

Caleb and Johnny traded nods. Saskia flashed the most cursory of smiles before going back to her phone.

'I can't believe you've come all this way,' Caleb said. 'What brings you to Electronicon?'

Penny considered her answer. She wanted to remain truthful, largely just to spite Johnny, though that seemed an exercise in pursuing virtue for an ignoble motive. She thought of what had happened to Alison Innis. Justice would not be served by a stubborn adherence to principle. But that did not mean she had to lie outright.

'I'm here to meet with Wesley Oswald.'

Caleb's face lit up with pleasant surprise.

'You know Oz?'

'Who really knows Oz?' she answered.

'Who indeed. What's your connection? Is it a St Andrews thing?'

'Kind of. I know him through mutual acquaintances.'

'Oh. Who might they be?'

He sounded genuinely curious rather than sceptical, but she knew she would be wise to make no assumptions.

'Miles Deacon? Crawford Nicholson?'

Caleb shook his head. 'Are they in games?'

'Movies, in Crawford's case,' said Johnny, 'and publishing for Miles.'

Caleb's expression remained blank. The names clearly meant nothing.

'So how is St Andrews these days?' he asked.

'As you might remember,' Penny said. 'It's not the kind of place that changes much.'

'I can't believe it's more than thirty years for me. They were such exciting times. I mean, you see all these people here acting weird about speaking to me? That's how I felt when I first met Oz.'

316

Caleb talked quickly, as if his mouth was trying to keep up with the thoughts piling up behind each other in his brain. Despite his obvious charisma before a crowd, there was something awkward about his manner up close. He was oddly restive, particularly when he wasn't the one speaking. Penny suspected she could use that.

'I understand you and Wesley were close.'

'I mean, we still are,' he countered, offering an uncertain smile.

Penny noticed that Saskia's eyes had been drawn from her screen, on alert.

'But perhaps not so much as once upon a time?'

'Well, yeah. That's no secret.'

Penny gave him her most sympathetic smile.

'It must be painful when so many of your and Wesley's memories of each other are bound up with someone you both lost.'

'Caleb, is there anything I can get for you?' Saskia asked. 'Another drink, something to eat?'

Her interruption was strategic. Protective, even. She was derailing what might be a painful conversation.

'My brother has a tendency to be over-candid,' she explained, turning to Penny but not quite making eye contact, possibly because her words were more intended for Caleb. 'He loves connecting with people, but he forgets that it's prudent to turn the tap off until you know who's drinking from it.'

'No, I'm cool,' Caleb insisted. 'It feels good to talk about it.' He eyed his sister as he said this, an assurance or perhaps even a rebuke. Whatever the corporate structure said, it was clearly family dynamics that were in play here. Saskia opened her palms in a 'whatever' gesture and went back to her phone.

'I think Wesley's problem is that he *doesn't* talk about it,' Penny said. 'I know you've spoken about your loss in interviews, and you've poured resources into your foundation. Has going public with it helped you?'

Caleb gestured for Penny and Johnny to take a seat on an upholstered lounger, conspicuously a few yards further away from Saskia. On a table next to it Penny spied a book, partially covered by a computer magazine. Something about dark matter. She wondered if it was Caleb or Saskia who was reading it; or whether they just wanted people to think they were reading it.

Caleb sat down opposite the pair of them, sending a wary glance his sister's way. She was apparently captivated by whatever she was typing, but Penny suspected she was still listening.

'Saskia is just looking out for me,' he said quietly. 'Always has, always will. I thought I'd lost my necklace last week, but she found it for me the next day. I took it off to go swimming and left it on a pool lounger.'

He put his hand to his neck, touching the pendant. It was a gold vessel, the blood contained in a glass capsule at the centre. Penny had imagined something macabre but in fact it looked more like a miniature spirit level than a reliquary. He looked into the distance while his fingers brushed the gold, as though trying to picture something. Someone.

'Oz acts like he's the only one who lost her,' he said. 'I think that's because he's never dealt with it properly.'

'When you say properly . . .'

'I mean he can't accept that Juliet killed herself.'

Caleb glanced towards his sister, as though checking she wasn't about to intervene again, or at least that she understood he didn't want her to.

'I get why that's hard for him,' he went on. 'I sure know how hard it was for me. But it's what goes along with it that's eaten away at him.'

'The unspoken corollary,' Penny said, lowering her voice and meeting his eye.

'I spent the longest time wondering if something was missed, if the right questions were asked by the cops. It put this distance between me and my family. All the time thinking: do you know something? Do you know that *someone else* knows something? Imagining alliances and conspiracies. It's insidious.'

'What got you past the suspicion?' asked Johnny, his tone soft also.

'Therapy. It helped me ask myself if I wanted to live in a world where someone close to me might have murdered Juliet. I accepted that sometimes random things just happen. I realised there's actually a security in randomness, because that's what we base encryption on.' He shrugged. 'I tried telling Oz this, suggested he try therapy too.'

'I assume it wasn't well received,' Penny said.

Caleb laughed. It wasn't dry or scornful, more like he had conjured a memory that was wistful yet amusing.

'God, no. But I did open him up to another idea. Kind of a Hail Mary play.'

'What was that?'

'I suggested he hire an investigator.'

'And he went for that?'

'He didn't exactly grab it with both hands, but I told him that even if it didn't give him all the answers, he would at least know someone had asked all the questions.'

'So he hired somebody?' asked Johnny.

'He did, yeah.'

'Do you know who?'

'Oz likes to keep things real close to his chest.'

Before they could ask anything further, Saskia appeared at Caleb's side.

'Caleb, we're skirting the edge regarding our schedule. I promised Mia Lee of Blastwave that we'd both be there.'

Caleb patted his sister's arm and looked up at her, nodding.

He turned back to Penny. 'Yeah, sorry. I've got to go press the flesh. But to be continued, yeah?'

Saskia escorted him from the gazebo, still tapping away on that phone as she walked.

Penny turned to Johnny once she was confident that they were out of earshot.

'Wesley Oswald believes someone in the Pierpont family killed his sister,' she said. 'And secretly Caleb thinks he might be right.'

'Or else Wesley Oswald wants everyone to *think* that's what he believes.'

'What makes you say that?'

'Two things. One, Vikram warned me that Wesley's whole gig is constructing deceptive games. But mostly it's something I've learned from reading classic noir: never trust whoever hires the private eye.'

The Silence Forever Echoes

Chapter Five

They're sitting in a rooftop restaurant looking out across the lawns and the marina as the sun sets over the Pacific. Johnny can see a few dozen people still out there under the lights, squeezing the last drops from the garden party. He and Penny bailed an hour or so ago, Johnny suggesting they should eat something ahead of the drive back to LA. That had seemed a sensible enough idea until Penny had to go choose the most upscale joint in the whole resort. Johnny ought to have guessed someone so hoity-toity would have expensive taste, so maybe that's on him. Either way, if this case doesn't kill him, it's at least gonna bankrupt him.

'Wesley ain't the only one playing games,' he says, forking a piece of his overpriced salmon teriyaki. 'Caleb seemed mighty keen to frame the narrative. Unless he's in the habit of pouring his heart out to complete strangers.'

Her mouth full, Penny makes a doubtful noise, one of a repertoire Johnny is picking up.

'What, you disagree?'

321

She finishes the piece of sashimi she's been working on as if it was a steak. The woman eats like a bird, something he's hoping ain't reflected in how they split the cheque.

'I read that Caleb tends to be quite open about the loss of his fiancée, which is why I gave him the impression I was close to Wesley. Don't forget, coaxing strangers to be candid is how I get results. People tend to trust me because they don't see me as a threat. Of course, it helps that I tend to *be* trustworthy.'

'Strangers find you trustworthy because they ain't spent enough time around you,' he tells her. 'And Caleb didn't open up because you got some kind of superpower. Remember how *he* gets results: he's a consummate salesman. We just need to work out what he's selling.'

'I think the most pertinent issue is what he's trying to buy,' she replies. 'And specifically why Wesley would rather *not* sell. He wants nothing to do with Pierpont Digital while he still has questions over what happened to his sister.'

There is a loud outbreak of hilarity from nearby, a big table down the centre of the room serving a party of tech types kicking back in cargo shorts and ironic tees.

Johnny works on a ten-dollar mouthful of fish while chewing on what Penny just said. The former feels easier to digest.

'What bothers me is that this all rests on the assumption Wesley is the innocent party,' he tells her. 'Maybe he is, but it's pretty clear he's got his own agenda, and he's at the heart of something *real* weird.'

Penny makes another of her non-verbal noises, but this time it's kind of neutral. 'We came into this with the concern that Wesley might be Miles Deacon's next victim,' she says. 'Loath as I am to give credence to your outlandish theory, if we follow your logic then in fact Wesley is the one in the Miles Deacon role. Whether that means we're wrong to assume Wesley's innocence or wrong to suspect Miles's guilt, I can't say.'

Johnny's eye is drawn to movement on the far side of the room, where a man and a woman are getting up from a booth. The man is facing his way, so Johnny immediately recognises him as Vikram Chaudhuri, and they've made eye contact before he realises the woman is Saskia Pierpont.

'Oh, shit.'

'What?'

'We got a problem. Don't look.'

Penny looks. She finds Saskia looking back.

'I said don't look,' Johnny moans, but he already knew it was too late when he saw Vikram. They're busted.

Saskia makes her way over, Vikram in tow. There's no way he hasn't told her who Johnny is. *What* he is.

Saskia slides into the seat opposite Johnny without being asked, Vikram opposite Penny. He gives Johnny a look, just to underline that this was what Johnny did to him earlier.

'Vikram tells me you're police,' Saskia says. 'You misrepresented who you were to me and my brother.'

'I'm not police,' says Penny.

'Yeah, but you're not any kind of professor either. I looked you up while you were speaking to Caleb under false pretences.'

'Penny is assisting with an investigation,' Johnny says. 'As Vikram mighta mentioned, we're looking into multiple homicides, as well as a credible threat to an unnamed person, which we believe to be Wesley Oswald, but could as easily be your brother.'

Saskia does not look placated.

'You're going to have to give me more than that. Vikram also tells me you've had access to a highly confidential memo that was acquired illegally. I hope you're investigating that too.'

'I already gave Vikram the names of who we got it from.'

Vikram wrinkles his nose. 'Yeah, reckon, mate,' he says scornfully. 'Some Scottish indie publisher and a minor-level Hollywood scribe. No clue as to why they might have access to top-secret internal documents. I think you were bullshitting me. Where did you actually get that memo?'

'Ask Penny. She never lies.'

'The information came to us via Miles Deacon,' Penny says. 'You are correct in that Miles is a publisher, but how the memo came to be in his possession we have no idea.'

'Well, whatever, it was no use to me,' Vikram says. 'You sold me a line.'

'Mr Hawke is not in the business of selling lines for information,' Penny says. 'He gives them away for free when he's doing that.'

Johnny bites his tongue. Vikram looks confused. Saskia ignores it.

'If there's a threat to my brother, or to Wesley, I'd like to know about it,' Saskia says. Johnny notes that she sounds concerned by the idea, whereas Vikram had been merely surprised and intrigued. It's a whole other thing when it's family in the cross-hairs, and he can use that.

'The more you can tell us, the better we'll be able to understand the situation ourselves,' Johnny replies. 'We're not here to get anybody in trouble or to obstruct this deal you guys are putting together. But we are interested in why Wesley is reluctant to let it happen.'

Saskia glances at Vikram, a hint of accusation at what he might have told Johnny. This is definitely a guarded area.

Saskia turns back to Johnny. 'You mean Juliet,' she says flatly. 'How does she factor into this?'

'We're trying to get a handle on that ourselves. Which is why I'd like to ask you a few questions.'

She stiffens. Shields up. 'You're talking about something that has caused a great deal of hurt to my family. To Caleb in particular.'

Johnny worries she's thinking about bailing.

'You're very close, aren't you,' says Penny, her voice soft and warm, like somebody's grandma. 'Always looking out for him.'

'Still his big sister, even in our fifties,' Saskia acknowledges, relaxing a little. It's not much, but enough to make the difference between her walking and talking. Johnny is starting to suss that if Penny does have a superpower, it's kindness. 'Caleb's a genius, but as a kid he was so distracted by what was in his head that I used to worry he'd walk out in front of traffic.'

'There's a rumour that you're the real genius,' says Johnny. 'That Caleb is the front of the operation, but you've always been the true computer whizz.'

Saskia wears an ironic smile, rolls her eyes. 'I think Caleb was the one who started that rumour. So that people think he understands less than he really does when they're showing him what's under the hood. Nothing is ever quite what it appears when it comes to Caleb. And that includes his façade of having got over what happened to Juliet.'

'Is that why you were trying to chaperone him earlier?' Penny asks, using that tender tone of hers.

Saskia swallows. 'Caleb carried so much guilt over what happened. I guess you always do when it's a suicide. Asking yourself what signs you missed, were you paying enough attention. He talks about therapy, he gives these candid interviews and he's all positive on the surface, but he's hiding so much hurt. That's why I get angsty whenever anyone starts digging this up.

He shut us all out before, for a long time, and I don't want that happening again.'

Johnny figures it's now or never for this question. He keeps his voice calm and low.

'Was there ever any suspicion that it wasn't a suicide?'

Saskia takes a beat.

'Only in Wesley's head,' she replies. 'The cops were satisfied nobody else could have been with Juliet when she fell. They found the keys to the lighthouse in the back of the door, locked from the inside.'

Johnny sends Penny a look, which she gives a damn good ignoring. She heard the same thing he did, though.

'Guess you weren't happy about this private investigator, then?' Johnny says. 'Did you try talking Caleb out of suggesting it?'

'Today is the first I've heard about it. Or at least, I heard Wesley hired an investigator, but today was the first I heard what for, or that it was Caleb's idea.'

'Caleb never mentioned it to you?' Johnny asks doubtfully.

'Are you kidding me? Nobody in this family tells each other shit. Caleb gives the impression he can't keep a single thought to himself, but like I said, impressions and reality are different things. My little sister's just as bad. Zoe only tells me what she's legally obliged to by rules of corporate governance. Even has her husband bound by the same omertà, despite us all being on the same goddamn board.

'That's why it's been a treat to team up with Vikram on this deal,' she adds. 'It makes a pleasant change to be working with someone who's pulling in the same direction, and who actually communicates.'

Vikram smiles bashfully and Johnny wonders if it's purely a professional relationship. He's not getting a vibe that it's more, but can't say for sure because they'd surely be trying to keep it discreet in a place full of game-industry types.

With that thought, something else slots into place, though Johnny's gonna have to verify the details, and he can't do that right now.

'But to answer your previous question,' Saskia says, 'damn straight I'd have tried to talk him out of suggesting it. Caleb thinks if an investigator finds nothing, that'll put Wesley's mind at rest. But what Caleb hasn't thought of is, what if this investigator does find something? And I don't mean anything dramatic. It would only take the slightest thing, then Wesley's paranoia would do the rest, and Caleb would be set back too, at a time when we really need his head straight. I know it might sound self-serving, but getting this deal over the line would be the best thing that could happen to both of them. Having no choice but to work together would be better than any kind of therapy.'

'Pierpont Digital were trying to buy Sea Monster before, weren't they?' Johnny says.

'Just before Juliet died,' Saskia confirms.

He's about to test a hunch, one bigger than the possibility that Saskia and Vikram are doing the deed.

'Juliet was part of Sea Monster, wasn't she? She wasn't just Wesley's twin sister and Caleb's fiancée. She was a material player in the deal.'

'She helped Wesley found Sea Monster. She was involved going right back to their teen years, with *Qubo's Quest*. People talk like Juliet was some silent partner advising in the background. She was a driving force, ambitious for the company.'

'Were you close to her too?' Penny asks.

Saskia replies flatly, same tone she used before: 'No. I'm not

327

going to lie about that. I didn't dislike her, but we were never friends, I think because we were too alike. We were both looking out for our brothers, worried someone else was trying to take advantage of them. Worried about who they were getting involved with.'

'What worried you about Wesley?' Penny asks.

'My fear was that Juliet would never love my brother as much as she loved *her* brother. I don't mean anything weird. I just mean it can be difficult getting between twins; they share everything, from DNA onwards. And I had the suspicion she was looking to tempt Caleb to walk away from us and go work exclusively for Sea Monster. I didn't think that would be a good move for either party, but these days I can see why he would be tempted. Working with your family can drive you nuts.'

Saskia has confirmed part one of Johnny's hunch: that just like Lilian founding a firm with Miles, Juliet had actually been Wesley's partner as well as his sister. Ordinarily this confirmation would be a positive thing, but it doesn't feel good to be verifying weird shit that he wishes he was wrong about. Nevertheless, he pushes on to part two.

'Back then, Pierpont trying to buy Sea Monster wasn't the only takeover in the air, was it?'

Saskia's eyes flash in brief surprise that he should know this. It's enough to count as another confirmation.

'There were rumours that someone was lining up a hostile bid for Pierpont,' Saskia replies.

'Who?'

'That was never clear. Supposedly a secret consortium of smaller players pooling resources. But my take is someone was flying a kite, trying to make something happen.'

'What makes you say that?'

'We're a family firm. Back then we held all but a couple of seats, giving us a controlling majority. There was a rumour the consortium had someone on the inside ready to sell, but that's all it was: a rumour started in an attempt to sow discord. Potentially self-fulfilling: get us all paranoid and pissed with each other, hoping one of us decides to sell out of spite.

'But then, you know, Juliet died and everything changed. Both parties backed away from the Sea Monster deal, and the consortium quietly disappeared. Pierpont Digital stayed a family affair, and Sea Monster got a whole load of independent investment after that. Whether that was from the same people who formed the consortium, we'll never know.'

Johnny spies an opportunity here: part bluff and part bargaining chip; the bluff part because he doesn't actually hold the bargaining chip yet.

'If you were able to persuade the Sea Monster board that Wesley is being driven by personal animosity, that would override his opposition to the deal, wouldn't it? I mean, if the Sea Monster board were informed that he had hired a private investigator to look into his sister's death, that would be pretty compelling.'

'We already know he hired a private investigator,' Vikram says with a dismissive shrug. 'We can tell them that ourselves.'

'No, what you can tell them is only hearsay. What you need is evidence. What you need is a name.'

Saskia's ear prick up. 'You can get that?' she asks.

'I'm a cop. It's what I do. But I'd want something in return.'

'What?'

'Me and Penny would like to know what Diegesis is.'

Vikram's expression says no way. Johnny pushes further.

'Better yet, we want you to *show* us what Diegesis is. We want a looky-loo, a quiet little visit to the Sea Monster campus, to give us some background on certain things.'

Vikram looks to Saskia. It's his company they're talking about, but she's clearly the key-holder in this situation. It's her firm that are waving $4 billion, after all. She weighs it up, then answers.

'Vikram will show you round the chocolate factory. But the name of that investigator is your golden ticket. You don't get in without it.'

Penny goes back to her morsels of sashimi as Saskia and Vikram walk away. Half of Johnny's salmon is still sitting on the plate, cold now, though he's gonna eat every last flake of it at that price. Meantime, he's checking the E30 app for the Pierpont Digital personnel profiles, scoping out the thing he couldn't verify earlier.

Yep, there it is. Tony Grant: chief financial officer and Zoe's husband.

'Bingo,' he says.

Penny gives him a withering look. 'Did you really just say "Bingo"?'

'The situation merited it.'

'How could it possibly?'

'Because I figured a way we can make the weirdness work for us.'

The Silence Forever Echoes

Chapter Six

Johnny has lost the ocean.

It was there on his left-hand side for the last twenty miles, then the road took them inland, down into a canyon that seems to have screwed with the sat-nav just as they're approaching a fork in the road.

He signals left. They're looking for a beach.

'I think you have to turn right,' says Penny.

'How can it be right? The ocean is that way.'

'It's not just the ocean we're looking for, though. It's Cinnamon Bay. You have to turn right, then the road descends under a bridge and doubles back beneath itself.'

Johnny has no idea what she thinks she's talking about, but he takes the counterintuitive right anyway. It's too early in the goddamn morning for an argument, plus he's curious to see how she handles it when they inevitably have to do a U-turn and come back.

The road pulls him into a wide sweeping bend, the gradient sloping sharply downwards between the canyon walls. After

331

about a quarter mile, he passes directly beneath the road he was on, and up ahead he sees a sign for Cinnamon Bay.

Son of a bitch.

'How could you possibly know that?' he asks.

Penny shrugs. 'I don't know. I must have seen it on television. I'm constantly surprised by the fragments of information that bubble up to the surface despite my having no recollection of where I got them from.'

Cinnamon Bay opens up before them as they emerge from the curving channel. It doesn't look the kind of place you would just happen upon. They've read that Zoe Grant likes to surf here most mornings before hitting the office. She was a keen surfer through childhood and right into her teens, when she became interested in more chemical-based ways to hang ten. She rediscovered her love for it during treatment for addiction issues.

According to a human-interest puff piece Johnny found online, she grew close to fellow Pierpont Digital exec Tony Grant after they both turned up to the same Narcotics Anonymous meeting, neither knowing the other had a problem. They recently celebrated their eighteenth wedding anniversary. The piece also said both have been clean twenty years and remain committed NA sponsors in their spare time.

There is a gnarly-looking shack of a café, currently closed, and a small parking lot with one car in it, a Genesis G80. Johnny parks the Cobra next to it and they climb out into the morning air.

Johnny looks again at the ocean and sees a lone figure rise amidst the spray, paddling with an unhurried but athletic motion then climbing onto the board as it catches the crest. She rides the wave with languid grace, almost nonchalant, like she's taking a travelator all the way to shore.

She wades back into the water, gently escorting her board over the incoming breakers until she's back in position, then she waits patiently and chooses her next ride.

Realising they might be here a while, Penny gets her phone out, like a freakin' millennial.

'Still nothing on the BBC,' she says. Johnny figures she's talking about Alison Innis.

'No news is good news,' he replies. Maybe the CCTV didn't catch them after all.

A few minutes later they're watching Zoe walk up the beach, board under her arm. They intercept her at the edge of the parking lot, where the blacktop meets the sand.

'Zoe, isn't it?' Penny asks, friendly, unthreatening. 'We met at the garden party yesterday afternoon.'

'Oh, yeah, hi. You're the professor, right?'

Zoe is slightly weirded out but riding it, keeping her balance. Yesterday she had looked skinny but now in her wetsuit Johnny can see she is wiry. Athletic. She is smiling but her quizzical expression says, with some justification, what the hell are you doing here?

'We had an interesting chat with your brother,' Penny tells her.

She puts the board down, resting it upright. There's a fine layer of sand stuck to the underside.

'Yeah, he was very keen to talk to you,' Zoe replies.

Johnny knows she's asking herself why they are so keen to talk to her that they tracked her all the way to this place for an ambush.

Her hair is wet and there's a smell of the sea off her. Johnny can see salt crystals forming on the back of her hand.

'He was surprisingly candid,' Penny tells her. 'He really opened up about the loss of his fiancée.'

Zoe looks wary. The waves are getting rougher.

'Caleb deals with it by talking about it. It's an admirably un-male technique.'

'We'd like to talk to you a little about what happened back then,' Penny says.

Zoe glances at the ocean, making them wait for a response.

'I don't have anything to say about that. I'm not my brother.'

'Talking about it to strangers is not how you would choose to deal with it?' Penny suggests with a leavening of humour.

'Partly that. But mostly it's that I don't have the same shit to deal with. I'm not the one it happened to.'

Good answer, Johnny thinks. She rode that one well. But they're just getting started, and he notices that she ain't heading for the Genesis yet. People with guilty secrets always want to know what you're holding.

'We've been reading about how you and your husband met,' Johnny says. 'Well, obviously you both worked for the firm. But you bonded through rehab: that's the story, ain't it? The cover story,' he adds.

Big wave on the horizon. She can sense it.

'What do you mean?'

Johnny is in cop mode now. No point hiding it.

'You were seeing each other before that, but you had to keep it on the down-low because of the politics: two members of the board in a relationship. Plus, Tony was a decade older, and you were the boss's youngest daughter.'

The wave is cresting.

'But mostly you kept it on the down-low so that nobody found out how the two of you had secretly become a block vote, ready to sell your shares to the anonymous consortium plotting to buy Pierpont Digital.'

Wipeout.

'How the fuck do you know this?' she asks.

Johnny can't tell her, because how could he possibly explain?

Saskia had mentioned Zoe binding her husband in an omertà. That caused him to recall seeing Lucy Stonebridge and Alan Brooks in the gardens at Crathie Hall: Brooks consoling Lucy, Johnny assuming this was grief and compassion overcoming mutual antipathy. In fact, the antipathy was all a front. He recalled how Lucy knew to tap Johnny for drugs. She claimed to have overheard his conversation with Brooks, when in fact Brooks must have told her directly.

Driving it home further was the clandestine relationship he had uncovered between Dominique King's son Damien and *his* fellow board member Peter Godfrey. Peter Godfrey who told him there were rumours of a hostile takeover for Kingdom Pictures.

'I asked you a question,' Zoe says. 'How do you know this?'

She's concerned that someone has been talking. Someone who was once part of the anonymous consortium, maybe.

'Well, we didn't for sure,' Johnny tells her. 'But you just confirmed it.'

She looks pissed now.

'Who are you people? Are you working for Wesley?'

'No,' says Penny. 'We are simply trying to get to the bottom of what happened back then.'

'You *are* working for Wesley,' she insists. 'If not directly, you're working with that rat-fink guy, Wesley's Hollywood gumshoe.'

'You spoke to his investigator?' Johnny asks.

'I told him I was done talking to him, and now I'm done talking to you.'

She lifts the board and makes for her car.

'We can talk to you, or we can talk to your family,' Johnny says. 'It's your choice. But I'm figuring it would be a bad time for them to learn this stuff about you and Tony and the consortium. What with them being on the brink of a deal that's gonna take you all to the next level.'

She stops, turns around, puts the board down again. She's looking even more alarmed that he knows *this* shit. Johnny presses the point.

'Buying Sea Monster will give Pierpont a head start on the next generation of games tech. If your family learn you tried to go behind their backs once, they might start wondering if you'd do it again: help kill the deal so that someone else can swoop.'

Zoe looks hunted all of a sudden. She runs her free hand nervously through her damp hair. The wetsuit rides up just a couple of mills at her wrist. Johnny sees the fine lines on her skin.

Scarring. Self-harm.

He feels this rush of guilt about how he tapped Lucy by giving her coke. He can't make sense of what is going on; he doesn't believe he's looking at some future version of Lucy, but he does know she and Zoe were both suffering. *Are* both suffering.

'That is so not what I . . .' she stumbles. 'Me and Tony would never try and mess with what Caleb's trying to do. But back then I was in a bad place. I was angry at my family. Feeling like they all thought I was a fuck-up, so I acted like one.'

'Why was Tony plotting to assist a takeover?'

'He was angry too. He had done a lot for the firm, but not being family, he never got the recognition or the respect.'

'Who was in the consortium?'

'Just minor players who saw a chance to consolidate. I can't name names. It would burn too many people.'

336

'And your father's wrath would be terrible to behold,' Penny says. 'Then as now.'

Zoe doesn't deny it.

'Juliet found out, didn't she?' Johnny asks. 'That you and Tony were planning to flip. Did one of you kill her to stop that coming out?'

She gives a hollow laugh, like the idea is pitiful.

'The rat-fink asked me the same thing. I'll tell you what I told him. I liked Juliet. Thought her coming into the family might help Caleb grow some balls and stand up to Dad.'

She runs a finger up the back of the board, drawing a stripe in the sand. Johnny knows she's considering a play.

'I did hear Juliet had hired her *own* investigator back then,' she says.

'Juliet hired a private eye?'

Zoe nods. 'I figured she was looking into the family ahead of the buyout. Juliet wanted to know all the potential pitfalls. Wesley just liked to build and tinker and didn't want to worry about the everyday shit. We thought we'd covered our tracks pretty well, but it's possible she found out about me and Tony. That said, I would have been real surprised if we were the worst thing she discovered.'

And there it is. The offer.

'You know, we're likely to forget all about the consortium if we're busy pursuing a different line of inquiry,' Johnny says. 'So why don't you tell us what you think *was* the worst thing she discovered?'

Zoe draws another stripe in the sand.

'I'll give you two names. Deal?'

He looks at Penny. She nods.

'Deal,' Johnny says.

'Melissa Neeson. Bradley Ignatieff.'

337

'Who are they?' Penny asks.

'Like the conspiracist assholes on the internet say, do your own research.'

'Okay, but one last thing. What was the name of Wesley's guy, the investigator?'

'I said two names.'

'How about one extra as a goodwill gesture?'

Zoe runs her finger down the back of the board a third time.

'Problem is, I can't quite recall. I think it began with a G, though. Oh yeah, I remember: Go fuck yourself.'

Death Is But the Overture

IV

Penny was amazed and a little disappointed at how much they were able to ascertain without even leaving the Cinnamon Bay car park. She preferred when detective work at least required the application of hot tea to fine china.

A brief search on social media immediately threw up no fewer than twenty Melissa Neesons but only one Bradley Ignatieff, so they concentrated on the latter for now. He was a roofing contractor based in Pismo Beach, but as Johnny put it, 'It's not like we can just ring him up and ask what connection he had to Juliet Oswald.'

After just a few minutes on his phone, Johnny had discovered that Ignatieff was the sole survivor of a fatal road-traffic accident back in 1995, one that had accounted for both of his parents and his two older sisters.

Though the crash had happened in the nineties, the article was more recent, a piece in a local newspaper about Ignatieff and his partner marking ten years since they had set up their business. It quoted Ignatieff as having 'gone off the rails for a little while', and made mention of the tragedy he'd had to overcome. Originally from Santa Cruz, California, the family had been on holiday in Vermont when the crash took place. His father was found to have been drunk-driving their rented RV, which veered off the road with catastrophic consequences. Ignatieff had been only ten at the time.

The article alluded to Ignatieff being frustrated in his attempts to get more details about what happened, but mostly it was a good-news story about a successful local business.

Johnny made some calls, clearly knowing which departments to ask for and what terms to use. He was breezy and charming, sweet-talking receptionists and trading banter with fellow officers. Penny noted that he could be polite and deferential when he wanted. Within about twenty minutes, he was talking to someone in the sheriff's department in Franklin County, Vermont.

'Yeah, I'm working a homicide case that has thrown up a possible connection to an RV crash your department investigated back in the nineties. Four fatalities, one survivor, same family, name of Ignatieff. I was wondering if you could send me a scan of the file, or at least take a look and give me the highlights.'

Penny could hear a female voice on the other end say, 'It's a good thing you called. We got so little to do out here in Vermont that we need California cops asking favours to keep us busy.'

There sounded just enough humour in her voice that it wasn't a blank No.

'I appreciate it's an ask, but if you can spare five minutes at some point . . .'

'No, you're in luck actually. The department's been digitising old files and I think it now goes back as far as eighty-nine, so I can run a search on the computer.'

'Fantastic.'

'What was the name again?'

'Ignatieff.'

There was a long silence, then the voice returned.

'Can I check the spelling? Is that with a V?'

'Two Fs.'

Another silence.

'Nah, still nothing. I said they're digitising the old files, but the department moved to a new building a few years back and some stuff must have got lost in transit.'

Johnny thanked her and disconnected the call.

'Lost in transit,' he told Penny. 'Sure it was.'

'What are you saying?'

'Somebody deep-sixed that report. We need to go to a primary source.'

They found Bradley Ignatieff on a roof in Pismo Beach around lunchtime, Johnny having posed as a prospective client to find out where he was working that morning. Penny recognised him from the photograph in the newspaper, though he looked considerably more muscular than the headshot had suggested. He and a workmate were dressed in matching yellow sleeveless tops, working on a two-storey wooden house with a view of the ocean.

Penny and Johnny watched from the car, waiting until he came down from the scaffolding to make their move.

'I'll take the lead on this,' said Johnny.

Ignatieff noticed their approach and Penny could see his expression darken, defences rising as a matter of instinct.

'Bradley?' Johnny asked.

'Uh-huh,' he said uncertainly. His name and profession were printed on the van parked a few yards away, so it was hard for him to deny it.

'I'm Johnny Hawke, we spoke on the phone.'

There was no sudden thaw. Whatever he hadn't liked about what he saw, Johnny introducing himself had not altered it.

'You ain't here about a job,' he said.

'No,' Johnny admitted. 'We just want to talk about something. Can I buy you a soda and a sandwich?'

'I don't break bread with cops.'

Bradley folded his muscular and heavily tattooed arms above the row of tools attached to his utility belt. His workmate noticed something was up and began striding towards them.

Penny took a step closer, deciding she ought to be the one taking the lead instead.

'What about librarians?' she asked. 'Would you break bread with one of those?'

Bradley looked her up and down, less sure of what to make of her than he had been of Johnny. He glanced at his workmate, something unspoken passing between them.

'One thing I learned when I was away,' he said; 'always stay tight with the person who hands out the books. Juanita's, on West Grand. I'll meet you there in five. But *he* stays outside.'

Juanita's was a tiny place, most of its tables situated in the car park it shared with the 7-Eleven next door. In keeping with the agreed terms, Johnny remained in his vehicle while Penny ventured inside, where the aircon was a relief. It must have felt all the more so to two men working on a roof in the sunshine.

Bradley was sitting with his workmate, who according to the sign on their van must be Rocco Hernandez. They had a jug of dark liquid in front of them, some of it poured into two glasses.

'We already ordered,' Bradley said. 'You want something?'

'Just tea, please.'

'Hey, Loupe,' he called, indicating the jug, 'another glass over here.'

Iced tea, Penny realised. She decided not to correct him.

'You got an accent,' he said. 'What are you, Australian?'

'I'm from Scotland.'

'Close. I knew it was one of those kinda places.'

She decided not to correct that either.

She cast an eye over his many tattoos. Most of them were intricate and done to an impressive level of artistic detail, but beneath certain of them were remnants of earlier, cruder designs. Homemade. Or prison-made.

The third glass arrived, and Bradley poured. Penny took a sip. It was sweeter than she was expecting, but not unpleasant.

'What does a Scottish librarian want to talk to me about?'

'I've been reading about you,' she answered. She sensed it would be wiser to build up to the subject of the crash gently. He was curious about her but clearly it wouldn't take much for him to decide he wasn't playing. 'How you set up your business and have been a successful concern for, what is it, almost ten years now?'

'We're doing okay. Margins are tight, always. But if you define successful as still going, then yeah. Why do you wanna know?'

'And you said you were *away*. Hence your mistrust of my friend Johnny out there.'

'Mistrust, yeah. That would be one way of putting it.'

'If you don't mind me asking, why were you in prison?'

He and Rocco exchanged another look.

'I do mind. When you done a little time, people think they can define you by the worst thing you ever did. Most folks, nobody ever finds out the worst thing they ever did, so they get defined by something better.'

343

'No, I appreciate that,' said Penny. 'I'm just trying to get a little background.'

'All I'll say is I was real messed up for a while. More messed up when I was inside, and still plenty messed up after I got out. But then I met Rocco here. He helped me get my shit together.'

They bumped fists, affection and solidarity in the gesture.

A waiter arrived, presenting them each with a large burrito, enough to feed Penny for a week.

'You're business partners,' she stated as they each took a bite.

They traded another look, a coy smile.

'A little more than that,' ventured Rocco.

'Is that enough background?' Bradley asked. 'What is it you came here to talk about?'

'With apologies for dredging up something painful, it concerns what happened to your family. Johnny and I are here because we think it is connected to four murders.'

Bradley's face became expressionless, a mask.

'What happened to my family *was* four murders.'

'We tried to access the Franklin County Sheriff Office's files on the crash. Apparently they've been lost.'

'Check out my astonished face.'

'Perhaps you could tell me a little about what you know?'

'Perhaps you could tell me what it's linked to?'

'At this stage it's very tangential.'

'At this stage I don't feel like talking.'

Penny nodded in placatory acknowledgement. She took a sip of iced tea. She knew she wasn't giving up anything meaningful here.

'Three were apparent suicides that we believe to be something else. A neurosurgeon named Juliet Oswald, a Hollywood screen-writer named Jed Mahoney and a Scottish publisher named

344

Lilian Deacon. The fourth death was a hotel manager, Alison Innis. She had her throat cut.'

Penny just about kept her voice steady saying this final part.

Bradley took another bite of his burrito, chomping it down fast, eating like he was afraid it might be taken away. The names clearly meant nothing to him.

'Nobody ever suggested my old man killed himself deliberately,' he said. 'Bullshit about drunk-driving, but not suicide.'

'As I said, the nature of the connection is unclear at this stage. We're hoping it might be clearer if we can learn some more.'

Bradley scrutinised her intently, like he was wondering whether he would regret trusting her, but she could tell he was going to take the gamble. She recognised a man who had spent his life looking for answers.

He glanced to Rocco, as though for reassurance. Then he began to speak.

'We were on vacation in Quebec. My dad had family in Montreal, so we started off there, but we hired the RV to explore further down the east coast. We crossed the border into Vermont after an early start, maybe around nine a.m. I remember us cheering that we were back in the USA.'

He swallowed, took a beat before speaking again. When he did, his voice was quieter, as though he was endeavouring to control his emotions.

'Here's the facts of it. Somebody was on the wrong side of the road, but because of where both vehicles ended up, nobody could say which one it was. I was just a kid. Your memory can play tricks, but I have this vivid recollection of seeing a car come straight toward us. My dad shouting "Jesus" and then everything going to shit.

'The other driver's statement said our RV was on the wrong

345

side of the road and they swerved to avoid it. They ended up with minor injuries. Crashed into a fence. The RV went down a steep slope and rolled.'

Bradley took a beat, eyeing Penny with the conviction of a man who needed to be heard and believed.

'Turns out my dad was, like, marginally over the alcohol limit because he'd been drinking the night before. This from blood tests they took . . . they took the blood from his dead body.'

He swallowed. Rocco placed a hand on his forearm.

'Listen, you'd need to drink a lot to still be over the limit the next day. I was ten years old, but the most I ever saw him have was two or three beers. My dad was a careful driver. A family guy. If he had been driving a fucking RV on the wrong side of the road, my mom would have been screaming her lungs out.'

Penny waited in case he had more he needed to say. He reached for his drink again, done for now.

'Do you know who the other driver was?' she asked.

He gave a dry, bitter laugh. 'Lawyers got all kinds of privacy clauses and redactions because of "their client's trauma at being involved in this tragedy" or some bullshit. Strongly implied they'd have sued my parents into oblivion if either of them had survived. To this day, I've been stonewalled at every attempt to find out. Which makes it clear there's something I'm not *supposed* to find out.'

Bradley sighed. 'I get what it sounds like. I can't accept that it just happened, so there has to be some deeper explanation, some grand conspiracy. Look, I'm not some kind of tinfoil-hat nutjob. I wore the masks, I took the vaccines, and I don't listen to assholes like Joe Rogan. But something about this just reeks of corruption. The cops were covering for somebody back then. One of their own, is my guess.'

Bradley glances out of the window towards Johnny's car.

'And here's me telling you all this when you got a cop in tow. For all I know he could be part of it.'

'I can assure you that today was the first time either of us heard your name,' Penny said. 'And we had to go to quite some trouble to get it.'

'Who did you get it from?'

'I'm not in a position to reveal that.'

'Spoken like a cop. When you say you're a librarian, that wouldn't be some kind of police librarian?'

'No.'

'So what you doing with Hawke?'

'It's complicated.'

Bradley raised his eyebrows in surprise. 'What, like, "It's complicated" complicated?'

'No. Like *Finnegans Wake* complicated.'

'I don't know what that is. You saying you trust him?'

Penny thought about it.

'Yes.'

Bradley looked at her for a moment. 'In my experience, the only people who trust cops are scumbags dirty as they are, or fools yet to find out they're being played. So which are you?'

Penny was about to reply that in her experience, the only people who were so openly disdainful of the police were criminals, but nothing felt quite so certain any more.

'He's a decent man,' she said, realising she had come to believe it.

Bradley looked scornful, even pitying.

'You ain't spent enough time around him yet. I've spent *too* much time around cops, and I can tell you they break down into three categories: grifters, crusaders and psychos. All dangerous in their different ways. I'm not saying there can't be other types. I'm just saying I ain't met any. What makes you think he's something different?'

Penny considered it.

'Between me and you, he's on suspension. Part of the reason we're here is that he broke the rules trying to get to the truth of a murder that was being covered up.'

Bradley and Rocco shared a look, a private joke.

'There you go,' said Rocco. 'Crusader.'

'He breaks the rules, he gets a suspension,' said Bradley. 'We break the rules, we go to jail. God save us from TV shows and mystery novels, making the world believe these assholes are the good guys.'

'Copaganda,' said Rocco.

'Cops are not the good guys,' Bradley continued. 'Cops are an unregulated militia: the world's most highly funded street gang. Listen, lady, I wish you good luck, but when you get to the bottom of whatever you're looking into, if you don't find police corruption at the heart of it, then that's only because police corruption is the reason you ain't got to the truth.'

The Silence Forever Echoes

Chapter Seven

In his rearview mirror, Johnny can see Penny through the window of the diner, having parked facing away from the building so that it doesn't look too conspicuously like he's eyeballing the meet. He wasn't surprised to find himself benched on this one. The moment Bradley came down from the roof, Johnny knew he was getting nothing from him. He was surprised that he would even talk to Penny. He recognised a guy who had been on the wrong end of the system much of his life, someone who wasn't gonna see a cop as anything other than an enemy, but he must have sensed something about Penny that he could deal with. Johnny figures it wasn't just her accent that gave Bradley the impression she came from somewhere very different than his and Johnny's world.

There is something disarmingly positive about her, but not naively so. He's coming to think that her optimism ain't born of a pampered existence or an absence of adversity. Johnny senses as much sadness and regret in Penny as in himself; it just manifests differently. That strict adherence to the rules, to protocol, etiquette: it ain't just because she figures that's the best way for everybody to get along, and wouldn't it be dandy if we were all well-behaved little kiddies. It's coming from someplace darker. Something very bad happened to Penelope Coyne once upon a time, and she's taking every precaution to ensure it doesn't happen again.

Johnny gets out his phone. Figures as long as he's cooling his heels, he should make the time count. They got lucky with Bradley Ignatieff. Not everybody has their name associated with a small business and their cell number listed on tradesmen's websites.

Johnny's on suspension but that don't mean he can't still work the system. It costs him a couple of markers, but he gets someone to look up contact details and whatever else they can find on all those Melissa Neesons.

He knows that's gonna take a while. Meantime he figures he better make a start on a whole bigger problem. Dollars to donuts, Wesley's PI is gonna be an ex-cop, so there will be plenty of ways for Johnny to bargain with him, but actually finding the sonofabitch is another matter. Making it even harder is the fact that these days so many of them have consolidated and gone corporate. Zoe referred to a Hollywood gumshoe, but the days of Sam Spade and Miles Archer running a little two-man operation are largely gone. Most of these guys work for agencies now, which means all kinds of regulations against leaking client-confidential information, starting with who the client even is.

He had promised Saskia and Vikram a name, but first and foremost, Johnny wants to talk to Wesley's guy himself. To do that, he's gonna have to trail some bullshit story, lean heavily on being a cop. 'Heard you were working for this dude Wesley

Oswald. Came across some information you might be interested in.' See who bites. Problem is, he's gonna have to work his way through a list of all the licensed investigators in the Southland, calling them one at a time.

He figures maybe he can narrow it down. When Zoe called this guy a Hollywood gumshoe, maybe she was speaking literally. He scrolls the list again, looking more carefully at the addresses. Then he sees it.

Daniel Rattigan. 3D Investigations, 1545 North La Brea Avenue.

That rat-fink guy.

Hollywood address.

Gotta be.

Johnny dials the number, gets an answering service: default automated synthesised female voice. He doesn't leave a message.

Death Is But the Overture

V

Penny sipped the last of her iced tea as she watched the roofing van drive away. Johnny walked into the diner shortly after.

'Is the tab still open?' he asked, glancing at the table.

'Well, I haven't been presented with a bill. And you did offer to buy him a drink and a sandwich.'

He walked to the counter, where she heard him order a soda water and ask for the cheque. The waiter brought both a few moments later. Johnny took a long thirsty gulp then lifted the slip of paper and examined it.

'Man, they sure went all-in with their burrito order when they knew someone else was paying. Was it worth it?'

'We had a constructive dialogue, yes.'

'Gimme the highlights.'

Penny told him what she had learned.

'Sounds like he's been picking up the pieces his whole life,' Johnny said. 'I've seen it too many times: somebody who doesn't die in a tragedy, but they don't quite live again either.'

This sentiment sent a wave of grief through Penny for reasons she could not quite understand. Or perhaps remember.

'He seems convinced the police have been complicit in covering up details of the accident,' she said.

Penny felt uncomfortable having to mention this. It wasn't that she preferred to believe police officers were incapable of being corrupt. It was that she preferred to believe most people were fundamentally decent.

'It sounds like somebody was getting their ducks in a row,' Johnny said. 'Creating a DUI scenario pins the blame on one driver and clears the way for the other to claim anonymity. Bradley's right. It stinks.'

'I appreciate this might be delicate,' said Penny, 'but have you encountered much in the way of police corruption? I mean, would investigating officers simply take a pay-off from someone to, as you put it, get their ducks in a row? How would that play out in practice?'

Johnny grimaced as he thought about it.

'Corruption is seldom about a bag full of money. It's about trading favours, influence. That way cops can tell themselves they never took a bribe. But someone powerful enough jerks on their leash, they do as they're told. That's how I ended up in Scotland. Dominique King didn't pay anybody off, but she exerted influence.'

Penny nodded in acknowledgement.

'Somebody in the Pierpont family was the other driver, weren't they?' she said.

'That would be my conclusion, yeah. Zoe knows who, but she ain't gonna tell us straight out. She wants us to follow the breadcrumbs.'

'But she's telling us this is a family that has covered up a death before.'

Johnny took a gulp of his soda water and stared out the window at the traffic.

'Saskia and Caleb would both have been old enough to drive back in ninety-five,' he said. 'The anointed first-born and the only son, both with big futures ahead of them. Can't have your whole life ruined by one little mistake just because it happens to kill four people. That *would* be a tragedy. But which of them's your money on?'

Penny considered it, and as she did so she looked at the bubbles rising through the clear liquid to the top of Johnny's glass. She pictured a champagne flute containing soda water, a waitress turning away with a tray of the real thing.

'Neither,' she said. 'See what you can find on their stepmother.'

Johnny lifted his phone and began thumbing. She saw his eyes widen moments later.

'Holly golly.'

'What?'

'First entry, Wikipedia. Viola Pierpont. Maiden name Adams, real New England blueblood. She was the eldest daughter of one of the wealthiest families in the state.'

'Which state?' Penny asked, though she barely needed to.

'Vermont.'

The Silence Forever Echoes

Chapter Eight

The 1500 block of North La Brea turns out to be a down-at-heel strip mall. It doesn't look like the kind of place some rich tech genius would rock up looking for help. Presumably Wesley never came here in person, just dialled a number or sent an email. Rattigan's agency does have a website, though it's hardly the slickest. When Johnny checked it out, several parts of it wouldn't load, including Rattigan's picture; or any pictures, for that matter. It was like the images were hot-linked from a server that doesn't exist any more.

Johnny and Penny step out of the car and approach number 1545, which is just a grey door sandwiched between the frontages of a bail bondsman and a store selling medicinal weed, the latter's previous incarnation as a sex shop still discernible on a partially painted-over sign.

Johnny glances above the storefronts at a row of windows, behind which is an assortment of blinds, most half-closed against the sun.

'Looks like there's a suite of offices on the second floor.'

'I can't see it,' says Penny.

'You can't see the offices?'

'No, I can see those fine. I can't see the second floor. I assume you mean the first.'

'There are two floors,' he points out.

'Yes. Ground and first.'

'Give me strength.'

The door opens into a cramped and gloomy lobby leading to a staircase. On the wall to the left is a short row of mailboxes, letters spilling out of one. Johnny lifts some of the uncollected mail clear so that he can read the nameplate beneath. It is marked 3D Investigations.

'Not a promising sign,' he says.

Rattigan's office is the third door down the hall, its name etched on a brass plaque beneath which is the motto: DILIGENCE DEDICATION DISCRETION.

Johnny presses the buzzer. There is no reply. He grips the door handle. It doesn't budge.

'Let's try Dan's neighbour,' he says.

Next door's plate reads LA BREA ACCOUNTING. INCOME TAX SPECIALISTS. There's a cartoon beneath the logo, showing a dinosaur in a suit sinking into the tar pits, accompanied by the caption: *Don't get mired in paperwork, leave it to us.* The tar pits are a ways south of here, but he figures they're just trading on the name.

Johnny knocks on the door. A voice calls out: 'It's open.'

They walk into a tiny office where they find a middle-aged woman behind the only desk.

'Hey there. What can I help you with?' she asks, smiling.

'Actually, we're trying to get a hold of your neighbour, Dan Rattigan.'

The smile fades. 'Yeah, that's not gonna happen. Ain't seen his happy, smiling face in maybe three weeks.'

Johnny can't miss the sarcasm. 'Any idea where we might find him?'

'Yeah. Cedars-Sinai. He had a car accident just two blocks south of here. I heard he got smashed up pretty bad. Wound up in the ICU.'

'Oh.'

'I didn't send flowers,' she adds.

The hospital is only a ten-minute drive, but it takes considerably longer before they reach the front of the line to speak to someone who might be able to help. The nurse's name badge says Rhoda Vincent. She looks tired and hassled, like she got at least ten other things she should be doing right now.

'We're looking for a patient who was brought in maybe two weeks ago,' Johnny says. 'Automobile accident, name of Daniel Rattigan.'

'Two weeks?' she asks sceptically, like it should be obvious he's wasting her time.

'Yeah. He might not be here any more, but we're trying . . .'

Even as Johnny speaks, she's rattling at the keyboard. Her eyes widen briefly at whatever she's seen on the monitor. She hits another key, then angles the screen further away like Johnny might lean over to peek.

'What's your relationship to the patient?'

Johnny doesn't want to lie until he has to. Never burn your bridges with medical staff.

'We're friends. I worked with him back in the day.'

'Can I have your name?'

'It's Johnny Hawke.'

She turns to Penny. 'And yours, ma'am.'

'Penelope Coyne. With a Y and an E.'

'And can I see some ID?'

Johnny's wondering why so belt-and-braces. It's not like they've asked for the guy's medical records. He produces his driver's licence and Penny her passport.

'Okay. Mr Rattigan isn't here any more. He was discharged three days after admission.'

'So just minor injuries?'

'I can't give out any information related to his treatment.'

'Sure. But we're having trouble tracking him down. Do you have any contact details?'

'Don't you?' asks Rhoda. 'You said he was your friend.'

Johnny's busted but intending to front it out. He's taking a beat to think of his next move when Penny suddenly bursts into tears.

'Please,' she says. 'I haven't seen Dan in forever. I flew in from the United Kingdom two days ago and I've only just learned he was in an accident. Surely there's some way you can help me out?'

Johnny is as impressed by her performance as Rhoda is taken aback. He notes, however, that Penny managed to pull it off without saying anything factually untrue. He can tell this woman will cling to the moral high ground until someone prises her cold dead fingers from it.

Rhoda lifts up a box of tissues and places it on the counter, handing one to Penny.

'Okay, here's what I'mma do. Why don't you take a seat while I make a call. It's gonna take a minute, because I got some other stuff I gotta deal with, but if Mr Rattigan is happy to speak to you, I'll put you on.'

'That's most obliging of you,' says Penny, dabbing her eyes.

'Don't go far,' Rhoda warns. 'I ain't tracking your asses down.'

'We'll be right over here.'

They walk around the side of the reception desk. Penny takes a seat in the waiting area while Johnny goes to the vending machines. He grabs a soda for himself and a cup of tea for Penny, glancing across to Rhoda as he sits down. She's on the phone. She notices his glance and makes a gesture with her open palm. He's not sure if she's saying five minutes or just stay put, but either way, something is in progress.

'How's the tea?'

'It's the best I've had since I got to California. Which is to say, dreadful.'

'You're welcome.'

Johnny's phone pings with an email. His contact at the department has got back to him. He shows Penny the screen, giving contact details for a whole list of women named Melissa Neeson.

'Why do you think Zoe gave us this name?' he asks. 'What's your gut instinct?'

'Well, she gave us Bradley's in order to point the finger at her wicked stepmother. My instinct is that the only person she dislikes more than Viola is her father.'

Johnny nods. 'Lucy Stonebridge told me about *her* father's MeToo stuff, and we heard those tech bros imply something similar with Lawrence Pierpont. What we don't know is Zoe's intentions toward Caleb or Saskia. She was ready to betray the whole family twenty years ago. But how this Melissa Neeson fits into that is anybody's guess.'

'What are you going to do?' Penny asks.

'Sometimes you just gotta throw out a line and see if anyone bites.'

That said, Johnny knows he can triage. Whatever this is, if Zoe reckons it could be related to Juliet's death, then like the Ignatieff crash, it has to pre-date that. He starts on the maiden names: women who were called Melissa Neeson back then. Further prioritising, he starts with those living in California.

The first one is a landline starting 619: San Diego area code. It rings a few times then someone picks up.

'Hello?'

'Melissa Neeson?'

She chuckles. 'Not for a long time. I'm Melissa Garvota now. Who is this?'

'Yeah, I'm a reporter with *Wired*. I'm just running some background on a story. Is it right you used to work with Pierpont Digital?'

She laughs again. 'No. I never heard of it.'

'You sure? Big video-games company.'

'I'm sure.'

'How about Pierpont Electronics?'

'Listen, I teach middle school.'

'Sorry, got my wires crossed.'

Johnny tries the next one, a Melissa Keating, living in Berkeley. She turns out to be a retired optician. Then he speaks to a dance instructor and an accountant before moving on to women whose married names are Neeson.

He thinks he's finally onto something when he gets an IT consultant. She has at least heard of Pierpont Digital, but that's all.

The next one is another landline, beginning 480. Arizona area code. The sight of it makes him think of Ibanez, but he can't let that inside his head right now.

'Is that Melissa Neeson?'

'Speaking. Who is this?'

'I'm with *Wired* magazine, just doing some background for a piece. Is it right that you used to work for Pierpont Digital?'

There is a pause.

'Who did you say you were again?'

'I work for *Wired*.'

The line goes dead. When Johnny calls back, there's no response.

He and Penny share a look.

'Will the real Melissa Neeson please stand up?' he says.

Johnny has just started keying her details into a search when someone in his peripheral vision causes him to look up. It's a woman, late thirties, her dark suit smart but sober, the material hard-wearing but comfortable. He knows what he's looking at in a heartbeat. He watches her approach the desk, sees the nurse point to the two of them.

Now he knows it wasn't Rattigan she called, and why she asked them to wait. Knows why she wanted names and ID. There was a note on Rattigan's file to alert the authorities should anyone come asking about him.

The woman walks up to them and produces a badge.

'I'm Detective Louisa Guadeloupe, LAPD. I'm informed that you are Penelope Coyne and Johnny Hawke, is that right?'

'*Lieutenant* Johnny Hawke,' he says. Johnny doesn't want this getting back to Nimitz but figures it will go better if she knows they're both on the job.

'Got your badge?'

'Not on me.'

She eyeballs him. She knows what's in front of her just as sure as Johnny does. Besides, they both know she can look him up, and that she will.

She glances quizzically at Penny. Johnny she can figure easily. It's what the old broad is doing with him that's taxing her.

'Can we talk someplace quiet?' she asks.

They take a walk outside to a bench in the shade, looking out on West 3rd. Guadeloupe walks with a machine coffee in one hand, her phone in the other, thumb busy on the screen.

'I understand you've been asking after Daniel Rattigan. What's your interest?'

'We want to talk to him about a case he's working.'

She looks again at Penny.

'We?'

'My role is unofficial.'

Guadeloupe looks sceptical but she lets it slide. She's got bigger questions.

'What's the case?'

Johnny decides he ain't gonna play hard to get. He's not giving away the farm either, but he knows that on this occasion he'll get more by playing nice.

'We don't know for sure. We believe he was hired by a tech entrepreneur we're interested in. Name of Wesley Oswald.'

Johnny watches for her response. There's very little. She's good.

'We were hoping Rattigan could confirm or deny,' Johnny adds.

'Why you looking for him here?'

'His neighbour told us he was in the hospital.'

She nods, expression still neutral.

'Assuming you're right,' she says, 'why was he hired? What is it you think he was looking into?'

Her earlier responses might have given him nothing, but these questions just confirmed that she is looking into Wesley too.

'A suicide twenty years ago. Wesley's sister, Juliet Oswald. Except Wesley has never accepted it was what it appeared.'

'What's your interest?'

'Two other suicides that might not be what they appeared either. One local, one in Scotland. And a straight-up, no questions murder. Slashed throat in a parked car, also in Scotland.'

Guadeloupe glances at Penny, making connections.

'What's the local case?' she asks, which is where she reaches the boundary of what Johnny is prepared to share. Mentioning the Jed Mahoney suicide would bring the house down on his head. But not giving her anything is gonna be conspicuous.

'We are unable to give you details without compromising a source,' Penny says, riding to the rescue and just about telling the truth once again.

Guadeloupe considers this.

'Are you guys also looking into Juliet Oswald's death?' she asks.

'It's in the scope of our investigation, yes,' Johnny says.

'What's your angle?'

He takes a moment, decides it's worth rolling the dice.

'I'd like to tell you, and it's good intel, but without trying to be an asshole about it, there's something I'd need in return.'

It's Guadeloupe's turn to take a beat. She's weighing up the whole thing. She knows there's something weird going on; probably smart enough to have already sussed Johnny is off the reservation. But that's gonna make her all the more curious as to what he might tell her.

Now she looks expectantly at him, like she's inviting him to name his terms.

'You're gonna look me up, soon as we're gone,' he says. 'You're—'

'Already did. You're on suspension. You want me to keep quiet about the fact that you're freelancing. This *better* be good intel.'

So now they both know where they stand.

Johnny takes a breath.

'Pierpont Digital are trying to buy Wesley's company, but Wesley doesn't trust them, so he hired Rattigan to investigate the Pierpont family. But here's the deeper context: twenty years ago, *Juliet* Oswald was investigating the Pierponts, not only because her brother was going into business with them, but also because she was about to marry Caleb Pierpont. We think the reason she died is that she found out something about one of them, but we don't know who and we don't know what.'

Guadeloupe eyes him intently. 'Will I be the first person you share this with when you do?'

'If my investigations have not been curtailed by my superiors finding out, then yes.'

She nods. 'My lips are sealed.'

'I'm figuring from the fact that there was an alert on his hospital file, and that you came running as soon as someone showed up asking about him, you don't believe Rattigan's accident was an accident.'

Guadeloupe looks out at the traffic on West 3rd and South San Vicente.

'His brakes failed at an intersection. We're not convinced it was bad luck.'

Johnny pauses a moment.

'What's Rattigan saying about it?'

'Not a lot. As far as we know, he's still unconscious.'

'As far as you know?'

'He was transferred to a private medical facility, some state-of-the-art place offering experimental rehabilitation for brain injury.'

'Wow. Who's paying for that?'

Guadeloupe gives him a knowing look. 'Wesley Oswald.'

'You've spoken to him?'

'Not exactly. Have you?'

'He has a reputation for shyness that seems to be well founded,' answers Penny.

'I've only spoken to his lawyer,' says Guadeloupe. 'She confirmed Rattigan had been working for Oswald but would *not* discuss what he hired Rattigan to look into.'

Johnny wishes he'd known this part two minutes ago. He had a stronger hand than he realised.

'Wesley must have been happy with his work, to be picking up his medical bills,' he suggests.

'Lawyer told me Oswald felt bad the accident happened on his dime.'

'Yeah. Because rich guys are always fair-minded and ethical that way.'

'You think there's another angle?'

'There usually is,' he says. 'If Rattigan was unconscious, who signed off on the transfer?'

'His ex-wife. Closest he has to next of kin. He's a real burnt-out loner. Anyway, it wasn't a difficult choice for her. Rattigan staying in the Cedars ICU was about to put a serious dent in her alimony, while the alternative was some sugar daddy takes him away.'

'Do you know where?'

'That's just one of many things I've been unable to get Oswald's lawyer to tell me.'

'If his vehicle was sabotaged, do you have anyone in the frame?'

She gives him an arch look. 'He's Dan Rattigan. We've narrowed it down to about two thousand suspects.'

'For those of us from overseas, perhaps you could provide some context,' says Penny.

'He was a homicide detective whose career imploded in a major scandal maybe twelve, thirteen years back,' Guadeloupe says. 'He was investigating two murders in West Hollywood. You understand West Hollywood?'

Penny looks blank.

'Boystown,' Johnny clarifies. 'Gay district.'

'Victims were both adolescent males, killed ten days apart, identical MO. I won't go into the details but it was real nasty. Ligatures, torture, nightmare stuff. Suddenly the gay community is concerned they got a serial killer loose in their playground. The department responds with more police on the streets. Then Rattigan finds out both vics had connections to a drug dealer named Latham, a real piece of shit. Rich-kid playboy with a rep for violent fetishism. Rattigan becomes convinced it's actually about drugs, and that Latham himself has seeded the serial-killer story as a smokescreen. Rattigan has a witness, a rival dealer who was once tied up and tortured by Latham as a warning.'

Guadeloupe takes a sip from her cup, makes a face like it's bitter, but Johnny knows it's not the coffee.

'It's a solid enough lead,' she goes on, 'but Latham's hard to get to. Expensive lawyers, uptown connections. Frustrations every detective has to swallow. Except Rattigan decides he's Dirty Harry or some shit. He busts into Latham's place without a warrant. Claims he was passing by when he thought he heard a domestic disturbance, some conveniently non-falsifiable pretext. He finds all the evidence he needs to get Latham arrested and charged.

'Everybody's relieved they caught the killer, not least the department, who can stand down all those extra officers and put them back to work elsewhere. Then two days later, while Latham is locked up awaiting arraignment, a seventeen-year-old kid becomes victim number three.'

Guadeloupe lets it hang for a moment.

'That's who Dan Rattigan is. A washed-out ex-cop who works solo because none of the agencies would touch him after he got his investigator's licence.'

'What was the third victim's name?' Johnny asks. A shiver runs through him as he realises there's an answer he really doesn't want to hear.

'Jayden Freil.'

Death Is But the Overture

VI

'I assume you're calling because you got a name for me.'

Penny heard Vikram's Australian accent boom through the speaker system inside Johnny's Cobra, making him seem a larger and more powerful figure than the rather slight individual she remembered from the restaurant yesterday.

'Yeah, I got a name,' Johnny told him. 'And a lot more besides. It's an independent operator too, not some corporate agency with a team of lawyers to counter your subpoenas.'

'What's the name?'

'I'll tell you that as you're welcoming us through the doors at Sea Monster, like we agreed. When is good for you?'

There was a pause.

'Can you get here around six? Most folks will have left by then, so I can let you have a look around without getting in anyone's way.'

Penny looked at the clock. It was just after five.

'You're near Westlake Village, right? Thousand Oaks.'

'Yeah.'

'We'll be there, long as the traffic gods smile on us.'

Johnny hung up and started the engine, hooking his phone into a holder on the dashboard. Penny watched him key an address into the navigation thingy, which estimated the journey would take just over an hour.

'What if we get there, we tell Vikram what we know, and he says it's not good enough?' she asked.

'Vikram will do whatever Saskia tells him. She's the one who agreed the terms. And she wants that name.'

Johnny pulled out onto Beverly Boulevard, heading east. They drove for a while without speaking. Penny was content to look at the cityscape scrolling past, but Johnny was not normally so withdrawn. She suspected he was mulling over what Guadeloupe had told them.

She had expected him to mount some kind of defence of Rattigan, perhaps making the case that he had acted in good faith with the intention of putting a dangerous man where he could do no further harm. Instead, she got the impression it had knocked him for six.

Johnny was taking them through Laurel Canyon, lost in his thoughts as he guided the Cobra through chicanes of parked cars and around endless switchback bends. He was heading north first and then presumably west after Studio City. Penny guessed this was to avoid Santa Monica Boulevard and then the 405, both of which would be choked at this time of day.

She pulled herself up, surprised by her own musings. How did she know this? The same thing had happened this morning, when she corrected Johnny on which route to take for Cinnamon Bay. She told him she must have seen it on television, but that wasn't true. She'd known instinctively, as though she'd been there before. She hadn't, though. This was her first visit to California.

Unless it wasn't and she simply couldn't recall. There were so many gaps: things she should know because she remembered knowing them once; as well as things she *shouldn't* know and couldn't remember learning. This was why her nephew worried about her. Penny told herself everybody forgot things as they got old, but the most troubling aspect of losing your memory was that you could never know how much memory you'd lost.

She just wished a loss of memory could explain all the other things that made no sense. She had stopped denying it to herself: Johnny was right. There were these parallels, these echoes stretching across twenty years between three otherwise unrelated deaths, and it wasn't even possible to say for sure which was an echo of which.

But what Penny *could* say for sure was that someone was trying to get away with murder, and that was territory where she always knew her footing. If she followed the clues and put the puzzle together, no matter how strange it appeared, the one thing she was always confident of was working out whodunnit.

They had passed an overhead sign saying the Ventura Freeway was two miles ahead when Johnny made a right turn, heading east.

'Change of route?' Penny asked.

Johnny didn't answer. She noticed that his eyes kept going to his rearview mirror. He drove another couple of blocks then made a sudden turn, veering sharply left and drawing a loud rebuke from the horn of an oncoming Jeep.

'What's going on? Are we lost?'

'No, but I'm hoping we will be soon. Lost from the Ford Bronco that's been tailing us since we crossed Sunset. I figured maybe it was a coincidence because if someone's behind you going into Laurel Canyon, chances are they're still gonna be behind you when you come out, but it followed me soon as I veered off.'

Penny turned and looked back.

'I don't see anyone.'

'No. That hard left I took was to let him know he was made.'

Johnny turned back onto Laurel Canyon Boulevard and stayed on it across the Los Angeles River. Then he took another sudden left, into a residential neighbourhood.

'I think I lost him.'

'You've certainly lost me.'

'I want you to open the glove box, just in case.'

Penny pushed the catch and the glove compartment fell open. There was an automatic pistol lodged inside, held by some form of clamp with a spring-loaded mechanism.

'I thought you had to surrender your firearm.'

'My police sidearm, sure. But I always carry a—'

Whatever he was about to say was lost in the crunch and jolt as the car was slammed sideways by a sudden impact. A black SUV blindsided them, slamming the Cobra down a narrow tree-lined lane between gardens. The car spun and skidded, its nose rebounding off a tree trunk, leaving Penny so dazed as to be unsure whether it had come to a stop.

There was movement around her, though. Through the windscreen she could see a burly man in an ill-fitting suit stride towards their vehicle, a gun gripped in his hand.

371

The Silence Forever Echoes

Chapter Nine

Johnny doesn't know why the airbags haven't deployed. Could be they weren't travelling fast enough at the moment of collision, or something to do with the angle of impact. Or perhaps he had just got what he paid for when he took the Cobra to that cheap-ass garage off La Cienega for its last service.

He turns to check if Penny is okay. She looks groggy but her eyes are open; gaping, in fact, as she takes in what Johnny should have been looking at. That corrupt asshole Arlo Waters has got out of the Bronco and he doesn't look like he's suddenly forgiven Johnny for putting his corrupt asshole brother away. He's bearing down on him, gun drawn.

Shit happens fast after that. Too fast. Arlo's got the door open and has hauled Johnny out onto the concrete of the alley while he's still seeing stars.

'What the fuck . . .' Johnny starts, steadying himself on all fours. Then Arlo cracks him in the head, a pistol whip to the temple with the butt of his weapon.

Johnny only catches a glimpse, but it looks like a Desert

Eagle 44. The model ain't what matters. More significant is that it is most definitely not a service issue, and that means Arlo ain't here on any kind of legitimate business.

Johnny sees the gun come down again and raises a hand to deflect the blow. It never comes, but what he does feel is the cold steel of a cuff fastening around his wrist. Fraction of a second later the other one clicks around the door handle.

For some stupid reason he worries about what it's gonna do to his paintwork. That's before he feels the next blow, an upwards swing into his gut, taking the wind from him. It's not with the Desert Eagle this time. Arlo's holstered it and is holding a wrench, which he's raising for another attack.

Johnny throws up his arm to deflect the incoming blow. Feels a dull but massive jolt of pain as it connects, somewhere on his forearm. Arlo swings again and again. There's only so far Johnny can duck and squirm. A glancing blow comes off his aching arm onto his head.

Johnny sees what this is. Arlo's gonna kill him: beat him to death with a wrench in an alley so it looks like some random incident. Except there's a witness. And with a horrible dread he realises Arlo's gonna kill her too.

That's when he hears her voice.

'Leave him alone.'

Penny's tone is full-on schoolmarm, though he can detect the fear beneath it.

'Stay in the goddamn car,' Arlo tells her. 'This is a police matter. It doesn't concern you.'

'Violence always concerns me,' she replies. 'It appears you have your suspect thoroughly restrained and he is not resisting.'

'I said get back in the fucking car. I already done told you, I'm a police officer.'

'Not once I've finished talking to your superiors, you won't be.'

'Run, Penny,' Johnny warns. 'Get the hell outta here.'

'No, you stay right there, lady,' Arlo commands. 'I'm gonna want a word with you too once I'm done here.'

Johnny is crushed as he watches Penny climb back into the Cobra. The woman always plays by the rules, always does what she's told, especially when it comes from the authorities. And today she's going to die for that.

Arlo raises the wrench again. Then he pauses as they both hear the Cobra's passenger door open once more. Penny is standing there, levelling Johnny's Glock.

'I said leave him alone.'

Christ, Johnny thinks, it's a miracle she disengaged it from the bracket. But she ain't gonna know the first thing about working the safety or chambering a round.

Arlo susses that too. He's reaching for his piece.

Penny racks the slide and flips the safety with her thumb. She looses off two rounds either side of Arlo's shoulders. One of them nicks the edge of his suit and the other is a couple of mills further in: just enough to draw blood.

Arlo shudders, reeling in shock and disbelief. When he turns and focuses again, she's got the Glock aimed directly at his head, the stock gripped in both hands, feet slightly apart, solid stance. She's five foot nothing and can't weigh more than seven stone carrying a purse, but you wouldn't fuck with her.

'Meet my new partner, asshole,' Johnny says.

'Motherfucker,' Arlo replies. 'Did you tell her what happened to all your other partners?'

Penny hasn't taken her eye off him, the Glock still levelled.

'Uncuff him,' she orders.

Arlo holds the keys in his palm where she can see them, then

374

throws them in the air as a distraction before scrambling back to the Bronco. He's driving away before he even pulls the door closed.

Seeing it from the rear as it peels away, Johnny flashes back to Fountain, outside Kingdom Pictures. He saw a similar vehicle hurry away then too, just after Ibanez died. Sonofabitch.

Penny keeps the gun on the retreating vehicle the whole time. Johnny's half expecting her to yell 'Yeah, you better run.'

'Who was that?' she asks.

'Never mind who was that. Who the hell are you?'

Penny looks at the Glock like she just noticed it and it's freaking her out. Her hands start trembling but she still has the presence of mind to engage the safety.

'I'm starting to wonder that myself,' she replies, her voice shorn of all the authority it was carrying a few seconds ago. 'My God, I just shot at a police officer.'

'You just *shot* a police officer, but I think he was fixing to kill *this* police officer, so it's cool.'

'It most definitely is not cool. We need to report this.'

'What, that you fired on a cop?'

Penny leans on the trunk of the Cobra, like her legs have gone weak.

'My God, what have I done? He's going to report it first. Then they're all going to come after us.'

'No, I know that guy. His name's Arlo Waters and he's as dumb as he is corrupt. Whatever he was up to, he ain't gonna say shit about it to anyone official.'

Penny's shaking her head gravely, not reassured. 'He's going to tell *somebody*, though. Or a witness will have seen what happened, and they'll report it. There are always consequences. When you break the rules, there are always consequences.'

Johnny can't fathom it. In the face of real danger, when she needed to be, Penny was ice cold. Now she's falling to pieces, terrified of some hypothetical retribution.

Finally he figures it out: Penny's not afraid of other people breaking the rules. She's afraid of what happens when *she* breaks them. Which means she's broken them before, and he's guessing it worked out as well for her as it did for Dan Rattigan.

Death Is But the Overture

VII

Penny applied a sticking plaster to Johnny's temple, that being the only visible damage of his assault. He assured her that nothing was broken, but he was holding his left arm rather gingerly. He was otherwise uncomplaining and disarmingly composed in the face of what had just happened. Penny felt more shaken up by her own part in the experience.

When people had related their own episodes of unexpected behaviour to Penny in the past, they often talked of feeling like they were possessed, but she had felt completely in control. Holding the gun had been natural and familiar, like something she had done a thousand times before. For an action to feel so accustomed required muscle memory, so even though her mind could not recall it, her body instinctively knew otherwise.

She was also troubled by the feeling that she had come full circle. This insane journey had begun when the police turned up and inexplicably started firing on her back at the library. Now, only a matter of days later, she was the one shooting at the police.

She felt a very long way from Glen Cluthar.

Johnny assured her he was still fit to drive, and though the car looked more beaten up than he did, they were able to resume their journey towards Westlake Village.

'Why would he do that?' Penny asked. 'Try to kill you, and in broad daylight?'

'I put his brother away on corruption charges a few years back.'

This was a motive, but not an explanation.

'But if that was years ago, why now?'

'I don't know,' Johnny admitted. 'He's greedy and he's stupid, but he's never been a psycho. His older brother was the scary one. Arlo looked up to him, got dragged along in his slipstream.'

'And you haven't done anything recently to provoke him?'

'No. It's usually the other way around, him goading me. He didn't even say anything: just started wailing on me. I don't like the guy, but I wouldn't have thought him capable of that. He was behaving totally out of character.'

'It's catching,' Penny said, glancing at the glove compartment.

Sea Monster HQ was an ultra-modern low-rise compound within acres of rolling lawns, the tinted windows on the two buildings reflecting the landscape like giant video screens. The greenery was punctuated by topiary carved into the shapes of, presumably, game characters, though the only one Penny recognised was Qubo, whom she was coming to detest. A fork in the avenue branched off left for Sea Monster Software and right for Seahorse Neuroscience, each route passing above a pale blue channel that encircled both buildings. As the car drove over it, Penny looked down, seeing a system of black objects submerged in about two metres of clear water, bubbles on the surface indicating a constant filtration process.

There was parking for maybe a hundred cars, several of which had passed them, on their way out. It was ten past six, the end of the working day. Almost every vehicle they saw looked new and electric, while Johnny's old Ford seemed all the more scruffy given the bashes it had recently sustained.

They walked into a two-storey reception lobby, its walls festooned with awards, framed magazine reviews and decades' worth of advertising artwork. Penny noted that there were no photographs of the founder, in keeping with Wesley's general reclusiveness. She wondered if he was nearby, watching them approach via CCTV, perhaps.

She was concerned they might be too late. Through the windows she could see the young woman on the front desk pulling on her jacket. To the left of reception there were two security gates: glass panels sliding apart to allow employees to exit. Beyond those she could see several doors, an elevator and the bottom of a staircase.

The young woman pulling on her jacket put on a professional face at their approach, but Penny read her scepticism that this pair could possibly be in the right place. Johnny was looking conspicuously roughed-up, and Penny would offer long odds on anyone else having turned up here in a twin-set.

'We're here to see Vikram Chaudhuri,' Johnny said.

The receptionist glanced at the clock. 'Do you have an appointment?'

'No worries, Michelle,' said a voice. 'I'm expecting them.'

Penny looked up and saw that Vikram had emerged onto the mezzanine level above reception.

'If you can just run off a couple of guest passes, I'll take it from here.'

Vikram disappeared from view then emerged at the foot of the stairs a few seconds later. He strolled through the gates and over to the front desk, where he held out a hand to intercept Michelle's as she was about to present the visitors with their security passes.

A power play, Penny recognised. Just for show. There was no way he wasn't letting them in. She remembered Johnny's words about Saskia, but furthermore she suspected Vikram was as curious to learn what they had to say as they were to hear from him.

'G'day,' he said.

'What's with the moat?' Johnny asked. 'You guys planning to install a drawbridge?'

'It's a highly efficient heat-exchange system for cooling our computers. This place uses heaps of processing power.'

'You have a server farm here?'

'Nah. That's hosted up in Palo Alto.'

'So what's generating all the heat?'

Vikram held up the guest cards. 'I'll need the password before I can answer that.'

He was smiling, but also serious.

'Daniel Rattigan,' said Johnny. '3D Investigations, North La Brea. He's an ex-cop who had to resign after a big scandal a dozen years ago. Works on his own because nobody else wants to be near him.'

'Why would Wesley hire a dag like that?'

'Hey, you know Wesley better than we do. That's why we're here.'

'Have you spoken to this Rattigan bloke?'

'Our deal was for a name. I'll give you more if we think your tour is worth five stars.'

'Oh, it's certainly worth that. But before I show you anything, I need you both to sign one of these.'

Vikram produced an iPad bearing a non-disclosure agreement,

presenting it to Penny first. She scrolled down, revealing that the document ran to pages and pages.

'I don't have time to read all this,' said Johnny.

'Who does, mate? But the gist is that we'll take every cent you own or earn between now and your death if you tell anybody about what you see here today.'

'We're investigating several murders,' Johnny reminded him.

'Yep, and if the murderer's name and the words "I confess" are written in stone on the other side of that wall, you're still gonna have to source that same information elsewhere, and *prove* you sourced it elsewhere.'

'What if we say Miles Deacon leaked it to us?' asked Penny.

Vikram gave her a shrug. 'Feel free to roll the dice,' he said.

Penny signed. So did Johnny.

Vikram handed them each a guest pass, then gestured towards the gates.

'Welcome to Sea Monster,' he said, once they had swiped themselves through.

He led them up the stairs and along the mezzanine, then down a long corridor. Through the glass wall to her left, Penny could see a cavernous room lined with rows of desks, each bearing huge monitors. There was nobody left working, but a few screens were displaying lines of code or still images. Lifesize cardboard cut-outs of characters were leaning against partitions, concept artwork in frames hung along one wall.

They walked slowly, Penny having the impression Vikram was rather proud of the place and wanted them to take it all in. It certainly didn't seem to trouble him that Johnny was taking pictures of things on his phone.

'Okay, potted history. The company was founded by Wesley and Juliet Oswald back in 1995. The original prem—'

381

'What about the garage in Dundee in the eighties?' Penny interrupted.

'That was Wesley's first company, Midge Byte, which he published Qubo with as a teenager. He then launched EMA Software, which first ported Qubo to consoles in 1993. *Qubo on the Moon*, *Qubo's Alpine Adventure*. Big hits.'

'What did EMA stand for?' Penny asked.

'Eat My Abbreviation,' Vikram answered apologetically. 'So you can understand that Sea Monster was when Wesley got serious, in every respect. He wanted to move on to more complex, narrative-based games. Sea Monster launched with the first title in what became the *Sacred Reign* franchise, and I joined in ninety-nine just as *Neon City* was being launched. It was like *Blade Runner* but with an emphasis on sleuthing rather than a shoot-em-up. Wesley has always loved his detective stories. Guess it runs in the family.'

'The family?'

'Yeah. Wesley and Juliet's aunt wrote like fifty mystery novels back in the day.'

'What was her name?'

Vikram wore a pained expression. 'I can't remember. I never read any. Not my genre, more of a sci-fi guy.'

'Somebody Oswald, perhaps?' Penny suggested.

'No, surname was different. Annabel something. Or Anne-Marie.'

Penny was running through imaginary shelves in her mind, looking for crime novelists whose first names were Annabel or Anne-Marie. Nothing leapt to mind.

'Why Sea Monster?' Johnny asked. 'Is it a Cthulhu thing? I know you video-game guys are crazy for Lovecraft.'

'No. That was Juliet's idea. It's a reference to the hippocampus:

the part of the brain that houses the imagination and looks like a seahorse. "Hippocampus" is Latin for "horse-like sea monster". After Juliet died, Wesley set up Seahorse Neuroscience, sort of in tribute.'

'And that's a separate entity, despite being right next door?'

'Not quite. It's actually why Wesley doesn't own the whole company any more. He sold off chunks of Sea Monster to generate investment in the neuroscience division, which he runs. Right now, Seahorse remains Wesley's personal fiefdom, but under the terms of the proposed takeover he would have to relinquish control.'

'Is there an overlap between the games and neuroscience operations?' Penny asked. 'It seems an odd pairing.'

Vikram beamed, like she'd asked precisely the question he wanted her to.

'Wesley always says a game has failed if it's using technology to replace imagination rather than enhance it.'

They were getting to the end of the corridor, approaching what Penny suspected Vikram was building up to. At the end on the right was a door with a sign on it, white text reversed out of a square of bright blue:

STRICTLY NO ENTRY

COBALT LEVEL AUTHORISED PERSONNEL ONLY

Before Vikram could tap his pass against the reader, the door opened and through it stepped Audrey Ireland. Penny thought again about CCTV, because Audrey didn't look surprised to find them there.

She didn't look happy either.

The Silence Forever Echoes

Chapter Ten

Back at Electronicon, Johnny had gotten used to Audrey popping up out of nowhere, like she had a sixth sense about when he and Penny might need her. He gets the impression something changed when they started asking the wrong kinds of questions about her boss, and that her superpower is now being deployed to the opposite end. He wonders if she still thinks they're from St Andrews University, or if she has sought out the truth, like Saskia did.

'I'm showing them around,' Vikram tells her. 'It's cool. They've signed an NDA.'

'Have you cleared it with Wesley?'

'Sure,' Vikram replies. Johnny doesn't believe him, and very much doubts Audrey will either.

It's clear there's a dividing line here. She's Wesley's assistant and fiercely loyal to him, which means she's gonna regard Vikram and the rest of the board as hostile.

Johnny looks at the door she came out of, with its stark debarment of all but 'cobalt level' personnel. If she verifies that her boss hasn't cleared it, then he and Penny will not be getting to see what's on the other side.

'Can I speak to you in private a moment?' Johnny asks her. 'It's concerning a professional matter.'

'Would that be an academic thing?' she replies, a hint of sarcasm in her tone. Yeah, she knows.

'No, it would be concerning my actual profession.'

Penny reads the play, sees he's running interference. 'Why don't you catch us up in a minute,' she says to Johnny, gesturing for Vikram to continue.

Vikram taps his card and holds the door open. Penny passes through as Audrey looks on, torn between dealing with Vikram and dealing with Johnny. The window for putting her foot down just closed.

'Is Wesley available to talk right now?' Johnny asks.

'He is unable to speak to anyone at the moment.'

'Is he *ever* gonna be available?'

'I assure you, Wesley remains very keen to meet you both, but now is not a good time.'

'That sounds like PR bullshit. I mean, if he doesn't want to talk to us, tell me now.'

'PR is not my remit. There are questions I can't answer or am not permitted to answer, but unlike some, I wouldn't accept a position that required me to lie as part of the job.'

'Touché,' Johnny says.

'Perhaps there is something I *can* help you with,' she adds.

'Yeah. Perhaps. We're told Wesley is paying for the medical care of a private investigator named Daniel Rattigan, whose services he engaged. Can you tell me anything about that?'

'Tell you what, specifically?'

'Can you confirm that he's paying Rattigan's medical bills?'

'That's outside the scope of my remit.'

'Can you confirm that he hired Rattigan?'

'That's also outside the scope of my remit.'

Johnny swallows his frustration. It's like talking to a machine. But like talking to a machine, sometimes it's a matter of working out what questions they're programmed to answer.

'We're told Rattigan was moved to a private facility. Is that facility part of Seahorse Neuroscience?'

'I am not permitted to comment. Medical matters are strictly confidential.'

'Wesley was involved in a court case, to do with the end-of-life care of a relative, we believe. Was that person moved to the same facility?'

'Like I said, medical matters are—'

Johnny's patience runs out. 'Jesus H. Candlesticks, lady. We're investigating four homicides and tracking a possible threat to Wesley's life. If you wanna help him, you should help us. Gimme *some* fuckin' thing.'

Audrey closes her eyes for a long moment. Johnny thinks she is preparing for another stonewalling response, but when she opens them, her expression is less professionally composed and her voice quieter.

'I can tell you *some* things, because they are in the public domain, just about.'

'Good enough,' Johnny concedes.

'Wesley's parents are both dead. Among his surviving relatives, the one he has always been closest to is Amanda Fraser, his father's older sister. She lives in California. The rest of the family are based in the UK.'

'Is she the mystery writer?'

'She *was* a mystery writer. She's long retired. She was suffering from Alzheimer's, then she had a stroke and her condition deteriorated. Her son wanted to bring her back home, but Wesley believed he could provide better care here in California.'

'What does her son do?'

'He's in publishing, officially. But what that really means is he manages the rights and revenues accruing from her books. I can neither confirm nor deny that Wesley has on occasion called him a parasite.'

'So he and Wesley are cousins, but not exactly close. How did her son react to losing the court case?'

'Not well. He called Wesley a body-snatcher.'

Death Is But the Overture

VIII

Penny followed Vikram down another corridor, this time one devoid of windows. He then used his card to open a door that looked imposingly sturdier than any of the ones she had seen already. The previous doors had unlocked with a quiet click, whereas this one gave way with a reverberating clunk.

He led her into an anteroom which looked a lot like the control booth in a radio studio: lots more computer monitors, but as well as keyboards there were consoles presenting hundreds of switches. One wall was dominated by windows looking into a larger space.

'I'm just nipping back to swipe Mr Hawke through,' Vikram said, leaving her alone in the booth.

She walked over to the windows and looked into the adjacent chamber. Were it actually a studio, it would have been filled with tables, chairs, microphones and headsets. Instead the space was dominated by a single object: a huge black electronic device that looked a lot like a CT scanner, a bed with a hexagonal surround forming a canopy over the head end.

Johnny appeared a couple of minutes later. Taking in the vast black lozenge they had apparently come here to see, his expression was much as Penny's had been.

'This is Diegesis? The future of the video-games industry?'

'Yeah,' conceded Vikram. 'It's not exactly the Nintendo Switch.'

'I have no notion what you're talking about,' said Penny.

'Maybe the ZX Spectrum is a better point of reference,' Vikram replied.

'That I *have* heard of.' She remembered her nephew getting one as a teenager, and being most excited about it.

'It revolutionised people's perception of computers,' Vikram said, 'because it was compact, cheap and unobtrusive.'

Penny looked again at the device beyond the windows. It was clearly none of these things.

'To be fair, back in 1962, the first ever video game was played on a computer the size of a fridge-freezer. Within a decade they had a version that could fit in a cabinet inside an amusement arcade. Seven years after that, you could buy the Atari at Sears.'

'So this is merely the prototype,' Penny observed.

'It's *a* prototype: the one we've been given by the blokes next door. I'm sure they've got a more advanced model by now, but this is the version we're allowed to play with.'

'And what does it do?'

Vikram took a breath.

'What Wesley has been trying to do all his life. It makes the brain generate a convincing simulation using internal rather than external stimuli. Which Wesley would say the brain already does when you experience a memory or when you dream.'

Penny looked at the machine. She had had fears she would struggle with the concept, but this made sense.

'So instead of looking at a virtual world projected on a monitor,' she suggested, 'you would be entering an enhanced version of your own imagination. Like a headset that works with your eyes closed.'

'Albeit a headset the size of a sideboard,' Vikram acknowledged. She was surprised at his candour. Perhaps it was his being Australian.

'What kind of games do you run on this thing?' Johnny asked.

'Not games. Books.'

Penny's ears pricked up.

'Books?'

'Wesley likes to say that games are just vehicles for narrative, whereas books are "concentrated story fuel". Our last *Neon City* game, we spent close to fifty million dollars and however many thousand man-hours simulating a futuristic Los Angeles. With Diegesis, you could feed in the text of *Do Androids Dream of Electric Sheep?* and a future Los Angeles would be instantly created by your imagination, and enhanced so that it feels completely convincing. It would let you experience the world of a book as though you're there.'

'What, you're saying you could feed in *Goldfinger* and get to be James Bond's new sidekick?' Johnny suggested.

'No,' Vikram replied, 'I'm saying you could feed in *Goldfinger* and get to be James Bond.'

'How does that work?' Penny asked. 'Do you feel like you're piloting another person's body? Or that they are piloting yours?'

'Yeah,' said Johnny. 'What if you're in a situation where James Bond would do one thing, but you want to do another?'

'That's where Wesley's secret sauce comes in. Sometimes the actions are predetermined, but it's designed so that it should always feel like you're the one making the decisions, even when you're not. We've found that it works best when there's a degree of overlap between yourself and the character.'

'Isn't that just like reading any book?' Penny observed. 'The better you can relate to a character, the more you're likely to bond with them?'

'Totally. Though we've found it works the other way too. Some people click with characters because they're so *unlike* themselves: they represent a person they'd rather be.'

'But how do you switch off from being yourself? I might bond perfectly with one of the Dashwood sisters in terms of values and temperament, but I can't forget what I know about the next three hundred years.'

Vikram clasped his hands together awkwardly, as though Penny had asked after a close relative who'd just been arrested for embezzlement. 'Did I forget to mention you have to be unconscious?' He cringed a little, while looking oddly amused by his admission. 'And that's not even the tricky part.'

'Wait,' said Penny. 'You have to be rendered unconscious?'

'Sparko.' Again, he was making no attempt to shrink from the shortcomings or put a polish on them. 'The technology was developed over at Seahorse as a means of reconnecting neural pathways. It's an experimental therapy for brain injury and deteriorative conditions. The patient can explore the world of a story like it's real, solving puzzles, having new experiences, all of it forging new neural connections.'

'And does that work?' Penny asked.

'Medical matters are—'

'Strictly confidential, I know,' said Johnny. 'But if *that's* not the tricky part, what the hell is?'

Vikram glanced through the window at the machine, which

could not look less like a marketable plaything now if had rotating razor blades attached and was on fire.

'Ms Coyne's question about the Dashwood sisters was bang on the nose,' he admitted. 'That secret sauce I mentioned? It's that the machine doesn't just stimulate your imagination. It also suppresses your memories.'

Johnny's eyes widened. 'Wait, what?'

Vikram nodded by way of confirmation that yes, he really did just say that.

'I don't know shit about marketing,' said Johnny, 'but nobody's gonna let a machine switch off part of their memory, because what if it don't switch on again once they're through?'

Vikram beamed again, exactly as he had done when Penny asked the question he wanted her to.

'I'd like to remind you both of the NDAs you signed, before saying that you've just outlined why the Sea Monster board believe this might be the biggest, most expensive white elephant in electronics history. Potentially, what it can do is staggering, but even if we get the cost and size down, there is Buckley's chance anybody's gonna buy what could turn out to be a home-brew lobotomy kit.'

'So why are Pierpont offering four billion for it?' Johnny asked.

Vikram let out a chuckle. 'Fucked if I know, mate. Wesley thinks he can get investment elsewhere, but me and the board can see bugger-all evidence for that, which is why I'm doing anything and everything to keep Saskia sweet and get the deal done. We need Pierpont Digital to sign on the dotted line before they realise they're not buying the ZX Spectrum: they're buying the Sinclair C5.'

Death Is But the Overture

IX

Night was falling as they stepped back outside, the temperature far warmer than Penny was bracing herself against. Darkness by seven back home usually meant she could expect a nip in the air, but it was still in the high sixties. She wasn't sure she would trade the heat for the extra light in summer long term, but California was beginning to grow on her. If only she could remember whether she had been here before.

Little seemed certain to her right now in fact, no matter how much information she gathered. Vikram had been as good as his word, showing them around Sea Monster and explaining, in depth, what Diegesis was. Unfortunately, Penny didn't feel that knowing any of it had shed much light on their case.

'I understand business about as well as I understand computers,' Penny said. 'But even I can grasp that Wesley might have poured everything into developing an invention nobody could sell. I would have thought he'd be biting Pierpont Digital's hand off, not rebuffing them.'

'Maybe it's some kinda double bluff to get them to bid even more,' Johnny suggested. 'Or to improve the terms of the deal.'

'Pierpont Digital don't need to, though. Wesley can be outvoted as it is. Perhaps it's simply as it appears: that regardless of money, he wants nothing to do with the Pierponts while he believes one of them killed his sister.'

'Yeah, except nothing about this has been simple or what it appears. I can't get a read on this Wesley dude, not least because we haven't got near the guy. And the thing I keep coming back to is that he's spent his whole life building super-complex games. It's not just that I'm worried he's working three moves ahead. It's that I get this feeling I ain't gonna find out what game he's even playing until it's too late.'

They made their way towards the car park, where Penny could see only a few vehicles remaining.

'Would you take a spin in Wesley's machine?' she asked.

'Not for a million bucks. Or at least not until a million other folks had a ride first and nobody came out like Jack Nicholson in *One Flew Over the Cuckoo's Nest*.'

'That being so, if the machine could put you inside a book, which one would you choose?'

Johnny glanced up at the stars, beginning to shine through the gathering dark.

'*The Hitchhiker's Guide to the Galaxy*. I wanna drink a Pan Galactic Gargle Blaster, and I'd like to see if I can't steal Trillian offa that asshole Zaphod.'

'Wouldn't it be rather traumatic in practice, discovering that the world you know is gone, and that everyone you care about is dead?'

'Vikram said it works better the more you can relate to the character.'

Penny rather got the sense he wasn't quite joking. She was about to ask him to elaborate, but he changed the subject, perhaps pre-emptively.

'Speaking of books, does the name Amanda Fraser ring any bells? That's Wesley's aunt, the mystery writer.'

Penny thought she had heard of just about every major novelist from Cervantes forward, but this meant nothing to her. And yet Vikram said she had written fifty books.

'I'm afraid not.'

'That's who the court case was about. I got Audrey to spill.' Johnny got out his phone. 'I looked her up – Wikipedia says very little about her personal life. All it mentions is that she had two younger siblings: Wesley's old man and a sister who died in childhood. But check this out. There's a list of titles, all of her books. Click on one.'

Johnny handed Penny his mobile. She tapped the first title, *A Death Most Inconvenient*. She was met with an error message: Page Not Found. She clicked on another at random: *Strong Fences Make Dead Neighbours*. Once again, Page Not Found.

'Weird, huh?'

'Indeed.'

Penny handed it back, and as she did so she felt her own mobile vibrating. She took it out and read a new email she'd received.

'Whatever *did* you say to Audrey?' she asked as they approached Johnny's Cobra, the new damage looking less raw in the softer evening light.

'Why?'

'We seem to be back in her good graces. She's just passed on an open invitation to a reception tomorrow.'

'What time?'

Penny looked closer and noticed that she had misread.

'Oh. It's actually tonight. Seven-thirty in somewhere called Calabasas.'

'Guess she figured, long as we're in the neighbourhood. That's like fifteen minutes from here. But why would she be wanting *us* to attend?'

'Because it's taking place at the Juliet Oswald Foundation. I think we might finally be about to meet the elusive Wesley.'

Death Is But the Overture

X

The premises of the Juliet Oswald Foundation turned out to be a two-storey modern building set amidst colourful gardens and flanked by rows of pine trees. The reception was being hosted in a lobby space that was bright and airy, as befitting a mental-health charity, but while Penny imagined it a quiet and calming space most of the time, right then it was thronging with bodies and noise.

The invitation had said nothing about a dress code, but many of those present exuded black tie even though they weren't wearing it; among them Lawrence and Viola Pierpont. Penny assumed the other conspicuously wealthy-looking attendees were donors.

She might have felt underdressed but for two less expensively attired cohorts. One comprised young people whom she assumed to have had dealings with the foundation, and the other media personnel, the open invitation evidently having gone out far and wide to publicise the foundation's work.

All of the Pierponts were present. Caleb was working the room, shaking hands and convening micro-gatherings. She saw

397

Zoe and her husband chatting to a trio of adolescents, and observed Saskia hovering on the fringes, ubiquitous phone in her hand, occasionally directing one of the servers circulating with drinks and canapés. Saskia gave Penny and Johnny a smiling glance by way of acknowledging the service they had rendered. Penny thought she might be feeling less grateful when she found out Rattigan was incommunicado, but a deal was a deal, and they had held up their end.

Significantly, Penny also saw Detective Guadeloupe, there incognito. She had evidently decided she wanted a closer look at the Pierponts. The detective traded subtle nods with Penny and Johnny, tacitly understanding that they should not acknowledge each other.

Conspicuously not present was Wesley Oswald, something they confirmed as soon as they spoke to Audrey. She was there to represent him, she said, adding that he never came to such events but did wish to be perceived as supporting the foundation.

Johnny looked palpably uncomfortable as they stood together by the front windows, and it wasn't because he was nursing a few injuries.

'I keep finding myself making chit-chat at champagne receptions,' he said. 'I'm happier kicking down doors in crappy neighbourhoods and having tweakers scream in my face. It's starting to feel like you've brought your world with you, and it's infected mine.'

'You infected mine first,' Penny replied. 'I never had to deal with graphic and bloody murder scenes before you turned up, to say nothing of machine guns and car chases.'

'At least you were on familiar terrain,' Johnny countered. 'A wedding at an upscale hotel in the countryside, dealing with lords and ladies and high society.'

'And yet no matter where we find ourselves, as you are at pains to point out, we are nonetheless confronted by very similar murders.'

'No,' Johnny insisted. 'Different versions of the *same* murder.'

Penny could hear the tinkle of polite laughter all around them. It was balm to her ears, both in its gentle familiarity and how it reassured her that they weren't being overheard.

'Indulging your hypothesis,' she said, 'Wesley is in the role of Miles Deacon, or Deacon is in the role of Wesley, depending which way you look at it. However, Wesley is trying to investigate his sister's death. Does that mean we're wrong about Miles killing Lilian and his alter ego Crawford Nicholson killing Jed?'

'That depends which way you look at it too. What if it means we're wrong to assume Wesley ain't the one who killed his sister?'

'Why would he be investigating it then?'

'Maybe that's not what he's really investigating. Like I keep saying, this guy's got an agenda we're not seeing.'

This was true. Penny shared Johnny's sense that there was a whole other game being played somewhere above their heads.

She glanced across the room to where Detective Guadeloupe was talking to a glamorous middle-aged couple.

'I've found a flaw in your theory,' Penny realised. 'You're missing a parallel. Wesley engaged Rattigan. Crawford-slash-Miles didn't hire anyone to investigate the deaths of Jed and Lilian.'

'Didn't he?' Johnny replied coyly.

'What do you mean?'

'Why would Miles invite *you* to his sister's wedding?'

Penny had to admit the question had long been troubling her. She gave him the only answer she had come up with.

'The same reason Lilian sought me out that night. They both knew I had experience of the Stonebridge family firm.'

'But that's not the main thing people know about you, is it?'

'What are you on about?'

'Your USP isn't that you used to work in publishing. Your USP is that you solve murders. So I'm wondering if maybe *that* ain't why Miles invited you.'

'That makes no sense,' Penny replied. 'Why, then, would he invite me if he was planning a murder?'

'I don't know, but just like Wesley engaged Rattigan, Miles engaged you.'

This was unsettlingly hard to dispute. She had never met the man, and yet not only had he sent her the invitation, he had paid for her room and board.

A server passed, offering canapés from a tray. Penny declined; Johnny grabbed a handful like they were popcorn.

'What about Jed, though?' she protested, once the server was out of earshot. 'Crawford Nicholson surely had nothing to do with you being assigned to his case.'

'No, he didn't. But he had a lot to do with me following the trail to Scotland. I didn't see it at the time because I was too focused on what happened to Ibanez, but thinking about it, my late partner found Nicholson's travel plans a little too easily. Not just his itinerary either: why would he write down the code for his secret room back in Edinburgh? We're being played, and we'll keep getting played until we start changing the rules.'

'You mean breaking the law,' Penny chided, feeling herself tense at the idea.

'Sometimes that's the same thing.'

'The fact that you cloak it in euphemism betrays that you know it isn't right. I won't be part of it.'

Johnny popped a canapé into his mouth and swallowed. She wondered if it touched the sides.

400

'You're on my turf now,' he said. 'Where I work, there *is* no right, just different degrees of wrong.'

'I would remind you that you only ended up on *my* turf because of mistakes you made here: because breaking the rules broke you.'

'You already broke the rules on your own turf when we hit Deacon's place.'

'Yes, and Alison Innis was murdered while we were busy doing that. There are always consequences. Can't you see that?'

'Alison dying was not a consequence of your actions, Penny. Can't *you* see *that*? It wasn't your fault.'

'I pulled her into this instead of going to the police.'

'The police were compromised. If you'd gone to them, you'd probably be dead by now.'

'Yes, but she wouldn't be. I'm an old woman. I've had my life. She was taken so young.'

Penny felt a wellspring of guilt and shame rising within, threatening to engulf her. Johnny seemed to sense it. He dumped the last of his canapés into a planter and stepped closer, grasping her frail, wrinkled hands delicately.

'Look at me,' he said, soft but insistent.

She raised her head. His eyes were at once fierce and sad and kind.

'It wasn't your fault. It was the fault of the motherfucker who killed her. So we gotta do whatever it takes to find out who that is, okay?'

Penny managed an uncertain nod. The tears that were threatening began to subside, feelings of guilt being slowly replaced by determination.

'Okay,' she said.

'Besides, you already shot a cop today. I think you crossed the Rubicon a ways back.'

401

The Silence Forever Echoes

Chapter Eleven

Johnny lets go Penny's hands and reaches into his pocket for a tissue, but she waves it away. He thought she was really gonna break down there, and in front of everybody too. It seemed to come upon her so suddenly. He gets that she's averse to going rogue in any way, but it's messed up that she's blaming herself for what happened to Innis.

Johnny can relate in that he knows it was down to him that Ibanez was inside Kingdom Pictures when the place went on fire, but there was a lot more cause and effect in play there. Innis, by contrast, was sitting in the car outside, so she wasn't part of any overt act.

'You good?' he asks.

She nods. 'I thought of another hole in your theory, though.'

'What?'

'*The Cracked Mirror* is a book about someone who steals a manuscript and kills the writer so they can pretend it's theirs. In the film adaptation, it's a screenplay. So where's the video-game version?'

It's an aggravatingly good question.

'Maybe one of those *Neon City* games Vikram talked about. We'll need to ask him.'

As he says this, he notices that Lawrence Pierpont is now making the rounds separate from his wife. Johnny's curious as to how loyal she'll be if he puts her feet to the flames.

'I want to talk to Viola,' he tells Penny. 'Hit her with what we know, see how she reacts.'

'She might react by having us ejected.'

'Nah. This is where we make the etiquette work for us. I'm betting she'll do anything to avoid a scene, so she's definitely not gonna have security strong-arm a little old lady out of the building in front of reporters.'

Johnny lets Penny choose the moment. She's better at reading these situations. He follows her lead as she manoeuvres them towards Viola. Penny stands close by, eavesdropping on the chit-chat and picking up on the signs that the encounter is winding down. Then she makes her move.

'Viola, so lovely to be here,' Penny says, all friendly and enthusiastic. 'We're so pleased we could attend.' She's leaning into the accent too. Johnny thinks she sounds like Mrs Doubtfire.

Viola is smiling, scrutinising them both, probably trying to figure why they look familiar. Johnny has read that she's fifty-seven, twenty-five years younger than Lawrence. If he didn't know this, it would be hard to peg her exact age, as she's had a lot of work done, and done well. She's got these straight, sparkling white teeth and perfect skin.

'Yes. I'm sorry, I don't believe I've had the pleasure?'

'Penelope Coyne. And this is Johnny Hawke. We had a lovely chat with Caleb yesterday, at the garden party. He cared so much for Juliet.'

403

Their names clearly mean nothing. Johnny can tell Viola's already fixing to move on.

'Well, thank you so much for coming,' she says, meaning get lost. 'We all appreciate it.'

'Just while we're here,' Johnny says, 'can I ask if the name Bradley Ignatieff means anything to you?'

He sees the briefest flash of alarm, swiftly covered up.

'No, I'm afraid not.'

She's still smiling, but there's suspicion in her eyes.

'What about Howard Ignatieff? Suzanne Ignatieff? Kathy and Deedee?'

Viola looks to Penny, confirming that she's complicit with Johnny in this. Still with the smile, because she is aware there are eyes everywhere, but all three of them now know this is a combat situation.

'No, I can't say that I'm familiar. Are they in the games industry?'

She's good. Poker-faced apart from that first glimmer. Time to turn up the heat.

'Perhaps if we mentioned the names to your husband,' Johnny says. 'Would they mean anything to him? Does he know the reason you moved out west? The reason you don't drink?'

She's no longer trying to make eye contact with other people as a route to escaping into a new conversation. She understands how much he and Penny know.

'What are you doing here?' Viola asks.

'Same as you,' Penny replies. 'We're here to honour Juliet Oswald. Which is why we're looking at who might have had reason to want her dead.'

'And you think that's me?'

'We know Juliet was investigating your family ahead of the

wedding,' Johnny says. 'We're wondering whether she found out the same thing we did. Or maybe you know something that could point us elsewhere.'

Viola glances away, looking towards her husband. Johnny's stoked that the play worked, but when she turns back again, there's scorn in her eyes.

'You really have no idea who you're dealing with,' she says. 'But there is one way to make you understand, which is to give you exactly what you're looking for.'

She signals to Lawrence, beckoning him. He swiftly disengages from the group he's in and walks across to join her, a glass of Scotch gripped in his fist.

'Lawrence, these charming people are Penny and Johnny. They were just asking me about someone called Bradley Ignatieff. Does that name mean anything to you?'

Lawrence's smile falters for only a fraction of a second, then his game face is back on. He looks Johnny in the eye as he answers.

'Yeah. Poor guy. The rest of his family were wiped out in an RV crash in Vermont, where Viola hails from. Cops discovered his father was driving drunk on the wrong side of the road. Killed himself, his wife and two of his kids, and from what I hear, it's a miracle he didn't kill the driver of another car he almost hit.'

The subtext is clear. Lawrence knows all about it. They're as one. Johnny's divide-and-conquer strategy is in ruins.

'They're interested in what happened to Juliet,' Viola adds, giving Lawrence the whole picture.

'What about the name Melissa Neeson?' Johnny tries, a desperate gambit at this point.

There's a blink, a flinch. It has rattled Lawrence more than the name Ignatieff rattled Viola, but Johnny doesn't know where he can go with it. He has tried to get in touch with Melissa Neeson again, but she's blocked his number. He got Penny to try a couple times too. It keeps going to voicemail. She's screening her calls.

'Never heard of her,' Lawrence says.

'There are whispers she was your MeToo,' Johnny suggests, a total stab in the dark. 'Back when a hash symbol was something you only saw on a telephone keypad. Back before the *first* time you tried to buy Sea Monster.'

The MeToo play got nothing, but that last one connected.

'You know about the bid?'

'We know about Diegesis too,' Johnny adds, grateful to look like he's still holding something. 'How it works. What it does.'

Lawrence doesn't say anything for a moment, then he nods, like he's decided something.

'What did you say your name was?'

'It's Johnny. Johnny Hawke.'

Lawrence takes a sip of his whisky, eyeing him over the rim.

'Okay, Johnny, I get why you're digging dirt. You think maybe Juliet found out something compromising and that I or maybe Viola had her killed, is that right?'

'We're not drawing conclusions,' Johnny replies. 'Just asking a few questions.'

'Then here's a question for you: why would I or my wife need to kill somebody? People like us have the resources to make bigger problems go away without resorting to such squalid means. Just ask Mr Ignatieff. Do you really think I would ruin my son's life by killing his fiancée, just to cover up some sexual indiscretion?'

Johnny doesn't have a comeback for this. Neither does Penny.

406

'Now, here's what's going to happen,' Lawrence says. 'There won't be a fuss. I'm not even going to ask you to leave. Stay as long as you like, mingle, have a few drinks and enjoy the canapés. But understand that by lunchtime tomorrow, you will both be subject to a restraining order, so that if either of you come near me or my family again, you're going to end up in jail.'

Lawrence smiles again, for the benefit of anyone looking their way. Then he leans in closer.

'I know where this is coming from,' he says. 'Saint Wesley has been pointing fingers in our direction for twenty years. Well, you know what they say: you point one finger at me, you're pointing four back at yourself. Maybe it's time someone asked a few questions of him.'

'Believe me, we've tried,' says Penny. 'But his reputation for being reclusive is well earned.'

Lawrence snorts. 'People say reclusive like it just means someone's shy. You ask me, it means someone who's got a lot to hide. Why don't you investigate what he's up to at that secret medical facility of his. My kids all think Wesley's some kind of genius, but the guy's experimenting with technology that can mess with people's minds. You don't build a machine like that without some poor schmuck finding out the hard way what happens when you turn the dial too far.'

407

Death Is But the Overture

XI

Lawrence and Viola all but pirouetted clear and air-kissed their way into their next conversation. Penny had quickly recognised them as people highly trained in hiding their true feelings behind a polite façade. The same could not be said of Johnny Hawke.

'Those preening, arrogant, amoral, over-privileged pieces of shit. Standing there bragging to our faces that they can make their problems go away because they got the money to do that. This is exactly why I'm saying we can't keep playing by their rules.'

'Yes,' Penny pointed out, 'but it's also why neither of them has a motive.'

Johnny looked around the room, his body language that of a caged animal.

'Sonofabitch is right about one thing,' he said. 'There's a big section missing from this picture, and its name is Wesley Oswald. I think it's time we found out what he's hiding behind the walls of his personal fiefdom.'

'There's no way we're getting into Seahorse,' Penny warned.

'Oh, there is a way. Just not one you're gonna approve of. But how badly do you want to solve this murder?'

'That's immaterial. The place is protected by state-of-the-art technology.'

Johnny flashed her a quite unnerving grin.

'The most effective component of any security system is the sign that says "No Entry". Getting in is seldom about being able to break through a wall. It's about being prepared to walk through a door.'

Penny had known this was coming since he started talking about changing the rules.

'You want me to help you commit a crime,' she said quietly.

Johnny shook his head and Penny enjoyed an unexpected moment of relief before he clarified: 'I want you to help me commit two.'

Johnny told her what she needed to do. It wasn't much, it wasn't difficult, and it wasn't remotely illegal. Not on its own. But it was part of a conspiracy, and it was premeditated, an overt act.

As she sidled over to where her target was standing, she noticed Caleb ascend halfway up the central staircase, preparing to address the room. She wondered if now would be too conspicuous, then realised she was just looking for a reason to back out. This was, in fact, the perfect time.

Caleb called the gathering to attention and began to talk about the work the foundation was doing.

Penny began to cough: a little catch in the throat at first, developing into a fit that had her hirpling off to the side, ostensibly so as not to disturb the proceedings. As anticipated, Audrey Ireland swooped in to assist, helping Penny to a seat and proffering a bottle of water. Out of the corner of her eye she saw

Johnny draw close very briefly then move away. Was that all it took? Or had he backed out again for fear of detection? She wasn't sure.

Penny started to cough some more, which was when she saw Johnny make a subtle sideways chopping motion to signal stop. Then she watched him move briskly towards the exit while all eyes were on Caleb.

Crime one had been successfully committed. Crime two was now in process. Penny had ceased fake coughing, but she genuinely felt sick.

Caleb spoke for a few minutes and Audrey stayed alongside her throughout. Penny felt doubly bad that they had not only stolen from her, but exploited her caring instinct to create the opportunity.

'Are you feeling better now?'

'Yes. Something just caught in my throat. I think it was the hypocrisy. The obscenely wealthy gathered here to convince themselves they care about something other than their own best interests.'

'I saw you speaking to Lawrence and Viola,' Audrey said, an observation that was not entirely a non sequitur. 'Did they tell you anything interesting?'

'I'm not permitted to say.'

'Touché,' Audrey replied.

'Was that why you invited us here? Did you do it at Wesley's request?'

'I'm here to serve,' Audrey said, which caught Penny on the blind side. She blanched with sudden sadness, recalling Alison Innis's voice as she used the same expression.

'What's wrong?' Audrey asked.

'I lost a friend recently. She was murdered. I am convinced

410

her death is linked to all this but I'm not sure how and I am fed up being caught in the middle of someone else's games. Aren't you? Or do you stand to make a substantial cut from what is going on between Sea Monster and Pierpont?'

Audrey stared at Caleb for a moment.

'Let's just say I'm not interested in money. But I *am* invested in the outcome. Did Vikram explain to you what Diegesis is?'

'He tried. As far as I understand, it is some kind of neural simulation that allows you to feel as though you are inside the world of a book.'

Penny's tone sounded rather dismissive, she realised. Perhaps if she was of Audrey's generation, she might be more enthused.

'Doesn't that excite you?' Audrey asked.

'I find books exciting enough as they are.'

'Sure, but what Vikram showed you is just the first generation of the tech. What it's ultimately about is the experience of *being* someone else.'

'That was the part that gave me pause. I'm in no hurry to dabble in something that would suppress my memories. My failing brain is doing a good enough job on its own.'

'Granted there are kinks to iron out, but what Wesley's working on now is not about suppressing memory. It's about *reading* it. There's a completely vivid, fully realised world inside of everybody's head: everything they know, every place they've been, every conversation they've had. A future iteration of Diegesis will be able to realise *those* worlds.'

It sounded exhausting to Penny, but she could understand the appeal.

'How far off is this future iteration? Years? Decades?'

Audrey gave her a coy smile.

'With Wesley, you never know.'

411

The Silence Forever Echoes

Chapter Twelve

It takes Johnny less than fifteen minutes to return to the campus in Westlake, having left Penny in place as his alibi.

'People are gonna assume I'm still around as long as you're here and as long as we leave together later,' he had told her.

'Also known as aiding and abetting,' she replied.

'Yeah, but it's aiding and abetting plus canapés.'

He stops the Cobra about fifty yards short of where the campus driveway meets the main road, putting on the parking brake and checking the cobalt-coloured pass is secure in his pocket.

He'd known this was a viable option the moment he saw Audrey walk out of that door marked 'Strictly No Entry'. She is Wesley's personal assistant, which means more than taking dictation and getting him coffee. She has high-level clearance. Audrey's swipe card means Johnny can literally just walk in the front door. No window-breaking, no lock-picking. But it would all fall down if one security guard asks to see ID, so he still has to play this carefully.

The thing to consider in assessing a place's security is what they're scared of. If it's a warehouse full of TVs, then what they're worried about is getting robbed. Likewise, a software company such as Sea Monster might be concerned about someone making off with a shitload of laptops, but mostly they're worried about someone seeing information that they shouldn't.

Bottom line is this place is not gonna be patrolled by teams of ex-special forces carrying shotguns and automatic rifles. He's guessing two guys at most, taking turns to watch the feeds and walk the perimeter.

He gets out his cell and dials the number for security. During his visit earlier he had taken a photograph of an internal directory posted behind the reception desk, so he doesn't just know which number to call, he knows which names he can use too.

It picks up after two rings.

'Security, Larry speaking.'

'Hi, Larry, this is Andy Bay, head of networks. Sorry to bug you but I'm getting a weird alert like there's a machine over-heating. It's probably a false signal but it won't let me shut it down remotely. It's probably nothing but I don't want to take any chances. If it *is* something, the danger is the whole place goes up.'

'Shit. Which machine is it? I can go deal.'

'See, that's the thing. Something's screwy with the network IDs, which has me worried about what system it's gonna knock over next. All I know is it's in Sea Monster somewhere. I know, right? Gotta be like two hundred computers. I'm just about to get in the car and drive over but I need you to go room to room in the meantime, shut down any machines still running.'

'Sure thing.'

'How many of you are working tonight?'

'Just me and Vern.'

'I'm gonna owe you guys big time. I need you both to drop everything and help me isolate this rogue computer before the problem gets out of hand. And when you find it, yank the plug out of the goddamn wall if you have to.'

'You got it.'

Johnny watches as a figure in a blue uniform emerges from the front entrance at Seahorse, gets in a golf buggy and starts driving towards the other building.

Time to go to work.

Johnny pulls into the Seahorse parking lot, where he can see four vehicles: a motorcycle and three cars. He figures two of them for Larry and Vern, meaning at least two more personnel on-site. Witnesses aside, this is a good thing, because it would support the theory that Rattigan and Amanda Fraser are being kept here. A private medical facility would need to be staffed twenty-four/seven.

Johnny walks up to the front door and presents Audrey's cobalt-blue card to the reader. Skips a beat when he gets a red light in response. He taps the card again. This time it works. He's just done it too fast. Less hurry, more haste, as his grandma used to say.

As he pulls open the glass door, he glances up at the camera pointed towards the entrance. It's far from the first he's seen, or that has no doubt seen him. One probably recorded his licence plate as he drove through the grounds. The sheer prevalence of cameras is a big part of the security strategy in a place like this, working two ways. One is to remind you that you're being recorded, and two is to make you think *those* are the cameras you need to worry about.

All of which is why Johnny's first task is not to find out whatever dirty secrets lie behind the Diegesis project, but to access the security console and start deleting all trace of his visit.

Having scrambled to find a rogue PC before the building burns down, Larry has left his station in a hurry, still logged on to the system. It takes Johnny a few minutes, but he navigates his way to a menu that lets him scrub all the CCTV from the last ten minutes and suspend recording. Next he turns off notifications, so that when Larry comes back, he won't get any pop-ups alerting him that nothing is being logged.

Johnny starts toggling through the feeds, a static slideshow of empty desks and corridors. Alpha labs. Beta labs. Admin. Archives. Data. Servers. Cafeteria. Parking lot. Driveway North. Driveway South. He keeps one live window showing the front entrance across at Sea Monster so that he'll have notice if Larry starts heading back.

His next keystroke toggles to a new feed showing two people sitting in a room stacked with more computers, more screens. A man and a woman, both dressed like paramedics. The woman is reading a book. The guy is playing a game on his phone. The feed is called Vital Systems Monitoring.

He toggles to the next feed. It's called Diegetic Therapy 1. It displays a chamber containing a machine similar to the device Vikram showed them earlier. Unlike before, there is a person hooked up to this one. The octagonal surround is covering the head end, but Johnny can see a body lying on the bed.

Diegetic Therapy 2 displays almost the same thing: a second chamber, a second machine, with someone hooked up to that one as well. In both cases there are tubes and wires, electrodes, catheters, IV lines. This is not like some private ICU, though. Sonofabitch got them plugged into his diabolical invention. Two guinea pigs who could not give consent.

This is why Amanda's son went to court and called Wesley

415

a body-snatcher. He couldn't know what Wesley was up to, but he had reason to suspect it wasn't good. Rattigan didn't even have someone to plead for him. Sounds like his ex would have been only too happy to sign the release.

Johnny hears Lawrence Pierpont's voice in his head: *You don't build a machine like that without some poor schmuck finding out the hard way what happens when you turn the dial too far.*

He doubts these two are the first subjects and wonders what happened to the previous ones.

Johnny needs confirmation of who is in those beds. He needs to get closer. He needs hard evidence.

He toggles back to the paramedics, monitoring their patients from an adjacent room. How is he gonna deal with them? His first thought is to pull an alarm to force an evacuation, but he doesn't want to trigger some emergency protocol that might bring more people than are here already.

Johnny photographs the building schematic from the fire evacuation plan pinned to the wall. There are no rooms marked 'Diegetic Therapy' on it, but there is an area marked 'Clinical Research' on the second floor. Or first floor if you're Penny.

He exits the security station and walks across the lobby where a tap of Audrey's card gets him through a door to the stairs. He's reached the second floor when his phone rings, sounding real loud against the silence. He rushes to answer, having forgotten to put it to silent. It's Larry.

'Good news. I think we found the problem. There was a machine in the design studio humming like a drone ready to take off. We shut it down.'

Christ, Johnny thinks. Of all the dumb luck. That machine's probably doing that every night, some asshole mining crypto on the sly.

416

'I'm afraid I'm still getting an overheat signal from someplace,' Johnny says. 'I gotta ask you to keep checking.'

There's a pause. Not a resigned sigh. A long pause.

'What are you seeing this signal on?' Larry asks, his tone altogether less cooperative than before. 'Aren't you supposed to be driving over here? You don't sound like you're in a car. What did you say your name was?'

Johnny hangs up.

He's blown. Nonetheless, he's gonna have to press on and do whatever he can right now because he ain't getting in here again.

He checks the photo of the schematic and navigates the maze of corridors until he finds what he's looking for. The door says:

CLINICAL RESEARCH
AMETHYST LEVEL AND
MEDICAL PERSONNEL ONLY

The words 'Amethyst Level' are in white on a square of dark purple. He's hoping this level is below Cobalt.

Johnny breathes in, taps Audrey's card.

No dice. Red light.

He remembers what happened downstairs. Taps it again.

Still red.

The door is similar to the one Vikram took him through at Sea Monster. Electromagnetic locking system.

Fuck. He's come so far to be denied now.

Johnny gazes up in exasperation, looks at the ceiling and laughs.

It's like he told Penny: so much security infrastructure is just there to stress where you're not supposed to be. Big strong door tells you it's gonna be hard to get inside, so best not try. But a research lab ain't built to keep out intruders, or even to hide someone's dirty secrets.

Through a door to his right is an office area, banks of desks divided by a line of storage cabinets. He climbs on top of the cabinets, nudging up the tile above his head. There is a cavity up there. It's a suspended ceiling: a steel frame descending eighteen inches from the concrete, and extending way beyond the walls either side of the maglocked door.

The number of times he's seen this. It's merely an illusion of a secure area, no less than what he saw at Kingdom Pictures had been an illusion of a ballroom.

Flexible ventilation tubing criss-crosses the space, held above the ceiling tiles by ties and brackets, but mostly the framework is there to support about a thousand miles of heavy cable, running along aluminum shelves. He figures if it can take that weight, it can take his too. He's gonna need someplace to hide when the security guards come searching anyways.

It's a tight squeeze but he's able to climb up there and haul himself onto one of the shelves. It holds. What he's not able to do is replace the tile, but chances are nobody will be coming into that office until morning. He drags himself forward. It's slow and his belt keeps snagging on the cables. The framework remains mostly steady, but it gets shaky at times, midway between anchor points.

He flashes back to Kingdom Pictures again, the ladders and gantries behind the ballroom set, and everything that happened there. Thinks of Ibanez, of that Bronco peeling away on Fountain, of Arlo Waters trying to kill him today. Wonders what truly links Lawrence Pierpont, Dominique King and Lord Stonebridge. This is truly the weirdest case he's ever worked.

Johnny figures he's got to be past the security door, but the shelf runs parallel to the corridor, so he's wary of what he might be directly above. Last thing he wants is to lift a tile and find those two paramedics staring back up at him. With that thought, he reaches for his phone and double checks he put it to silent.

He comes up on a vent sitting a couple of feet to the left of the shelf. From this angle he can mainly see wall through it. He can hear a pulsatile hum, though: something powerful. Johnny gets out his cell and starts recording video. He feels movement in the framework as he manoeuvres but it steadies.

He angles his phone above the vent to act as a mirror, the screen showing that he's above one of the Diegetic Therapy chambers. He can see one end of the machine, see the shape of legs and feet beneath a sheet. He'd expect to hear beeping from an EKG or whatever, but that's from watching too many TV shows. Plus it's all being monitored from a different room.

With the octagonal surround forming a hood, it's like one of those split coffins, except that it's the bottom end of the casket that's open. He can see a name tag at the end of the bed. He zooms in. It says 'Amanda Fraser', then her date of birth. She's eighty-three. He can't see her face, though. If he could just get the phone a little further across. Johnny pushes down with his right hand, leaning out to the left. There's movement in the framework. More than a tremor: a lurch. Johnny freezes, holding his breath. It steadies. He dares to raise his phone again. Then the framework ahead of him comes away and drops through the ceiling with a crash, tipping him off the shelf and onto the polished floor beneath.

He lands at the side of the bed, his cell and his gun clattering amidst fragments of broken tiles. The paramedics might have been reading a book and playing a game, but even if they weren't looking at the video feed, there's no way they didn't hear that.

Johnny gets to his knees. He's dazed. He can't see his gun, but he can see his cell a few feet away. He has to get proof. He hauls himself unsteadily upright, gripping the edge of the bed, which is when he finds himself finally looking at Amanda Fraser's face.

Except it's not Amanda Fraser's face.

It's Penny's.

Johnny stares, uncomprehending. Her eyes are closed but there's no mistaking it. It's the face he has been looking at constantly for the past few days. Amanda Fraser is Penny's twin? No, that's impossible. Penny said she'd never heard of her. Amanda had a brother, and a younger sister who died in childhood.

There's no time to make sense of it. He can hear hurried footsteps approaching the door to his left. He looks to his right. There's a door there too. A way out.

Johnny is scrambling towards it on unsteady feet as he notices the sign saying 'Diegetic Therapy 2'.

He tumbles through into the second chamber, where he discovers that he's come through the only door. There's no other exit, but it wouldn't matter if there was, because there is no escaping what he sees in that room.

The card at the foot of the bed says 'Dan Rattigan', but the face beneath the hood is one he sees every day.

In the mirror.

Death Is But the Overture

XII

Penny looked at her watch as discreetly as she could, not wishing to give the vapid socialite she was talking to the impression she was planning to leave. Insincere as Lawrence Pierpont's invitation had been, she had done as he suggested, mingling for all she was worth so that it did not become obvious that she was now unaccompanied. But as time ticked by, she couldn't help noticing that the crowd was starting to thin. She had begun to worry how much longer Johnny might be, and worse, what she would do if he didn't come back.

If something went wrong, he would say he acted alone, she knew that. But if Johnny was arrested, and this ahead of a restraining order being served by Lawrence Pierpont, there would be no way of keeping it from his superiors. The fallout would be devastating. It would be the end of their investigation, and possibly his career.

Penny would then have little option but to go home: if home it still was. Even before leaving for California, she had found herself in a world where very little made sense the way it used

421

to; where black and white had become a smeared miasma of grey; and where she could no longer even trust the police. Perhaps it really was time to consider her nephew's offer.

And yet that tugging sense of unfinished business felt stronger than ever. Wherever it came from, it felt connected to this, and murky as the waters had become, she had the sense that she was closing in on the answers.

She noticed Detective Guadeloupe heading her way. The sight of a determined, bright and assured young policewoman made Penny think of Saeeda Sattar, which reminded her that there were police officers she *could* trust. However, remembering who Saeeda reported to underlined that from now on, that trust would be extended on an individual basis.

Guadeloupe nodded to Penny and then to the bathrooms. Penny excused herself from her current conversation and met the detective in the Ladies a short time later.

'Where's your partner?' she asked.

'I don't think he's allowed in here,' Penny replied, by way of deflection.

Guadeloupe didn't follow up.

'How's your evening been?' the detective asked. 'You got the skinny on the Munsters out there?'

Penny told her about Bradley Ignatieff and what little they had learned from the name Melissa Neeson. Guadeloupe's brows danced at some of it.

'That ain't nothing, but I don't know where it gets us. I'm sure Rattigan found out a lot more, only we can't get into his computer. It's all password protected.'

'And what about you?' Penny asked. 'Have you found out anything more since we spoke?'

Guadeloupe gave a slow solemn nod.

'I started looking into what we've got on the death of Juliet Oswald. I tried to talk to the investigating officer, figured he'd probably have retired by now. A Sergeant Lars Olin. Turns out he's dead.'

'I don't suppose that's surprising,' Penny admitted. 'It was twenty years ago. Or did he die before he could retire?'

'No, but that's where things do get surprising. Olin retired only a few weeks after signing off on the Juliet Oswald case. Seems he came into a whole lot of money all of a sudden.'

'So when did he die?'

'Three weeks ago. Boating accident. Crashed the cruiser he bought with some of that windfall.'

'Folk do keep having accidents around these people,' Penny observed.

'Don't they, though. And I'm getting a strong smell of death around one of them in particular.'

'Do you mean Lawrence, Viola or Caleb?'

'I mean Wesley Oswald.'

The Silence Forever Echoes

Chapter Thirteen

He stares at the face, at the figure in the bed, looking down at himself like it's some out-of-body experience. Johnny is standing upright but he is just as paralysed, as motionless as his reflection. He is also trapped. Through the window in the door he can see the two paramedics entering the other chamber.

Johnny knows he can get past them. They've come to investigate but they're not gonna take him on, and he likes his chances if they did. There's gotta be multiple ways out of this building, a maze of corridors and emergency exits. If he triggers a fire alarm, that should automatically unlock all the doors to allow a safe and swift exit. Then he's only gotta worry about evading two security guards. He's suspended recording on the cameras, so once he's gone, he's gone. He can get away clean, if he can just get his fucking feet to move.

First step is tearing his eyes off the face on the bed. He manages that, turns to the exit and starts towards it.

The door closes automatically.

He tugs on the handle. It's locked. There isn't a card reader, though the cobalt card would be useless here anyway. It's been locked remotely, but not by anyone he can see. The paramedics are checking on Penny.

On Amanda.

Larry the security guard appears, looking like he got here in a rush. Johnny didn't hear any alarms, but some kind of alert has been triggered, clearly. The paramedics are pointing towards the second room. Larry is going for his holster.

Then a fourth person walks into the chamber. He is slight, maybe five-five at the most. Grey-haired, head bowed just a little like he's reluctant to make eye contact. He's wearing sweatpants and a black t-shirt that says 'Quake 2'. He's also wearing this sleeveless gilet thing that isn't quite closed over, a utility vest full of pouches and pockets for tools. Johnny would have figured he's here to fix the computers, except he recognises him from that video at Electronicon.

This is Wesley Oswald.

The man behind the curtain. The great and powerful Oz.

He is signalling to everybody to stand down. To calm down.

Wesley looks up semi-reluctantly, almost like the view is too bright, and gives Johnny a wave. He smiles shyly, self-conscious, almost apologetic.

'Are you okay?' he asks through the glass.

Johnny doesn't know the answer to that.

'Are you cool? You're not about to do anything crazy if I open this door?'

He's got that weird accent from the video, part Californian, part Scottish.

Johnny raises his hands to signal he's calm.

'I'm coming in,' Wesley says.

He presses a button on a device he's holding then slips it into one of the pouches on the gilet. Johnny hears the door unlock.

Larry has holstered his weapon, but his hand is hovering close to it. Wesley tells him to back away.

One of the paramedics is still checking on Amanda. The other is clearing broken pieces of tile.

Wesley starts towards the second chamber then pauses, like he's changed his mind. He bends down and picks up something from the floor. It's Johnny's cell. He walks through the door and holds it out like some kind of peace offering.

Johnny accepts it wordlessly, not sure at this point if his voice even works. It hits him that he could still make a run for it but he's feeling meek as a lamb. As meek as Wesley appears.

The door closes. Just the two of them.

There is a long moment of silence, an inadvertent stand-off between a cripplingly shy individual and a guy who's temporarily too brain-fucked to speak.

Eventually Johnny finds his voice, and it sounds weirdly quiet, like it was a long way down inside.

'Who is that?' he asks, pointing at the bed alongside him.

Wesley angles his head, his right hand rising to rest against his temple like a support.

'That's you,' he says. 'Dan Rattigan.'

Johnny knows it's true. In his gut he knows it's true even though he can't make sense of it. Some part of him can't deny it. He just needs someone to explain how the hell it can be so.

'And you're Wesley.'

'That's complicated.'

Wesley is slight, his skin weathered like he spends a lot of time outdoors, which is surprising to Johnny. Figures him for someone permanently in front of a computer. He guesses these days you don't need to be indoors to be doing that.

'How can that be me? I'm fucking standing here.'

'In truth, neither of us is really standing here. You know about Diegesis, right? Vikram explained it to you.'

Johnny nods. 'I thought Diegesis put you in the world of a book, a story.'

'Yeah, that's where you were, at first. A Johnny Hawke book. You've worked your way through several Johnny Hawke books, in fact.'

'But Johnny Hawke isn't real?'

'No. He's the creation of the late Donovan Colt, 1937 to 2006. Featured in seventeen novels between 1981 and 2005.'

'You said "at first". So where am I now?'

'Since you and Penny got here from Scotland – the Scotland of Amanda Fraser's novels – you've both been inside a version of southern California constructed directly from human memory. Call it Diegesis 2.0.'

'But how can this be a memory? I've never been in this building before.'

Then he gets it.

'It's *your* memory,' Johnny says.

Death Is But the Overture

XIII

The catering staff were starting to gather glasses and uneaten nibbles from tables and other improvised resting places. The piped-in Mozart had been turned off and all of the Pierponts had long gone. Penny was one of maybe fifteen guests still hanging around as if they had nowhere else to go. Which for Penny was precisely the case.

Her instinct was to call Johnny, an urge so strong she felt it in her hand like an itch. She had thus far held off, concerned that she might cause his phone to ring out while he was trying to be stealthy.

Detective Guadeloupe was gone too, but Audrey was still here. Penny wasn't sure if the latter was a good thing or not. Audrey would surely have noticed that she hadn't seen Johnny in at least an hour, but his alibi plan did rely on being seen leaving with Penny at the end of the night, and the ideal witness was someone who could confirm he had been present earlier. That said, Audrey knew the campus was only fifteen minutes away, so that absence was going to be all the more significant if she later learned there had been an intruder.

Johnny hadn't been able to say what he was looking for. It was a fishing expedition. But whether or not he had found anything, he surely wouldn't be leaving it this late to return. Something was wrong.

She had to make contingencies. Her first consideration was where she was going to go. She didn't have keys for Johnny's house. Would she check into a hotel? And if so, how was she going to get there? As the night had worn on, she heard people talk about calling an Uber, though they didn't actually *call* anyone. Penny didn't have an Uber account on her phone. All she had was the number of Glen Cluthar Private Hire, and she couldn't see Kenny making it here from Perthshire.

There was a rather drunk man veering towards her, an old Ivy League friend of Lawrence Pierpont by the name of Sam Howard. Penny knew this because she had spoken to him twice already, the second encounter indicating he was drunk enough to have forgotten the first, regaling her with the same conversational gambits. Consequently she had been avoiding him since, but now there was no hiding place.

'It's Penny, right?'

'That's correct.'

'Sam Howard,' he said, slurring his words. 'I'm an old college buddy of Lawrence. We were both majoring in electronics, back when we thought hand-held radios were going to be the future of communication.'

'How times change,' Penny replied politely. For the third time.

She saw headlights coming into the car park. Was this finally Johnny, or just another Uber pick-up?

'Yep. Who'da thunk it. Games,' he said, also for a third time. 'Did pretty well for himself. But not without so much tragedy. That's why I'm here for him tonight. The foundation. Poor Caleb. And that poor girl.'

As the vehicle drew closer, she could see it was definitely not Johnny's Cobra, but a black SUV. Penny immediately thought of their encounter with Arlo, but these vehicles were not in any way bashed up. The first was a Mitsubishi and the one behind it a Lexus.

'Juliet,' Penny said, in case Howard had forgotten this detail.

'Juliet, yeah. So much tragedy.'

It was not to Penny's credit that it took this third time for her to pick up on the significance of his wording.

'There was more than one tragedy?'

'Oh, sure. Lawrence's older brother, Travis. Fell down the stairs on a visit to Lawrence's house. A terrible accident, though there were rumours he had, you know, done away with himself.'

'How awful.'

As she spoke, Penny watched the SUVs not so much park as slew sideways across several spaces each. She recalled a similar vehicle pulling up outside the library, an image that set her on edge.

'Yeah,' Howard said quietly. Or what he thought was quietly, anyway. 'Travis was a bit of an oddball. Let's just say that wasn't the only rumour about him. If I were Lawrence, I wouldn't have had him around the . . .'

Howard's words faded as Penny saw who was emerging from the SUVs. It was Chief Superintendent McLeod, accompanied by the three policemen he had had with him in Glen Cluthar. The ones who had tried to kill her. The ones who most likely killed Alison Innis.

'You'll have to excuse me,' Penny told Howard, and began walking briskly away from the windows. She reached for her phone. She had to call Johnny now, regardless of the consequences.

It rang out, went to voicemail.

'Is everything all right?'

It was Audrey who spoke, appearing by her side and walking in step.

'No. There are four gentlemen heading towards the building, and I can assure you they're not here for charitable purposes.'

The Silence Forever Echoes

Chapter Fourteen

Johnny glances through the window into the other chamber, at the woman he knows as Penny Coyne, but whose name is listed otherwise.

'And her?' Johnny asks. 'Is she just a part of your memory?'

Wesley shakes his head solemnly, a look of sadness and regret on his face, mixed with something warmer.

'No. Not yet.'

'Your aunt,' Johnny says. 'Amanda Fraser.'

Wesley swallows, his eyes misting.

'I wish you could have met the real her.'

'Could have? Wait. Is she dead?'

'No, but . . .'

Wesley looks through the window too. One of the paramedics is checking a tube.

'That's why I did this. Well, why I started doing this. I had my own selfish reasons too. Maybe all my reasons are selfish.'

'Hey,' Johnny says. 'Start making sense.'

Wesley does that thing of holding his head again, like he's worried it's gonna roll off.

'Sorry. I'm not dealing with this well. For the longest time, she's been all I had left. I lost Juliet twenty years ago, my parents not long after that. They went within weeks of one another. I was always close with Amanda. Juliet and I both were, growing up. After I moved out here, Amanda visited California a lot. Book tours, vacations. Then she moved out here too, a semi-retirement. Writers never really retire.

'She was still publishing, but then she started losing track of things, losing her memory bit by bit. It was crushing to watch. This brilliant mind, with such unparalleled command of detail, suddenly fragmenting. It was slow and gradual, then she deteriorated quite rapidly over the past year, physically as well as mentally. The doctors said she didn't have long.'

Wesley taps the hood of the machine absently.

'I got the court order to stop her son taking her back to the UK. We had made a breakthrough with Diegesis, and I got this idea . . .' He shakes his head wistfully.

'You thought you could cure her?'

'No. Maybe. I don't know. I knew that Diegesis could create new neural pathways and possibly repair connections, but mostly I thought I could give her something good before the end. She didn't know who she was any more: couldn't remember her life, her work. I knew that with Diegesis she could be Penny Coyne. She could fuse with her own great creation, solve all these mysteries she'd written; mysteries she'd forgotten.'

Johnny gets it, he thinks.

'Like her idea of heaven, maybe?'

433

'I've always imagined heaven having fewer murders. But certainly somewhere comforting. Somewhere she'd be happy.'

Johnny looks through the window at Amanda Fraser. She is the woman he knows and yet not her at all. She looks gaunt, older, paler.

'That's what she looks like in the real world right now,' Johnny says, trying to clarify for himself. 'But I'm inside a simulation of the real world, based on *your* mind, *your* memories.'

'That's right. Updated a few hours ago.'

'So if I call Penny on her cell, she'll answer?'

Wesley nods.

Johnny wakes his phone. Before he can dial, he sees he's missed a call from her.

He dials. She picks up fast.

'Johnny. I can't talk.'

He feels a lump in his throat when he hears her voice.

She sounds breathless. Afraid.

'What's going on? You okay?'

'McLeod is here. With men. Cars. Guns. I'm with Audrey.'

'Understood. I'm—'

It cuts off. Johnny hangs up and looks at Wesley.

'She's in danger.'

'I know,' Wesley says. 'We need to go.'

Johnny follows Wesley as he hurries through the building, all the doors opening automatically as he approaches them.

'She's slipped out through an emergency exit and has just made it to Audrey's car,' Wesley says, running down a long corridor.

'How do you know that? And how are you doing *this*? Isn't the real you unconscious and plugged into one of these machines too?'

'No. I'm watching a lo-res approximation on screen right now, controlling an avatar of myself. It's just a monitoring programme: a back door into the system to allow real-time tweaking.'

'And this back door, could somebody else have opened it?'

'Not without me knowing. My security is as good as it gets.'

The door to a stairwell opens before them and they hurtle down two storeys, skidding around each landing.

'What happens if this McLeod asshole kills her?' Johnny asks. 'Doesn't she just get to start over?'

'Yes, but it would be a total reset. The machine is doing all her remembering for her. She won't recall you, or anything you've done together, and we really need her to remember.'

They bust out into the downstairs lobby. Same as all the doors, the glass barriers swing open as Wesley nears them, like he's got superpowers. Which is a thought.

'Can't you just teleport her out of there or something?'

'The system won't allow it. Actions have to be within the parameters of the world.'

'You made the goddamn parameters. Can't you change them?'

'I could rewrite the protocols, but doing that would take far longer than we've got.'

'Can you give us a helicopter, then?'

'Can you *fly* a helicopter?'

'No.'

'Then there's no point in me giving you one.'

'Fuck.'

They make it to the parking lot, Johnny's Cobra sitting there looking all beat up.

'You couldn't give me a fuckin' Ferrari or something?'

'Don't look at me. Blame the author.'

Death Is But the Overture

XIV

Penny was able to pull Audrey out of sight behind the lobby staircase before McLeod and his men reached the building. She could feel her pulse racing from the moment they stepped out of their vehicles, becoming a growing throb in her chest as she tried to get out of sight. She didn't know whether she had been seen, but it was a certainty that McLeod was here for her. Less certain was why this dull, predictable, gong-chasing functionary of a man had suddenly transformed into some avenging angel.

'Who are they?' Audrey asked, as Penny urged her along a corridor away from the lobby.

'Ostensibly they are policemen, but they're not here in any official capacity. They killed my friend Alison back in Scotland, and they tried to kill me and Johnny too.'

'No point dialling 911, then.'

They reached a fire door exiting to the side of the building. Penny opened it quietly and tentatively popped her head out.

'Do you have a car?' she asked.

'Sure. Blue Mazda MX-30. Far side of the lot.'

Penny looked at the expanse of tarmac. It was no distance at all under normal circumstances, but all of it was in full view of those huge front windows.

'It's you they're looking for, right?' Audrey asked.

'Me and Johnny, I assume.'

'Okay.'

Audrey slipped through the fire door and began walking briskly but unhurriedly across the car park. Penny thought for a moment that she had taken this as her opportunity to escape alone, then she understood Audrey's plan. They weren't looking for an unaccompanied woman in her thirties.

Penny pressed herself against the outside of the door, keeping out of sight of the windows. From inside she could hear voices and heavy footsteps echoing around the corridor. They were searching the place. She barely dared breathe, though the sound of her heart against her chest was surely just as loud. It seemed not just faster, but harder, something not alleviated by her phone ringing. It was Johnny calling her back. She rushed to answer.

'Johnny. I can't talk.'

'What's going on? You okay?'

'McLeod is here. With men. Cars. Guns. I'm with Audrey.'

She hung up as Audrey drove past the two SUVs and pulled in at the side of the building, only a few yards from the doorway. Penny broke from cover and climbed into the passenger seat. She ducked her head down as Audrey pulled away, driving a little faster than Penny would have considered discreet.

'Were we seen?' she asked, awkwardly pulling on the seat belt from her sunken position.

'I don't know.'

She was aching to sit up and look but they were still in sight of the building.

'Shit,' Audrey said.

Penny couldn't stop herself. She sat up and turned around, gazing through the rear windscreen. She saw the four policemen running for their vehicles, McLeod pointing towards the departing Mazda.

Audrey put her foot down hard, no need for discretion in her driving now. The car accelerated impressively fast, but that only prompted another worry. Penny looked at the dashboard, though she was able to make little sense of it.

'How much petrol do you have?'

'Petrol?'

'I mean gas.'

'None. It runs on electricity.'

'And how much electricity do you have?'

'I really wish you hadn't asked that.'

The Silence Forever Echoes

Chapter Fifteen

Johnny puts the Cobra into drive and hits the gas, peeling out onto the boulevard as fast as he dares. A pick-up swerves to avoid them, blaring its horn.

'It doesn't matter if I hit anything, right?' he asks. 'It's just a simulation.'

'It will matter if you flip this thing and we spend the next two hours being cut out of the simulated wreckage.'

'Understood.'

Johnny floors it, taking the 23 towards the Ventura Freeway. Wesley's riding shotgun, looking anxious as hell even though none of this shit's real.

'Okay, I got about a million questions,' Johnny says.

'I'll do my best.'

'I was in a car accident, right? I'm Dan Rattigan and I was in a crash.'

'Yes, all of that's true. I hired you to look into my sister's murder. I suspect that's *why* you had an accident. You were on your way to tell me something.'

'Why wouldn't I just call, or email?'

'I don't know, because you never got to say. The doctors were worried you might have memory loss, possibly a serious brain injury. What you definitely didn't have was decent health insurance.'

'Diegesis being something that can repair brain damage . . . you wanted to make sure I could remember whatever it was I found out.'

'I also wanted you in a place where whoever did this couldn't finish you off.'

'What, a place with just two security guards, that I was able to walk right inside of?'

'You're still alive, aren't you?'

'Right now I'm not sure.'

Johnny turns onto the 101. There's barely any traffic. Seems right for this time of night, but maybe it's just how Wesley's mind imagines it. He doesn't know anything for certain any more.

'Why Johnny Hawke?' he asks.

Wesley pauses a moment.

'I'm not going to sugar-coat it. Inside Diegesis, the more you want to be him or her, the better you will inhabit your character inside the fictional world.'

'A maverick hero cop who breaks the rules and gets the job done,' Johnny says. 'As opposed to an ex-cop who broke the rules and fucked it for everybody.'

'We find that it works best on people who have reason to suppress part of their own memory.'

They pass a hotel on the right. Sheraton Agoura Hills. Johnny thinks of Crathie Hall, which he now knows doesn't exist, and that makes him surprisingly sad. Maybe it's based on a real place. He'd like to go there some day. That prompts another question.

'How come I ended up in a Penny Coyne story?'

Wesley shrinks into himself, like he's afraid Johnny's gonna slug him when he answers.

'I looked at the two of you, hooked into these simulations, solving murders from old novels as therapy, and I had this idea. Dan Rattigan had gathered all this information about what happened to Juliet, supplementing everything I had found out down the years, but it still didn't point to a solution. I had been looking at the puzzle for two decades, going round in circles. Then I thought, what if I can get these two great detectives, Penny Coyne and Johnny Hawke, working this case from different perspectives, examining the information every possible way?

'I had the system generate speculative versions of Juliet's death. A Johnny Hawke version, a Penny Coyne version. I let the AI do it so that I wasn't infecting the stories with my own assumptions. It took the ingredients and put them together with new variables – gender flips, new settings – but ultimately versions of the same people with the same agendas, the same personalities. I wanted to go further, though. Reckoned two heads were better than one.'

'You set it up for multiplayer,' Johnny says, overtaking a minivan.

'I let the AI create a combined narrative. It put you into Penny's world, folding your story into hers. But I realised I could take it further still. I took a gamble on the next-generation tech we've been working on at Seahorse. I had it scan my own memory to create a new world from that, and added it to the mix. There were glitches though, conflicts between LA as I know it and the writer Donovan Colt's LA.'

'Like there being no Crawford Nicholson living in your Marina del Rey.'

'Yes. But it allowed the pair of you to investigate the here and now, based on everything I know, including stuff I might have missed. And crucially it allowed the AI to speculate based on stuff I might only have been aware of subconsciously.'

Johnny looks in the mirror, checks his six. The freeway is still real quiet.

'Why do I keep getting flashbacks?' he asks.

'The memory-suppression algorithm is still pretty shonky. We can't have it block out everything, because you need to remember how to read and write, drive a car. As a result, other stuff can get through: usually related to extreme emotions, unfortunately. It's all a work in progress.'

Johnny is coming up on a black SUV. Between Arlo Waters going psycho and hearing McLeod has shown up, anything bigger than a sedan has got him on edge. His right hand starts reaching towards the glove box.

Johnny passes on the left-hand side, sees it's a Lyft with a passenger in the back. Just part of the interactive landscape Wesley is projecting into his head. But clearly some parts interact harder than others.

'To be clear, you're saying Penny and I have only been able to find out information you already know?'

'No. The system can access anything on the internet. If you drove to a place I've never been, it would draw upon maps, photos and schematics to fill in the blanks. And if you were to search for something right now, that's real-time, real-world information that gets pulled into the mix. Certain search parameters are filtered though, to prevent conflicts that would break the world.'

'Like us finding out Penny Coyne and Johnny Hawke are characters in books.'

'Or you seeing a photograph of Dan Rattigan on his website.'

'When Ignatieff talked to Penny after he refused to talk to me, where did that information come from?'

'Things you passed on to me. Ignatieff spoke to Dan Rattigan.'

Johnny thinks about it, trying to piece together the logic, which leads him to one obvious question.

'If I was to wake up right now, in the real world, might I know who killed Juliet?'

'I think if you knew that, you'd have told me straight out, before the crash. You said you had found something significant, something you needed to show me in person. That's all I know.'

'So why not wake me up and ask me?'

'Two reasons,' Wesley replies. 'One, there's no way of knowing how much you'll remember from before the crash. Typically, events immediately pre-trauma are the ones most likely to be affected by memory loss. Bringing us to two, which is that wrenching you out of Diegesis before you're fully recovered poses a not-insignificant risk of frying your brain.'

'Okay. Let's not do that.'

Johnny passes a sign telling him he's two miles from Calabasas. He glances across at his passenger. What Wesley has said is making sense, just about. But there's one thing that really doesn't.

'You're in here. Interacting via a computer, but you're in here. You couldn't just tell us all this shit?'

'What would you make of information I simply handed you? I needed you to discover it for yourselves, assess it from angles I never thought of. Ideally, I would have had you both work through dozens of versions of the murder and see if you always came to the same conclusion. But Amanda is running out of time. And the vote is imminent.'

'*Now* we're getting down to it,' Johnny says, hackles rising. 'Ultimately this is about controlling your company, and you're using me and Amanda. Jesus. You couldn't just let her die in peace?'

'This is *how* I give her peace,' Wesley replies. Guy sounds like he's on the verge of tears. 'Amanda was haunted by Juliet's death as much as I was. We were also both tormented by the irony of it. The designer of complex puzzles and the writer of murder-mysteries, neither of them able to solve the one that had taken Juliet from us. I wanted to give her one last chance.'

They're approaching Deer Springs on the right. Getting close.

'Call her up,' Johnny says, handing Wesley his phone. 'Get her on speaker.'

'You can't tell her about this.'

'Don't worry. I literally couldn't tell her about this. I'm barely understanding it myself.'

Penny answers, her voice sounding through the stereo.

'Johnny. Where are you?'

'On the 101, coming into Calabasas now. You?'

'Where are we, dear?' he hears her ask.

'Just off Topanga Canyon Boulevard,' says Audrey in the background. 'Got two cars following. Not sure how I'm supposed to lose them.'

'Let me worry about that,' Johnny replies. 'You just stay ahead of them.'

The call disconnects.

'What's with this McLeod motherfucker? I ain't read any Amanda Fraser books, but I'm guessing the local police chief never went rogue and started shooting up any libraries.'

Wesley grimaces. 'That's the problem with AI. It doesn't always work the way you anticipate. These entities need to have a degree of autonomy, even ones based on my impressions of real people. It's fascinating watching them make their own decisions, until they start trying to kill you.'

'Can Audrey handle this?' Johnny asks. 'I mean, is real-world Audrey a fast driver? Does that even matter?'

'There is no real-world Audrey.'

'What?'

'I needed to have someone help you both out in here; nudge you in the right direction and stop you getting stuck. An assistant who would work independently, to minimise the extent to which I was prejudicing the experiment.'

'But Audrey only showed up when we got to Elec—' Johnny says, then it hits him. 'Audrey Ireland. Alison Innis. Alessandro Ibanez.'

'The problem is, the rogue characters keep targeting these assistants. Like they've been identified as a virus in the system.'

'That doesn't explain why they'd go after me and Penny. Not just McLeod, neither. I had Arlo Waters come at me with a wrench. I think he set the fire at Kingdom Pictures too.'

'Of course,' Wesley says, sounding kind of freaked, which Johnny takes to be a very bad sign, 'it hadn't occurred to me that part of the system might regard you and Amanda as intruders too.'

'You're saying the system you built is trying to expel us?'

'It's a work in progress.'

Death Is But the Overture

XV

Audrey was driving like a demon, running red lights, slaloming past slower cars and taking corners screechingly hard. After each turn Penny looked back and felt the tightness in her chest worsen as she waited to see whether the two SUVs would reappear in pursuit. They always did. It seemed to have a ratchet effect on her pulse: always increasing, never easing off.

'You don't happen to have a gun in your glove compartment, do you?' she asked Audrey.

'No, why?'

'Never mind.'

As they approached another interchange, Audrey suddenly veered right and drove across the lawns surrounding an office building. She cut through a quarter of a block before emerging onto another boulevard, continuing east in an S-shaped manoeuvre.

When Penny looked back, she could only see the Mitsubishi.

'I think you lost one of them.'

Audrey accelerated hard.

At the next interchange, the Lexus reappeared, bearing down from the road on the left, trying to flank them. It was a few seconds too slow, but it still made Penny realise that *not* being able to see their pursuers was actually worse.

'I just don't understand what these people want,' she said. 'Or on whose behalf they're operating.'

'Not that hard to figure out,' Audrey replied. 'You're investigating the Pierponts. I'm guessing someone would rather you didn't. There's a multi-billion-dollar deal being negotiated, remember.'

'I do remember,' Penny said, as Audrey swerved to overtake a flatbed truck. 'It has been my privilege, if that is the word, to be around extremely wealthy people for much of my life. And what I've never been able to fathom is why they strive always to acquire more when they could never spend what they already have should they live a thousand years.'

'You're looking at it the wrong way round,' said Audrey. 'It's the *not* living a thousand years part that they're accruing money to deal with.'

'I don't follow.'

'Musk, Zuckerberg, Dorsey and every other tech-billionaire asshole: they're all looking for ways to live forever. They have teams of medical, fitness and diet consultants to extend their physical longevity, but that's just the short game. In the long term they all want to digitise their consciousness so that when they die, they can upload their minds to some virtual paradise. Creating that is going to be very, very expensive. But whoever is first to sell it to them will be the richest tech-billionaire asshole in the world.'

The Silence Forever Echoes

Chapter Sixteen

'We should be seeing them soon,' says Wesley. 'Blue Mazda MX-30. They're coming up on Ventura Boulevard, right beneath us. Two black SUVs on their tail: a Mitsubishi Barbarian and a Lexus LX.'

Johnny is still on the 101. He knows the boulevard runs parallel to the freeway, but it's thirty feet below and a hundred yards south of the other carriageway.

'How are you seeing that?'

'I'm looking at you on one screen, Penny on another.'

'And yet you're sitting right there in my passenger seat. When I wake up from this, I'm gonna have serious mental problems. You do realise I'll be suing you, right?'

'Your ex-wife was very amenable with regards to waivers.'

Christ. He had forgotten Rattigan had an ex-wife, meaning *he* has an ex-wife, someone he can't remember. He wonders why it didn't work out. Doesn't imagine it was a no-fault divorce. Doesn't imagine the fault was evenly spread.

But picturing the real-world Wesley logged in at a keyboard takes him back to a hunch he can't shake.

'McLeod going rogue and coming after us. Are you sure that's a glitch in your system? Because it feels to me like an *intrusion* in your system.'

'Not possible,' Wesley insists. 'I told you: my system security is as good as it gets.'

Johnny recalls being precisely that confident telling Ibanez about their encrypted radios when they were chasing that truck-jacker, Istvan Kulic. But the reason they could never catch the Jackrabbit was because he was always listening in.

'I'm betting every tech genius who was ever hacked thought it was impossible right up until it happened.'

Wesley's shaking his head. 'If someone else was live inside the system, I would be seeing sustained spikes in data going in and out. I'm seeing nothing.'

'What if it was a real smash-and-grab job, like implanting a virus? The hacker wouldn't need sustained access, only a few seconds.'

Wesley's expression changes, goes from adamant to looking like he just put his faith in the wrong fart.

'Oh fuck. Fuck. Let me just check the . . . Christ. There are two short TCP spikes, both just beneath the level that would trigger an alert. Each for only a few seconds, but long enough to upload a rogue script.'

'What's all that in English?'

'I'm saying it's possible Arlo and McLeod have been subtly reprogrammed. Infected by something. They wouldn't be under direct control, and they would still have to operate within the parameters, but they would be following the hacker's agenda.'

'When you say parameters, you mean they wouldn't suddenly get turned into the Terminator. They still gotta follow the rules, right?'

'Up to a point,' Wesley replies, in a tone about as reassuring as a dentist with the DTs.

Johnny takes the Cobra down the off-ramp a little too hot. It skids across the blacktop just after the two SUVs shoot past from beneath: the Lexus first and then the Mitsubishi. He can see a blue Mazda up ahead. Audrey's done well to stay in front of them.

'She's going to run out of juice in about a quarter of a mile,' Wesley warns.

'Anything you can do about that?'

Johnny realises he knows the answer before he's even finished asking the question.

'The parameters are fixed,' Wesley replies.

Johnny can see that there is a tunnel dead ahead, by his estimate a quarter mile. It would be the worst possible place to break down. Nowhere to run or hide.

Johnny watches a guy climb out of a rear side window of the Mitsubishi, dude with a stupid little ponytail. He flops into the flatbed, disappearing beneath the tailgate. The road is straight and clear, and it occurs to Johnny that this would be a real deadly time for McLeod's guys to open up with those machine guns. He figures that's what Ponytail is retrieving.

He's wrong, though. It's so much worse than that.

When Ponytail stands up again, he's holding a fucking RPG, prepping it for use.

Johnny reaches for the glove box. That's when he remembers he took his gun into Seahorse, and the last time he saw it, it was skidding across the floor of Diegetic Therapy Chamber 1.

Johnny looks at the target. The Mazda is headed in a straight line towards the tunnel, and Audrey won't even see the danger because the Lexus is blocking her line of sight: deliberately, he figures. It will veer out of the way as soon as Ponytail signals he's ready to fire.

He remembers countless shootouts, final battles, taking down the Big Bad at the end. Even though he understands the memories are not real, it doesn't change that Johnny Hawke is an implausibly tough sonofabitch.

'You merged it with your memories, but this is still Johnny Hawke's LA, right?' he asks.

'The parameters are fixed,' Wesley repeats.

'Okay. Get us close.'

Wesley scrambles to grab the wheel as Johnny abandons the controls, opening the driver-side window of the Cobra and hauling himself onto the roof.

Wesley accelerates, bringing the Cobra alongside the Mitsubishi. Ponytail doesn't react, as he's busy lining up his shot.

Johnny feels the wind in his hair, the vibration underfoot on a vehicle travelling at least fifty miles an hour. He wonders how that memory-suppression stuff is holding up, because the part of him that is still Dan Rattigan knows what he's about to do is one-hundred-per-cent batshit.

He dives across onto the flatbed, grappling Ponytail to the deck and causing the RPG to clatter onto the metal alongside them. They both scramble to their feet, Ponytail going for his holster, but Johnny is already pirouetting into a roundhouse kick. He sends the guy flying over the tailgate and onto the road, where he gets pancaked by an oncoming dump-truck in the other lane.

Through the cab's rear window Johnny can see the driver of the Mitsubishi draw a gun, swerving as he leans around to take aim. He ducks as the driver fires, but there's only sound. The rear windshield is bulletproof. The guy tries again, like a fucking idiot.

Johnny looks ahead, sees the Mazda is almost to the tunnel, the Lexus gaining. He knows Audrey's gonna run out of juice any second.

He picks up the RPG and hefts it to his shoulder, getting his target into its sights.

'Pick on someone your own size, fuckwad,' he says, finger on the trigger.

He's about to fire when the Mitsubishi suddenly swerves beneath him. The driver has sussed his plan and is zigzagging all over the road. Johnny tries to hold his aim steady, but the Lexus is zigzagging too, keeping a tight pattern thirty or so yards behind the Mazda. Smart. If Johnny misses the Lexus, he's hitting Penny and Audrey.

Then he realises he doesn't need to aim for the Lexus.

Johnny holds off two more seconds until the Mazda disappears into the tunnel. Then he squeezes the trigger.

The rocket flies over the LX and impacts above the mouth of the tunnel in a blinding explosion. The Lexus brakes, but not fast enough, smashing into the shit-ton of rubble Johnny just brought down to block the road.

It ain't over, though.

The Mitsubishi skids to a rapid halt, Johnny struggling to stay upright in the back. The driver is climbing out of the cab, pistol in hand as McLeod and another guy emerge from the crashed Lexus. Fuckers are both carrying those HKs they shot up the library with. Johnny's holding nothing.

Johnny dives from the flatbed, slamming into the emerging driver and taking him down. When he rolls clear into a crouch, the driver is unconscious and Johnny has his gun, which he uses to shoot the gas tank of the Lexus.

It goes up in a fireball, engulfing McLeod and his last buddy.

Boom.

'Ooh,' he says. 'That's gonna leave a mark.'

He feels the adrenaline course through him, the relief and the exhilaration. He fucking *loves* being Johnny Hawke.

But all good things must come to an end.

The Silence Forever Echoes

Chapter Seventeen

Johnny's cell rings as he watches Wesley bring the Cobra to a stop about twenty yards away, presumably as close as he dares. He can feel the heat and smell the gasoline from the burning Lexus. There's a hint of barbecue in the breeze too, but it's comforting to know that nobody really died.

He fishes the phone out of his pants pocket, where it has miraculously remained.

It's Penny.

'We've broken down,' she says, sounding anxious, breathless. 'I mean, we've run out of power for the car.'

'It's okay. We'll come and get you.'

'But they're chasing us.'

'Not any more.'

'I heard explosions.'

'Yeah, that was me.'

'But you're all right?' she asks. She sounds relieved but still kinda breathless.

'I am, but Glen Cluthar's gonna be needing a new Chief Superintendent.'

'Oh. Oh dear,' she says gravely.

'Yeah.'

'There are always consequences when you break the rules.'

'He had a machine gun. It was him or me.'

'No, I mean he murdered my friend and he destroyed my library. *You* were the consequences.'

Johnny allows himself a smile.

'You're welcome.'

'I think I might have found something,' Penny says. 'Guadeloupe told me that the local police chief who investigated Juliet's death came into a lot of money soon after, allowing him to retire.'

'Interesting.'

'More interesting still is that he died in a boating accident a few weeks ago. I also spoke to a drunk old man who told me Lawrence's brother Travis died after falling down the stairs at Lawrence's house.'

'Another accident,' Johnny acknowledges.

'Yes, though apparently there were rumours he took his own life. What about you? Did you find out anything interesting at Seahorse?'

Jesus. Where to begin. He glances across to the timid figure emerging from the Cobra, parked a cautious distance from anything that's on fire.

'I met the elusive Wesley. He's here with me. I think he's one of the good guys.'

'Glad to hear it. I always had a warm feeling about him. I couldn't say why. Does he know anything about Miles Deacon and Lilian, or about Crawford Nicholson?'

Johnny swallows. He comes up with a plausible lie. Some of it is even true, but he's glad he doesn't have to say it to her face.

'No, but I discovered McLeod was working for the Pierponts. I got him to talk before he died. Lilian and Jed both found out something about one of the Pierpont family, but I don't know what and I don't know which one.'

'Oh,' Penny says. 'Oh.'

It's not an intrigued 'Oh'. It's not even a disappointed or frustrated 'Oh'. It's a weak and distressed 'Oh'.

'You okay?'

'There's something wrong with the power,' she says, her voice faltering.

'Yeah, it's okay. The Mazda just ran out. Needs recharging.'

'No, I mean the tunnel. The lights are fading. I can't see.'

Then it goes quiet.

Johnny all but shouts into the phone.

'Penny? Penny?'

It's Audrey who answers. 'Something's wrong,' she says.

'Yeah, she said the lights went out, probably to do with the explosion. We need to clear some wreckage, then we can—'

'No. Something's wrong with Penny.'

Wesley has stopped dead on his way from the Cobra. He's staring over Johnny's shoulder towards the tunnel.

Johnny turns to see what he's looking at. The lights this end seem to be working okay. He turns back to Wesley, and finds he's gone. Not fled gone, physically gone. The Cobra's still there but Wesley simply isn't.

Johnny doesn't have time to worry about that. He needs to get to Penny.

He starts running towards the tunnel entrance, which is

when the lights inside do go out. He can't see anything in there. The lights behind him go out too. Every streetlight, even the headlights on the cars.

Then there is no light anywhere.

The Silence Forever Echoes

Chapter Eighteen

He's back in the second therapy chamber, next to the simulated version of himself. It's like he blinked and went from standing at the mouth of the tunnel to standing right back here in Westlake. Wesley is standing there too. He looks distraught.

'What the hell? I thought you said you couldn't teleport us.'

'I didn't. There was a major glitch in the system, most likely caused by a large electrical discharge nearby. It pulled us right back here, last place we were at rest.'

'An electrical discharge: like a power surge? What caused it?' Wesley swallows.

'The defibrillator. Amanda had a cardiac arrest. It was all too much.'

Johnny feels it like a pile-driver.

'I thought you said if you died in Diegesis, it doesn't affect the real you.'

'You ever had a bad dream, woke up and your heart was pounding?'

Johnny understands now.

Except he's not Johnny. He's Dan. But nobody calls him Dan. People call him Rattigan, and they say it like it's a cuss-word.

'Is she . . .?' He can't say it out loud.

The window into the other chamber shimmers, dissolving and then reconstituting itself.

'What you're seeing now is a live feed, not a simulation. They stabilised her but I don't know how long she's got left.'

Johnny walks closer, looks through the window that is not really a window. He already saw her like this, helpless beneath the canopy, but it hits him harder because he can't pick up his phone and talk to her now. It also hits harder because she looks a lot worse in the real world. Inside Diegesis, he had been shown a woman whose final days were being rendered more pleasant by technology: the version Wesley wanted to believe. Here he sees a woman who is only being kept alive by machines.

Johnny pictures Arlo and his wrench, Penny's vital intervention.

'She saved my life,' he says. 'In there, I mean. Still counts as far as I'm concerned.'

'Ultimate manifestation of it being the thought that matters,' Wesley replies softly.

'She knew how to handle a gun. Where did that come from?'

'Her father was a military man. An officer, not a conscript. That's why she had such a rigid attitude to rules and authority. He taught her to shoot. He'd fought the Germans and worried the Russians would be next. My grandfather, Graham Oswald.'

'Did you know him?'

'A little. He died when I was thirteen. He was a prick.'

There is surprising vehemence in this. Johnny fails to hide his response.

'I shouldn't say that,' Wesley adds. 'He lost his wife young,

459

was left to raise three kids on his own; or at least until he could find a new wife to do it for him. In the meantime, he had Amanda looking after my dad and their little sister. She was seven. My dad was five and Janine was two.'

'That ain't right.'

'My dad told me all about it. Graham had Amanda drilled with a thousand rules. Military discipline. Had her doing every kind of chore. One day he had her cleaning the bathroom and she forgot to latch a cupboard when she was done. Janine came in later and drank from a bottle of bleach.'

Johnny thinks of the sparse little line he read, the rest perhaps censored out by Wesley's filters. *Died in childhood.*

'He was a thirty-five-year-old man who put a seven-year-old in charge of his other two kids, but he made Amanda believe it was her fault. I mean, once she grew up she understood how unfair that was, and everybody kept telling her, but it was hard-wired by then. Seventy-five years of self-recrimination. She spent her whole life primed to anticipate the possible consequences of every minute action. And always expecting rules to be obeyed.'

There's a growing silence as the two of them stand there, witness to a situation they can do nothing about. No sound but the hiss and soft clicks coming from the ventilator, streamed in from the real world.

Wesley swallows again, filling up now.

'It hit her so hard when Juliet died. I think we got closer because we both knew what it was to lose a sister. Even though she can't remember being Amanda, or what Juliet meant to her, I wanted to give her a chance to solve this, to know it had *been* solved.'

Johnny feels a crushing sense of failure immerse him.

'But we've still got nothing,' he says.

Then he remembers: Johnny's got nothing, but he isn't really Johnny.

'Wait. You said I was on my way to tell you something when the car crash happened. What if you were to wake me up right now? How risky is it?'

Wesley weighs it up. 'Best-case scenario is it's just like waking from an extremely deep sleep. Worst-case is that it triggers a state of total confusion.'

'That sounds like most mornings to me.'

From Wesley's expression, this ain't something to joke about.

'Do you know what the word "confusion" means, literally? It's the fusing together of two things so that you can't separate one from the other. The danger is you'd never be able to separate who you are from Johnny Hawke, and you'd never again be sure which world you belong in: his or Rattigan's.'

'And how likely is that?'

'The problem is we just don't know.'

He thinks about it. Looks to the window, at the woman on the bed.

'It's the only way to find out what Rattigan knows,' Johnny says.

'It's not, though. The medics say it should be safe to revive you in another two days. We'd find out then.'

'Amanda doesn't have that kinda time.'

'I can't ask you to do that for me,' Wesley says.

'I wouldn't be doing it for you.'

Wesley thinks about it, then gives him a sad, grateful smile.

'If you're absolutely sure.'

'I am. Just tell me the drill.'

Wesley doesn't move or answer for a few seconds, Johnny figuring he's busy in the real world. That shimmer thing happens

461

again, except this time it's the simulated version of himself lying in the Diegesis machine that dissolves.

Wesley speaks again, indicating the now empty bed.

'For what it's worth, I'm hoping if you wake up in the same place you lay down, it might help smooth things.'

'Okay.'

Johnny lies down, looks at the metal and plastic above, the potentially brain-frying electronic machine. Takes a breath.

'Say "Ready" when you're good to go,' Wesley tells him.

He wants to do this for Penny, for Amanda, but he's suddenly assailed by the possible real-world consequences. *Confusion.* Spending the rest of his days totally schizoid, never knowing what is real.

'Wait,' he says.

'What's wrong?'

'I got one question. How am I gonna know I've really woken up?'

'You'll have your memories back. You'll be Dan Rattigan again.'

'Yeah, but how will I know the world I'm waking up in is the real one?'

Wesley nods, sincere but smiling. 'I built in a fail-safe so I don't need to worry about precisely that whenever I take this thing for a test drive.'

Johnny is about to ask what the fail-safe consists of, then decides he doesn't want to know. He's got enough shit to worry about.

He closes his eyes.

'Ready.'

PART FOUR

PRIVATE INVESTIGATIONS: WESTLAKE

There's just a blur at first, shapes and colours merging into one another.

'Pulse is steady,' someone says. 'Pressure normal.'

Things start to come into focus. A room with spartan white walls. A shadow above. A window: blue sky and clouds.

There are people here. Medical people.

'Just take it easy,' says a woman's voice. 'You've been out for a long time. Don't try to sit up.'

He tries to sit up. A lot of stuff hurts. He must have cracked some ribs. He lies back down.

He looks directly above his head. The shadow above has resolved into a canopy: metal and plastic, made up of four panels: one half of an octagon.

He knows what that means. Or at least he knows that somewhere in his mind some part of him knows what that means. Some part he can't access quite yet.

'I want to get up.'

His voice works, only just. It comes out in a whisper, a croak. His throat is dry.

'Hold on, you came up a little quicker than we were antici-pating. We've just de-catheterised. Let me . . .'

The woman pulls out a cannula from his left arm. There's a little spot of blood. She sticks a band-aid on it. She's forties, Black, short. Got a name badge he can't quite make out.

Someone else hands him a cup of water. A man. Twenties, white, tall, athletic.

He sits up a little again so he can drink. Ribs hurt like hell, but the water goes down like the best thing he ever tasted.

He knows where he is. He knows what this is. *Who* he is is harder to deal with, but it's not because he doesn't know. There's no confusion. It's because he does know. He's a piece-of-shit loser, a washed-up ex-cop with an ex-wife who hates him. His ex-colleagues hate him too. Everybody hates him.

No. That's not true. There's one person who likes him. Then he remembers: she likes Johnny, not him.

'Penny. Amanda.'

He attempts to get up, swings his legs over the side of the bed. It hits him that he has no idea how much time has passed since the crash, though the fact that he still hurts means he's not gonna look out the window and see flying cars in the year 2300.

Someone tries to sit him back down.

'Where's Wesley?'

He attempts to get up again.

'Okay. Let me take you to him,' the woman says.

Rattigan can read that name badge now as she leans in to help him: Dr Angie DeRosa. She was in the simulation. She's a doctor though, not a paramedic.

'Take it slow,' she warns.

He slings his legs around and lets his feet touch the floor.

Then he stands. He feels woozy but his legs are working just fine. She walks him slowly down a corridor.

Wesley is waiting for him inside some kinda control room, this miniature Cape Canaveral he's got going. Johnny Hawke never saw this place on the camera feeds. There's a wall of monitors, some showing views inside the world he just came from: the Cobra sitting there beyond the mouth of that tunnel next to burnt-out wreckage, everything frozen in stasis. On another screen he can see the empty Diegesis machine he was plugged into, and on another he can see Amanda Fraser. Arlo Waters's words sneak back into his head.

Did you tell her what happened to all your other partners?

Arlo Waters was never real, but Rattigan knows this partner *is* going to die. And he is going to take it a lot harder than Johnny Hawke ever did.

Dr DeRosa helps him to a seat.

'We need the room,' Wesley tells her. 'We'll be okay,' he adds.

She looks reluctant to leave but does as she's bid.

'How are you doing?' Wesley asks him.

'My brains aren't scrambled, if that's what you mean. I know who I am, though truth be told I felt a lot better when I thought I was Johnny Hawke.'

'What are you complaining about? You're getting paid and you haven't even got out of bed in two weeks.'

Wesley smiles as he says this: shy, still sad, but there's something warm in there. Almost as if Wesley likes him.

'I've had worse gigs,' Rattigan admits.

Wesley does that thing of cradling his head. There's no difference between real-world him and Diegesis him, apart from he's got a little band-aid on his thumb. He's even in the same clothes.

'What do you remember?'

467

Rattigan closes his eyes, blocking out the distraction of the monitors. When he thinks back, everything is kinda fuzzy. The memories of being Johnny Hawke feel so real, and it's like he's got to block that out so he can access a separate section of his mind.

'I remember my brakes not working, pumping the pedal as I hit the intersection. I know they had been working okay just before that because I used them at the junction, waiting to pull out of the mini mall.'

'Police found a device they believe was remotely triggered to cut your brake line,' Wesley says. 'They checked CCTV to see if the person operating the device was close by, but turns out all of the cameras went dead shortly before. Not by coincidence.'

'The police: would that be Detective Guadeloupe?'

'She's real. You've met her. So have I, but—'

'But you edited yourself out of the picture, so as not to prejudice the experiment. I get it.'

'What else do you remember?'

Rattigan's mind goes blank for a moment, that pop-quiz freeze when being asked a question jolts the answer right out of your head.

'What were you doing in Scotland?' Wesley prompts.

'I was in Scotland for real?'

Then it all comes back. Starts as a trickle, but soon it's flooding in.

'You told me a witness saw Juliet checking her emails, morning of the wedding,' Rattigan says. 'It was the last time anybody saw her alive. I had a hunch that she'd hired an investigator. I phoned and emailed dozens of them, guys who were active twenty years ago. Got nothing. Then I had the idea: what if the investigator wasn't in California. I switched focus to where Juliet was from.

'Took a while, but eventually I spoke to a PI based out of Edinburgh, name of Jenny. The case was before her time: it was her father who took it, and he's dead now.'

'Another suspicious accident?'

'No. Natural causes, a few years back. Jenny was able to find a file. Juliet hired her father to look into the death of a student who was at St Andrews same time as you and Caleb. The file was light on details. Just a few names. I had to rework the investigation myself.'

Wesley looks tense.

'What did you find?'

'The student was found dead in his flat. Carbon monoxide poisoning from a faulty heater. Ruled accidental death. I visited the landlord. He took a lot of flak at the time, but he had the paperwork to prove the heater had been serviced recently and everything was up to code. Just amazingly bad luck that a fault suddenly developed.'

'What was the student's name?'

'Toby Delamere.'

Wesley nods solemnly. 'Toby. I remember. He was into games too. Told me he was writing one. Back then half the people who spoke to me told me they were writing one.'

'I went to see his old man. He's still got his son's stuff: his computer and all his notebooks and magazines and shit. He remembered the original PI, said the guy had asked about what Toby was working on just before he died. The old man still had it on a disk, made him a copy. Made me a copy too. I tried opening the file but it wouldn't work. As I understand it, Juliet got some kinda message the morning of the wedding. My hunch is it was that. Which is why I was bringing it to you in person.'

Wesley looks agitated.

'Where's the disk now?'

'It was in my jacket. Wherever that is.'

'Shit. There was a lot of blood on your clothes when you were brought into the ER. Apparently your ex-wife told the nurses they could bin them.'

'Ah, yeah, Carla. She'd have enjoyed that. Don't sweat it, though. I backed it up before I left Scotland. Had me a time finding somebody who still had a disk drive, but I wasn't taking that thing through any airport scanners until I had a copy of the file.'

'And where's the copy?'

'On my phone. I'm guessing they wouldn't throw that away, even if Carla said they could. You know where it is?'

Wesley reaches into a pocket on his gilet. He takes out Rattigan's cell and hands it to him.

'I'll admit I tried to open it, using your biometrics,' Wesley says. 'Seeing as you weren't in a position to object. But I notice you've got all that switched off. Password only.'

'I'd never trust all my information to a fingerprint. Always worried some asshole could hold my thumb to it while I was asleep. Turns out I'm not as dumb as everyone thinks.'

'Long as you can remember your password.'

'No problem.'

That's one thing Rattigan could never forget. It's 'jaydenfreil'. He chose it so he'd be forced to remember the consequence of his fuck-up every day. A lesser price than the kid paid.

He keys it in.

The phone wakes up. There's like fifty new emails and a hundred missed calls. It takes him a couple goes to remember where he stored the file, but he finds it. Sends it across to Wesley. It appears in a window on the bank of monitors a few seconds later.

470

Wesley runs some weird script to launch the file. Rattigan never got further than double-clicking, to no effect. It opens, sort of. Another window pops up, filled with lines of code. It's just weird phrases and numbers to Rattigan. Wesley scrolls down it like he's speed-reading.

'Do you remember what kind of computer it was?'

'A white one.'

Wesley sighs. He opens another window, moves the one with the code into it, runs some kind of analysis.

Wesley lets out a tut at whatever he's seeing, like he should have known.

'Going to need an emu.'

'A what?'

Wesley's fingers rattle the keyboard again, and a few seconds later he's located something labelled 'Amiga Emulator'. He drags Delamere's file into it and hits launch.

Rattigan watches a big section of the monitor bank form a single screen, which fills with what is obviously a game. The graphics look real blocky, but the figure in the centre is clearly a knight in armour: one he recognises from the Pierpont garden party, some poor schmuck going around dressed as the character.

Wesley rears back in surprise. Not good surprise. His fingers move tentatively towards the keyboard now, like he's afraid what will happen when he touches a key. Rattigan wonders how he even knows what keys to touch, as there's no instructions.

At Wesley's prompting, the knight advances across the screen, or rather the screen scrolls sideways around him, until he comes to a goblin. Rattigan's anticipating a fight, but Wesley lifts his hand from the keyboard.

He's frozen, unblinking. Rattigan's worried for a second that the guy's glitched out, proof he hasn't really woken up after all.

471

It hits him he's gonna be spending the rest of his life worried he's still in a simulation.

'It's *Last Knight*,' Wesley says, his voice real quiet.

'What was last night?'

'*Last Knight*. With a K. The game Caleb showed me as his work-in-progress when we were students. The first game he published when he convinced his father to launch a software arm. Christ almighty.'

Rattigan looks at the screen: the knight standing with his sword drawn, the goblin holding a club. Wesley slides his chair back, like he wants to physically distance himself from what he's seeing.

'Caleb stole it,' Wesley says. His voice sounds kinda hollow. Horrified. Broken. 'He stole it and killed Toby so he couldn't tell anybody it was his. Then he got Saskia to polish up the code. She was the first person he lied to. All these years she's been thinking he's the great talent in the family. All these years of people thinking he's a visionary, when he's a thief. And a killer.'

Wesley is physically shaking with shock and anger. Rattigan can barely begin to consider the enormity of it. The guy Wesley thought was his best friend: that's who killed his twin sister. Her fucking fiancé.

'Juliet loved old Amiga games,' Wesley says. '*Lemmings*, *Populous*. She had an emulator on her laptop. I'm guessing the PI sent this file to her on the day of the wedding. When she saw what it was, she worked it out, and . . .'

He doesn't say the rest. How could he.

'Caleb set up a foundation in her name,' Wesley continues, his voice trembling. 'Was that to assuage his guilt, or just to allay suspicion?'

'It was worse than that,' Rattigan realises. 'He made it part of his brand. Always honouring her memory.'

Wesley swallows, fighting back tears and rage.

'Caleb basks in being thought of as a visionary,' he says. 'But the real vision he's been selling is an illusion of himself.'

As Wesley speaks, Saskia's words come back to Rattigan, responding to the rumour that she was the real coding genius.

I think Caleb was the one who started that rumour. So that people think he understands less than he really does when they're showing him what's under the hood.

People like Wesley.

'He's our hacker,' Rattigan says. 'And if he could hack Diegesis, he could sure as shit hack my emails. Maybe even monitor my phone. I assume you told him who you'd hired?'

'I didn't need to,' Wesley says. 'It was Caleb who suggested you, after he had convinced me to engage an investigator. But why would he do that, if he was the one who . . .?'

Rattigan tastes something bittersweet as he sees the answer.

'Caleb wanted to put your suspicions to rest, so as to clear the path for the deal. He suggested you hire me because I'm a washed-out fuck-up and he thought I wouldn't find anything.'

Then it hits him: the irony of it.

'Which means that, technically, *you* didn't hire me. Caleb did.'

'Why does that matter?'

'Because in classic noir, the person who hired the private eye usually turns out to be the killer.'

Private Investigations: Westlake (II)

Wesley cradles his head in one hand for a few moments, then decides he needs both. He holds it there a long time, dealing with what he's just learned. Rattigan figures even a brain as big as his don't have any shortcuts for processing this kind of hurt.

Rattigan is patient, sitting there saying nothing, giving him time. Wesley's spent two decades wondering, but Caleb must have been bottom of his list of suspects: the guy who still pretended to be his caring friend throughout the estrangement of their mutual loss.

Eventually Wesley speaks again.

'All those years I wrestled with how the only set of keys to that lighthouse were found inside the locked door, which indicated nobody else could have been with Juliet. But I was told that by the investigating officer, Sergeant Olin, and what Guadeloupe found out suggests he had been paid off. It was that simple and I never saw it.'

'You can't beat yourself up for assuming what the cops told you was true,' Rattigan says.

Wesley glances at the monitor showing his beloved aunt lying

474

there motionless. The guy's whole world is in pieces. But despite that, his next words are: 'Thank you. For everything. I appreciate Caleb only recommended you because he expected you to fail, but he sure backed the wrong horse.'

'Another noir trope,' Rattigan replies. 'Washed-out hack proves he's still got what it takes. Don't seem like there's a whole bunch to thank me for, though. I wish I had found out something different, but it is what it is.'

Wesley sniffs, wiping his nose with a paper tissue.

'At the very least I'll be able to stop the sale. Because this isn't only about Caleb: not everybody can bribe a senior police officer, or even consider it an option.'

'Lawrence,' says Rattigan. 'Lawrence knew.'

'He knew and he covered it up, for the sake of his firm. He's always been the one I didn't want getting his hands on my company. He's never been interested in games: he's only interested in money and power. Lawrence wants Diegesis because he thinks he can sell it to billionaires looking for an electronic afterlife. I mean, if there was to be a digital heaven, would you want the Pierpont family owning it?'

It doesn't sound like a question that needs an answer.

Wesley closes the emulator window and makes the stolen game disappear.

'What are you planning to do now?' Rattigan asks.

'I'll go to Guadeloupe in the first instance, but we'll have to tread delicately. This isn't the end of an investigation. This is the beginning. I'll be bringing her three murders that we know of – Juliet, Toby Delamere and Sergeant Olin – as well as conspiracy and aiding-and-abetting charges against Lawrence.'

'Not to make it about myself, but don't forget attempted murder too.'

'Don't worry, I won't miss a thing. If you've learned anything about me, it's that I am all about the details.'

Hearing this, something occurs to Rattigan, one last detail that he couldn't make anything of.

'Melissa Neeson,' he says. 'That name mean something to you?'

'I know Zoe gave it to you, that's all. Did it lead you anywhere?'

'Kinda. Someone who might have a story to tell about Lawrence, but I suspect she's too scared to talk.'

'That might change now,' Wesley suggests. 'Everything is about to change.'

Rattigan looks to the monitor showing Amanda, Dr DeRosa standing at her side.

'Is there still time?' he asks.

'I hope so,' Wesley replies. 'Though what are you going to tell her?'

Rattigan's been thinking about it. He can't give her the whole truth, but there's gotta be a version of it that will make sense to her.

'Gonna take a leaf out of Amanda's book,' he says. 'Make up a story that pulls it all together at the end.'

Wesley leads him back towards the chamber, where the Diegesis machine is waiting.

'Just so you know, you'll have to go in without memory suppression, otherwise you'd forget everything we've discovered out here. You'll appear to Penny as Johnny Hawke, but essentially you'll just be acting.'

'That's okay. I could use the practice. From here on out, I want to be more like Johnny Hawke and less like Dan Rattigan. But above all, I want to be more like Penny Coyne.'

Death Is But the Overture

XVI

The room was unexpectedly bright as Penny came to, sunshine streaming through gaps in curtains that were never much good at keeping the light out anyway. She could hear a twitter of birds just outside, and a little further off, the gentle splashing of waterfowl on the oxbow lake. The sounds of Silverbank Cottage. The sounds of home.

Wiping her eyes, she observed with minor embarrassment that according to her bedside clock it was after eleven: an unacceptable hour to still be in bed unless she was ill. She did not feel ill, just bleary. That in itself seemed unusual; she ought not to feel so disoriented in her own home. But when the haze started to clear in her mind as well as her vision, she understood that it was not so much down to where she was as where she had been. And in particular how rapidly she had returned.

It was all coming back now, albeit the fragments seemed jumbled and incomplete. She had collapsed in that tunnel following the car chase. Stress and exhaustion, Wesley's doctor had said. She had been taken to Wesley's house for her immediate recovery, but the doctor suggested that the best place for her to recuperate was in her own home. That had seemed as desirable as it was unfortunately impractical, until it became apparent that Wesley had the use of a private jet. She had subsequently been flown from Los Angeles all the way to an airfield less than ten miles from Glen Cluthar. She had no idea what time it was when she got home, remembering only that it was dark and that she was exhausted.

Then she heard a knock at her bedroom door and remembered one other important detail: she had been accompanied all the way back to Scotland by Lieutenant Hawke.

'Are you awake?' he called through the door. 'Would you like some breakfast?'

Penny realised she was hungry, though given the time difference, for what meal she could not rightly say. But she knew a place where all possibilities could be catered for.

'You know, given the hour I'd quite like to go out for breakfast. Would you care to join?'

'You buying?'

Penny walked into her living room once she was showered and dressed, finding Johnny standing by the window as though on sentry duty. Given the events of the past week, she did not consider this unnecessarily vigilant.

'The doctor suggested I not over-exert myself. I'd best call a taxi to get us into town.'

'Why don't we take your car?' Johnny asked.

'Because the last time I saw it, I was climbing out of the driver's door at the bottom of the Tay.'

'I meant your new car.'

Johnny beckoned her closer to the front window, where she

saw that there was a shiny new vehicle in her drive, connected to an equally new electric charger on her garden wall.

'Courtesy of a grateful software magnate.'

Penny did not trust herself with machinery quite yet, far less sparklingly new and expensive-looking machinery, so Johnny did the driving. The short journey proved considerably less eventful than any of the previous ones she had shared with him, and she was soon ensconced in the happily familiar surroundings of Tayview Brew. That familiarity less happily extended to the sight of Mr Toal, the indefatigably miserable newsagent, who noticed Penny as he shuffled past on his way out.

'Terrible business about the library,' he said with an ostensibly grave shake of the head: one that incorporated a degree of alacrity to those who could recognise it. So much bad news of late, he must have been beside himself with quiet glee.

'Shocking,' Penny replied.

'The world's falling to pieces if such a thing can happen in Glen Cluthar. And whoever would have thought a man like Chief Superintendent McLeod could be bought off to act as some mercenary?'

'Who indeed,' Penny said, eyeing Johnny quizzically.

She leaned in once Mr Toal had made his exit.

'I know the gist of what emerged following my collapse, but I remain unclear on some of the finer points. I understand the business with Caleb sabotaging the gas heater and stealing the video game, but I can't quite follow the ripples outwards.'

Johnny nodded. He took a moment, as though carefully ordering his thoughts.

'Okay. As you know, Crawford Nicholson was an alias for

Miles Deacon. What you didn't know, and I have subsequently learned, is that Jed had an alias too: Alex Gillen.'

'The mysterious author of *The Cracked Mirror*?'

'Exactly. The screenplay for *Everybody Dies Alone* was based on his book. And it turns out Jed was a close friend of Lilian too.'

'But why were they all murdered?'

'Remember when you asked me where the video-game version was? There *is* no video-game version. There was a real-life version, and it came first.'

Her eyes widened. 'Of course!'

'Somehow Jed had found out the truth about Caleb's first video game, then Miles and Lilian found out through him. Miles was a target too, but he was too quick off the mark.'

Penny nibbled at a scone as she took this in.

'That all makes sense, I suppose. But it feels just a little too neat. How did Jed find out? Is there something you're not telling me?'

'There are several things I'm not *allowed* to tell you. But you don't want me to stop playing by the rules now that you just got me into the habit.'

Penny smiled. Well played, she thought.

'Is anyone under arrest yet?'

'Detective Guadeloupe has the information, and a complex police operation is underway, but we're not making anything public until we have everything in place. These are powerful, resourceful and highly connected people.'

'Goodness,' Penny said. 'It just goes to show how wrong one can be. I got the sense of something genuine about Caleb: of true affection and regret.'

'Wesley admits he had a blind spot for him too. As did, tragically, Juliet.'

Penny sighed, a familiar fatigue washing over her.

'I don't think I understand this world so well as I once thought I did. Yes, there were always smiling psychopaths, people skilled at putting a benign public face on the most malign secret agenda. But I used to be better at reading them.'

'Caleb was the consummate salesman,' Johnny replied. 'I don't think I've ever encountered anyone more skilled at hiding in plain sight.'

Penny washed the last of her scone down with a sip of tea. It was a relief to have it made properly again.

'At least Lilian will have justice now,' she said, but she did not feel the satisfaction she normally did when she got to the bottom of a mystery. Perhaps it was due to having had a passive role at the end: she had played her part, but it was Johnny who had found the crucial evidence.

She didn't quite understand how he had unlocked Rattigan's computer to reveal this information. If she had known the technical details, would that make the resolution feel more satisfying? Possibly. But as it stood, she still felt a restlessness, a hunger for answers that was not quite sated. Perhaps it simply never could be.

'What are your plans now?' Johnny asked, after she had paid the bill.

'What I would really like most is to take a walk. Would you join me for a turn around the village?'

'That would be my pleasure.'

'I'd like you to see what the place looks like when there are no bullets flying.'

Johnny gave her an oddly knowing smile.

'There's something I'd like *you* to see too,' he said.

Death Is But the Overture

XVII

'There is something different about you, something I can't quite place,' Penny said as they strolled along the Main Street, past the late Brendan Gault's ill-starred patisserie.

'You could say I'm a changed man,' he replied, checking his stride to avoid a group of tourists disembarking from a coach.

He glanced across to Leven Square, where Dougal Keogh's art-deco cinema was advertising a screening of *Kiss Me Deadly*.

'Is Glen Cluthar where you've always lived?' he asked.

'No. This is where I retired.'

'Where did you live before that?'

'Oh, many places,' Penny replied, to cover up the fact that she could not in fact remember. 'But I've lived in Glen Cluthar the longest. I've been happy in this place.'

'I can see why. I guess not much changes around here.'

'It didn't used to, anyway.'

'But then I showed up.'

'No. Things were changing even before you came into my life.'

482

They were approaching St Bride's. Penny took in its familiar lines and crenellations, a looming presence that had once brought reassurance. Now, she was not so sure.

'Are you a religious man, Johnny?'

'My old man walked out on us when I was seven. It was hard to sell me the idea of a benevolent all-powerful father figure after that.'

'I still have my faith,' she told him. 'But I don't think that extends to institutions in the way it used to. Whether that be the police or indeed the Church itself.'

'I get that our recent shenanigans might have tarnished your perspective on the boys in blue, but what has the Church got to do with it?'

'I'm talking about before that. My last murder case, just before I was invited to the wedding.'

She told him all about it: poor Mr Gault and the secret sins of Father Driver.

'I'd like to go inside for a moment,' Penny said.

She wanted to light a candle for Alison and for Lilian. She would light one for Juliet too: though they had never met, Penny felt as though she knew her somehow.

They walked into the church, the echo of their footsteps and the smell of incense instantly calming: a salving balm to Penny's soul. She saw Mrs Crichton, the housekeeper, quietly working away at one corner of the altar, polishing the handrail. Inside this sacred place, even after it had been desecrated by murder, it appeared things were going back to normal. Perhaps she could go back to normal too.

Penny knelt before the votive stand, where she would reflect upon the three women who had died to cover the wickedness of one man. She picked up a taper and lit her three candles,

483

noticing as she did so the spatters of wax on the metal trays, gathered over the course of the week.

She looked across at Mrs Crichton, who gave her a polite smile. Then Penny gazed back into the gently flickering flames, and saw that everything was wrong.

She remembered speaking to Mrs Crichton at the first service after the church reopened, seeing the tiny flecks of wax in her hair from cleaning the votive shrine that morning. It had been the first chance Mrs Crichton got since the body was discovered and the church closed off by the police. Except that Father Driver claimed to have discovered the body first thing on Sunday morning as he prepared to say mass. Mrs Crichton always cleaned the candle wax on Saturday evening. Why would she not have done so on the night Mr Gault was strangled?

Penny recalled her gossip-hungry tendency to be polishing the pews closest to the booth whenever Father Driver was hearing confession. It was Mrs Crichton who claimed she had overheard Mrs Gault say her husband was having an affair, and feared what she might do. Casting suspicion upon an innocent party.

Penny also recalled Saeeda saying that Father Driver had written his resignation letter, acceding to Mr Gault's demands. But, as Penny had asked, if he intended to resign his priesthood, why then would he commit murder? Father Driver claimed that Gault had vowed to go public after all, and that he had consequently snapped and killed him in his rage. It had not sounded quite right to Penny, but perhaps that was because she'd shared Saeeda's intuition that the killer was a woman, and it was always difficult to accept that one's reading of a crime had been wrong.

But now she could see the truth of it, laid bare in a few spatters of red. Mrs Crichton had actually overheard the discussion Mr Gault secretly recorded: of him confronting Father Driver with his accusations and demands.

Perhaps she told herself Mr Gault had made it all up, or perhaps her instinct to protect the things she loved – Father Driver and the Church – over-rode any other considerations. Mrs Crichton was larger and physically stronger than the slight Mr Gault. She was the one who had strangled him with a stole.

Father Driver had known this. Perhaps he had seen something, or Mrs Crichton came to him in the aftermath and confessed. Either way, he had pretended to discover the body on the Sunday morning, and had hoped the police would not be able to solve the crime. But when Saeeda confronted him with the recording and his letter of resignation, he knew he was undone. He had been prepared to pay a penance for his own crimes, and decided to take the blame for Mrs Crichton's too.

Penny looked at the housekeeper again, and Mrs Crichton looked back, suddenly apprehensive.

'It was you,' Penny said.

Mrs Crichton stood up, dropped her duster and bolted from the church, her soles squeaking on the tiled floor she had lovingly buffed.

Johnny observed her rapid exit and walked across to the shrine. 'What was that?' he asked.

'A confession,' Penny answered, getting to her feet.

She looked at the candles once more, and reeled to see that this tiny twist of the kaleidoscope had altered a bigger picture also.

'It wasn't Caleb,' she realised. 'It was Saskia. It was always Saskia.'

'*What?*'

'Remember what you said earlier: that you'd never encountered anyone more skilled than Caleb at hiding in plain sight. But you had. Groomed to take over, but reluctant to be in the spotlight. An engineer who comes up with pragmatic solutions.'

'Reputed to have been a hacker in her youth,' Johnny said, understanding. 'At St Andrews the same time as Caleb, and credited with cleaning up his code back in the early days.'

'Think of how adoring she was as she watched her brother on that stage,' Penny said. 'She loves him and admires him. She would do anything for him. But she was using him too. She must have told Caleb *she* wrote the game, and that she wanted him to be the face of it because she was too shy. She was the power behind the throne, the arch-manipulator.'

'I think someone hacked my emails,' Johnny said. 'That tech bro said there's nothing Saskia doesn't know about what's going on inside her company. She hacks *everybody's* emails. She read Juliet's messages: that's how she knew Juliet had found out about Toby Delamere.'

Penny looked down at the duster Mrs Crichton had dropped. She took her phone from her handbag and began walking towards the front doors.

'I need to ring Saeeda Sattar.'

'Yeah,' said Johnny. 'I gotta make an urgent call myself.'

Death Is But the Overture

XVIII

Dorothy Crichton gave herself up with little struggle and even less grace.

'He violated the sanctity of the confessional,' she screeched at Penny as she was escorted to Saeeda's police car. 'They make up lies to cover their own depravity, their own filth. Why should a philanderer get to cast his aspersions over a good man like Father Driver?'

A philanderer, Penny thought. Like the late Mr Crichton, perhaps. The man she was truly angry at.

Johnny was standing at Penny's side as she watched Saeeda drive the prisoner away.

'Did you make your calls?' she asked.

'Yeah. There's gonna be a lot of work to do, but it'll sure help to be looking at the right target. You solved the case, Penny. Like nobody else could.'

'That's what I do. It's my— what did you call it?'

'Your USP.'

'Quite. Now, I believe you said you had something to show me.'

She let him lead her along the Main Street, back the way they had come. As they passed where Johnny had parked her new car, she realised that she was nearing the junction with Marshall Street. She was not sure she was ready for what awaited her there, but even before she reached the corner she could see a shimmer of glass. Drawing closer, she observed that all of the library's windows had been replaced.

There was a sweet scent of freshly cut wood in the air. Through the new windows she could see that there were half a dozen people working inside the building, constructing new book-shelves.

'Wesley's got deep pockets,' Johnny said. 'He's paying to have the library completely refurbished. And he's gonna fund it in perpetuity.'

Penny felt quite overcome. Having made her deductions about Mrs Crichton and about Saskia, she had finally experienced the sense of resolution that had been missing. Now she felt something more: a lifting of responsibility, a reassurance that all would be well without her.

'I think I'm ready to go home now,' she said.

The Silence Forever Echoes

Chapter Nineteen

Rattigan parks in the driveway of Silverbank Cottage. He holds the door open for Penny as she climbs out of the car. He can sense the warmth of her as she passes, smell that old-fashioned perfume she wears.

He's in danger of welling up, has to swallow it back so that she doesn't see. He knows that what he's looking at, what he's smelling and what he's hearing isn't real, but he has no question what he's feeling for her is.

He wishes he'd known the real her, the woman who dreamt up Penny Coyne. But he got to meet her creation in a way no one else ever has.

'So, what now?' he asks.

Penny looks around, at the house and the woods and the oxbow lake down the hill.

'I think I'm going to retire.'

'Yeah, the jetlag is catching up with me too.'

'No, I mean I've solved my last mystery. I don't think Glen Cluthar needs me any more.'

'You deserve to retire,' he tells her. 'You've earned it.'

'I'm going to call my nephew. Tell him I like what's in the brochure. But yes, retire in the other sense too. I feel very sleepy and it's getting dark.'

Rattigan looks around. It's broad daylight.

'You'll be here when I wake up, won't you?' she asks.

'Sure.'

And in that single word, there are two well-meant, gentle lies. Because he's not really here now. And she ain't never gonna wake up.

'Penny, before you go, can I just give you a hug?'

Her eyes fill and she nods. She moves towards him. He puts his arms around her, holds her for a while, then she fades away.

PRIVATE INVESTIGATIONS: LAX–LHR

Ten days later, Rattigan is at LAX, killing time before his flight. And he's definitely at the actual LAX, though it's taken him this long to fully accept that he's back in reality.

He was wrong that he'd spend the rest of his life worried he was still in a simulation. He was like that for a while: looking for proof of what's real, worrying whether events feel too much like a story. But you can't take every irony and turn it into something it's not: that way madness lies. Like, he'd thought it was classic noir that the person who hired the private eye turned out to be the killer, but in the end that wasn't true. Appropriately, it was Penny's words that set him straight: *I'd advise you not to become so distracted by what is strange that you lose sight of what is plain and factual.*

For the most part he's also stopped worrying about his own memories becoming merged with Johnny's. He's stopped sounding like Johnny inside his own head, though he is aware of consciously trying not to, so he isn't sure what that proves either way.

*

He's browsing the stores in the departure area when a woman walks past carrying an Amanda Fraser novel under her arm. It's the second one he's seen at the airport, and must be like the fifth he's seen this week. That's the kind of weird coincidence that might have made him suspicious, but he knows this is how it goes: once your attention has been drawn to something, you start noticing it everywhere. Plus, it's no surprise her books are selling, given she's been in the news.

Rattigan is checking the departure board to see if they announced a gate yet, when his phone rings. He fishes it out of his pocket and sees the caller ID'd as Melissa Neeson. Wow. He'd all but given up on getting a response out of her, and she's phoning him out of the blue.

He walks across to a quiet corner to take it.

'Mr Rattigan,' she says, her voice kind of shaky, nervous. 'I know you've been trying to get in touch for a while, and I apologise for stonewalling you. It's delicate stuff. Scary stuff. I need to tell somebody, though.'

'I appreciate how hard this must be for you,' he tells her, keeping his tone real soft. 'But would I be correct in assuming you were subject to sexual harassment by Lawrence Pierpont?'

'No,' she replies, which takes him aback. But what she says next floors him.

'I was sexually abused by his brother, Travis, when I was twelve. He was a youth pastor at our church. I didn't tell anyone. I was ashamed and I was scared what would happen to me. But I came forward after he died, because I knew there would be others. Lawrence paid me to keep the family name out of the media.'

'When you say you came forward, who did you go to? How did Lawrence find out and not the media?'

492

'You don't understand. It was Lawrence I approached. Something Travis once said made me think he was abusing someone else, someone close to him. I thought it might have been one of Lawrence's children. I came forward because I thought it might help them to know they weren't alone.'

Rattigan pictures Zoe. The drug problems. The marks on her arms.

'I don't know what Lawrence did with that information,' Melissa says. 'He paid me to keep it to myself. Made me sign an NDA. I thought it was just so that the family didn't suffer by association for Travis's crimes, but over the years I came to wonder. The reports said Travis fell down a staircase drunk and broke his neck. Some people suggested he might have killed himself, but if you knew him, you'd never believe that. Travis had no shame or guilt.'

'You think he was pushed.'

'I don't know what I think. I'm telling you because I've seen the news. I know what you've been investigating, and I want you to know that there are victims in that family too.'

The flight touches down at Heathrow a little over thirteen hours later, and when he takes his phone off airplane mode, he sees an alert telling him Guadeloupe has been trying to call. He had phoned her from LAX as soon as he finished talking to Melissa Neeson, passing on the details. It took a while for his memory to separate his real-world interactions with Guadeloupe from the ones he had had as Johnny, though much of the content is the same.

'You got an update, Detective?' he asks.

'Sure have. Caleb confirmed everything Neeson said. He's gonna be our star witness. He's real angry about his family, and

493

let me just say, it is one fucked-up family. He told me Saskia witnessed Travis abusing Zoe, so she pushed him down the stairs. Seems Travis had abused Saskia first, when she was younger, then moved on to Zoe once she hit the right age for his tastes.'

There's noise in the background. Sounds like she's at the precinct, talking over the hubbub but trying to keep her voice down at the same time.

'Caleb knew that Lawrence covered up what Saskia did to Travis. I think that's made it easier for him to accept that Lawrence covered up what Saskia did to Juliet too. Also made it easier for him to understand that in Saskia's messed-up mind, anything was acceptable when it came to helping and protecting her siblings. She thought she was helping Zoe when she killed Travis, like she thought she was helping Caleb when she killed Toby Delamere and stole his game.'

Rattigan pictures Caleb in Santa Barbara as he opened up to Penny underneath that gazebo. Hears her talking about him later.

I got the sense of something genuine about Caleb: of true affection and regret.

'Poor bastard,' he says. 'Penny's instincts were right all along.'

'*Whose* instincts?' asks Guadeloupe.

PRIVATE INVESTIGATIONS: DUNKELD

Rattigan is back in Scotland. Who'da thunk it. A few weeks ago, he'd never been here, now it's his second trip in little over a month; third if you count Diegesis. He's with Wesley, who's flown Amanda Fraser's body back to her native land for the funeral.

They're standing on a hillside overlooking the town. It's maybe not quite as pretty as Glen Cluthar, and definitely not as old-fashioned, but it's where she grew up. The weather ain't so sunny here in the real world either. There's light drizzle and it's about fifty degrees. Nobody got the memo that it's supposed to be July.

'You still recovering okay?' Wesley asks.

'Yeah. The headaches have eased off and my ribs don't hurt so bad any more. Plus the phone has been ringing a lot since Guadeloupe credited me in the press. Pity she couldn't credit my partner, though.'

'We both know the truth. That's what matters.'

'I'm gonna miss her real bad,' Rattigan tells him. Not because it's what he feels he ought to say, but because it's true.

'You've only just started to miss her,' Wesley replies. 'I've been missing her for years. Since her mind . . .'

He chokes up. Rattigan places an arm on his back.

'We're blessed, though,' Wesley says, wiping his eyes. 'These days everybody has a thousand photographs of the people they've lost, but nobody's got what we have. That's why I gifted you the complete works.'

It takes Rattigan a moment, then he gets it. If he wants to feel what it's like to be in Penny's company again, he just has to walk over to the shelf and pick up a book.

Wesley taps the side of his head.

'And what about . . .? You recovering okay from all that too?'

'Just about. Though now and again something happens that makes me worry I'm still in somebody else's fantasy-land. That me talking to you now, me talking to Guadeloupe, is all part of some illusion to let Saskia get away with it while really I'm still in a coma.'

Wesley nods like he did that time before: sincere but smiling. He holds up his left thumb. Rattigan thinks it's just a goodwill gesture, then he notices that he's got a little band-aid on there again.

'What's that?' Rattigan asks.

'My fail-safe, so I can be sure nobody else has access to the highest levels of the system. I'm the only living soul who can authenticate my identity, because it requires my DNA. And I'm not talking about a few skin cells or hair follicles: it needs what's known as a high-volume sample.'

'A drop of blood,' Rattigan says.

'Means I have to stick myself with a needle every time I log in, but it's a small price to pay for peace of mind. Peace of knowing it *is* my mind when I wake up from the simulation.'

496

Wesley reaches into his jacket and produces his phone, handing it to Rattigan. The screen shows the *LA Times* story from a few days ago, covering Saskia's arrest, accompanied by her police mugshot.

'If anybody is in a fantasy-land right now,' Wesley says, 'it certainly isn't Saskia Pierpont. And that's down to you, Dan.'

Rattigan smiles. Reading about Saskia's perp walk and knowing his own part in it makes him feel like a cop again, just for a while. And somebody just called him Dan.

He's about to hand back the phone when he notices Caleb's picture on there too, just a stock shot for story background. He's wearing that pendant. The one containing Juliet's blood.

Rattigan hears Saskia's voice in his head:

It can be difficult getting between twins; they share everything, from DNA onwards.

Holly golly.

Acknowledgements

On 16 June 2022 my editor, Ed Wood, tweeted: 'People often ask what editors are looking for – I would kill for a really clever meta whodunnit that plays with the genre. So there it is, gauntlet thrown.'

I couldn't resist, so I'd like to thank him for that challenge, but I'd like to thank him more for pushing me to take this idea further than I had initially dared. You need an editor who really believes in what you're doing, so when he is describing his own suggestion as 'probably too insane' but encouraging you to do it anyway, you know you're in good hands.

I would also like to thank the rest of the team at Little, Brown, where they have been believing in what I'm doing for almost thirty years, as have Caroline Dawnay, Sophie Scard, Charles Walker, and the team at United Agents. Thanks also to Fiona Brownlee for never missing a chance to thrust me under the spotlight, both as myself and with Ambrose Parry.

I would like to thank Greg Dulli for kindly allowing me to quote from 'Debonair', those lines of which were playing in my head on a loop while writing this novel.

I would like to thank Marisa Haetzman for her wisdom, judgement and patience in helping me create order from chaos by pulling a highly complex concept into focus.

And finally, I would like to offer a huge thanks to the one and only Doug Johnstone for letting me borrow Jenny and Jim Skelf.

Chris Brookmyre was a journalist before becoming a full-time novelist with the publication of his award-winning debut *Quite Ugly One Morning*, which established him as one of Britain's leading crime writers. His 2016 novel *Black Widow* won both the McIlvanney Prize and the Theakston Old Peculier Crime Novel of the Year award. Brookmyre's novels have sold more than two million copies in the UK alone.